The Traitor of St Giles

MICHAEL JECKS

The Traitor of St Giles

**SIMON &
SCHUSTER**

London · New York · Sydney · Toronto · New Delhi

A CBS COMPANY

First published in 1999 by Headline Books Publishing

This edition published in Great Britain in 2013 by Simon & Schuster UK Ltd
A CBS COMPANY

1 3 5 7 9 10 8 6 4 2

ISBN: 978-1-47112-631-4
eBook ISBN: 978-1-47112-632-1

Printed and bound in Great Britain by CPI Group UK Ltd, Croydon CR0 4YY

For Jane Conway-Gordon,
because without her help, advice,
and occasional criticism,
I would not be a writer.
Many thanks!

CAST OF CHARACTERS

Sir Baldwin de Furnshill   The Keeper of the King's Peace in Crediton, who is known as a shrewd investigator of crimes in his jurisdiction. He has a reputation for helping those who have been persecuted.

Jeanne   The widow of Ralph de Liddinstone has now married Baldwin. She has the nagging fear that her husband may be sent to fight for his Lord.

Edgar   Baldwin's servant, formerly his man-at-arms, and for several years now his loyal companion.

Bailiff Simon Puttock	The long-standing friend of Sir Baldwin. With his own legal experience as a Stannary Bailiff, Simon has often joined forces with Baldwin to investigate murders.
Lord Hugh de Courtenay	The head of one of the country's important families, Lord Hugh is worried by rumours of impending war and seeks to consult his most loyal men as to which faction to support.
Sir Gilbert de Carlisle	A renegade Templar, one of the many who escaped the vindictive persecution of the French King. Now he is being used by the Despensers as a messenger. He hopes to regain a little of his dignity by joining a Lord's retinue.
William the Small	Man-at-arms to Sir Gilbert. William was with Despenser as a sailor, but he left the ship when he saw that Sir Gilbert needed help.
Joan Carter	The raped and murdered daughter of Matilda Carter.

Matilda Carter
Married to Andrew Carter, Matilda is sister to Nicholas Lovecok. She came down to Devon with Nicholas when he had to leave his old home in Lincolnshire.

Nicholas Lovecok
A wealthy and powerful merchant in Exeter, he built up his business from nothing. He is visiting Tiverton to help with the provisions for the feast at Lord Hugh's castle.

Andrew Carter
Husband to Matilda and step-father to Joan, he has been Nicholas's close friend for several years. Their wealth has grown as a result of their shared business interests.

Philip Dyne
An apprentice spicer who was Joan Carter's lover. He has confessed to killing Joan but managed to escape capture by gaining a place of sanctuary. Now he must leave the country.

Harlewin le Poter
The Coroner of Tiverton – a bluff, vain womaniser who has Lancastrian sympathies.

3

Father Abraham

The local priest in Tiverton who has a loathing bordering on hysterical fear of heretics in general and the Knights Templar in particular.

Father Benedict

The old Templar priest for Templeton. He refused to leave the area and desert the small parish flock when the Templar manor was closed.

Avicia Dyne

Sister to Philip. She never believed that her brother could have killed the girl he loved.

Sir Peregrine of Barnstaple

A bannaret and trusted follower of Lord Hugh, he is the Keeper of Tiverton Castle.

Felicity

A well-known whore who works in Tiverton.

AUTHOR'S NOTE

I have always had a fondness for Tiverton. It's one of those old market towns which has been altered almost out of recognition in recent years: one-way systems and, more recently, pedestrianisation make it a difficult place to get to – it's even worse finding a parking space – but local councils and central government haven't managed to entirely destroy its atmosphere. My own ties with the town extend to my being married in Tiverton's Register Office – and I can recommend it as a venue!

It was while on honeymoon in Devon that my wife and I visited Tiverton Castle, Bickleigh Castle and Fursdon House, the three places which inspired *The Last Templar* and subsequent stories. For some time recently I had been promising myself that I would return north of Crediton to base another story in Tiverton itself. This book is the result.

Tiverton was founded under the Saxons; the name comes from *Twyfyrde*, or 'Two Fords' because it lies between two rivers, the Exe and the Lowman. In 1106 King Henry I gave it to Richard de Redvers and it was Richard's son Baldwin who became the first Earl of Devon. The castle was built by the de Redvers family, but they died out in 1293 and the castle then passed to Hugh de Courtenay, who became Earl himself in 1335, a mere five years before his death.

Little remains of the early castle buildings, but there is enough to give you a good feel for the place. It was held by Royalists in the Civil War, and when Fairfax and his Roundheads captured it they 'slighted' it (i.e. destroyed it as a defensible fortress) to prevent its being held against Parliament again: the curtain walls to west and north were blown up or pulled down. A huge southeastern tower survives, there are fragments of a hall visible and some of the 14th-century solar block remains but there is little else from the 1300s.

Although Tiverton Castle has been badly knocked about over the years it is well worth a visit. Its museum holds a fascinating collection of Civil War arms and armour. Equally interesting are Bickleigh Castle a few miles to the south, and Fursdon House near Cadbury. I can also recommend a visit to Templeton, a beautiful little village to the west of Tiverton.

Lord Hugh de Courtenay was an interesting character. The early 1300s were dangerous times to live in and yet he managed to survive in a world of richer and more powerful magnates.

King Edward II was very fond of his favourites. The first was Piers Gaveston, the younger son of a Béarnaise knight, who compounded the jealousy that better-born men felt for him by giving them disrespectful nicknames. For example, he referred to the Earl of Warwick as 'the black dog of Arden' and the Earl of Gloucester as 'a cuckold's bird'. During the reign of King Edward I, Gaveston was banished from the realm, but as soon as Edward I died, his son recalled his companion (and, most believe, homosexual lover) from exile. He smothered Gaveston with titles and lavish presents, giving him the Earldom of Cornwall and the honour and castle of Berkhamstead among others, and arranging for Gaveston's marriage to Margaret de Clare, the King's niece.

Gaveston was thrown from the kingdom when Parliament selected Ordainers – among them Lord Hugh de Courtenay – to control the realm better and stop the King's spendthrift habits from ruining the country. During the Parliament of 1311 they forced the King to accept new counsellors, but their success was short-lived since the King soon invited Gaveston back. Certainly the barons and earls believed that Gaveston had returned because, that same November, Lord Hugh was one of two men ordered to seek him in the West Country.

The end of Gaveston came the next year, when he was executed by lords sick of his greed and fearful – or jealous – of his hold over the King. However, this wasn't the end of the King's troublesome selection of his friends, because now he chose young Hugh Despenser as his favourite; Despenser being the greediest and most corrupt baron the King could have fixed upon as advisor – and again, probably, lover.

Hugh Despenser the Younger, as he is now known, was if anything more ambitious than Gaveston. His marriage to Eleanor de Clare (arranged by the King) ensured his wealth when, at Bannockburn, her brother Gilbert de Clare died without an heir. The Clare estates were subsequently split up

7

and divided between his sisters and their husbands, and Despenser, being favoured by the King, was able to extort those pieces of land he wanted. He was arrogant, determined, and prepared to use violence whenever it suited him.

The Despenser War of 1321, which was precipitated by Despenser's blatant avarice and during which the Despenser lands were wasted by a loose confederation of Marcher Lords determined to remove this threat to their properties, marked a turning point in King Edward II's reign. Afterwards the Despensers returned to rule the nation with an iron hand, but for a short time – again – it appeared that wiser counsel would prevail and the King might be better advised.

In 1321, the year of this story, the Despensers were exiled. As with Gaveston it was only a short time before the King allowed them back, and the result was the Despenser tyranny, which lasted for four years before the two Despensers, Older and Younger, were overthrown and executed as traitors.

The Young Despenser is said to have stated that he wanted to be rich. When Gilbert de Clare died, the Younger's share of the Clare inheritance was some £1,507 each year, mostly from Welsh property; by the time he died in 1326, Despenser was worth more than £7,500 each year, as well as holding over £3,000 worth of moveable goods and, at one time, having nearly £6,000 on deposit with Italian bankers. One can only guess at the level of corruption involved in his government.

However, through all of the madness and mayhem of the civil wars, through the arguments with the King, the disputes between the barons and eventually the war between King Edward II and his Queen, Lord Hugh survived. There is little in any book about someone who was ever on the fringes of power and never made himself hugely rich, but I hope that if he were to read my description of him, Lord Hugh would not be overly upset. I think he has to have been shrewd and capable, to have lived to die of old age!

Other characters have been entirely invented. There *was* no Sir Gilbert of Carlisle to my knowledge, nor was there a Sir Peregrine of Barnstaple. My merchants, breadmakers, whores, men-at-arms, ratcatchers and others are also the result of my imagination.

For those who wish to learn more of the history of the period, I can recommend Mary Saaler's book *Edward II* and May McKisack's *The Fourteenth Century*. For more about the Templars, look at John J. Robinson's *Dungeon, Fire and Sword* and Edward Burman's *Supremely Abominable Crimes*, while for a marvellous summary of the persecution itself, Norman Cohn's superb book *Europe's Inner Demons* shows how the Order was destroyed through malicious propaganda – and how such persecution continues down the ages.

There are some terms and concepts in these pages which might cause readers to think I have not checked my proofs or that my copy-editor missed whole pieces of text. Life was considerably more simple in those days. Justice was more a means of ensuring that revenues to the Crown were protected, rather than ensuring that villeins and other subjects had *their* interests protected.

It was the duty of the jury in the first instance to report to the justices what crimes had been committed and who they thought was responsible. This was the jury of presentment. They reported by issuing their *veredicta*, which were their charges, and the miserable felon would then be hauled off to wait for the trial of gaol delivery, which was when he would be tried by the visiting justices. Here again the jurors would present the facts and the justices would make their decision.

As well as the jury presenting their indictments, other folk could *appeal* a man's offence. This was a formal accusation of felony which was laid by the victim against the criminal and meant that a jury's indictment wasn't necessary – although there were risks. If a felon was found to be innocent, he could then immediately accuse anyone who had appealed against him of 'conspiracy' and demand damages.

For those who wish to learn more about criminal trials and the processes, look at J. G. Bellamy's *The Criminal Trial in Later Medieval England*.

One last topic may arouse interest and that is the subject of fighting. Throughout history the English have exercised a series of martial arts. At times practitioners have been lauded and given approval by governments and kings; at others they have scared those in authority and have had their rights to practise curtailed.

That does not change the fact that experts in fighting have existed for centuries. The *Liber Albus* (c. 1180) mentions them, King Edward I tried to ban the teaching of fencing in London (unsuccessfully) and it was King Henry VIII who finally gave a Royal Warrant to 'Maisters of Defence', effectively a martial arts commission. This put the group on a professional footing, like lawyers, and gave them monopolistic rights over controlling all aspects of training men in fighting.

The sole remaining sport which provides evidence of those days is boxing. Hundreds of people flock to watch boxers demonstrating their skill, stamina and speed; in the past there were similar exhibitions, but our forbears were rather more sanguine in their approach to life. Their fights were conducted by men with swords, knives, cudgels, or bare fists – and their weapons were not blunted. Savage wounds were inflicted or received, and one must assume that many of the contestants must have died.

In the twentieth century it is hard to imagine anyone being prepared to fight in this way, but that is because we are conditioned to think differently. To gain an insight into how our ancestors' minds worked, I cannot recommend Terry Jones's thoroughly accessible book *Chaucer's Knight* strongly enough. For evidence of the fighting arts you need look no further than Samuel Pepys's *Diary* for 1 June 1663, 9 September 1667 and 12 April 1669. On each of these dates he mentions watching bouts. Other letter-writers and diarists also give us tantalising glimpses into the way professional fighting was organised. And of course there were female fencers, dagger-fighters and bare-knuckle fighters as well; this was *not* a male preserve.

The British have exercised with a wide variety of weapons over the centuries. Bows and arrows gave way to swords and sabres, pistols and rifles. However, one type of deadly weapon which has been in constant use for defence in this country is the simple stick. Films show us Little John fighting with Robin Hood, both using staffs, but up to the turn of the last century men protected themselves about town with weighted walking sticks. And back in history, we read in *Piers the Ploughman* that a man would go to protect his wife with his 'cudgels', beating off the crowd that beset her.

If you are interested in the history of the English fighting arts, you should read Terry Brown's *English Martial Arts*. This shows many methods of fighting which have been painstakingly researched by Terry as well as giving the best history of the 'Maisters of Defence' I have read.

For my other readers whose interest lies in the stories themselves, I can only hope that this book will be an enjoyable diversion. I had great fun writing it and I sincerely hope you get as much pleasure out of reading it.

Michael Jecks
Dartmoor
July 1999

CHAPTER ONE

In the servant's hall of her father's house in Tiverton, Joan Carter yawned and stretched. She had been working hard removing the old rushes and strewing fresh ones, but now the light was fading she had to stop. Soon the servants would be finishing their own work for the day and returning out here to the hall where they ate, drank and slept each night.

This room was always dim, set as it was at the back of the house and overshadowed by the merchants' houses at either side, but Joan was used to the gloom. She had spent much of her young life in this place, here at the back with the servants instead of in the main house with her mother. Not that she slept here with them. Even that comfort was denied her.

She went to the door and peered out. Earlier there had been a thin mizzle falling but it had cleared and the air was dry, with thick clouds hanging apparently motionless in a clear sky. Although it was late and the church bells had already rung for Vespers, she could hear the people in the streets trying to divest themselves of the few remaining goods they had to sell. That meant there were still some four hours until dark, and Joan was determined to enjoy them. She had been cooped up indoors all day, and felt she deserved a rest.

Pulling on a loose-fitting coat she strolled out into the busy cobbled thoroughfare; a quiet, contemplative young woman not yet in her twentieth year. In the lanes it was dim and intimidating, and the smell from the open sewer was foul, mingling with the scent of decomposing flesh from the tanners to create a doubly unwholesome stench. Joan hardly noticed it, however. The alleys and lanes were always fetid in summer, and the people who lived in Tiverton were used to it.

Hucksters bellowed their wares, alewives scurried about filling pots and jugs, prostitutes lounged at corners smiling at the men and boys who visited from outside the town, and Joan felt her mood lift. The atmosphere was happy, bustling and enthusiastic, especially at the small ring where a couple of men had set their dogs against each other; spectators cheered on the two, particularly the winning animal as he ripped open his foe's neck, spraying blood over a pair of young girls who screamed with glee and giggled, taking shelter behind their mother's skirts as she smiled indulgently.

Joan grinned, at first because it felt good to see people enjoying themselves, but soon she was smiling simply because she felt happy to be away from the house – *free*!

It was rare for her to feel this light-hearted. Lonely, desperate for the comfort of a companion, she tried to make friends with the servants but they were scared of her and withdrew. They knew her secret. She was outcast from their company: solitary and shunned.

That was how she sometimes saw herself: a separate creature of sadness and despair, almost otherworldly, unable to join in festivities or engage in normal conversation. Yet she generally managed to keep from gloom. She told herself that God would reward her if she endured.

Turning a corner she found herself before a small tavern. Standing there she had a moment's nervousness: it was daunting to enter a common alehouse on her own. Her father would be appalled if he heard. The thought made her stiffen her back proudly and almost before she realised, she'd made the decision and walked in.

She bought a quart of wine and looked about her for a table. A man glanced up as she hesitated, giving her a smile and casual glance up and down. He was quite good-looking, Joan thought to herself, square-faced and robust-looking. Well-dressed without being showy, with his clean shirt and velvet cotte. At least he didn't appear drunk. When he stood, she saw he was tall, at least six inches above her, and he had warm, dark eyes set beneath a high, intelligent brow.

'You want to sit?' he enquired.

'No, thank you, I'm only here for a short time,' she said, ducking her head and walking on to a space near the window. It was so rare for a man to speak to her that she hardly knew where to look. It was embarrassing, silly, for a stranger to talk to her. Why should he? What did he think she was? Some kind of strumpet from the streets? The hot blood of shame leaped into her cheeks and she determined to leave as soon as she could.

Sitting at last, she glanced back and saw that although his friends around the table were laughing as they drank, the man who had spoken was still smiling admiringly at her. The

15

sight sent a thrill of warmth flowing through her veins. Perhaps she needn't leave *quite* so soon.

In the dark the boat rocked alarmingly as Sir Gilbert of Carlisle climbed in, and he grabbed the sides swearing as the sailors began pulling on the oars.

Yet another ally of Despenser had resiled. It was difficult to find any men who would hold true to their oaths of support for the Despenser family now that armies were marching against them; no one wanted to be on the losing side. It was hard for Sir Gilbert to see how to advise his master, Hugh Despenser the Younger, when all the men he attempted to negotiate with either refused to see him at all or, if they did, laughed in his face. Everyone was now convinced that Despenser would have to leave the kingdom. And that meant Sir Gilbert was faced with a stark choice: face exile with Despenser or stay and seek a new lord.

Not an easy choice. Sir Gilbert had suffered once before from membership of an outlawed group. As a Knight Templar he had been an honoured warrior monk, revered wherever he went, until the French King invented foul lies about the Order so as to steal their wealth. Templar lands had been taken, shared out among the notaries and clerks who had persecuted members of the Order in France; Sir Gilbert himself had been cast aside, evicted from the lands he managed for the Order and forced to wander, masterless. He could still remember the loneliness and despair of his time on the road; he was too old now to go through all that again and to rebuild his life afresh – but the idea of following Despenser into exile filled him with dread.

As the boat rustled through the water towards the sea and the moored Despenser ship, Sir Gilbert had a clear view of both shores of the Thames, and he eyed them unenthusiastically as he passed. This city of London was a swirling pot of lies and intrigue. The King had sowed dissatisfaction by overtly favouring his friends – and now he was reaping the harvest of war.

It was Despenser's avarice which had brought this disaster down upon all their heads. Hugh Despenser had set about snatching land from brothers-in-law, from neighbours, from anyone weaker than himself, with the sole aim of becoming rich. Then he had set his heart upon the Gower, an obscure piece of southern Welsh territory. With it, Despenser would control the Bristol Channel. William de Braose owned it and was happy to sell to the highest bidder, but then he died and before Despenser could act, de Braose's son-in-law, John Mowbray, seized it.

Despenser was furious. Going to the King, he persuaded his friend to confiscate the lands. King Edward complied, but neither had realised the strength of opposition. The action confirmed the Lords of the Marches in their concern that their own lordships were threatened. If Despenser could force one lord to lose his inheritance, he could do the same to others, they reasoned, and all rose in arms against Despenser, declaring him to be an enemy of the King and demanding that he should leave the country. Earl Hereford, the Mortimers, Audley, Maurice Berkeley and Damory, were jointly ransacking Despenser lands, marching behind the King's own banner, declaring themselves to be fighting *for* him against an evil counsellor. Soon they would be here in London – and what then for Sir Gilbert's chances of survival?

While the King sulked in his palace, refusing to see any ambassadors from the Marches, men machinated: those who had sworn fealty to Despenser negotiated with new lords in anticipation of Despenser's exile. The whole nation felt like a keg of black powder on glowing coals, ready to explode at any moment. When the explosion came, Sir Gilbert was determined to be sheltered. But abroad with Despenser – or in England with a new lord?

The King himself supported Despenser, of course. That must count for something. If there were to be a fight, the King would stand at the side of the Despensers – and surely villeins and knights would prefer to remain loyal to their monarch rather than follow upstarts from the Marches who had been declared to be in revolt.

In the meantime, the King had ordered the Marcher Lords to London where he could hear their complaints. If the rumours were true and they *were* bringing their armies with them, Sir Gilbert might have to change his allegiance. It was hard to see where else he could go – but then, while thinking of the Templars, Sir Gilbert remembered Devon.

When the Templars had been destroyed, he had been living in a small Templar manor near Tiverton. In those days he had often met Lord Hugh de Courtenay, a baron who, like Sir Gilbert himself, was keen on his hunting. Sir Gilbert hadn't been back for over a decade, but he knew de Courtenay was an important man, one who could control his own small army, a man who was potentially useful. And someone who could give good advice.

At last – some sort of solution! Sir Gilbert smiled to himself. He would suggest to Despenser that he should sound out de Courtenay. That way, he could see how influential barons viewed the Despensers and decide whether his own loyalty was misplaced.

Feeling a little less anxious now, Sir Gilbert settled back in the boat, unaware that his decision would lead to his death in a matter of weeks.

*　　*　　*

Joan drained her cup and set it carefully down on the table before her. As she contemplated getting up and leaving, a shadow fell over her and she looked up to see the handsome stranger. He was holding a fresh jug in his hand.

'I wondered if you would like a drink with me,' he said.

'Why should I?'

'Oh, I don't know. You looked lonely, and I thought perhaps we could talk.'

'Why are you here?' she asked, peering around him at the crowded table he had just left.

He beamed. 'My friend Daniel there has just finished his apprenticeship and we're here to help him to celebrate!' To reinforce his words he up-ended his pot and set it down empty next to hers with a belch of content. 'Sorry!' Filling both their cups, he shot her a look. 'I haven't seen you here before.'

'You haven't been looking hard, then,' she rejoined tartly.

'You've lived here long?'

'Almost all my life. What of you?'

'I was born in Exeter. My father wanted to make sure I learned a decent trade so he sent me here thirteen years ago, when I was eight.'

'What trade?'

'I am to be a spicer, although,' his eyes took on a thoughtful expression, 'I am not sure that I should remain here. I think there's more money to be made in Exeter.'

'Really?' she said cynically. His words sounded boastful to her.

'Yes,' he grinned and mimicked her. '*Really*! I work for John Sherman now, but when I'm trained, Exeter will beckon. There's more potential for a spicer there.'

'You're bold enough, anyway. Coming over here without introducing yourself. Or did you think me . . . '

'Forgive me,' he said laughing, and gave a mock-serious bow. 'I am called Philip Dyne, or Phil of Exeter. And no, I did not think you a common tavern girl. You don't behave like one.'

'I am Joan. Joan Carter,' she said.

'It's a good name. Can I buy you a jug of wine?'

She thought a moment. Philip Dyne had already chased away the residual dregs of her gloom and made her laugh. With another sip of wine strange but exciting thoughts beset her. She noticed that his lips seemed very full and attractive, and the thought of kissing them was appealing.

Later, much later, the noise in the tavern grew deafening. When there came a loud guffaw and roar from an adjacent table, Dyne gave a fleeting frown, and she could guess what he was thinking: it was not conducive for talk here.

She knew men and their earthy desires. They weren't like girls. But she felt she'd be happy to satisfy this man; she'd be happy to stroll with him, or better, lie with him in the long grass that bordered the riverbank down in the meadow.

Sipping her wine, she considered him speculatively. With a boldness that surprised her, she knocked back the remainder of her pot with gusto, then refilled it. This too she drank quickly. A fire started in her belly, warming her whole body.

She wanted him, but not here. As another burst of laughter exploded at the next table, she gave him a shy, coquettish grin and nodded towards the doorway. He eagerly took her hint and stood; with delight he helped her from her seat. They interlaced their fingers while they drained their jugs, and then walked from the tavern, still hand-in-hand, and Joan led the way to the riverbank.

CHAPTER TWO

Sir Baldwin de Furnshill, Keeper of the King's Peace for Crediton, mounted his wife's Arab mare and set spurs to her flanks.

With something of a belly, now that his wife ordered his kitchen, Sir Baldwin was a tall, dark-haired man with a weathered complexion from his years of living in the Kingdom of Jerusalem. Unlike his contemporaries he wore a black beard that followed the line of his jaw. Proof of his fighting background lay in the scar which stretched from his temple to his jaw, but the lines of sadness and despair that had once scored his features were gone. He felt comfortable and happy as he followed the smooth track that led along the front meadow to the roadway. Here he paused and glanced behind him, waiting for his mastiff.

'Uther! Uther, come here.'

The dog ignored him. Nose deep in a bush at the roadside, tail moving slowly, the huge beast joyfully inhaled.

'*Uther*!'

The dog's head turned to him, tilted a little as if in enquiry. Sighing, Baldwin gave up. 'Chopsie!'

At his call the tawny dog padded quietly to his side and looked up with an expression that was so much like a smile, Baldwin had to chuckle despite his annoyance. Uther was young but there appeared to be nothing Baldwin could do to teach him his real name. No matter what he did, the dog only responded to the silly name which Baldwin's servant, Edgar, had given him.

But it was impossible for Baldwin to feel angry at the renaming of his dog, least of all towards the dog himself. For Uther Baldwin felt only affection, especially on a fine day like this. The sun shone brightly while a cool breeze stopped the heat becoming overpowering; high overhead, larks sang busily, shooting up as he came close, then dropping silently back to their nests after he had passed. A blackbird flew off close to the ground, its harsh warning call alerting all other creatures to Baldwin and Uther's presence.

It was good land here. Trees covered much of the landscape still, for few town-dwellers could be bothered to travel so far to fetch firewood or building materials, and there were not enough peasants to clear areas for growing crops. From here he could see many areas of agriculture, but each was discrete, separated by swathes of woodland through which the roads cut meanderingly, following hillsides or riverbanks. At this time of year, July, the trees still wore their covering of lighter-coloured, newer leaves. Oak, elm, chestnut and beech gave the hills a pleasing verdant tone, while in those areas where there was space the ground was bright with the yellow of buttercups or scattered with daisies.

Baldwin rode slowly, enjoying the sights and scents of this, his land.

But for all the pleasure of the journey, his mind could not leave the threatened war. No matter where he went, it was the main topic of conversation and he was worried that the whole country could soon be engulfed in flames.

His concern was for his wife, for Baldwin had only recently been married. He knew perfectly well that if war came he would be called away to fight for his master, Lord Hugh de Courtenay. If Baldwin died, or worse, if the war came here to Furnshill, he would not be able to protect her; that thought tore at him with each fresh rumour of battle.

Lady Jeanne, his wife, was a tall, slender woman with red-gold hair and the clearest blue eyes he had ever seen; to him she was the very picture of perfection. Her face was regular, if a little round; her nose short and too small; her mouth over-wide with a full upper lip that gave her a stubborn appearance; her forehead was perhaps too broad. And yet to Baldwin she was the most beautiful woman he had seen.

When they first met, he had been filled with reticence; his affection for her had felt wrong, because he had taken the Knight Templar's threefold vows: of obedience, poverty, and *chastity*. Sir Baldwin had felt confused, knowing his desire for Jeanne was unchaste, and it had taken some time for him to come to terms with his new position as a married man.

And now he had more or less accepted it, the kingdom was threatened by the greed of a few lords. He reined in at the top of the hill looking south towards Crediton and Dartmoor, surveying the sweep of the land while Uther snuffled in the ferns that lined the roadside.

Baldwin had been a Templar and survived the persecution of his Order. The experience had given him a loathing of intolerance of any kind. It was this that made him an effective official. Many times he had investigated murders and other felonies, convinced that an arrested man was innocent and fired with the determination to see justice prevail.

But justice would go by the board if there was a new war. Baldwin had a gloomy certainty that no matter who won a war it was the peasants and poorer knights like himself who would lose all – perhaps even their lives. His wife had already been widowed once; Baldwin was not sure how she would cope with losing a second man.

Suddenly, a black shape exploded skywards from his side, giving a harsh shrieking cry like metal scored with rough stone, and Baldwin's mount reared. When he had the beast under control, he saw Uther, who had sprung the black grouse, chasing off after the bird, paws windmilling as he tried to equal its speed. Baldwin laughed for joy and spurred his mare on.

A canter, then a gallop, and Baldwin tore past Uther, who lumbered at full speed staring up at the grouse, ignoring the land ahead. Baldwin too failed to notice the change in the grasses before him. Suddenly there was a splash and a jerk; Baldwin's mare stopped dead, and the astonished knight found himself flying through the air. For a brief moment he saw the ground racing towards his face and then he landed with a splash in a foul-smelling bog.

An hour or so later, when Uther had been installed for the night in the stable, a groom instructed to clean the mare and a servant called to fetch a clean robe so that Jeanne would not see the state Baldwin was in, many miles away Sir Gilbert of Carlisle was clambering down from the moored Despenser ship, clutching the leashes of his own two recalci- trant hounds. While the small craft rocked and bucked under the weight of the three passengers, the sailors took up their oars for the trip back to shore.

It was cloudy and a thin wind was blowing a fine spray at them. Sir Gilbert's coat of best wool was soggy, its smell reminding him of old, wet sheep. Compared with the foul odour of sewage and putrefaction that hung over London, it was almost pleasant.

Before they set off, an iron-bound chest was let down on a whip, caught by a sailor and thrust quickly at Sir Gilbert, who stowed it away between his feet. He rested his hand on it for reassurance.

It was his own fault, he reflected; he had suggested this journey down to Devon. At the time he hadn't realised the wind was blowing from the west. It would take an age for the old single-masted cog to beat up into the breeze; she was ever a slow ship, but tacking constantly would take an age, and Hugh Despenser the Younger had need of speed. He proposed that Sir Gilbert should land in London and make his own way to Devon using horses owned by the Despensers.

So here he was, setting off for a long journey with his dogs and two guards for company, and this box. With a grim smile Sir Gilbert patted his dogs' heads. With the wealth held inside he needed all the protection he could get.

There was a sharp intake of breath from one of the sailors. Sir Gilbert ignored it: he wasn't used to paying attention to the feelings of menials and servants. He assumed it was simply the gasp of a tired man pulling at oars. Shrugging himself lower into his sodden coat, he tried to protect his neck from the chill breeze. In his gloomy mood he thought there was a dull blanket of dampness over everything, even smothering the torches and braziers at either bank.

It was only when he realised that the breath was hissing through the teeth of the nearer sailor, a swarthy, pox-scarred man with a shock of tawny hair and small, shrewd eyes, that Sir Gilbert glanced up. The man was staring over Sir Gilbert's shoulder and after a moment the knight peered back as well.

There, casting a great white bow-wave, was a small ship, a galley-type, moving speedily towards them. 'What is it?' Gilbert asked.

'It's that whoreson Badlesmere, I'll bet. Whoever it is, they mean to catch us – board us or ram us.'

The vessel was closing fast now, and instinctively Sir Gilbert pulled the chest up to his lap, cradling it protectively as he might a child. When he next looked over his shoulder their pursuer was scant yards away.

An order was grunted. Without warning the sailor and his mate behind him lifted their oars from the water; the other men on the opposite side hauled. Sir Gilbert was no expert seaman and he was thrown bodily to one side, almost losing his grip on the box, while one dog yelped in alarm, ears flat back in fear, and the other stood scrabbling on the slippery wood trying to remain upright. The boat lurched once, then again, and there was a loud crack as the ship struck their side, knocking him from his seat.

A man sprang down, axe in hand. Sir Gilbert was on his back in the bilgewater and could only stare up in horror. He saw the axe swing and embed itself in the head of one of his guards: the man shrieked. A kick sent him overboard as a second boarder leapt down. The first pirate made a hideous gargling sound deep in his throat and Sir Gilbert saw him clutch at his neck even as a warm, fine spray settled on his face. Then he saw the knife's hilt showing. All at once the pock-marked sailor was up. He grabbed his dagger from the one, shoved, and in an instant both boarders were over the side.

'What . . .?' Sir Gilbert managed, clambering to his seat and gazing about him in the murky light.

'They tried to overhaul us; we slipped aside before they could ram us,' the sailor grunted, once more at his oar. 'They'll need to tack to come back at us. Can't do that in a hurry, so they'll try to land some men to catch us as we moor. We'll just have to beat them to it.'

They ran the boat scraping up a shallow ramp and one of the crew waded to land and held the boat while the others helped Sir Gilbert out. There was no need to help the dogs: Aylmer jumped quickly from the boat and hared to the top of the ramp away from the water, while Merry stepped lightly onto land and stood there sniffing at a wall.

'Wait here,' said the sailor and darted silently across the yard to a gate in the encircling wooden fence. Soon he was back, the knife in his hand shining in the light of the torches. 'It's safe enough.'

Sir Gilbert glanced at his remaining guard, who hefted the chest. The sailor glanced at it, his face twisting with sympathetic amusement. It was the same expression that Sir Gilbert had seen other sailors wearing as they watched lubbers clumsily moving about the ship.

'What?' he demanded sharply.

'You're in London, Sir Gilbert. You may be on the Surrey and Kent side, but this is still London, where sluts, cutpurses, horsethieves and footpads mingle. What are you going to do? Walk up to an inn, bold as a cock, and ask for a horse, holding your little box at your shoulder?'

'No one would dare attack me with my dogs here,' Sir Gilbert said coldly, but the man had a point. Sir Gilbert hadn't expected to be put ashore here, he'd been hoping to be further upriver, nearer the London Bridge. Instead, here he was, with a long walk ahead of him and no horse or carriage. And only one guard, not two.

The sailor saw his expression and shook his head. Turning, he issued instructions to the other men before walking ahead to the gate again, beckoning to Sir Gilbert.

'What is this?' Sir Gilbert demanded.

'You need help to cross London. This is a seaman's land, not fit for a country knight.'

'We can protect ourselves.'

The sailor watched him tap his sword. 'You think so? While protecting the box?'

Sir Gilbert considered.

'Come, Sir Knight. I'll join you. You can be certain that I won't betray my Lord Despenser, not while he wins me rewards from the ships he takes. With two guards there's more chance of your mission succeeding.'

It was hard to believe he'd come to this. Philip Dyne squatted on the floor by the altar within the sanctuary and gazed ahead of him unseeing. It was dark now, and the place was lit by a few candles this late in the evening. The priest himself, the sepulchral Father Abraham, had gone to his bedchamber hours before, and Philip was alone in the great cold room.

He shivered. The memory of men pounding after him lingered; never in all his years had he known such terror. It was one thing to be found pilfering the odd spice and being soundly thrashed by his master for trying to supply it on the quiet, but *this*!

His legs ached, and he shifted uncomfortably while keeping a grip on the altar cloth. He wanted no mistake about his right to claim sanctuary here, not while he had no knife, no staff, *nothing* with which to protect himself.

Moving his legs, he carefully avoided the small pile of excrement where a dog had relieved itself. He was astonished that the priest hadn't cleaned the spot, but then Father Abraham was very jealous of his position, proud of his standing. He would refuse to clean the place; that was the job of the sexton, not the priest.

From here Philip could see the pictures on the walls, large, round, flamboyant depictions of biblical scenes, of the seven deadly sins and the seven cardinal virtues, with angels on one side receiving Christian souls into Heaven while on the other angels sternly pointed the way to Hell for sinners.

He stared at them despondently. Every now and again he sniffed, too exhausted to sob; his emotions had been used up over the last few nights.

This church held no mystery – he'd been here so often, watching Father Abraham thundering on about the evils of sin from this very place, pointing out the pictures, ranting wide-eyed as the spittle flew, berating his congregation as he tried to instill his own loathing for pride, covetousness, lust, anger, gluttony, envy, and sloth. Philip and his friends had enjoyed those sermons with the priest roaring away, scaring maids and upsetting children. It had been fun. He could still grin weakly, recollecting the time when a pigeon had been startled from the rafters and left a deposit on the priest's tonsured head.

His face hardened. It was all over now. His only escape was to leave England, to abjure the realm and become an exile. All for the death of Joan. Whenever he thought of her his eyes filled with tears. She was fun, exciting and bright. That was why they became engaged.

That first night together down by the river, she had thrilled him so much, lying almost naked in his arms. Then they realised how late it was and she breathily giggled into his shoulder that she couldn't get home now: the house's doors would be locked. It was already too late; with her warm flesh filling his hands he wouldn't have let her go anyway. Not that she wanted to. Her hands pulled impatiently at his tunic, untying the thongs that held up his hose, releasing them so that she could lift the cloth from him before he rolled her on her back and covered her body with his own.

Her father had gone mad when she got home, she told him the next time they met. He knew she'd been up to no good. Joan laughed as she described Andrew Carter's towering rage. Then she pulled Philip along behind her, back to their meadow, and made love to him again.

'You won't leave me, will you?' she asked seriously afterwards.

'No, 'course not.'

And he hadn't. She had left him.

By dying.

CHAPTER THREE

As the end of July drew near, Sir Gilbert of Carlisle gratefully approached the West Country. Reaching the top of a rise, he gazed ahead and halted. There before him he could see the hills and woods of Devonshire.

The journey had not been easy. Before long he had been forced to appreciate the stolid sailor who stayed with him when his second guard was lost. His name was William, the sailor said; William the Small.

It had been the panic of London's folk that had cost him his second guard. Not only were Londoners anxious at having Hugh Despenser aboard his ship in the Thames, they also had the country's great magnates ringing the city with their armies. The Mortimers were the guests of the Knights of St John at Clerkenwell, Hereford was at Holborn, Damory at the New Temple, and Audley at St Bartholomew's Priory at Smithfield. The city was enclosed and while the King vacillated, reluctant to banish his friend, yet fearful of the response of the Marcher

Lords if he refused to do so, the lords themselves grew annoyed to hear of the King's trips to the Despensers' ship, or young Despenser's visits to the shore to feast with the King.

The unease in the city had come to a head the day before Sir Gilbert landed. Parliament had met at the great hall at Westminster, and the lords demanded that both Despensers should be exiled. They were guilty of greed and treachery, they were enemies of both the King and his people.

In the streets, supporters of the Despensers hurled stones or fired arrows at the men from the marches; their attacks were returned with gusto. Before the parliamentary meeting there had been threats to fire the city of London, and that brought out the burgesses to protect their homes. Now, instead of running fights between two groups, there were battles between all three and Sir Gilbert arrived with his men in the middle of it all. London Bridge was closed, as were all the main gates while the emergency continued, and Sir Gilbert and his servants were forced to seek an inn in which to stay until they could continue their journey.

They found one close to the Black Friars' Priory, down at the Thames where the River Fleet met it. Sir Gilbert would have been happier to have been nearer London's bridge, but William pointed out that here they had two rivers over which they could make an escape at need.

On the second day the situation changed: the King finally agreed to exile the Despensers. Sir Gilbert breathed a sigh of relief, paid his reckoning, and he and his men left – but they had forgotten the armies about the city.

Horses had been promised, but in the new climate friends of the Younger Despenser were hard to find. Sir Gilbert had to threaten one of Despenser's grooms to provide him with three horses. The fellow agreed with a bad grace and it was while he was preparing the mounts that Sir Gilbert went to see the Temple: he couldn't resist taking a look at the symbol of his old Order. However, as he and his men turned a corner, they found themselves confronted by five scruffy men-at-arms.

One sat at a table drinking, while two stood behind him in a tavern's doorway. All had the bleared voices and ruddy faces of men who have been drinking for many hours. They were egging on two more men who were practising fighting with daggers. As soon as Sir Gilbert and his little retinue appeared, the fighters stopped and eyed them with interest.

Sir Gilbert avoided meeting their eyes, but hefted his wooden chest beneath an arm and carried on.

'Oi! Stop a moment, my Lord.' It was the large, broad-shouldered man at the bench who spoke, his face remarkably smooth and youthful, with light-coloured brown hair, and only one blemish: a thick, pink scar which followed the line of his eyebrows like an obscene crease. Bright blue eyes gleamed with humour but, when he motioned, the men with daggers moved to stand in Sir Gilbert's path.

Instantly the dogs were at Sir Gilbert's side, Aylmer standing still, head low as he scowled forward, Merry crouching slightly before taking two stiff-legged steps towards the men blocking the path.

Sir Gilbert paused, his hand falling to his sword.

'Master, there's no need for violence,' the seated man said mildly, and his men chuckled. 'But I think I should like to peep inside your little box there, just to make sure you haven't got something you shouldn't.'

'The box stays shut,' Sir Gilbert said flatly, staring at the dagger men.

'That's a pity, isn't it, Toker?' said one of them, address-
ing the seated man.

'I think it is, Perkin. Owen thinks so too, don't you, Owen?'

The other dagger-fighter said nothing. If anything he
looked unhappy about the way things were developing.

Sir Gilbert heard a slight noise: the man called Toker had
spanned a crossbow. It was a powerful modern one with a
metal bow and it rested, cocked, on the table. As Sir Gilbert
watched, the man placed a quarrel in the groove and shifted
it until it pointed at him. Sir Gilbert weighed the distance. If
he could throw the chest, it would make the man duck. He'd
almost certainly miss his aim, and that would give Sir Gilbert
time to take on the leader. Sir Gilbert was a Templar: he had
no fear of the odds, not with his dogs at his side.

Before he could move, his plans were wrecked. His
remaining guard sprang forward, sweeping out a short
sword. The crossbow moved and the string hummed as it
spat out the bolt which passed clean through the guard, who
nonetheless ran on at full tilt. Lifting the crossbow, Toker
lazily blocked the clumsy sword-thrust before punching the
guard to the ground.

Simultaneously Sir Gilbert heard a sharp rap, then a cry.
Turning, he saw that William, smiling mildly, was grasping
a six-foot pole. At his feet were the two men from the doorway, one lying on his back and snoring, the other retching
drily into the gutter, gripping his belly. William held his
quarter-staff aimed at Toker's face. Shrugging good-
humouredly, Toker let his crossbow fall to the table.

Aylmer had forced the man called Perkin up against a wall,
while Merry had knocked the other to the ground and now
stood guard over him, snarling each time he moved, his bared

teeth at the man's throat. Sir Gilbert almost pitied the fellow when he saw the grimace of terror on the silent man's face.

Sir Gilbert called and the dogs returned to his side – Merry with a certain reluctance. William Small the sailor took out his knife and slashed at the crossbow's string, which snapped with a loud twanging report. A small crowd had appeared, and for a coin or two one man agreed to fetch a physician for the wounded guard. Meanwhile the man called Toker remained calm and smiling, even calling for more ale.

Sir Gilbert and William left the scene as soon as they could. The moment they had put some distance between them and the inn, the knight asked: 'Where did you find the staff?'

'It was one of theirs. I noticed it leaning by the door there,' William told him.

'I thank you.'

'There's no need,' the other said. 'I have a duty to see that the money gets to Devon, just like you. But rather than trying to set ourselves up as targets for every footpad and outlaw between here and Devon, let's lose the chest.'

'Lose it?'

'Throw it in the river,' William said shortly. 'You can put all the stuff into a sack. At least it wouldn't be so conspicuous.'

Sir Gilbert considered. 'You're right.' He found a merchant and bought a pair of small sacks. While William mounted guard, Sir Gilbert crouched in an alley and transferred the contents of the chest to them.

That was many leagues ago and now, as Sir Gilbert approached the country where he had spent so much of his youth and young adulthood, he felt his mood lifting. The weather was poor (just as it always used to be, he sighed happily), with heavy, storm-filled clouds hanging threateningly in the sky and puddles on the ground. At each step of his horse the mud spattered, and the two dogs kept their distance.

William was a curious man. Sir Gilbert had discovered a little about him: he had been a man-at-arms serving in the King's army in Flanders in 1297 and later in Scotland in 1303; not long afterwards he had turned to the sea.

'Why?' Sir Gilbert had asked.

William had a badly pock-marked face, but his hair was thick and curling, his shoulders broad, and he had a steadiness in his green eyes that spoke of a stable nature. He glanced now at Sir Gilbert. 'The sea is clean compared with the land, sir. On land, everyone is owned by someone and tied like a dog. At sea, when the wind blows we're all equals. The man is a king who can save the cog, and if there's discipline, there's freedom too; on land a man has to behave as he's told.'

Sir Gilbert nodded and left the matter there, but he was aware of something else. William was a fighter; it was obvious in the way he had handled his staff. There was good money to be earned by a fighter on a ship – especially one like Hugh Despenser's which was about to turn pirate and steal whatever it could. A sailor would be unwilling to jump back to land just to help protect his master's cash from felons. He would want to be at sea with his boat where he could help win prizes and make his fortune.

Perhaps William was with him less to guard Sir Gilbert, more to protect his mission and Hugh Despenser's money.

Unless William was a thief and simply sought an opportunity to take the lot for himself, of course.

*　　*　　*

While they continued on their way, Matilda Carter was sitting in Tiverton with her eyes closed, the tears running down her cheeks. This part of her garden had always been a delight to her. It was peaceful here at the back of their burgage plot with the stream running along the lawn's edge; the noise and bustle of the townspeople seemed a thousand miles away. Here the turfed seats stayed cool in the hottest weather and the scent of the little dog roses wafted to her on each small breeze. It was her sanctuary; she came here when she had need of silence and reflection, but now she would never know peace again because that man was safe in the sanctuary of her church.

It was obscene! Andrew, Matilda's husband, had railed against Joan for being no better than a whore when she eventually returned from her first meeting with the lad, but Joan had appeared unimpressed with his rage. She was handfast, she said; she would marry Philip Dyne. But before she could, her lover had throttled her.

How a man could murder a sweet, innocent child like Joan, Matilda didn't know. Her daughter was never spiteful or unkind. If anything, she was a little too quiet. And for her murderer to be granted safety in church was mad. There were rumours that he would be allowed to escape justice completely. While Joan lay in her grave, he might be allowed to run away.

Hearing steps on the gravelled pathway, she hurriedly wiped at her eyes, composing herself.

It was her maid, Clarice. 'Mistress? Can I fetch you a cup of wine?'

'No. I am all right, Clarice. Quite all right.' Matilda sniffed, then she burst out: 'I just miss her! I feel so alone without her. You know my husband only values me for my money and the ties I have with my brother.'

'Oh, no!'

'It's true. What's the point of denying it? He only comes to me in our bed when he is desperate and there are no whores to tempt him. And to keep him happy, I allowed him to shut poor Joan away.'

'I'm sure Joan was happy, Mistress.'

Clarice's words went ignored.

'And she was so pretty. So pretty. As she grew older she became more so, but I missed her growing. I should have been there to watch her, to guide her; I should have been there for her to describe the first man she was attracted to, to help her dress and learn how to comport herself. I should have been there.'

'You were there when she needed you.'

'How can you say that?' Matilda flashed. 'She needed me when she met that bastard Dyne! She needed me to tell her that the man was evil – that he would kill her!'

'You couldn't predict that,' Clarice pointed out reasonably.

'How do I know?' Matilda wailed miserably. 'How can I tell? But at least I would have been there for her, instead of ignoring her for so long.'

'It is the way of children that they are put to their work,' said Clarice, who had left her mother and home when she was eight. She patted her mistress's hand sympathetically. 'You did all you thought best for her.'

'And now whenever I go to celebrate Mass, he's there, watching me with his piggy little eyes, like a demon,' Matilda said. 'He killed her, and now he claims the protection of the altar in my own church. Even Father Abraham supports him.'

'It is the law.'

'Stuff the law! I want *revenge*!'

It was a relief when August came and Baldwin could see how well his crops were doing. To him this time of year was rewarding and reassuring, proof of Dame Nature's fruitfulness.

There was always much to be done, but at least his manor was heading towards the culmination of the annual effort. Soon the men would be trooping off to the fields to rake the corn for the harvesters. Those with scythes would be sweeping the great blades from side to side, mowing the slender yellow stalks; women in thick fustian aprons would bundle up the sheaves and stack them in stooks, while the children, chattering and laughing, their slings or bows in their hands, would prepare to shoot the rabbits and hares that would bolt from the fields as their cover was cut down. Afterwards, while the threshers flailed the grain from the stalks, the gleaners would crouch among the stubble, picking over the dirt to gather as much of the fallen grain as possible before the birds got it all.

And overnight many would celebrate, drinking heavily from cider or ale jars, snoring under the stars, both because walking home was too strenuous, and because Baldwin's haywarden would willingly pay them to stay in the fields to prevent thieves taking the precious crop – and nine months later the parish priest would have a rash of squalling children to baptise.

But Baldwin was not content. Although his land was fertile and the harvest looked to be good, he heard that the fighting in Wales was spreading and he wanted more, much more: enough to fill his granaries and give him the confidence that his people would have plenty of food for the winter in case war came to his lands.

He had altered his routine now. Rising soon after dawn, he practised with a sword or cudgels on the flat grass before his house. It was normal for a man-at-arms to perform such ritual dances with weapons of all types, but Baldwin knew that many of his peers did not bother. They relied on the cavalry charge, the weight of steel, chargers and knights welded together in an unstoppable phalanx.

Baldwin had seen the shattering effect of a troop of heavily armoured knights on horseback, but he was not convinced that modern fights would be won that easily. He had kept in touch with developments across Europe where resolute Swiss farmers had destroyed an Austrian army at Morgarten and Flemish peasants had massacred France's elite at Courtrai, while nearer home the Scots had slaughtered the English at Bannockburn. There was an unpleasant sense of the natural order being overturned, if the chivalrous could be killed by villeins.

Whatever nasty surprises battle might hold, Baldwin intended to ensure that his own lack of preparation would not be a contributory factor. That was why he spent his mornings swinging weapons in the guard positions while balancing solidly on both legs, moving to protect his right flank then his left, striking at imaginary foes, thrusting, parrying, stepping quickly to one side or another. Sometimes his servant Edgar joined him and the two would cautiously dance about each other, their sword-blades shimmering and gleaming in the sun. Both men gathered fresh scars. They only used unrebated weapons, and if one or the other lost concentration for a moment he was likely to regret it.

After a bout or two, whether with a real or an imaginary opponent, Baldwin would go for a ride, usually up over the hill towards Bickleigh but sometimes south to Crediton, to attend court or just to pick up whatever gossip he could from the inns. The news was rarely good, and it concerned him to see how men had taken to wearing weapons. It wasn't only he who practised; there were enough fighters in Crediton from old King Edward I's wars to form a small army.

When he returned to his manor, he would often soak in a bath. This was a luxury he had been forced to live without when he was a Templar, for the Rule of the Order forbade bathing, but now he saw to it that all the wood ashes were gathered from the fires, and these were boiled with mutton fat to produce his solid soap cakes. While bathing he could forget the troubles besetting the kingdom. Cleansed, he would dine with his wife before walking with her over his lands, or taking his dogs to hunt some kind of venison – boar, deer, rabbit or hare.

But even as he chased his game, always at the back of his mind was the anxiety of the political situation. War would come. It might not be this month or the one after, but the loathing between the King and his lords was strong, mutual – and irreconcilable.

That was why, when he received the invitation to visit Tiverton Castle during the feast of St Giles, he was not overly surprised. The de Courtenay family would want to test the loyalty of their knights if they were soon to be tried in battle. The saint's feast and the fair which celebrated it would give Lord Hugh de Courtenay the excuse he needed to speak to all his men.

CHAPTER FOUR

Once they arrived in Exeter Sir Gilbert began to wonder where their next destination should be. The noise was deafening, the city heaving. It was a Friday, and the whole place seemed full of farmers and other peasants who had turned up to sell their produce at the market or to buy provisions. Sir Gilbert dropped from his stallion and gave the reins to a boy. Glancing at the teeming marketplace in the Cathedral precinct, he saw it was packed with what looked like the whole of Christianity. Men and women shouted their wares, gaily dressed girls bustled about offering drink, beggars shuffled on crippled legs, piteously calling for alms; a child with a belly distended by starvation squeaked for food at his mother's feet, a scrawny woman who sat with her back against a wall feebly watching passers-by with eyes made immense with hunger; Sir Gilbert threw the pair some coins.

He paused at the ring, where a massive bull was trampling a dog, spraying blood and gore with defiant tosses of its head. Bulls had to be baited before death to tenderise their flesh, but Sir Gilbert was confident this hoary beast would have iron bands for muscles: even after baiting and hanging he would be inedible.

An official jostled him, hurrying by with two scruffy men carrying long staves; behind them, a man was led by a rope, bawling his innocence – he was a tavern-keeper found selling short measures. There would be little sympathy for him here. Sir Gilbert's dogs both lunged at the little procession, but he had put them on leashes as he entered the city and now he hauled them back. They were unsettled in so large a crowd and the knight decided to find somewhere to sit and rest.

Overhead, flags fluttered gently in the breeze. Fresh air was certainly welcome, for the high walls of the city trapped the air within and Sir Gilbert's nostrils were assailed with the stench. Sweat from the men and women all about him vied with animal and human excrement and the persistent tang of urine, thickened by the reek of putrefaction from the tanners on Exe Island. Fanning the air disgustedly, Sir Gilbert bought a bunch of herbs and held it beneath his nose in a vain attempt to drown out the surrounding odours.

At Nobles Inn, Sir Gilbert paid off the boy and he and William ordered ale, sitting at a bench outside, the leather saddlebag containing the sacks at Sir Gilbert's feet. Merry sat at his side, but Aylmer rolled over and was soon snoring gently.

'Where to now?' William asked, glancing up at the sun.

Sir Gilbert emptied his pot and waved at the surly tavern-keeper for more. There was no point in concealing their destination. 'We try to find out where the Lord is. He may well be here or at Oakhampton. Maybe up at Tiverton.'

'You're planning on seeing Lord de Courtenay?' William asked, aghast.

'Yes.' Sir Gilbert held out his pot to be refilled and cast a quick look at the sailor.

William was blank for a moment, but nodded. 'I could ask about: find where he is, if you want.'

'You know this city? I didn't think the river was navigable.'

William shrugged. 'It's not got its own port, but down at the head of the estuary there's another town, Topsham. Ships delivering goods for Exeter go there, and sometimes after we've paid the customs we load up smaller craft to ferry them up the Exe to the city. I've been here several times.'

'Good. In that case, ask your friends where we might find de Courtenay and his retinue. I shall be here waiting.'

William stood, glanced up and down the narrow thoroughfare, and strolled off towards Cook Row. Sir Gilbert meanwhile ordered himself a coffin filled with fish, this being Friday and a fast day, and munched on the pie. Once they were outside the city he was determined to rest in a river and clean himself. His flesh itched from dried sweat, and he was unpleasantly aware that he had grown verminous. There was an unpleasant tingling at his armpits and groin as if creatures were scuttling.

But he had other things to occupy his mind.

No man would entrust a large fortune to an emissary without trying to ensure its protection. But the two men Despenser had sent to accompany Sir Gilbert were dead or wounded before they had left London. When William Small showed himself willing to join him, Sir Gilbert had been grateful. On a ship no secrets could be kept; Sir Gilbert had assumed that

William had heard of the money and chose to stay with Sir Gilbert to see that his master's bribe was protected. But he was no fool and now he considered once more the other possibility. William plainly hadn't thought Sir Gilbert ever intended delivering the chest – he could see that now. He obviously believed Sir Gilbert was going to steal it for himself, and if so, William was determined to share in the profits.

The knight sat back and eased himself into a comfortable position, cradling his pot in his large hand, resting it on his flat stomach. Merry looked at him, then scratched idly at an ear and lay down, chin on paws, but watching every passer-by.

Sir Gilbert smiled down at his dog and patted the tawny flank. If William wanted to rob him, he would find it very difficult.

Two days later, Philip Dyne blinked as he left the safe confines of the church. The sun was blazing in a clear blue sky, painful to his eyes after so many days locked in the dark. He had to shield them with a hand. The gloom of the church was preferable.

As he blinked, wincing at the pain, colours appeared before him; brilliant hues and stunning shades. His head ached with the magnificence of the greens of grass and leaves, the brightness of coats and tunics, dull-coloured hose for the poorer, parti-coloured reds and blues for the rich. His legs buckled beneath him and he was struck with a feeling of vertigo as he saw the faces ranged before him.

'Get your hand off me!' Father Abraham snarled as Philip grabbed at his sleeve to stop himself falling. Father Abraham snatched his arm away and strode on to the Coroner's side by the little gate.

The waiting crowd stood silently at the other side of the fence and Philip eyed them with a sense of doom. If they decided to attack him, the thin palings would be no protection. There was an occasional curse uttered in his direction, but for the most part they stood quietly, waiting. Oddly he found that their loathing pricked at his pride, gave him a little strength, and he willed himself on, alone, dressed only in his threadbare tunic and coat, a pilgrim's cross stitched to his breast. The felon about to flee the scene of his crime.

Father Abraham, at the gate to the churchyard, held up his hand and scowled at the folk about him until they were silent, awed by the slim, regal figure clothed in the garb of a priest. When their muttering had died away, he beckoned to Philip and snapped, 'Come here, Dyne.'

He could not watch Dyne approach. It was disgusting that the pervert should have entered his church at all, let alone dare to claim sanctuary and stay inside for so long. Quite deplorable. Better that the mob should catch him. It was vile that he, a priest, should be expected to give such a creature food. It was enough to make one sick! He would order the sexton to see the whole sanctuary scrubbed clean to remove Dyne's foul contamination.

It was at times like this that he wished he had not joined the Church and instead had joined a warrior Order, something like the Knights of St John. Better to fight for God than to pander to felons.

The crowd agreed with his view; he could see that at a single glance. There were some who were merely observers: farmers and others from outside town come to visit the market who had spotted the huddle at the gate and strolled over to investigate; others were locals who had gathered out of mild interest to see what the sanctuary-seeker looked like before he fled. These were no trouble; it was the others who gave Father Abraham concern.

Andrew Carter was at the back, a large, grossly proportioned man, red of face, with fleshy lips and heavy jowls, dark hair under his velvet hat, and a vindictive frown twisting his features. Next to him was the merchant Nicholas Lovecok, Carter's brother-in-law, a weakly-looking man with unnaturally bright eyes in his pale face and little hair on his bare head. The sight made the priest purse his lips. He could see Lovecok's lips moving, and he held his hat in his hand, twisting it and turning it as he prayed, no doubt, for the felon's painful death. About these two was a small gathering of what looked like the dregs of the nearby alehouses. Rough, drink-coarsened men, some still with jugs or pots in their hands, were watching the solitary figure with ill-concealed hatred, measuring interest or vague bafflement, the degree of concentration depending upon the quantity of ale they had already drunk.

It was understandable, Father Abraham thought. Even the expression of sheer loathing on Coroner Harlewin le Poter's face was justified. No one liked the murderer of a young wench.

Coroner Harlewin's face was bleak as Philip approached the low picket fence. He held up his hand both to halt the felon and silence the crowd, which had begun to murmur.

'Quiet!' he thundered, glaring about him, then crooked his finger at Philip. 'Come closer, boy. You can't reach the fu— . . .' he swallowed the automatic expletive when he felt Father Abraham stiffen '. . . um, Gospels from there.'

Father Abraham hadn't missed his near-lapse and made a mental note to demand a severe penance. The Coroner was a brutish knight, low-born and with the manners of a hog. He disgusted Father Abraham.

The Coroner continued, 'We all know why we're here. This man, Philip Dyne, apprentice to the spicer John Sherman, murdered a young girl from this town: Joan Carter. The posse nearly caught him, but he managed to escape by claiming sanctuary within the church. Unless someone saw him outside the church during his imprisonment, or saw him eating anything other than the water and bread supplied by the priest here, he can abjure the realm . . .' He peered at the crowd, a hopeful tone creeping into his voice. 'Did anyone see him outside?'

Father Abraham was sure that this was not a part of the normal procedure for an abjuration; the Coroner was tempting the audience to bear false witness. 'He did not leave,' he said sharply. 'I was there all the time. If he had left I would have known.'

Harlewin grunted without satisfaction. 'In that case,' he mumbled, then cleared his throat. 'Very well, Father, let him confess. Come here, Dyne!'

Philip Dyne cast a look at the people before him, and Father Abraham saw him shiver. Pathetic! he thought. A typical peasant. He jerked his head, saying shortly, 'You heard him, Dyne. Come here and make your confession. If you don't, you cannot abjure; that's the law.'

'I admit that I took the girl, um . . .'

'Go on, you bastard! Tell us all about it, how you raped my daughter and slaughtered her!' roared a voice. Father Abraham turned and made a swift cutting movement with his hand.

'*Enough*! Carter, be still! I will not have men here incited to murder to the ruin of their immortal souls – no, and you must not risk your own, either. You regret the loss of your daughter, but you forget yourself; this place is proof of God's mercy, and this lad may be able to serve God's purpose if he contritely and honestly confesses. Don't presume to question His judgement. There has been a terrible crime committed, don't let's make things worse.'

Philip, eyes closed, made his confession, shivering slightly. 'I killed her. I met her down near the river where we always met and wanted her body. When she refused me, I took her anyway and strangled her to make sure she couldn't tell anyone. I sincerely regret it, and beg God's forgiveness. As I live this is true.'

The Coroner nodded and Father Abraham turned to his sexton who carried the immense book. Taking it, Father Abraham bowed his head over it, making the sign of the cross, then held it out. Philip Dyne swallowed and rested his hand on the cover with a wide-eyed, wondering fear.

Harlewin then spoke. His voice, filled with the authority of his position, carried over the whole crowd with ease, scaring the rooks in the oaks and elms of the churchyard and sending them fluttering upwards, chattering and squawking to each other.

'Philip Dyne, you have remained in the sanctuary of this church for forty days. You have made a free confession of your guilt, and now you must make your oath of abjuration. Repeat after me: "I, Philip Dyne . . ."'

'I, Philip Dyne . . .'

' "Do swear to leave this realm . . ."'

49

Father Abraham saw Philip Dyne's cheeks were running with tears.

'Never to return . . .'

The book felt heavier in his hands, as if Dyne was leaning on it for support.

'Unless with the permission of the King or his heirs . . .'

Using the Gospels in that manner was irreverent. Father Abraham considered snapping at him to refrain.

'I will hasten by the most direct road to a port . . .'

No. He decided not to: it would only create more fuss. Better that this ceremony should be completed swiftly and this beggarly creature should finally be ejected from the town.

'Never leaving the King's highway . . .'

Father Abraham saw the young man swallow again as if he feared the next words.

'On pain of arrest as a felon and being beheaded instantly.'

There was a slight quiver in his voice. Good, thought Father Abraham. Perhaps the immensity of his crime is driven home to him at last.

'And on arriving I shall seek diligently for a passage across the sea.'

'Very well!' said the Coroner and stood back as Father Abraham passed the precious book back to the patiently waiting sexton. 'I order that this man be allowed to leave the town by the road to Bickleigh, thence to Exeter, from whence he must find a ship to remove him from King Edward's lands. He must not remain at any inn or vill for more than one night. At Exeter's port he must seek diligently for a passage, delaying only one tide. If there is no ship when he arrives, he must walk into the sea up to his knees each day in demonstration of his willingness to cross it, and if he has still failed after forty days he must take sanctuary again at the port.'

He stopped and fixed Dyne with a stern, unsympathetic eye. 'His goods are all forfeit: he can take with him only a wooden cross and a bowl. Nothing else.' He pointed southwards towards Crediton. 'Go! Don't delay, but leave the country as soon as you possibly can.'

Philip Dyne's head hung low; the crowd began hissing again, jostling forward, a young boy on his father's shoulder cried out as an inaccurate stone hit his cheek, raking a long scratch. Harlewin le Poter's head shot round, and seeing the boy weep, a hand touching the bleeding scar, he swept out his sword. Two men-at-arms thrust their way through to his side, their long polearms swinging like heavy, iron-shod clubs, prodding away any who came too close.

'*Back*, you lot!' the Coroner roared. 'Serfs and bastard whoresons, the lot of you! *Back*, I said: give him space, in the King's name – and no more rocks. If I see any of you with one you'll be in the castle's stocks so fast your feet will burn – *is that clear*? The man's not to be pilloried, he's abjured.'

A thin gap appeared as reluctant, muttering people pulled away from each other.

'That's better. Now, felon, *sod off!* And never come back!' the Coroner said. He shoved his sword away, then pushed Dyne along the channel, crossing his arms and watching.

At his side Father Abraham curled his lip. Watching Dyne scuff through the people, his head low, avoiding all the eyes on him, wincing and turning away when a man hawked and spat, the spittle running down his neck, Father Abraham muttered vindictively: 'And if you should stray from the road so much as a single foot, I hope you will be seen and executed on the spot. God protect your executioner!'

In her room Matilda Carter chewed her lip and rubbed her hands together in a tortured near-frenzy. She didn't know where her husband was, and she needed his support. Andrew Carter and Nicholas, her brother, had both left the house earlier with their horses without telling her where they were going. What was she to do? The murderer who had killed her child was escaping.

Until today she had known hope: that Dyne could be struck down in the church, that he might commit suicide, that someone might slay him as he went to abjure – but *no*! Even that small comfort was denied her. She must sit and tolerate his escape. Let him go without a murmur.

She wouldn't – she *couldn't*! There was a resolve within her. She wanted Joan to be avenged so that her only child could rest peacefully in her grave. Matilda walked to her chest and lifted the lid. Inside was Joan's clothing from the day she had died. Matilda lifted it aside and reached beneath. Her hands closed upon her knife.

Tying it to her waist, she pulled out a green cloak and draped it over her shoulders before walking composedly out to the stableyard.

CHAPTER FIVE

When he died, it wasn't with a whimper but a great howl. Baldwin had seen many deaths in his time, but he knew that poison was evil, and since the time of Eve the serpent's bite was the death that revolted all men.

He and Jeanne had been riding with their hounds seeking quarry for their lunch. It was the first time that he had brought Jeanne to this hill since their marriage; it was a sheltered area over to the eastern edge of his demesne, largely left as waste, with the nearest barton some mile or more southwards hidden deep in a valley near Sir Baldwin's own mill.

They had ridden here in the bright sunlight of midday. Jeanne's high-spirited Arab mare, which he had given her on their wedding day, was eager for exercise. As the land opened up and they left the trees behind, the thoroughbred began tossing her head, whinnying and prancing, and at last Baldwin had laughed and pointed ahead through the gorse bushes to a lone oak. 'I'll wager a new Baltic Squirrel skin to a penny that I can beat you to the tree there!'

Jeanne showed her teeth in a smile and before he could say more, she applied her switch to the Arab's rump and felt the animal explode into action beneath her.

It was startling whenever she allowed the beast to run at her own speed. Jeanne felt the muscles bunch and jarr as they propelled the animal forward into a rough, unbalanced gallop, but then the roughness was gone and in its place there was a smooth, steady regularity to the mare's movement. The wind was in Jeanne's face, tugging at her wimple, and suddenly it was gone, torn away, and she felt her braided hair whip loose. Unconsciously she crouched over the mare's neck; the sense of motion, of speed, of onrushing bushes which were before her, level, and then gone in a moment, was so exhilarating Jeanne had an urge to scream with an almost pagan delight.

As she approached the tree she glanced over her shoulder to see where her husband was. He was taking a longer route, and she gave a brief frown wondering why – but then her mare turned. Startled, Jeanne tried to wrench the horse back, but she refused to obey and continued up the hill a way before heading back towards the tree.

When they arrived, Baldwin was there already, innocently picking at his teeth with his fingernail, a knee crooked over his horse's withers. 'You took a while.'

She glared at him before studying the ground carefully. 'You cheated! That's a bog.'

'It can get damp,' he agreed cheerfully. 'But it's not deep, only wet.'

'And I could have gone straight through it!'

'Not with your mare, my love,' he laughed. 'She fell into it once before, and never goes near it now. I think you owe me a penny.'

She lifted her chin in imitation of disdain and looked down her nose at him. 'Certainly, Sir Knight. If you think the wager that important, I shall be glad to pay you when we return.'

Catching hold of her bridle, he grinned, glancing all about them with a meaningful air. 'If you can't pay, I shall be forced to demand payment in kind.'

'And how could a poor woman pay?' she demanded, then squealed with delight when he tickled her ribs and pulled her towards him.

'Only a kiss, my Lady, for now. In a moment, we could leave the horses to feed while we take some wine and rest in the grass.'

'What do you think I am, a milkmaid?' she asked, but could not maintain the pretence of indifference and began to chuckle.

He dismounted and stood at her side, holding out his hands. She took a quick look about her, checking that they were alone, before letting herself drop down, feeling his arms encircle her. Soon she was lying on her back, her husband above, smiling down at her, his hand on her belly, stroking and teasing, his face coming closer.

At that moment they heard the loud, tortured bellow of agony.

Uther had wandered idly away from Baldwin and Jeanne. He was used to occupying himself when his master dithered and there were plenty of odours to entrance him here: rabbits, a hare, foxes, and dogs, plenty of dogs. And when he saw the

55

burst of movement nearby – a swirling of dust in the sunlight and a shimmer of green silk – he shoved his short nose closer to the viper . . .

When the old priest coughed, he brought up blood. Squeezing his eyes tight shut with the pain, he prayed for a speedy release.

He had sent the boy from the nearest farm to fetch Father Abraham from Tiverton, but neither had returned yet. Father Benedict found it hurtful that Abraham should not have responded more urgently to his summons, for after all they were brothers in God's service.

The Father lifted his head at the sound of hooves clattering down the track, an exhausted man old before his time. He sipped water from his bowl and unsteadily rose to his feet, feeling the phlegm in his lungs threatening to choke him, and hobbled to the doorway to see who it was, but when he squinted into the daylight he felt as if he was seeing a ghost.

'Merciful and gracious God! Is it really him?'

Sir Gilbert dismounted and tied his horse to a tree, removing a saddlebag before he realised he was being watched. Whirling around he glowered fiercely, his hand flashing to his sword.

'Brother Gilbert, there's no need for that!' Father Benedict exclaimed with a low chuckle. As it degenerated into a hacking cough, he saw the knight's face fill with solicitous concern.

Spitting out a gobbet of blood, he waved a hand. 'Do not fear for me, Brother Gilbert. I'm dead. It's just that this old body of mine refuses to topple over.'

The Father allowed his visitor to help him inside, and once there Sir Gilbert insisted on Father Benedict lying on his palliasse. He curled his lip at the rank-smelling water and instead went and fetched a wineskin from his horse, holding it to the priest's mouth until he sipped a little.

Father Benedict tried to reject his ministrations, but Sir Gilbert refused to leave his side until the priest from Tiverton had come to listen to his confession. 'If I don't wait here, you might die unshriven,' he said. 'What are you doing here?'

'Where else would an old fool like me go? Here there is water and the locals are kind to me. None of them believe the nonsense told about us.'

'You have stayed here at Templeton all this time?'

'I did think about leaving – but who would then look to the interests of the parishioners here? I doubt whether Father Abraham could be bothered to come so far, and although Witheridge should be in charge of this chapel, the priest there prefers his wine and food to travel. The folk about here are used to me, they remember me from my time as the chaplain to the chapel for the Order, and while I was seeing to their souls, I felt I was doing God's work.'

Sir Gilbert rested with the elderly and dying cleric. He daren't leave. If no one else came along he must listen to Father Benedict's confession as was his duty as a Christian. It was good to see the chaplain from his past, but it was also a relief to hear hoofbeats approaching. Going to the door Sir Gilbert saw a cleric and a young lad riding down the lane. It reminded him why he was here, but first he knelt at Father Benedict's side. 'I must go, Father. Please, could you bless me?'

Father Benedict choked, but the tears in his eyes had nothing to do with the illness which held him in its grip. He smiled, muttering in Latin, finishing with the sign of the cross. 'Go with my blessing, my son.'

'First, where is the reliquary, Father?'

The surprised priest told him, and Sir Gilbert took his hand and kissed it reverently. Rising, he took up his bags and strode off. A short while later Father Abraham appeared.

'I am sorry to take so long. A man was in my sanctuary and I was witnessing his abjuration. Who was that?'

Father Benedict would have been more cautious if he hadn't felt so ill but his pain made him careless. 'Sir Gilbert of Carlisle. He used to be here with me when I was chaplain for the Order.'

It was hot in the heavy fustian tunic in which a pilgrim should be clad, and Philip Dyne was taken by an itch that he couldn't clear. His sweat was soaking into the cloth, and each drip seemed to attract a number of hairs, each of which prickled and irritated.

The road was thankfully flat now. Left was the slow, meandering river, while on his right the hill rose up, covered with tall, ancient trees. The road itself was a mere slash through the trees and grass, although wild plants fought for prominence at the roadside: gorse, valerian, foxglove, buttercups and daisies. Occasionally he inhaled their strong, sweet scents. There was a constant gurgling from the river here and another, less welcome sound. At first he thought he had mistaken it, but as he continued, gripping his little wooden cross firmly in his left hand, head lowered devoutly, he heard it again: horses.

Once more he was filled with foreboding. It was the same every time he met someone on the road. His guilt was apparent from his garb and demeanour, and he felt the shame that both conferred upon him, although most travellers he had encountered tended to ask him with interest what he had done, rather than try to insult or threaten him. One girl had even appeared to be fascinated with his crime, stating her conviction that he must be a murderer and asking what it was like to have killed a man. She offered him her body, but her ghoulish curiosity repelled him.

Now so taken with his gloomy thoughts, Dyne hardly heard the horses as they came close. It was only when one was almost upon him that he darted from beneath its hooves, stumbling over a stone to fall flat on his face at the verge.

'You can move fast enough at need, then.'

Rolling over he saw it was Andrew Carter and he hurriedly climbed to his feet. The hatred in Carter's eyes told him his life was in danger. Carter was pale, his features twisting with emotion, and as Philip Dyne watched him, the man's hand strayed to his knife's hilt.

'Wait, Andrew,' said the man at his side, Nicholas Lovecok, putting his hand to his brother-in-law's before Andrew could pull his dagger free of its sheath.

Andrew threw him a furious look and spat on the ground between them. 'Christ! But he'll escape – and after he murdered poor Joan.'

'The evil shit won't get away with what he did,' Lovecok said, glancing coolly at Dyne, who knelt gripping his cross with hands that shook.

That look, the expression of malevolent certainty, told Philip Dyne that he would never succeed in getting to Exeter.

These men would destroy him long before then. As the realisation burst upon him he heard more hooves. The relief was so acute he felt his head whirl. A large group of men and women on horseback were coming along the road, chattering and laughing as they rode. Some shot Philip Dyne a curious look, no doubt wondering what a man dressed like a penitent was doing, talking to two merchants so far from a town – or maybe it was the tense expressions on all their faces.

Philip was torn. If he were to admit to his position, he might be saved by the folk, but then again it was as likely that he would be held by them and slain – either with their consent or their active participation. Looking back up the hill towards the protection that the trees offered, he saw that he could never make it. Even at full tilt, it would take so long to cover the thirty or so yards that the horses would hardly need to hurry to catch him. What's more, even if by some miracle he made it up the hill, the brambles there would trap him; pinioning him as effectively as a felon in irons. A perfect target.

He opened his mouth to shout for help, but as he did so Andrew Carter kicked his horse and rode on. Nicholas Lovecok smiled coldly at Philip Dyne, and as he moved away, he whispered in a chilling voice: 'I look forward to seeing you again soon . . . *Very* soon.'

Baldwin was up in a flash, his hand on his riding sword, and he swept it out in a shimmering arc of blue as he crouched, seeking the source of the terrible cry.

In a moment he saw Uther, reeling drunkenly, shaking his head, and Baldwin almost laughed. He thought the dog had bitten a bee – Uther had done so before, snapping them from

the air before regretting his temerity – but then he realised
that the dog was in too much pain; was too terrified. And
then Uther crashed to the ground in a frenzy, and Baldwin
felt as if his own heart had been stabbed.

He ran up the incline to Uther's side and dropped to his
knees. The dog's eyes had disappeared, rolled back so that
the white alone showed, and foam whitened his mouth. A
small, ridiculously small, speck of blood showed near his
eye at the dog's temple, and Baldwin smoothed it away,
murmuring soft endearments.

For a moment Uther seemed to rally. His eyes reappeared
and Baldwin could see him look up at him. Baldwin managed
a smile although he felt as if his heart was bursting. His face
felt hot, his eyes ready to flood with tears, and there was a
clenching sensation at the back of his throat.

Uther gently took his forearm in his mouth and closed his
eyes as another spasm burst through his body and Baldwin
was scarcely aware of his own pain as the teeth gripped
tighter and tighter before Uther died.

Andrew Carter spurred his horse on furiously, riding pell-
mell along the road, ignoring Nicholas's calls until he had
worked the demonic anger from his system.

'Brother, you cannot keep on like this,' Nicholas panted
when he had caught up with him.

'Christ alive! I want the bastard dead for what he did!'
Carter spat, his fat features mauve with his emotion. 'You
know what he did to your niece – or had you forgotten?'

'By St Peter, of course I do! How could I forget?'

'He raped her, didn't he? He admitted as much, and when
he had done enjoying himself, he throttled her, right?'

'For God's sake, Andrew, keep your voice down,' Nicholas said urgently.

Looking up the road, Carter saw a small group of travellers approaching. He kicked his horse and wandered off the road a short way, and when he spoke again his voice was a low, bitter rumble: 'How do you expect me to keep calm when the girl has been murdered, eh? God's blood, I want Dyne to suffer for what he did to her. An eye for an eye, that's what the Bible tells me I deserve, and that's what I want! *His* damned eye for hers; his blood for hers. I'll make the shit suffer.'

Nicholas studied his brother-in-law's face for a moment. 'You'll have his heart for what he did to Joan,' he said softly. 'But if you keep shouting your intentions to the world, you'll be arrested yourself.'

'Not if . . .'

'I know,' Nicholas interrupted, his patience wearing thin, and reaching forward he grabbed the bridle of the other man's mount. 'And if our plan works, we'll be able to see to him, but if you keep breaking out into this sanguine temper every time we meet people on the way to Tiverton, not only will you not succeed, you'll end up being attached at the nearest court as well. Is that what you want?'

'I want his head on a plate!'

'Then use *your* head, man, and stop this ranting. Jesus save us!' His voice dropped to a low whisper. 'Because if you don't, much though I adored poor Joan, I'll leave you here on your own and go back to Exeter. I won't risk gaol or death to help a fool.'

Carter stiffened, meeting Nicholas's solemn gaze with a sullen glower. After a moment he looked down, suddenly ashamed, and Nicholas released his horse.

'And now, brother, let's carry on and see whether we might be able to execute – ha! – your revenge.'

Andrew and Nicholas would not have ridden away so quickly had they known that Matilda was watching them. She had missed Dyne's abjuration, but she asked men in the town's square and soon learned which road he had taken. Riding off after him, it was not long before she saw him ahead of her, and she was about to ride up to him and slash at him when she saw her husband and brother approach him. She watched, half-thrilled to think that she was about to see Dyne die, but also jealous not to have the savage joy of executing her daughter's murderer herself.

From her vantage-point partway up the hillside, Matilda couldn't hear what her husband and brother said to the evil wretch, but she saw the way that the two men rode off, and saw the outlaw who had killed her daughter drop to his knees and cross himself, praying as a band of travellers appeared.

The sight made her shiver with contempt. This was a man who dared rape and murder, yet he begged God's protection when others sought to avenge his victim. She was tempted to spur her mount, draw her blade and run him down there and then; there could be no doubt that she had justice on her side. Her feet swept forward to hack at her mount's flanks, but then she hesitated, irresolute.

Executing the felon in full view of travellers on the way to St Giles's Fair could lead to an unreasonable attack on *her*. Others might not realise the depth of Philip Dyne's crimes. They might disbelieve her, or take his side and protect him, perhaps killing her if she attacked him. Matilda was only a woman. If she were to stab Dyne, she could be overwhelmed or run through as a madwoman – possibly before she'd killed Dyne.

She wanted him dead: she craved justice for Joan. But for that her blow must have a chance of success.

Fleetingly she wondered where her husband could have gone, and then she realised that Andrew and Nicholas must be setting a trap for Dyne further along the road. They were good men, her husband and brother. They wouldn't feebly moan and complain about Dyne escaping. She was unfair to accuse them of such a thing. No, they were here to ensure Dyne's execution for his sins. They would see to him.

But how could they? They had left the rapist here alone, riding off at speed. What if he were to leave the roadway and bolt? Matilda Carter gritted her teeth. He would not get away. She swore by Holy Mother Mary that she would shadow the lad and make sure he couldn't escape.

When he stood, shakily wiping at his face with a sleeve, Matilda took her horse's reins and pulled the mare after her, resolutely trailing the weeping penitent as he continued on his way south.

On foot she walked after him, growing tired now but filled with bitterness and the angry determination to see Philip Dyne dead.

CHAPTER SIX

They set off to St Giles's Fair early the next morning. Baldwin did not enjoy going to town, but once he knew he must endure an unpleasant duty, he was resolved to begin it as soon as possible. Today he looked upon the journey as a useful distraction from his sadness.

Their retinue was as small as he could make it. There was no point in dragging half his servants with him, not on a political visit like this – although it was a fine balancing act knowing how many to bring. If Baldwin brought a large entourage it might make him appear too rich, as though he was trying to score points off other knights; too few people with him and Lord Hugh de Courtenay could feel that there was some slight intended: that his lordship didn't warrant a show of respect. On the other hand, the harvest would soon be ready, and for that the manor needed every spare hand. Baldwin had no intention of denuding his demesne of men.

Jeanne knew all this, but she was concerned that he could have brought too few with him. He had only his servant, Edgar, the cattleman's son, Wat, and Jeanne had brought her maid, Petronilla. Petronilla had given birth only a month before and baby Stephen was proving to be a handful; Petronilla had grown pale and apathetic, yawning and dozing whenever she might. Her obvious exhaustion made Jeanne wonder how she herself might cope with childbirth.

Usually a child was welcomed wholeheartedly into a household but Stephen had caused no little complaint among the other servants. All slept communally in Baldwin's hall and when the child was being difficult, demanding his mother in the darkest hours of the night, Jeanne knew that others dreamed black thoughts of smothering babies. Edgar had been heard to wonder aloud why Herod had never been canonised.

At least now he was sleeping, rocked gently in the wagon, lying among the gifts which Baldwin and Jeanne had brought for Lord Hugh de Courtenay, and while he slept Petronilla had regained much of her animation. She was fairskinned and blonde, and incarceration indoors had made her pale, but the walk had already put roses in her cheeks, making her look much younger. Wat's hand was in hers as she pointed out flowers, birds or animals, a habit which Wat, who had fallen in love with Petronilla when he first met her in Throwleigh, scorned. At his age – about fourteen; no one was quite sure, least of all his father – he was almost old enough to marry, and the scowl on his face demonstrated his belief that inconsequential chats about flowers and blackbirds were demeaning.

Trying not to grin to herself as she caught sight of his expression, Jeanne glanced at her husband.

Baldwin had been dreadfully saddened by the death of his dog. Uther had been an uncomfortable companion, as much as Jeanne liked dogs, because his habits of slobbering over those whom he adored, of farting beneath the table at meal-times, of resting his head in a lap and dribbling, tended to make some people fractious about him. And the more unpopular he felt, the more poor Uther tried to endear himself, usually with disastrous consequences, like the time he knocked Baldwin over in his enthusiasm to welcome the knight home after an extended absence of less than an hour.

But there was no denying that the beast had adored Baldwin, nor that he had reciprocated Uther's affection. Even when the dog died biting on Baldwin's arm, Baldwin hadn't complained. His forearm was a mass of scabs where Uther's teeth had sunk in, and Jeanne had seen her man touch the scabs every so often, as if reminding himself of his hound's death. Although Baldwin smiled as often as before, it was clear to Jeanne that he felt the hound's death keenly. She had suggested another dog, but he had smiled sadly and shaken his head. No replacement would be able to fill the space left by Uther. Perhaps in a year or so.

Jeanne sighed, but she was not used to inaction. She was sure that her husband needed another dog to bring him out of his odd, quiet mood, and she would find him one. Perhaps a pleasing little pet-dog, something small enough to sit on his lap? Some knights thought them the height of fashion, so she had heard. It made for a wonderful companion, something so small and cuddly.

The word cuddly brought to her mind a vision of Uther's head, massive, dark-jowled, sombre, panting, with a long dribble of slime forever dangling. Shuddering slightly, she decided to act. Maybe there would be something suitable in Tiverton.

Tiverton. It was an odd-sounding place. Although Jeanne had lived in Furnshill for some months now, she had never made the journey north: there had never been the need. Crediton held all that they needed in terms of those food-stuffs they couldn't grow themselves, and if there was anything else they required, they tended to send to Exeter. That great port could provide anything that was available in the world and there was little point in going elsewhere.

Being a Devon-born woman, Jeanne had been raised in the county, but she had been adopted by her uncle and taken to live with him in Bordeaux when her parents were murdered by a gang of trail bastons. Many such outlaws had killed, raped and thieved their way through the country over the last twenty years and Jeanne had been lucky to escape with her life. The axe-blow intended to kill her had glanced off. She still had a dent in her skull where it struck.

Jeanne had learned much about gracious living in Bordeaux, but her first husband, Sir Ralph de Liddinstone, was a rough, heavy-handed bully, who had lost all affection for her when she proved unable to conceive a child for him. He had beaten her whenever he was drunk, and when he died some three years before, his passing had been a source of real relief to Jeanne. And then she had met Sir Baldwin de Furnshill.

Where her first husband had been hot-headed, untutored and ill-mannered, Baldwin was calm, educated and courte-ous to a fault. When it came to their bedchamber he had been almost embarrassingly respectful, a condition which Jeanne had not been prepared to allow to continue, for not only did she long for a child, she knew that Baldwin did as well. She had seen his tenderness towards Petronilla's, even though the poor baby was illegitimate.

It was as she was contemplating the possibility of a baby of her own that she realised that they had almost reached the town. It was clear above the trees lining the far riverbank ahead and she surveyed it with interest.

The castle was a massive grey building; the town huddled south-east of it in the gap between the Rivers Lowman and Exe, an accumulation of limewashed, timber-built places which sprawled haphazardly up the hillside, with gardens, orchards and burgage plots radiating out. Thin fields lay further down the hill, as did pastures and meadows: cattle and horses, sheep and lambs could be seen browsing or dozing in the warm summer sunlight.

They clattered over the timber bridge to the main street leading up to the castle, and Jeanne began to feel the strength and power of the place. It would be strange to live beneath such a massive symbol of a lord's power, she thought. Strange and intimidating.

Baldwin turned to her as if reading her mind. For a moment he appeared to have forgotten his loss, and he gave her a broad smile. 'Does it look a glum place to you?'

'I have no idea how you guessed that was what I was thinking, but yes. It doesn't appeal to me.'

'It's not so dreadful inside,' he said. 'My Lord de Courtenay enjoys a comfortable life.'

'But imagine living beneath these walls all the time,' she said, shivering as they rode towards the great gatehouse. 'I heard once of the King's castle at London, and how the tall walls and towers threatened any who came near. I begin to understand how people must feel when their whole lives are lived in the shadows of a place like this.'

Baldwin cast her a sympathetic glance. Although she had lived in Bordeaux during her youth, she had spent most of her life in England in places where there appeared little need for strong defences. Devon was not like the Scottish or Welsh marches where warfare was a way of life. 'Didn't you feel the same at Bordeaux?'

'Bordeaux? No, of course not! The whole town was enclosed and protected. The castle was only for the last resort, there to protect the King's subjects.'

Baldwin nodded but wasn't convinced. The King's father, Edward I, was perfectly capable of bullying his people into submission, and a place like Bordeaux was protected because it made sense to look after the citizens so that their wealth could be defended and saved for the King himself, rather than handing it to his enemies. No king was truly altruistic.

He glanced up at the castle walls. Strong, solid, unblemished, they looked impregnable – yet he wondered how they would cope with the might of the King's artillery pounding them. The walls of Bristol had not survived long in 1316 when the King had exercised his will over the townspeople, raising the whole posse of the county against the rebellious folks who would not obey his will . . .

But his reverie was halted by a cry.

'Baldwin! About time!'

He spun in his saddle and then smiled as he recognised his old friend Simon. 'Bailiff Puttock, did they invite you as well? I thought it was to be a select gathering!'

'Is Margaret with you?' Jeanne asked as she and her husband dropped gratefully from their mounts.

'No,' Simon said, and there was a reticence in his manner. 'You know she has often miscarried? The midwife told her to stay at home and rest in her bed to prevent another, and I agreed.'

'What of Hugh?' Baldwin asked. They were inside the great hall now, sipping drinks, and Baldwin was surprised not to see Simon's truculent servant making a nuisance of himself among the castle's own men.

'Er, no,' Simon said. 'Hugh has decided to stay and help Constance with her garden.'

Baldwin's eyebrows shot heavenwards. He had no idea what sort of woman would want so morose a companion.

'There's no need to look like that, Baldwin. Hugh can work well enough.'

'Really?'

'When he wants to, yes.'

'Does he ever want to?' Baldwin enquired.

'He's loyal.'

'Ah!'

Seeing his expression Simon added defensively, 'I gave him permission.'

Baldwin snorted derisively. 'One always agrees with a servant who wishes to do something – if one intends to keep him, that is!' he scoffed, and glanced around at Edgar, who stood aloof from other servants nearby.

'Edgar is handfast to Cristine in the tavern at Crediton,' Jeanne chuckled in explanation. 'Baldwin is not sure yet that it is a good match: he fears Cristine will tempt Edgar away from his side and, to be honest, I fear it myself. I don't know how Edgar manages to keep Baldwin so obedient!'

Baldwin gave a dry smile but didn't answer. He had not told his wife how he had met Edgar in the disastrous battle to defend Acre. Saving Edgar's life had conferred a curious obligation upon both men and Baldwin was as aware as Edgar of the bond that tied them. It was hard to conceive of life without Edgar. They had been together since Acre, first as refugees, then as Knight and Sergeant in the Templars, more recently as land-owning knight and servant.

Not that Baldwin was an enormously wealthy knight. Certainly not in the same league as some of Hugh de Courtenay's other knights – and not in the same league as Simon either, he realised as he took in Simon's fur trimmings at neck and hem, the brilliant vermillion cloth of his cotte and surcoat, the ruddy linen of his hose, and most of all the two gold rings on his fingers. 'You should be careful, Simon,' he said seriously. 'If you flaunt your money like that,' nodding towards the rings, 'you'll be made a knight.'

Simon grinned and was about to reply when he saw that Baldwin was serious. 'Me?'

'You could be forced to accept a knighthood if Lord de Courtenay considers you rich enough.'

'I don't earn enough to justify it,' Simon protested.

'An income of £40 a year is all it takes, and I would think that the chief bailiff of the Warden of the Stannaries would probably have that each year as well as the money he might win from his old farm at Sandford and other investments.'

'Hmm,' Simon grunted thoughtfully. 'I never liked the idea of distraint. Compelling people to become knights when they've got no inclination seems foolish.'

'Certainly you'd be more use as a shield to protect a worthy man from arrows than as any sort of warrior,' Baldwin observed critically, glancing askance at his friend's jutting belly.

'I resent that, Sir Baldwin!' Simon laughed. 'It takes a large investment to build a temple to the epicurean arts like this.' And he slapped his stomach.

Baldwin shook his head as if in disgust, but couldn't help but smile at his friend's cheerfulness. Simon had lost the haggard look of two years before when his only son had died, but the greying hair was a feature that he would never again be without. For all that his guts were expanding, his face's ruddy colouring showed that he still took his regular exercise, riding over the moors to impose his lord's will on the ever-rebellious miners who scraped a meagre living on Dartmoor. His dark grey eyes had more wisdom, more experience than when Baldwin had first known him. The loss of his boy had affected him badly, as had his wife's miscarriages since.

'Anyway, Baldwin, what of your own people? I see you've brought Jeanne and Edgar; have you decided not to impose Chops on our poor lord?'

As soon as he asked the question Jeanne saw the sadness return to her husband's face and she took his hand comfortingly.

Piers Bakere eyed the road sourly as he jogged along on his cart. It was a stupid waste of his time, this journey, but since he must use the manor's mill, he had to load up with grain every so often and take it down the roadway here to get it ground down to flour.

Normally the portly baker wouldn't have come: there was no point in his performing menial tasks like this when he had an apprentice, Jack, to do it for him. But Jack had some kind of sickness and was laid up, shivering as if he had the ague, sweating and throwing up. Piers's wife had fetched the physician, who had inspected Jack's urine for fully an hour, then his most recent stool, before declaring solemnly that the boy needed to stay in bed, get bled, and eat only food and drink for a hot, dry humour. Then he ran off to fetch the necessary potions. In the meantime it was obvious that the boy must remain in his cot in the hall. He could hardly lift sacks of flour in his present state.

His day was ruined, Piers brooded, and all because of that good-for-nothing brat. Jack was nearly eleven, or so his father had said, almost a man. Piers had never taken days off when *he* was an apprentice. An employee abed was no use to him. Yet while he irritably listed Jack's faults, the anxiety wouldn't leave him. The baker was fond of his apprentice and, much as he tried to conceal the fact from himself, he was worried about the boy.

He was just contemplating the next few days without Jack when he came across a man standing in the middle of the road.

'Sir, sir – have you seen a knight on this road?'

Piers eyed the panting fellow doubtfully. From his pock-marked face to his tatty hose and tunic, made of the cheapest-looking cloth, this man looked more like a draw-latch or some other form of felon than a traveller. 'No one. Why?'

'My master, he's gone missing!' It was William Small, Sir Gilbert's companion.

'He's probably gone to have a shit,' Piers said dismissively.

'It can't be that. He went last night,' William said. 'Anyway, he wanted me with him.'

'Really?'

'Don't look at me like that, man. I've guarded him all the way from London because he feared attack, and now he's disappeared!'

Piers was about to speak when a call came from the woods. 'What in *God's name*?' It was a shuddering howl of anguish, mournful and doom-laden.

'Christ Jesus!' Piers said, fingering his rosary.

'God's cods!' said William with feeling, and drew his dagger. 'Come on, help me.'

Piers jumped down and dug about in the back of his cart, dragging free a pair of cudgels – good, strong blackthorn clubs that could break a man's skull. He cast an anxious look at his cart, fearing that it might be stolen, then grimaced and made off after the sailor.

The woods here were thick and overgrown. Brambles tore at Piers's hose, snagging at threads and wrecking them. He glanced down fretfully, knowing how his wife would rail at him for making such a mess of his clothing, but then smiled grimly. There was little likelihood that she would worry too much about them when she realised he had lost a morning's work chasing about in the woods after someone who could well have knocked him on the head.

'This way!'

The baker was no fool. He knew that life was full of risks, and also knew that the man he was following could well prove to be the advance member of a gang of trail bastons, but no gang of thieves would bother to rob him. He wasn't carrying money and if felons wanted to get rich they'd attack someone nearer the road. No one would steal a cart of flour. Unless they intended stealing his horse . . .

He hesitated. He was already some distance from the road, and he couldn't see his cart or horse anymore. Chewing at his lip, he listened to the crashing of the other man as William sped forward. Another gloomy cry broke on the air, and now Piers could recognise it as a dog howling dolefully. He felt torn, unsure which way to go. To his right was a gap – he could see the sunlight falling on a pretty, buttercup-strewn glade – and deciding he could move faster across such a clearing, he made for it.

Long grasses rustled past his knees. His feet felt as though they were sinking into a thick carpet of the softest silk. Up ahead was the source of the noise, and Piers hurried along, his eyes fixed on the darkness beneath the trees from where the noises appeared to issue.

Thus it was that he didn't see the lump until it was too late, and he went flying, falling on his cudgels and dropping both. 'What in God's name?' he muttered angrily. Rising, he kicked out at the thing.

Before his terrified gaze he saw a man's head fly up into the air, only to fall a short distance away, the eyes wide in horror, the mouth slackly open, the neck a red and bloody mess.

CHAPTER SEVEN

'God! . . . Christ alive!' Piers declared in shock, and the head stared back.

The baker clutched at his belly, trying not to vomit. Remembering himself, he made a hasty sign of the cross, then tugged his rosary free and muttered a prayer. There was something wrong with his beads; they felt slick and oily in his hands, and he looked down to see that they were smothered and beslobbered with semi-congealed blood. Then, a couple of paces away, he saw the headless body. He winced with revulsion. The ground all about him was red with blood. It was repellent to be covered in this filth. Flies buzzed about him already: he would stink by the time he got home if the sun stayed as warm all the way.

Hearing an anguished shout, he wiped his hands on clean grass, snatched up his cudgels, and ran towards the call without once glancing backwards. Jumping a low barrier of fern and bramble, he found himself in a darker area where the sun was blotted out by thick growth overhead. Dried leaves and twigs snapped and rustled under his feet as he hurried on, and then before him he saw another clearing.

When he broke in, he slowed in his onwards rush and gradually came to a halt. In the trees above him, three large black carrion birds noisily launched themselves into the air and flew away.

On the ground before him knelt William, but as Piers took in the scene he gasped and clapped a blood stained hand over his mouth.

Before William was the dead body of a dog, who lay in a thick pool of his own gore. A second large dog lay a few yards from William, and hearing Piers's approach, this one raised his head and stared at him, head tilted a little as if in vague enquiry. The expression on the animal's face was one of unutterable sadness, and after a moment he looked away, resting his chin on his paws and gazing at another corpse.

It was that of a man in his prime of life; a tall man, his head resting on a tree root, his hands clasped together at the hilt of the sword lying on his breast like one already laid in his grave.

A knight.

Tiverton Castle was not the largest Baldwin had ever visited, but it was in a strong position to guard the bridge over the river. South and west it was protected by the River Exe; north were marshes, and the castle had good, massive walls to enclose its lord. The court was oddly shaped, designed to fit the space, and stables and outhouses were filled. Men and women hurried on their duties, guards lounged and guests wandered around getting in everyone else's way.

The great hall had been cleaned and decorated in honour of the feast – *and* to show off the best silver and pewter plate of the de Courtenay family, Baldwin added to himself. It was set out on a heavy sideboard, taking up four shelves – a proud display of the power and money the family commanded. On the walls hung tapestries with rich embroidery showing scenes of chivalric magnificence: unicorns and lions fought, knights tilted at each other or knelt praying while their serfs tilled the fields, sheared sheep, and drove carts filled with produce. The floor had been laid with fresh rushes, and their scent reminded Baldwin of long days idling in fields, although they did pose something of a risk to some of the ladies in their long gowns and skirts. Baldwin noticed several stumble as, unwittingly, they managed to sweep the rushes before them, building up a small rampart which they then tripped over.

The hall was crowded. Music from the minstrels in their small gallery over the screens meant people were forced to speak more loudly, although the freely-flowing drink encouraged them. Baldwin looked about him, recognising some of his peers from other towns: knights, esquires, clerics, advocates. More were arriving and he began to wonder whether they would all fit, especially with the numbers of servants on every side, passing jugs of wine and ale, handing platters of small pastries, tarts and titbits.

He saw a face he knew: Sir Peregrine of Barnstaple. Baldwin looked away hurriedly and walked off with his wife in the opposite direction.

There were many others he knew. The Coroner, like Sir Peregrine, Baldwin avoided. Men gained reputations when they won positions of power, and Coroner Harlewin le Poter

had earned that of a womaniser, politician and corrupt official. It was a sad comment on the officers of justice that so
many were similarly labelled, but Baldwin's personal loathing of injustice led him to keep away from Harlewin.

Jeanne and he migrated to a corner with people whom
Baldwin did not recognise. It was here that he met Andrew
Carter and Nicholas Lovecok for the first time, two men
whom he was to get to know well. Andrew, he heard, was
one of Tiverton's leading merchants, while Nicholas hailed
from Exeter – which was clearly not his original home: his
accent was softened with the years, but there were strong
traces of Welsh. Baldwin was struck by their appearance:
both were pale as if from lack of sleep, and Andrew in particular was curt almost to the point of rudeness.

His wife Matilda was a slim woman in her late thirties.
She appeared utterly indifferent to the people about her –
indeed, Baldwin thought she was intentionally ignoring
them, but then he saw the tic fluttering beneath her eye, noted
her gaunt appearance and realised she was suffering from
some deep inner sadness.

'This is Cecily Sherman,' Jeanne announced.

The newcomer was shortish, attractive, plump and dark-
haired. Constantly smiling, she had a gushing manner that
was in no way irritating, but more entrancing: the residual
girlishness of a young woman. Baldwin placed her in her
early twenties. While the men talked she rarely interrupted, but her comments were succinct and often very
witty. Baldwin gained the impression that she was a skilled
flirt.

When her husband John was pointed out to him, Baldwin
saw a heavy-set man, tall, with grizzled hair, cleanshaven

and heavy of shoulder. In appearance he looked much like a knight or some other trained martial artist, strong and proud. Baldwin was interested to see that Cecily Sherman rarely glanced at her husband. Her attention, Baldwin noticed, was more often upon the Coroner.

The party was proving enjoyable, if loud, but the jolly atmosphere was ruined when a guard hurried in with the bedraggled figure of Piers Bakere.

'Did you recognise the corpses?'

'No, Coroner. The beheaded one I didn't give more than a glance to. I've seen dead men before – who hasn't? – but tripping over a man's head . . . well, it's not something I've done before. As to the knight, I've no idea who *he* was.'

Harlewin le Poter was a vain man, Baldwin thought. He appeared to be listening intently to the baker – but Baldwin was sure that he was merely putting on an act and that belief rankled. The affair sounded too serious to be treated in a frivolous mood.

Baldwin could see the baker clearly. He looked nervous, and there was no surprise in that, with the poor fellow having to stand in front of the most important people in the shire. Piers was unkempt, and his hands seemed to be streaked and spotted with rusty stains. Only later did Baldwin realise that this was, in fact, dried blood.

'You say that both men were outside the verge?' Harlewin asked, studying his pot and sipping. He was dressed in bright reds and blues, with a plain white shirt under his blue cotte and red surcoat, and parti-coloured hose hiding his legs. From the size of his belly Baldwin guessed he was not a particularly dedicated officer of the law. If he were, he could not have grown so fat, for there were only two Coroners to cover the whole of Devonshire at present, and since they had the responsibility to investigate all sudden deaths so as to ensure that fines from the vills were all paid whenever the King's Peace was broken, both should cover many leagues each week.

'Yes, sir. They were in the woods a long way from the road, far from the town.'

'And you are sure both were dead?'

A small frown passed over Piers's brow. 'You mean the beheaded one?'

'Don't be frivolous, fool! I can have you gaoled if you don't behave respectfully,' Harlewin snapped, flushing. 'This knight: how do you know he was dead?'

'He didn't wake when his dog howled,' Piers said as if reciting a story. 'He didn't wake when I called him, didn't wake when I touched him, and his face was cold.' He paused as if suddenly remembering and added, 'Oh, and there was a stab-wound in his back.'

'How did you know he was a knight?'

'By his golden spurs and his belt,' Piers said scathingly. 'How else would you recognise a knight?'

'Damn your soul, learn courtesy!' Harlewin snapped, dashing his pot to the ground. 'You can learn your position in the town's gaol, if you prefer!'

'I apologise,' Piers said with oily sincerity, but Baldwin could see the contempt in his eyes. For some reason Baldwin found himself alerted to Harlewin's stance and gestures. The man seemed unsurprised by the news, his actions and voice geared more to impressing his audience than extracting information.

Harlewin snapped his fingers to a servant and took another pot of wine. 'You left these two bodies in the care of this other man?'

'Yes, sir.'

'Then I suppose I must organise the posse,' Harlewin yawned. 'Although it is most annoying.' He glanced at the door through which at any moment Lord de Courtenay was expected to enter. 'Since both were dead, you'll both have to pay the sureties. You can consider yourself attached.'

'Sir, I have to get back to my shop,' Piers protested. 'If I'm arrested, how'll I be able to pay the fine?'

'I hope you have the money. You know the law: if a man is found dead, the finder must be amerced – he has to pay a surety to show he will attend the inquest. You and this other fellow were the first finders, so you must both pay, as must those who live nearest the place where the bodies were found, although . . .' he meditated a moment '. . . God only knows who lives nearest. Ah, well. I suppose we'll have to attach and amerce everyone who lives along the road.'

Baldwin shrugged. There was nothing new in murder at the roadside. He felt sure it would turn out to be trail bastons who came across two unwary travellers; nothing to interest him. He was about to turn away when he caught sight of the Coroner. He was staring at Andrew Carter suspiciously. Andrew was looking away, but his wife clung to his arm and she stared up at him with an expression of pride and joy.

'Take the baker away. I shall see to him later,' the Coroner commanded gruffly at last. Two men-at-arms each grabbed one of Piers's elbows and conducted him away. Immediately Harlewin spotted Baldwin. 'Keeper, how are you?'

'Very well, Coroner.'

'You must have come up the very same road. Did you see anything suspicious? A man behaving oddly?'

'Nothing. But a gang would surely have remained hidden until they could see an easy target. They would not have attacked me, for I had my man-at-arms with me, and two men properly armed can travel in safety except from a very large band indeed.'

'True enough.' Harlewin appeared bored by the affair. 'I don't suppose you saw this knight on the road?'

Baldwin gave a faint smile. 'The baker did say that the man was cold. Surely that would mean he had been dead for some little while? He must have died overnight or yesterday.'

Harlewin frowned, contemplating a dish of tarts held temptingly before his nose. 'Hmm. Perhaps. Although it's always best, I find, to wonder at the honesty of first finders. Take this man, Piers. Why should he have come forward so eagerly?'

Simon had joined them and he broke in sharply. 'Because he's an honest man and wanted to help capture the murderer, of course.'

'Ah, Bailiff Puttock! It's pleasant to see faces from so far afield. So you think the fellow was honest? Let me tell you, I have seen that same man in court more times than I can count for breaking the assize on bread. He often sells underweight loaves.'

'Miserable thief!' Simon muttered, throwing an angry look after the disappearing baker.

Baldwin grinned. Simon's views on people who cheated the poor out of their food were trenchant and well-known to him. 'But the fact that he came here to raise the Hue and Cry is evidence of his honesty. The man whom you should question is the one who was already there, this man who called Piers from his journey.'

'Good point, Sir Baldwin,' Harlewin said. 'Yes, I shall question him most carefully.'

A sneering voice made Harlewin whirl. 'You do that, Coroner, you do that. And don't allow anyone to escape, will you? Earl Thomas might be upset!'

Baldwin felt rather than saw Edgar join him, and looking at the man who had appeared, he could understand why Edgar should have sprung to his side. It was John Sherman.

Harlewin had gone quite white. At first Baldwin thought it was fear, but then the Coroner spoke and his tone was one of rage. 'You dare accuse me of bribery? Of corruption? That is a deplorable suggestion, even for you, Master Sherman.'

'Well, take independent witnesses so that you can prove me wrong then, Coroner.'

Harlewin leaned forward, his face suddenly mauve. Baldwin stepped between the two men before he could speak.

'Gentlemen, please remember where you are,' he said urgently. 'This is your lord's hall, and we are here to feast, not quarrel. Come, Coroner, you have to visit the scene and begin your inquest.'

'Be damned to that,' Harlewin rasped.

'Silence, Coroner!' said another man at Baldwin's elbow and Baldwin had a sense of foreboding. He recognised that voice: it was Sir Peregrine of Barnstaple.

'Who are you?' Sherman demanded of Baldwin, but then he caught sight of Sir Peregrine, who smiled thinly.

'This is Sir Baldwin de Furnshill, Keeper of the King's Peace in Crediton.'

'Oh, a Keeper?' His eyes registered interest, then amusement. 'Well, why don't you go along with this brave Coroner of ours and then he can prove his innocence!'

Harlewin pursed his lips with fury. 'You dare to suggest that I—'

'Coroner, this is your lord's hall,' Baldwin repeated. 'He would not wish to see you fighting with another of his guests. Now, sir,' he said, facing Sherman, 'I don't know what you intend by this display, but you are provoking the good Coroner without reason.'

'You think so? Then go with him and help his investigation. Or does he have something to hide?'

'God damn your eyes, Sherman! I have nothing to conceal, but next time I'm at your shop I'll have the assizes check your weights.'

'Do so, Coroner. You'll find everything above the boards, nothing hidden,' Sherman shot back.

'Oh, yes? What of . . .?' But Harlewin choked off whatever he was about to say. Sherman leaned forward, an intent expression in his eyes. Harlewin waved a hand in angry rejection. 'I'll not be drawn into debate with a fool. Sir Baldwin, since this cretin wishes my inquest to be witnessed, I ask you to join my posse.'

'Me?' Baldwin said, and felt his heart sink. The last thing he wanted was to be cossetted with the Coroner; he was here to be presented to his lord, not to join another investigation. If he had time he wanted to show Jeanne the sights of the town, not spend it chasing over the countryside looking for a band of murderers. 'Oh, I do not think I should intervene in . . .'

'I would look on it as a special favour, Sir Baldwin,' Harlewin pressed him. 'My integrity, my honour, has been impugned. I must ask that you assist me.'

Baldwin glanced over his shoulder. Jeanne saw his strained visage, and gave him a gay smile. It was his own fault for intervening between the two men, she thought. He could expect little sympathy from her.

Then came the smooth voice he feared. 'I am sure it would be an excellent idea.'

'Good. Thank you, Sir Peregrine. That's settled, then,' Harlewin said, rubbing his hands together.

'Oh, very well,' Baldwin agreed despondently. An esquire carrying a plate was moving past him, and Baldwin picked off a handful of pastries and thrust them into the wallet at his belt, moodily reflecting that he might not see any other items from the feast that day.

CHAPTER EIGHT

Cecily Sherman breathed a sigh of relief. The bloody fool had almost given away their secret. It was hazardous enough trying to meet while John was so suspicious, but if Harlewin was to give away every secret she had mentioned to him while they were in bed, she would have to seek another lover.

She turned her charm on to Father Abraham. He looked most distracted, unhappy and nervous. 'Father, won't you have some wine with me? It is the best that Nicholas Lovecok could supply and the flavour is splendid.'

He shuddered and turned away.

'Father, what . . .?'

'You know what it is. Last night,' he rasped.

'Father, don't be like that, please!' she entreated, touching his shoulder and exerting a slight pressure to make him face her. He tried to avoid her eyes, but she remained still, gazing up at him with an expression of sadness. 'I know you don't approve of me or my behaviour, but I can't help the way I'm made.'

'What were you doing last night?' he grated. 'Seeing your lover again?' He didn't wait for her reply, but averted his face and stalked away, disgusted. His demeanour made her smile as she walked to her husband's side. She beamed at him with every sign of warmth, but he returned her only a grimace.

'Husband, I am glad you didn't go with them. Would you like to go back home soon?'

'Why are you so glad to find me here still? Are you bored now your lover's gone?'

'John, believe me, I would never seek another.'

'Then where did you go last night?'

'Last night? I . . .'

'You were with *him* again, weren't you?'

Cecily gave him a look of pain. 'How could you think that?'

'It's true, isn't it? You were with your lover again – that fat fool Harlewin.'

'You saw him off well. He is gross, isn't he?'

Sherman eyed her furiously. While she could treat his accusations with such calmness he had to doubt his own sanity, but he knew she was lying. The trouble was, he couldn't accuse her now. That would mean confessing what he had been doing last night, and he didn't want everyone to know he had been out there in the woods.

Simon volunteered to join them although Baldwin insisted that Edgar should remain with his wife in case she chose to visit the market.

It took some time to find a pair of mounts. Neither Simon nor Baldwin wanted to use their own: Baldwin's had travelled far enough already for one day and Simon's had a strained fetlock. Instead, both went to the hackneyman nearest the castle. He had been recommended to them by a steward, but Baldwin gave an inward groan on seeing the proprietor, a fawning man with filthy fingers and thin, waxen features. 'Oh yes, masters, yes. I have some of the best horseflesh in Devon, yes.'

His words were far from the mark. In the stalls they found several sumpters, rough pack horses, a couple of rounseys, both badly spavined, and some worn and ancient hackneys. One heavy beast like a draughthorse stood out, but it was filthy, plastered with mud over neck and thighs. Nearby was a young mare which tempted Baldwin, but when he went closer he saw that she had cut her forehead on a splinter or nail, and the wound was flyblown: maggots squirmed and wriggled. Baldwin felt his stomach heave and called the man over.

While the hackneyman tried to hold her head steady so he could pick the maggots out, Simon and Baldwin looked about them with near-despair; they had to have something. They settled for a couple of the less exhausted-looking beasts. Soon they were mounted and met the Coroner at the castle gate.

The Coroner had brought a man-at-arms with him, and Piers was seated on his wagon, his expression bitter as he thought of the dough he should even now be mixing. For all his insistence of hurrying to report the dead bodies, Baldwin noticed that his cart was empty of the flour he declared he had collected, and was sure that the baker had gone to his home and off-loaded it before going to seek the Coroner. It made Baldwin grin to himself. The baker was no fool – he knew he must report the murders, but that was no reason to ruin himself.

'I should have taken a second apprentice,' Piers mumbled disconsolately.

'What's that?' Baldwin asked, kicking at his horse to urge it alongside. It wasn't easy: he had picked a mare, and she resolutely fought every tug on the reins. Simon's mount was no better – it preferred to wander off the road to the grasses that grew thickly nearer the riverbank.

Piers sighed and spread his hands. 'An apprentice, Sir Baldwin. Mine is sick, and all the time I spend wandering down here, my business is wasting. I've got a cartload of flour sitting in the yard and if it rains it'll be ruined. My wife does all she can, but without my apprentice or me she'll never get it done. Oh God! I wish I'd never seen the bugger.'

'The man who stopped you?'

'Yes. If he'd missed me and found someone else I'd be indoors now, baking, all my flour safely locked away. Instead here I am, amerced and riding away again. Daft, I call it.'

'The man who stopped you – was he a local?'

'I didn't recognise him. His voice was odd, too. Very strong accent.'

Casting a look ahead, Baldwin asked, 'How much farther to the place where this stranger found you?'

Piers shielded his eyes. 'About another half mile. You see where the trees follow the curve of the river over there? I think it was about there.'

'I see.' Baldwin nodded and was about to drop back when Piers nodded meaningfully at the Coroner ahead and said, 'Sir Baldwin, I understand how these things are done. If I pay you as well as the priest and the Coroner there, will you speak for me?'

Baldwin's voice was icy as he replied, 'I am Keeper of the King's Peace. I cannot be bought, you fool!' He dragged viciously on the reins and went to join Simon.

'What is it?' Simon asked. He could see that his friend was peeved, but he hadn't heard the baker's quiet offer.

'That idiot asked me to accept a payment. It is probably true that he needs to get back to work, but to offer me a bribe . . .' His voice tailed off in disgust.

'It's common enough, isn't it?' Simon pointed out reasonably. 'Especially for Coroners. How else are they expected to cover their expenses, always riding here and there, inspecting corpses along the way, and all for no pay?'

'Hah! They get paid all right,' Baldwin burst out. 'They charge fortunes for looking at dead bodies, and if the people of the area don't pay up, the Coroner won't visit, which means the folk have to leave the corpse lying in the open, rotting, eaten by wild animals, until they agree to cough up. And then the Coroner will add a fresh fine as like as not, just to signal his displeasure.'

'They aren't all like that,' Simon soothed.

'No – some are worse! They gain their post as a result of a great magnate's favour and use their position to serve his interests, releasing his servants and imprisoning his enemies.'

'And you've obviously made up your mind that this fine fellow is of that ilk.'

'Look at him! Fat, foolish, a sluggard . . . what would you think?'

'I would think we've arrived,' Simon said.

The Coroner was waving to the baker, and Piers kicked his little pony forward, pointing in among the trees. Baldwin wrenched his horse's head around after a struggle; Simon's was still more recalcitrant. It obstinately tugged at the grasses and flowers at the side of the river, and Simon had to kick it hard, swearing, to make it obey. It turned, and then, for no apparent reason, bolted. Caught off-balance, Simon clung to the reins even as his feet flew from the stirrups. He could feel himself gradually toppling backwards but by fighting he managed to remain in his seat and, as he passed Baldwin, who was ambling along gently, he turned and called, 'My beast has more fire than yours, anyway!'

'*Simon!*'

He saw Baldwin's anguished expression and turned just in time to see the branch.

Jeanne had felt the mood of the hall lighten after Simon and Baldwin left with Harlewin. It was as if the presence of the Coroner had put a blight upon the proceedings.

Petronilla had gone to a quiet room to feed Stephen as soon as they had arrived, agreeing to come and help the servants in the hall as soon as her child was sleeping. A maid in the castle also had a young child and had agreed to look after Stephen while Petronilla helped her mistress. Now Jeanne saw Petronilla enter carrying pots of wine for guests and sent Edgar over to help her – and to ask where Wat had got to. Jeanne was always nervous if the cattleman's son disappeared when there was ale or wine available. Wat enjoyed alcohol and was often to be found snoring in a hidden corner of a buttery when left to his own devices.

'It's all right, my Lady,' Petronilla said quietly. 'He's in the dairy. I sent him there to help since so many of the maids are in the kitchens.'

'Well done,' Jeanne said. If Wat was occupied there was less chance he could embarrass her or her husband. Glancing up, Jeanne saw Petronilla move away from a passing man. 'Are you well?'

Petronilla nodded, but didn't speak for fear of shaming herself. It was daunting in here, with knights, bannerets, even lords and their ladies. Some might think the same as the Coroner.

Horrible man, she thought, shuddering. All greasy and slimy, like a fat reptile. As he'd gone out, he'd put his arm around her in the hallway, his hand grasping her buttock, trying to force her to kiss him. It was only for a moment, and his thick-lipped face had been so close, slobbering like a great dog inches from her.

'Come on, pretty little maid, give me a kiss or later you might regret it!'

Petronilla was revolted. She had turned her head away, and before he could do more than grope her breast and back-side, Edgar had appeared. He quickly stepped close and the Coroner hastily fell back. 'Yes?'

Edgar instantly moved between them. With a muttered prayer of relief she had fled back into the buttery. At the door she had glanced back. The Coroner had looked angry, but before he could say anything there was a call: Simon and Baldwin had arrived with their horses. The Coroner stalked out.

Now Petronilla was determined to remain close to Edgar. He would protect her. He was like that: kind and generous.

Jeanne was unaware of the anguish in Petronilla's face.

All she saw, she thought, was petulance, as if Petronilla resented having to help serve guests in another household. 'Edgar, take Petronilla out and see if you can help in the kitchen or the buttery.'

Nodding, he led the way. As she left, Petronilla threw Jeanne a look of immense gratitude, which Jeanne recognised but couldn't understand. Musings as to her maid's feelings were cut short as Sir Peregrine called loudly: 'My Lords and Ladies, Lord Hugh de Courtenay.'

Baldwin's cry of warning reached Simon a second before his chest struck the branch squarely with a hollow thud that made Baldwin wince.

The breath was forced from Simon's lungs with an audible '*Oof!*' and Baldwin gave a bellow of laughter as his friend hooked both arms over the branch to stop himself being knocked to the ground. However, his horse kept going, leaving Simon clinging to the tree. The white-faced bailiff was held in mid-air staring after his mount as it stopped and began to crop the grass once more. With a slow inevitability, Simon's weight begin to bow the branch, until with a report like black powder exploding, the tree gave up its limb and Simon dropped smartly onto his rump with a curse. Snorting and snuffling, desperate not to laugh, Baldwin persuaded his reluctant beast to walk to Simon's side.

'God's Saints! If all you can do is grin,' Simon growled from beneath the branch, 'I'd prefer you to get someone who can help. Better still, fetch yourself a bow and shoot that bloody horse!' He lifted the branch and threw it aside. 'Rotten! Typical! I get flung from a horse by a twig that's not got enough strength to cleave to its tree.'

Baldwin set his features into a stern mask of agreement, but before he could ride off in pursuit of Simon's horse, Piers appeared and caught it by the reins. 'Didn't you see the tree?'

Simon ignored him as he took the reins. His backside had hit the ground with a solid thump, and he was aware of tension in his lower back and arse. He daren't rub it for the delight he knew he would see on his friend's face and, largely to take his mind off the pain as he settled gingerly in his saddle once more, he spoke to the baker.

'How far?'

'It's close, sir.'

They ducked under more boughs, avoiding the thicker brambles. Soon Piers pointed. 'That's where the headless one lies.'

Simon allowed his pony to move at a slow walk. He had no intention of asking it to move in a jerking trot, up and down. Ahead was a clear area, bright in the sunshine, and it was a pleasure to be in the warmth after the shade of the trees. At the furthest corner of the glade he saw the Coroner and his man-at-arms.

'Come on,' said Baldwin, and even his voice was subdued as they approached the patch of blood-reddened grass.

The Coroner picked up the head and stared at the battered face of Philip Dyne.

There were many who believed that all Coroners were corrupt. Harlewin le Poter knew better. Some no doubt were, but Harlewin was committed to his job. It might be a regal pain in his backside – having to ride to all parts of the shire at a moment's notice, seeking the bodies of the suddenly dead, holding inquests before all the men in a village or the neighbours in a town, making a decision before this or that jury, formally demanding the deodand (the value of the weapon that had killed the dead man), while old men hissed angrily on hearing the level of the fine to be imposed on them . . . yes, all this *was* aggravating, but when there was a murder, Harlewin was proud of his reputation of commitment. Justice was important. Killers had to be caught and must pay the price for their crimes. Harlewin believed that a man's life was too important to go unavenged.

He tossed the head to his man-at-arms with a feeling of satisfaction. 'This won't take long. Recognise him?'

It was good to have a case in which the whole sordid story could be seen at a glance. So often there were surly crowds who denied all knowledge as he manhandled their dead. Commonly the cause of death was mundane: a stab-wound or a throat slitted like a pig's. Occasionally there was a broken skull or a drowning, but usually it was just a fight that had gone too far.

And the reasons were just as earthy. A man who found his wife lying in an adulterous bed – that was a little close to home, Harlewin acknowledged – or a woman who retaliated after a heavy beating and committed the hideous act of petty treason, stabbing her man while he lay abed.

So many murders were incomprehensible, but with war looming Harlewin knew more deaths would occur. When men grabbed their swords and knives, people began to die even at a distance from the battlefields. Especially when there was a thieving, avaricious bastard like Despenser running the place.

At least this death was straightforward.

'Dyne?' the man-at-arms asked, peering into the half-closed eyes.

'Yes. Looks like he left his road.'

Baldwin heard him muttering to the guard, but his own attention was fixed upon the body sprawled on its back in the long grass near the trees. There were marks about the wrists which Baldwin could not miss: he had been bound before his head was swept off. While Harlewin muttered in an undertone, Baldwin cast about and in a few moments he had found a thong lying atop a flattened expanse of grass nearby; it had been cut in two and its thickness matched the bruises on the wrists.

Continuing with his hands, he felt around the flattened area. 'Ouch!' Carefully he parted the grass to discover what had cut his hand: a knife. Within a few inches, broken pieces of wood; a snapped crucifix, while a short distance away was a purse, large and made of good leather, with some coins inside. The cords which should have bound the purse to its owner's belt were cut through with a sharp blade.

'Coroner, would you like to see this?' he called.

'Interesting, eh?' Harlewin sniffed. 'Let's get on with it, then.'

The whole figure had stiffened, and it was only with an effort that Harlewin could drag the tunic off, swearing as it caught. 'Oh, God's teeth!' he snarled and took the dagger from Baldwin, slicing up the sleeves to the shoulders, then easing the cloth free. Baldwin noticed how sharp the blade was, like a fighter's.

Beneath the tunic was a simple, rough shirt and hose. These Harlewin cut off as well, to reveal the figure of a young man.

Harlewin pointed with the knife. 'As I thought: extensive bruising on the chest, more here on his belly, and he has been kicked hard in the bollocks from the look of it,' he said, indicating the swollen groin. 'No stab-wound.'

'No,' Baldwin agreed. 'It looks like someone beat him, bound him and beheaded him like a common felon. And broke his cross.'

'Killed him like a wolf,' Harlewin agreed, grunting as he pushed himself up into a standing position, and gazed down. Leaving Sir Baldwin at the side of the corpse, he strode off. The whole affair was tidy, he reflected. The outlaw had been caught and despatched. There must be a good reason why someone had done so without complying with the law.

The second body was a few hundred feet away in the next clearing. Harlewin was almost at its side when he heard the low rumble.

'Leash that hound,' he snarled. The dog had moved forward menacingly as he leaned over the body.

The man-at-arms reached for its collar, but it crouched, growling in a long, ferocious, steady timbre and the man hastily withdrew his hand.

'Fetch a bow or something,' Harlewin said irritably. 'I can't be standing here all the damned day! I'm supposed to be seeing my Lord de Courtenay. Go on, shoot the blasted mutt.'

'All right.' Wandering to his horse, the man pulled his crossbow from the saddle. It was a powerful one built of wood and bone, and he put his foot in the stirrup, bent his legs and caught the string in the hook at his belt. Slowly straightening, he spanned the string until he saw it catch on the sear. Walking to the Coroner's side, he selected a steel-tipped quarrel from his belt's quiver and set it on the bow's groove.

'Go on, man!' Harlewin rasped.

The man-at-arms lifted it and aimed the arrow's tip at the dog's throat. His hand moved to the long trigger and he was about to fire when he heard a bellow at his side. Startled, he caught a glimpse of something moving before a bunched fist struck the stock of his bow, releasing the bolt high over the dog's head to thud into an oak.

'Don't you dare slay the hound for protecting his master's body,' Baldwin roared, enraged. 'The beast is a good servant.' He walked slowly towards the dog.

'You may regret it, Sir Baldwin,' Harlewin called. 'The damned thing looks almost mad to me.'

Baldwin ignored him, squatting near the dog. Unconsciously, he suddenly realised, he had started kneading the flesh of his forearm where Uther had bitten him in his death-throes. It made Baldwin feel a sharp pang. This dog was very different from Uther. It growled, more from fear than anger. It was stupid, Baldwin reflected, to try to save the beast for no purpose, especially since he might get bitten. He glanced at the other dog a few yards away, dead. The pair were *raches*, hunting dogs which relied more on scent than sight. Handsome animals, with sleek black coats, brown eyebrows and cheeks, strong jaws and powerful chests, they were built heavily, like mastiffs.

He recalled the pastries he had grabbed before leaving the hall. Some were still in his purse, and he pulled them free, much crumbled and broken, and tossed a piece on the ground. The dog glanced down but didn't eat. Baldwin held out his hand with a piece of pastry in it.

'Come on, it's been a while since you ate, hasn't it, old fellow?' he asked gently.

'Aylmer won't eat like that from a stranger, he needs the order. Aylmer: feed! Good boy.'

The dog dropped his head and snuffled at the pie on the ground. Behind Baldwin stood a swarthy man with a pock-marked face.

'I am called William the Small, sir. I was servant to Sir Gilbert.'

For the first time Baldwin looked at the dead man, and as he did so, he felt the breath catch in his throat as he recognised the face.

CHAPTER NINE

Andrew Carter wiped a hand over his face and walked to his buttery where he bent at a large cask and filled a jug with an unsteady hand, carrying it through to his small hall. His belly rebelled, but he forced the wine down, and soon its soothing warmth calmed his nerves again. In his mind's eye he saw once more the great gout of blood as the head fell from Dyne's shoulders. God! It made him want to heave again.

And he had so much to do for St Giles's Fair. Tomorrow was the vigil, marking the start of the three-day event: vigil, feast and morrow of St Giles. There were other fairs at Tiverton, three others through the year, but there was an especial significance to this one, as Andrew Carter knew only too well. At this fair all Lord Hugh de Courtenay's senior advisers and knights were present. And while their women and victuallers strolled among the tents and stalls of the fair, while all that money was being made, Andrew

Carter, merchant, sat here in his room with his belly roiling after bringing justice on Philip Dyne.

He couldn't keep from worrying at the memory like a dog with a marrow bone. Swallowing, he tried to force his mind to business instead.

It was an anxious time. Andrew Carter knew as well as anyone how fragile was the kingdom's peace; much of his business was conducted with the north of the country, for there were good profits to be made from importing good English wine from the King's lands in Guyenne and sending them up to the wild lands of the Scottish marches, especially to certain clients of his, such as Thomas of Lancaster.

Not that Andrew had ever met Lancaster, of course. Earl Thomas was the son of King Edward I's brother and Queen Blanche, and thus of higher birth than almost all the other nobles in the land. Powerful men tended not to soil their hands in dealings with the lowly, such as Andrew – and, by God's saints, Thomas *was* powerful! Five earldoms were his: he had inherited Lancaster, Leicester and Derby, and acquired Salisbury and Lincoln when he married Alice Lacy. When the government decided to buy peace with him at Leake, they had to negotiate with him in the same manner as they would a separate, independent state.

That was three years ago, when Andrew Carter had decided to tie his purse-strings to Lancaster's future. The Earl was the Steward of England, the most powerful man in the land, even more so than the King in many ways, and he was happy to pay a merchant for information about affairs down in the south.

It had been the obvious choice. King Edward II, as every-one could see by then, was a weak, effeminate waster. He

103

spent his time in idleness, employing actors and jugglers and flattering parasites in his court. Whereas his father, King Edward I, had lived an austere life, dressing simply, keeping his hair trimmed, and practising the skills which made him a good king – sword-fighting, riding, tilting with the lance – his son delighted in wrestling with peasants or swimming: fine accomplishments, these, for a king!

Thomas of Lancaster was in every way a better leader. Andrew had no doubts on that score, but the question that exercised him was whether his Lord de Courtenay would see that. If the news was to be believed (and Andrew invested a fair amount of his own money in good networks of information to protect his business) the two Despensers had fled the kingdom. The armies which had camped outside London's walls had forced the King to accede to their demands. Hugh the Younger and his father had gone: the older man had taken up a relaxed life in France, but his whelp couldn't. He would find life difficult in the French King's domains, for he was Edward II's father-in-law, and the French King resented how his daughter had been supplanted by the royal favourite even in their bed, if the rumours be true. Despenser the Younger had taken a ship and now he raided shipping in the Channel, whatever flag it flew. No vessel was safe.

Lord de Courtenay showed little inclination to go over to Lancaster's side. If anything, he was more keen on supporting the King than before. Still, that was all right so long as the Despensers were abroad and Earl Thomas had power.

Andrew stared into his cup, lips pursed into a single white line, then hurled it against the far wall. The earthenware shattered, shards flying, and wine spattered and dribbled like blood sprayed from a wound as he rested his aching head in his hands again.

He'd been over and over this: the risks of the Younger Despenser's return and the strengthening of the King compared with Lancaster's continued grip on the reins of power. All he could do was pray that Lancaster remained all-powerful. And if the Despensers did come back, maybe he could join them instead. They were dangerous enemies.

'Brother? Are you all right?'

'Nicholas! Yes. Yes, I am fine. Just thinking again about . . .'

'If you're thinking about *him*, don't. He deserved his end,' Nicholas said thinly.

'But what about the knight?'

'Christ Jesus, Andrew, did *you* kill him? *I* didn't! I never even knew him! The bastard probably deserved it. More important now is that you come back to the hall.'

'Very well, brother,' Andrew sighed, rising to his feet. Nicholas was studying him with a jaundiced eye. 'Well? What in God's name's the matter now?' he flared up.

'Nothing. Just keep your temper under control. You don't want people to see your mood.'

'I've got nothing to fear.'

'I know that as well as you!' Nicholas said sharply. 'My concern is that people don't get the wrong idea – or the *right* idea: that we have both forsworn our loyalties to de Courtenay and tied ourselves to Lancaster.'

'Who would guess that?' said Andrew dismissively.

'You damned, whoreson *cretin*,' Nicholas spat, and took a pace forward, clenching his fists. 'You think you're so clever, and yet out there I've heard three men commenting on your absence. Sir Peregrine of Barnstaple has already asked me whether you find the food of a loyal subject to the King less flavoursome than a traitor's!'

'The castle's keeper said that? The bastard should—'

'Let's hope he keeps his views to himself, but in the meantime you, brother, had better come with me; because war is on its way, and if any man doubts your loyalty to de Courtenay, you will be removed from Tiverton – and if you are *very* lucky you will have a swift death!'

Simon disliked William Small on sight. There was something about his pock-marked face that singled him out for dishonesty and faithlessness.

The bailiff had joined Baldwin as he tried to feed the dog. Seeing his friend's shock at the sight of the dead knight, Simon decided to say nothing in front of the other men; instead he moved to the sailor while Baldwin gentled the dog and tied him to a tree.

'You say you're a sailor?' Simon demanded.

'Yes, sir. But I agreed to help this knight in his journey. To guard him.'

'Not very successfully.'

'That wasn't my fault, sir!' William flashed back.

'Perhaps. Where did you meet him?'

'London.'

'And you came all the way here?'

William shrugged. 'He said he wanted to come to Devonshire, and I brought him to Exeter. I know that city from sailing.'

Simon eyed him cynically. 'Why were you coming up here?'

'He wanted to go to Tiverton,' William said hesitantly.

'For St Giles's Fair?' Harlewin asked. He had walked to over to the two men and now stood on Simon's left watching the sailor with suspicion.

'I don't think so, sir. I think he was intending to meet with my Lord de Courtenay.'

'What makes you think that?' Harlewin burst out. 'You've been drinking, man. Ach! I've got better things to do than listen to this.'

'Why do you think a lord would speak to someone like him?' Simon enquired, jerking a thumb at the dead man.

'Sir Gilbert was a Knight Templar from a village not far from here, a place called Templeton. He knew Lord de Courtenay and wanted to speak to him.'

Sir Peregrine of Barnstaple had been called to the gatehouse soon after Lord Hugh entered the hall. He went reluctantly; if he could, he would have gone to see his woman, Emily, but he had to locate his man Toker and learn what news he had. Still, as the knight crossed the yard to the gatehouse, his thoughts were not on the realm's political troubles or London; his mind was fixed upon the little room where Emily was in labour with his child. It was only as he entered his room that he could force himself to consider the business at hand.

Toker was one of his better finds. A Devonshire man through and through, Toker had been one of the survivors of King Edward II's army that had been destroyed at Bannockburn. There he had been a squire in the retinue of Gilbert Clare, Earl of Gloucester, a man he respected and loved as lord and warrior. When Clare died at Bannockburn

Toker was distraught, but being a loyal servant to his master, he had gone to Clare's widow, Maud, Countess of Gloucester, and sworn fealty to her in her husband's memory.

But even the most loyal servant is feeble protection against an army. In an act of cynical opportunism, Despenser the Younger seized the Countess's castle at Tonbridge and from that day Toker had been the implacable enemy of the Despensers: their intolerable greed was the spark that fired his loathing. Chivalry demanded responsibilities, but the Despensers ignored duties and followed their own avarice.

It was his history which made Toker so invaluable. His hatred was boundless. Not only had Despenser cruelly shattered Toker's belief in chivalry, he had stolen Toker's future. Toker had dreamed of being knighted, but without a lord he had no opportunity. Without the largesse of a lord to support him, he had become what he himself detested: a wandering, lordless, impecunious scavenger. During the famine, starving, he became an outlaw.

Sir Peregrine had rescued him. Toker had been caught poaching Lord Hugh's venison and something in Toker's eyes intrigued Sir Peregrine. Little by little he pieced together the man's story. He felt certain Toker could prove useful.

And useful he had been. Now Sir Peregrine's only concern was that he might one day find himself without a focus for Toker's energy, and then he would have to work hard to ensure that the man's resentment did not become targeted upon him.

Toker was seated negligently in one of his chairs, waiting.

'You're back, then, Toker,' Sir Peregrine said, walking to his own chair.

'It was interesting, Sir Peregrine, and worthwhile.'

'Tell me about it.'

Sir Peregrine had sent Toker, together with Perkin of Croydon and the Welshman, Owen of Harlech, off to London to gather information on the latest developments to do with the Despensers – to find out what the people of London thought, and how the Lords of the Marches planned to get rid of them.

Everyone who could afford to had sent men to watch. Abbots, merchants and lords – all had observers there to witness the unfolding events. No man could afford to be ill-informed when the kingdom was so near to civil war.

'The Despensers have gone?'

'Yes, Sir Peregrine,' said Toker. 'The King wasn't happy, but he had little choice. Now the sire is in France while his whelp lies in the Channel and robs any ship he can.'

'Let's hope one of the ships he stops is full of men-at-arms ready for him. The bastard deserves death for the ill he's stirred in the country.'

'Yes, my Lord. The sooner they're dead the better.'

'What was the mood in London?'

'Evil. The people are sick of a King who spends his time with actors and the like.'

'What of Lancaster? Any news?'

'Badlesmere has tried to join him, but I heard Lancaster wants nothing to do with him. A man like that, who'll change his alliances almost at a whim – it's hardly surprising if Earl Thomas ditches him.'

'You must be tired. Would you like some food?'

'I could eat a team of oxen and still chew on their harness,' agreed Toker with a grim smile.

Sir Peregrine walked to the door with him. 'It was lucky you came from the northern road,' he said as they went down the stairs. 'A man was murdered on the Exeter Road.'

'Who?'

'I don't know yet. Some knight, apparently,' Sir Peregrine said dismissively as they came into the sunlight. He waved Toker to the table near the kitchen where others were already chewing at cold meats and swilling the castle's best ales.

If he had known of Toker's meeting with the Templar in London, he might have found out that Sir Gilbert of Carlisle had been seen travelling with a chest containing riches of some sort. Thus he would have been alerted, and might have been able to rescue the gold, but he didn't know to ask. As for Toker, he had already forgotten the man with the intriguing little chest. There had been too many things to watch, listen to and remember since then.

Baldwin rolled Sir Gilbert over. The back of his tunic was cleanly punctured where a sharp knife had been shoved in, and when Baldwin lifted the cloth, he found that directly beneath was a thin slit in the man's flesh. It had wept scarcely a drop of blood.

'One stab and his life was ended,' Baldwin reflected, resting on his heels. Sir Gilbert's sword now lay sheathed beside the knight's body, but Baldwin was interested to see that where his purse had once dangled, there were only two thongs hanging, both with cleanly slashed ends. They matched those of the purse. The knight's spurs were valuable, as was the belt and sword from the look of them, but his dagger's sheath was empty. When Baldwin pushed the knife found by the other body into the sheath, it fitted. Must have been a straightforward theft that had gone wrong. Someone had had time to take the purse and dagger, but had then run off empty-handed.

He turned his attention to the dead dog. It lay a short distance away, and there was a goodly-sized stab-wound in its chest, at the front beneath its neck. When he opened the jaws, he saw no cloth or anything to link the dead beast with who had killed it.

'You poor brute,' he said sadly. 'You tried to save your master but you had no chance, did you?'

CHAPTER TEN

At the gate to the church, Father Abraham stood with arms akimbo watching people arrive for St Giles's Fair. Folk travelled from many miles away to come to a place like this, and he could see many rich-looking merchants; not that they were alone. Jugglers, actors and other good-for-nothings were tagging along. Gamblers, barbers, quacksalvers trailed past, all hoping to enjoy a few days' holiday, perhaps also making profits from some of the more foolish people in the town.

Father Abraham muttered a short prayer, avoiding the eye of Felicity, the whore from Cock Lane, who stood at the other side of the road with her arms folded, eyeing the crowds with a similar professional measurement in her gaze, but with a view to a more immediate reward than that which Father Abraham could offer.

He shook his head. That poor man Father Benedict had died late in the evening the previous day and Father Abraham had sat up with him until after dark. Fortunately the boy who had come to fetch Father Abraham that morning had returned with his mother, and the priest had commanded them to sit up with the body all night.

It was a great shame, though. And a waste. The man had been devoted to his damned chapel, that centre of heresy, sodomy and sinfulness, but he was still a Godly man in his own way. He personally lived the pure life of a priest – and was now dead, while the whore Felicity lived on. Father Abraham sighed. Truly God's way was sometimes difficult to comprehend.

He turned and almost tripped over Hick, the rat-catcher. 'What is it?' he demanded testily.

'Father, I'm sorry, but it's Emily. She's awful sick and the midwife asked if you could come and see her. Give her the last rites.'

He had noticed her looking unwell recently, but she had a brood of eleven children. 'She's too old for another. I did tell her,' he pointed out.

The rat-catcher agreed hastily. Emily wasn't his wife and he had no wish to irritate the priest. This was a man who could add a few words to tip the balance in favour of a dying person, someone who could either help a soul on its way to Heaven or – God forbid! – aid the angels in tumbling it down to Hell.

Father Abraham went to his church and fetched a small bottle of holy water to take with him, picked up his wallet and set off, reminding himself that he must send a cart to collect Father Benedict's body at some stage.

Emily was a foolish woman, Father Abraham knew that. She was too much the victim of her passions. That was the trouble with so many women today, they thought they could indulge their most sinful whims with impunity. With all those children, Emily was surely the prisoner of her lusts.

The house was one of the shabbier places out to the north of the town, one of a line straggling along the road near the marsh, and Father Abraham stood back with a disapproving expression on his face as he considered it: small, only perhaps some ten feet square, with no second storey, a hole for a door with a piece of tattered and threadbare cloth to cover it, and a window that had a broken shutter. The thatching was holed, green, and compacted in a thin layer over the roof.

Sighing, he walked to the door. Her husband had deserted her some years before. He had never controlled Emily when he was still with her. Always drunk, feckless by nature, he was rarely at home when he had money to spend in an alehouse.

Inside the hut, the air was filled with the rank odour of twelve bodies living in close proximity. A ladder stood at one corner, leading up to a series of rough planks nailed to beams to provide a little space free of mice or rats, but apart from that everything was set out on the floor or on the table formed by a plain board resting on trestles.

The earthen floor held a fire, whose dull flames shed a small amount of light and showed the family's belongings. Scraps of cloth and straw made the communal bed; all shared the same blankets to keep each other warm. There was a single large pot by the fire, the only cooking utensil they owned.

It was near this that he saw Emily, lying in the corner gripping the forearms of the midwife. Her face was waxen and yellow in the gloom, and sweat glistened on her brow as she clenched her teeth on the leather strap, whimpering with the pain as it washed over her in waves.

Father Abraham looked enquiringly at the midwife, who wiped her brow with exhaustion and motioned towards a tiny object lying in the corner of the room. A cat was sniffing at it. He crossed the floor, aiming a mistimed kick at the cat, and squatted.

Death came in many forms. This was sad, and he felt the small cheek with a sense of awe that so small a creature could have been created so perfectly, only to be ruined and die in the fight for birth. But it was not for Father Abraham to try to gauge God's reasons, and a grunt from Emily brought him back to the present. He slowly got to his feet and walked to the midwife's side.

'Emily hasn't yet produced the afterbirth,' the midwife whispered, stepping away a moment and rubbing at her temples. She had been with Emily since the previous day when the labour had begun, and now she was close to the end of her tether. Occasionally a woman would have a difficult birth; sometimes a baby would die – but this time the midwife knew that her patient was fighting for her life and she had no idea how to help her.

Spitting out the strap, Emily shouted, 'It's tearing me apart – I can *feel* it! Oh God, have pity!'

Father Abraham recoiled. There was little he could do. The midwife was professional; he could see the scrap of paper tied to Emily's upper thigh where it must do the most good: all good midwives knew they must write down prayers and bind them close to the woman's groin to ease her pain. There was nothing else to be done for her. She was in God's hands. He bent his head and prayed before enquiring of the midwife in an undertone whether she had been able to baptise the child before it died.

'He came out already dead, Father,' she said sadly. 'There was no chance.'

'I shall pray for it.'

'What about *me*?'

Grumbling to himself, Father Abraham shot a look at the midwife. She shook her head again, mouthing the word, 'No.' Resignedly he began the seven questions.

'Do you believe in God and the Holy Scriptures and reject heresy?'

'Yes, Father,' the dying woman moaned.

'Do you recognise that you have offended God?'

'Yes, Father.'

'Are you sorry for your sins?'

'Yes, Father.'

'Do you desire to make amends and, if God grants you time, will you do so?'

'Yes, Father.'

'Do you forgive your enemies?'

'Yes, Father.'

'Will you make all satisfaction?'

'Yes, Father.'

'And finally, do you believe that Christ died for you and that you may never be saved except through the merit of Christ's passion, and do you thank God with all your heart as you should?'

'Yes, Father.'

He could see the muscles at her temples clenching and the perspiration breaking out over her face. Swiftly he gave her

Extreme Unction and touched her forehead with oil. She had not been confirmed so he couldn't anoint her temples, but as his cool fingers touched her brow she closed her eyes in obvious relief, the proof to him, if he needed it, that she was a true Christian as she professed, eager for the life to come. Murmuring the *viaticum*, he reflected that she could be buried in his churchyard. He wasn't sure where her child could go; unbaptised, it could be installed anywhere. There was no need to worry about protecting it in hallowed ground.

'Oh *God*!'

As Father Abraham watched in horror, a stream of bright blood spurted from between Emily's legs. He stumbled back as the midwife rushed to her side, wringing out a damp cloth and draping it over her brow while Emily tensed, arching her back, clutching her still swollen belly, and screaming again and again. Father Abraham remembered his vial of holy water. He grabbed it from his wallet, pulled off the stopper, hesitated irresolutely, then sprinkled it over her stomach. Even as the water touched her, she appeared to relax, slumping back.

'Save your water, Father,' said the midwife sadly, closing Emily's mad, staring eyes.

It took a little time to carry the two bodies to the wagon ready to be carted back to Tiverton.

'Well?' Simon said when Baldwin came back to the road, the dog still on his leash.

'His purse was stolen, but what thief would take that and leave the spurs and belt?' Baldwin asked, patting the dog's head.

'A thief who was interrupted.'

'And who arranged the dead man in that manner?' Baldwin wondered aloud. 'Laid out like a corpse under a hearse. One stab in the back: a professional job. The fact that one blow was struck is significant.'

'Someone who knew how to kill.'

'Yes. A soldier. Or perhaps a sailor.'

Simon nodded. Both had seen too many corpses in their time. An inexperienced murderer stabbed several times to make sure of his victim; only a man who knew what he was doing selected the correct place carefully, killing with one blow.

Harlewin joined them. 'Not much to learn here. It's getting late – we may as well return to the castle.'

Simon looked at Baldwin.

'William, you will need to pack your things,' Baldwin said. 'We will wait for you. Coroner, you carry on.'

Harlewin le Poter glanced at the sailor. 'If you wish . . . but first I need a surety. Come, master Mariner. Open your purse there!'

'I only have four pennies,' William said mournfully, holding his wallet open in proof.

'Give me them. That will do.' Harlewin gazed back at the trees, his mouth askew with dissatisfaction. 'It's a bad day; a bad thing! Two men dead, and little enough for the King.' He nodded to the man-at-arms, who already sat waiting on his horse. 'We'd best return to town. We can hold our inquest there, before the town's jury.'

The doleful Piers clicked his tongue and the wagon jolted off behind the Coroner. Baldwin found his attention fixed on the bodies jerking in the back of the cart as it rattled and clattered over the ruts in the road. He was convinced the head would bounce out long before they got to Tiverton.

'What's his problem?' William asked.

'He was hoping for more money, I expect,' Baldwin said shortly. 'The *murdrum* fine.'

'So? You think he won't be able to charge *murdrum* now?'

'The *murdrum* is levied where no one can swear to the corpse being that of an Englishman,' Simon told him. 'If my Lord de Courtenay knows this man, how could the Coroner refuse to accept *his* word? A dead felon is free of fines anyway, he doesn't rate. No, only the knight matters and now the Coroner can get nothing for him. Most galling.' He looked about him. 'Did Sir Gilbert say he had been here recently?' he asked William. 'You mentioned that he knew Lord Hugh.'

'No. He told me it was the first time he had been here in almost thirteen years.'

'Thirteen years?' Baldwin asked. 'That's interesting. Tell me, this dog appears unhurt, yet he looks a sturdy enough creature. Why did he not protect his master?'

'He was with me in the camp. Sir Gilbert only took Merry with him.'

'Take us there and on the way you can tell us what happened.'

William nodded and led the way to the riverbank. 'We'd been travelling for ages when we got here three days ago. We stopped here latish and made camp. Then the day before yesterday, in the morning, I remained here while Sir Gilbert rode off.'

'Did he say where he was going?' Baldwin asked.

William gave him a steady look. 'He said he was meeting friends in Tiverton.'

'Who?'

'How should I know?' William said with exasperation. 'He went, that's all I know.'

'But he returned?'

'Yes. During the night. He seemed in good spirits, as if he'd heard good news. Reeked of cheap wine too. In the morning he said we should wait a day longer before going to town. And no, he didn't tell me why! I didn't care, it was good to take a day to rest. Dogs didn't like it, though.'

'Why do you say that?'

'The pair were restless. Unsettled. Kept barking at the trees.'

They had arrived at a small enclosed area of grass inside a stand of young oaks and sycamores which formed a natural windbreak. At the other side of the greensward was the river, swift-flowing here, and William had laid out their camp in a natural hollow near the water.

Baldwin walked to the horses. Two were tethered, one strong-looking mount, the other a packhorse. 'You had only the two horses?'

William blinked. 'I . . . No, my master's never came back last night.'

'It probably ran off. I daresay it will be found sooner or later,' Simon nodded. 'You were talking about the dogs.'

'Oh . . . um, yes. Sir Gilbert cuffed them and pulled them back, but they'd settle a moment, then stare at the trees again.'

'Weren't you afraid of outlaws?'

'Look how far it is to the trees there,' William said. 'Anyone wanting to attack would have to cover the verge, the road, and then the grass to get to us here. If they tried it, the dogs'd be loosed and me and Sir Gilbert armed before they got halfway.'

Simon nodded and the sailor continued. 'Anyway, in the afternoon two men rode past heading for Exeter. Didn't think about them at first, but . . . What with the dogs being uneasy, I'd kept an eye on the trees and after a while I saw a man peering at us. He realised I'd seen him, and ducked down out of sight. I was about to tell Sir Gilbert when we heard hooves approaching fast. It was the same two men I'd seen earlier. Both well-seated on expensive mounts.'

'Names?' Baldwin pressed.

'One was called Andrew. A big fat man, red-faced and enormous girth. Bigger than the Coroner himself. The other was thinner, but with really dark, nasty eyes. When he fixed those eyes on you, you could feel them.'

Baldwin found himself recalling Andrew Carter and his brother Nicholas from the castle. The descriptions fitted both.

'And you say they approached from behind you? From Exeter?'

He nodded.

'What did they do?'

'They stopped and asked whether we'd seen a felon on the road, an abjurer. Said they were there to make sure he didn't run and hide in the woods. I told them I'd seen a fellow in the trees. Soon as I did that, they were all set to be off after him, but the thinner man, he called the other one back, said: "Andrew, slow down! We don't want to get separated".'

'They went off together?' Baldwin said.

'Yes, but Sir Gilbert was fretful afterwards. It's every man's duty to help the Hue and Cry chase down a felon, yet I think he was dubious about them.'

'Why so?' Simon demanded.

'He said that the two looked more bent on murder than on justice. If an abjurer is forced to leave the road given to him against his will, it's the same as forcing him to leave his sanctuary. It's not his fault and he should be protected. Sir Gilbert fancied that these two men would give their victim little sympathy. He told me to stay here, released Merry and set off after them on his horse.'

'Why take only the one dog?' Baldwin mused.

'Perhaps because Aylmer hasn't a good nose? He hunts by sight.'

Baldwin glanced at Aylmer, who lay with his head on his forepaws watching them. 'Why take a dog hunting when the animal doesn't know which scent to follow? To hunt the two from the road?' He shrugged. 'Continue.'

'That was all. He disappeared among the trees, but never returned. When daylight came, I went to the road but I couldn't see anything, so I came back and released Aylmer. I was sure something had gone wrong. That carter appeared then and I asked him to stop and help me. It wasn't long before we came across Sir Gilbert's body, the dog a few yards away as you saw them.'

'I see.' Baldwin walked to Aylmer and untied him. The dog was reticent and growled, unhappy to be led away by someone other than his master, but Baldwin cuffed his backside and growled back, 'Learn obedience, you bastard!' The dog showed his teeth but walked with him.

Simon said, 'You say he left the dog at the camp to protect you? Was the knight carrying anything valuable with him that needed protecting?'

'No, sir. Nothing,' said William innocently.

CHAPTER ELEVEN

When Father Abraham got back to the church, the baby, wrapped to make a neat bundle, had been set in the arms of its dead mother. The midwife – superstitious old soul – had insisted and Father Abraham considered it preferable to leave the matter to her rather than continue arguing. The daft besom was determined to have her way, even though it was practically heretical. After all, the mother, whoring bitch that she was as far as Father Abraham was concerned, had at least been baptised, and the child would have to be buried far from her. No unbaptised child could be placed for eternal rest in *his* churchyard.

He was content that he had done his duty, though. He had given the woman the seven interrogations, which she had been able to answer satisfactorily, and she had received Extreme Unction and the *viaticum*. Even through her pain, Father Abraham had been pleased to see how her face eased as he murmured his way through the words and anointed her forehead.

Back at his churchyard he walked past the church to his own little house. This, a two-roomed building set into the church's wall, was already warmed from the fire his sexton had lit for him that morning. The cosy glow gave him a sense of comfort and ease which he had not known for some hours; especially after the ride yesterday. That reminded him: he went to the door and called for the sexton, ordering him to fetch Father Benedict's body.

He returned to his room and sat on his chair by the fire. There was much to consider, especially now that all these lords and ladies were arriving. Father Abraham knew that he must make notes about each together with their political leanings for his lord, Bishop Stapledon of Exeter. The Bishop had been one of the key political leaders in the country, becoming the Treasurer of the Exchequer. He would want to hear how Lord Hugh was being advised.

Father Abraham shuddered as he recalled the gloomy clearing with the dead bodies of the knight and his dog. Stapledon would want to know of Sir Gilbert's mission.

The warmth made his eyelids droop and he found himself nodding. The late night yesterday, he told himself. He let his chin fall forward onto his breast, and before long he was asleep.

At the castle's gate Baldwin called to a man-at-arms and nodded towards William. 'This man is a witness to the murder of Sir Gilbert and the felon on the Exeter road. You should keep him until the Coroner has decided what to do with him.'

William apparently saw no reason to protest and trailed along after the man without demur, the dog at his heels. Baldwin watched him for a moment, then shook his head and sprang down from his horse, giving the reins to a passing hostler. 'Take them to the hackney man,' he said, grateful that he would never again have to ride the nag.

Simon and he strode up to the hall and entered, keen to rejoin the throng.

In their absence food had been served on trestle-tables; the guests had watched it arrive, had sat and eaten, entertained by jugglers and musicians, and had risen again to drink large pots of wine or strong ale while servants came in to eat at the same tables before clearing away the debris and removing the tables again. By the time Baldwin entered glancing about for his wife, Simon casting about just as eagerly for food, all remnants of the midday meal had been disposed of: almost half had gone into the bellies of the guests, another two-fifths into those of the servants, and the remainder into the platters and bowls of the poor waiting hopefully at the door.

Already disappointed by the lack of food, it was with a feeling of the inevitability of his destiny that Baldwin saw his wife talking to Sir Peregrine of Barnstaple.

'Oh my God!' he groaned.

Simon looked at his friend. 'What is it? Upset about missing the feast, old fellow?'

'That man! Sir Peregrine!'

Baldwin spoke in an undertone, and Simon eyed the tall knight in conversation with Lady Jeanne without any idea what his friend meant. Simon himself had never heard of Sir Peregrine. Barnstaple was many miles from Lydford, and all he knew of the man was that he had instantly gone to

Baldwin's side when the Coroner and Sherman had begun their row earlier.

'Sir Baldwin . . . I hope you managed to keep our good Coroner in check?' The stranger said lightly, and Baldwin nodded as politely as he could.

His manner intrigued Simon, who was already sure that the man before him was not viewed by Baldwin as a courteous philanderer, nor as a serious physical danger. The fact that Edgar stood nearby without apparent concern also indicated that Sir Peregrine was not a dangerous lunatic who might threaten Baldwin's life.

Sir Peregrine was as tall as Simon, with a high forehead and intelligent green eyes in a long, narrow face. His brow rose up to a shining dome as clear of hair as a cleric's, and all about it was a thick fringe of golden curls, looking strangely out of place, like a child's fluff on a middle-aged man's head. His mouth smiled easily, and Simon could believe that Sir Peregrine would be popular with women, but he showed no sign of embarrassment, which he surely would have, had he been trying to cuckold Baldwin. Instead he studied Baldwin and appeared to like what he saw, his mouth widening into a calm and appreciative grin.

When Simon was introduced, Sir Peregrine cast a glance all over him, from boots to head and down again. 'The Bailiff of Lydford under the Warden of the Stannaries, Abbot Champeaux of Tavistock? My friend, I have heard much about you. You are growing famous.'

'I thank you, Sir Peregrine,' Simon said, feeling foolishly flattered.

'Oh no, I assure you, your name has been brought to my attention on several occasions, particularly by my very good friend Bishop Stapledon of Exeter. Do you tend towards his views on politics?'

Baldwin intervened smoothly. 'My friend and I serve our masters as best we may.'

'Of course, Sir Baldwin,' Sir Peregrine said agreeably, his eyes creasing in merriment.

Simon was struck by a sudden certainty that there was some kind of verbal jousting going on and although he had little idea what the matter was that the two men were warily skirting, he was happy to leave Baldwin in control of the conversation.

'And I am sure you would agree that Simon's master, his lord, Abbot Champeaux, is the only man with whom he could truly discuss allegiances? Any political decisions must be made by the good Abbot. It is Simon's duty to obey,' Baldwin continued.

'Absolutely. Although he could, if he so wished, advise.'

'Not if he wished: if he was *asked*,' Baldwin said shortly.

'Naturally,' Sir Peregrine agreed suavely. 'And another matter we should discuss is this affair of our Lord de Courtenay and the Despensers. And the King, of course.'

Baldwin glanced at Jeanne and to his relief she instantly read his mind. 'Oh, Sir Peregrine, do you think we could return to this matter at some later hour? I know I am exhausted after our ride here this morning, and since our arrival I have had no time to recuperate. Could we take some little rest now – and I am sure that the good bailiff and my husband would be glad of refreshment, for both have been out to view the dead men and assist the Coroner.'

'Of course, my lady,' Sir Peregrine said and took his leave with a calm smile. As he walked away, he turned and spoke to Baldwin. 'But we shall need to talk very soon, Sir Baldwin. Very soon.'

William walked from the stable with Aylmer at his heels, having seen the two remaining mounts into their stalls. He'd ignored the offers of a young groom and rubbed them down himself with handfuls of straw before running a hand over their legs to make sure all was well. He had learned early, when he was still a man-at-arms, that a horse should be protected and looked after more carefully than a companion. A companion might run away, while your mount could save your life.

'You going to take all day?' his guard had demanded.

'Not much longer.'

'Oh, Christ's bones!'

Standing in the yard with the man, William breathed in the mixed odours: woodsmoke from the kitchen's fires, roasting meat, pies and bread baking adding their wholesome scents to the tang of the horse and cattle droppings, human shit and urine that permeated the place.

They were the smells of life itself, he thought happily. Only one thing could improve matters: ale. The hall above the gatehouse looked best. There was bound to be a buttery in there.

'Ale?' he asked.

'Why not?' the guard grunted.

With a cheery determination William strode across the yard to the door. Aylmer sat and scratched an ear, then wandered off to a corner near the stairs where he cocked a leg and decorated the wall, before strolling about the yard inquisitively.

William didn't notice Toker at the kitchen door, nor the way the blue eyes narrowed, watching as he climbed up the stairs to the hall's doorway. Toker was sure he recognised William's face, but couldn't place him right away. But it would come back to him eventually. It always did.

Jeanne could see her husband's mood even before he muttered a curse and snapped his fingers at Edgar, a rude method of beckoning his servant that he would normally have shunned. 'My love, what is it?'

'That primping, vain, conceited cockscomb . . .'

'Sir Peregrine?' she asked with genuine confusion. 'But he was perfectly correct and chivalrous, husband. He offered no insult to me or to you.'

'He wouldn't. He is not that kind of man. No, his danger is more indirect. More insidious.'

Simon gazed at his friend with utter bafflement. 'Baldwin, what are you talking about? As far as I could tell he was a pleasant man, better versed in courtesy than many others of his rank.'

'You realise what his rank is?'

'A knight, of course.'

'Well, of course he is a knight, but *not* a knight *bachelor*; he's a bannaret,' Baldwin shot back. 'Do you realise what that means? He can command other knights. In theory he could command *me* to fight with him.'

'He'd be a good man to stand beside, wouldn't he?' Simon protested, still confused. 'I don't understand what your problem is.'

'The man is not a loyal Courtenay knight. He is on the side of the Marchers.'

'Surely he wouldn't commit treason against my Lord de Courtenay,' Jeanne burst out.

'There is no telling what he might do,' Baldwin said heavily. 'He's a politician.'

Simon frowned uncomprehendingly. 'If you're sure of this, you should warn Lord de Courtenay.'

'That one of his trusted advisers has taken a line tending towards one party? That in itself is no crime and Sir Peregrine is too shrewd to leave himself compromised.'

'How can you be sure he's loyal to the Marchers?' Simon asked.

'It is a matter of discussion in the shire,' Baldwin said. 'I have heard his allegiance talked about in Crediton and Exeter – I am surprised news of it has not spread to Lydford. There are many men who wonder what will happen now that the Despensers are banished from the kingdom. But it doesn't do to speculate too much. Not when there is so much possible danger here.'

'What danger?' Simon asked.

'Simon, have you not understood? We are confirmed as loyal subjects of King Edward because with all his faults, he was rightly anointed King; we are known to be friends of Bishop Stapledon, one of many Lords who deprecates the illegal expulsion of the Despensers. Sir Peregrine supports the Marcher Lords who forced the King to expel the Despensers. If you were a political creature trying to persuade Lord Hugh to throw his weight behind the Marcher Lords like Sir Peregrine, would you want two men like us advising Lord Hugh?'

'Christ's balls!' Simon breathed. 'Oh, sorry, Jeanne.'

'I've heard worse,' she said, but her voice was far away, and she stared with perplexity at Sir Baldwin.

'What is it, my love?'

'It occurs to me, if you are correct and Sir Peregrine is loyal to the Marchers, he is prepared to support those whom the King has declared his enemies. Would he be prepared to use violence against you?'

Simon watched his friend and saw the smile and brief shake of his head, but Simon also saw Baldwin's expression harden as he glanced towards the screens where Sir Peregrine had left, and Simon was convinced that Baldwin thought Sir Peregrine would stop at nothing in support of his friends.

Striding through the castle gates late the next morning, Harlewin le Poter nodded to the porter before he crossed the yard and climbed the low staircase to the hall. It was the eve of the feast of St Giles, not a good day for an inquest. He walked into the buttery, where he found a small group of men sitting on benches, drinking and chatting. Their noise stopped as the Coroner entered and eyed them coldly.

Harlewin was not given to threatening people unnecessarily, but now and again he felt it was useful to demonstrate his position. This was one such occasion. He said nothing but stared coldly until the men moved aside, and only then, when he had a clear passage to the barrel, did he march forward and fill himself a quart pot.

His position was an important one. The Coroner enforced the King's laws on the region. Gone were the days when a lord could impose a death penalty on any man he disliked: the Coroner had to agree and confirm the sentence. Coroners were among the most important of all the King's officials, especially now that corruption and bribery had reduced bailiffs, sergeants and sheriffs to the standing of liars and thieves in the eyes of many.

Of course there was dishonesty among Coroners, just as there was in many professions. Harlewin had heard the stories: his counterpart in western Devon who had refused to visit the body of a dead woman for nine weeks at the height of summer because his extortionate fee had been rejected. He only agreed to go and inspect the stinking remains once his money had been paid. Then there was the story of the Coroner eastwards who had refused to hold an inquest into a baby's death, stillborn as the result of a quarrel and fight, because the man accused of striking the mother had been the Coroner's own servant; or the rumours that this same Coroner released men from gaol in return for gifts.

Harlewin grunted to himself, standing in the screens passage sipping at his drink. Many of these stories were perfectly true, and sometimes he had himself followed the example given. Once, as John Sherman had said, he had helped Earl Thomas, but what else could a man do when he came up against someone as powerful as the Earl? And he had not released a murderer. He wouldn't stoop so low, not even for a lord.

For all the accusations of corruption levelled against Coroners which were correct, Harlewin had a shrewd suspicion that often the wrong man was accused. He knew that Father Abraham was, like many clerks, an enthusiastic collector of coins. Often enough he'd seen the priest pocketing a shilling or even two for recording the details of a peculiarly repulsive corpse. Andrew Carter had paid five shillings when the priest wrote up the inquest of young Joan's body. A man like Andrew wouldn't want salacious facts being scribbled down for any sick bastard to read. Yet no doubt many would assume Harlewin was corrupt because *he* was a despised Coroner, whereas Father Abraham was a holy servant.

'Ah, Coroner. I hope I find you well?' Sir Peregrine asked.

Harlewin grunted noncommittally. 'I've sorted out the death of the felon, though why the knight should have died is anyone's guess.'

'Surely the felon murdered the knight? That is what felons do.'

Harlewin sourly studied his drink. 'Perhaps.'

'It would make the life of your lord a great deal easier, Coroner.' Seeing he had Harlewin's attention, Sir Peregrine spoke softly. 'Our Lord Hugh is a little perturbed that a murder has been committed here just as he's preparing to hold a feast. He'd be much happier if I could inform him that the matter is closed, that you've found that the murdered man was killed by a felon, a man abjuring the realm, who was then himself shortly afterwards executed by two upright citizens of Tiverton. You understand me?'

Harlewin watched the knight stride away down the stairs and out to the yard. 'So why do you want this knight forgotten, Sir Peregrine?' he muttered cynically. 'Or is it your Marcher Lords whom you seek to please?'

True, the knight's suggestion would save a lot of difficulty; it was a logical explanation; and he had a duty to his Lord. Draining his pot, he marched back to the hall. Seeing Simon and Baldwin with Jeanne at the far side of the hall, Harlewin smiled broadly.

'Bailiff Puttock, Sir Baldwin? Congratulate me! I have slept on the problem and already I have solved both murders!'

CHAPTER TWELVE

Toker stretched and walked into the bright daylight of the castle's court. He didn't notice Aylmer, who had found a cool patch of grass at the entrance to one of the servants' rooms and lay down blocking the doorway. Toker knew he had come across the man he had seen the previous evening fairly recently, but much had happened over the last few weeks and he had met a great many new people.

Idly, he ran his mind over the last few days. He had detoured on the journey back to Tiverton, taking his men with him on the road to Bristol to hear the latest news from Wales.

The Despenser lands, he learned, were being systematically ruined, their crops destroyed, houses and castles burned or otherwise wasted. Eight Despenser castles were already wrecked. All the family's possessions were being ransacked, their luxurious belongings stolen. The list of goods was proof enough of their greed: tables of ivory and ebony, chessboards with chessmen of fine crystal, rich clothing, silver and jewellery.

It wasn't enough that the Despensers had lost it all: they had escaped into exile. If Toker could have had his way, both Despensers would have been hanged, drawn and quartered. They were an abomination: power-crazed thieves whose robberies were all the more obscene in the light of their already enormous wealth.

Toker spat and took a long draught of ale; William was completely forgotten now. The waste of the Despensers' lands was good to hear. It proved that the tyranny of that deplorable family was ended. No Despenser would ever again be able to hold the kingdom in his hand. Even the King must recognise the damage done to his realm.

The attitude of people up towards Bristol had surprised him. They appeared to think the Lords of the Marches were acting from self-interest and were no better than the Despensers. Toker was convinced they were wrong. Without the Despensers, the country could be ruled once more by the King with wise and pragmatic advisers: men who looked more to the chivalric codes than to their own advantage; men who could be trusted. Perhaps he might even be able to find a little honour and forget the lawless period of his life. That thought brought a wry smile to this face, for he knew that when he had the chance he couldn't help but return to his felonious ways. In London he had joined his men in looting a shop during a riot; on another occasion, while bonfires lit the night sky, he'd slipped inside a merchant's house and walked away with a good collection of plate. The instinct to take what he could was too strong; the urge to serve himself in case he lost his lord again.

Toker knew himself. He would always tend to resort to theft when he could. He needed a war, a means of winning money. If the Despensers returned – *then*, Toker thought, he would be able to get enough to set himself up for life. He'd never have to work again; he could just sit in a tavern all day and drink.

'Whose dog is that?'

It was Perkin; he was staring at the hound. Aylmer lay in a doorway out of the sun, but Perkin glared at him with loathing.

'I've seen that mutt somewhere,' Perkin said.

As he spoke Wat walked towards Aylmer. His foot caught a stone, which flew through the air and hit the dog's shoulder. Instantly Aylmer woke and rose fluidly into a menacing crouch, his head below his shoulders, his legs bent ready to spring, while a low, vicious growl rumbled from deep in his throat.

Wat froze in fear. 'Christ!'

A groom laughed: a maid from the kitchen cried, 'Don't touch him – he must be rabid.'

'Yeah, mind out, dog!' someone called with a laugh.

Toker's men sniggered as Wat nervously retreated. 'I only wanted to get to the storeroom. Someone call the dog off.'

'Who owns the thing?' shouted Owen.

Toker listened but didn't look at him. The little Welshman was always nervous, and the anxiety in his voice was proof, if Toker had needed it, that the man was unreliable. Sir Peregrine had foisted him on Toker before going to London saying he was a good archer, but so far he'd been useless in fights. Anyway, why call the dog off? Toker was like his men – he was interested to see how the dog would see off the brat. Yet the dog's stance looked familiar . . .

'He doesn't like being kicked,' said William. He lounged at the door to the hall, a large pot in his hand, leaning on the rough wooden handrail. The sun was warm on his face and he felt good. He didn't notice Toker or his men, he was watching Wat with an amused grin. Taking a deep, contented gulp of ale, he said, 'Aylmer gets angry when people prod him.'

Toker lifted his eyes to stare. It was that man again, and his voice was familiar . . . and then Toker remembered a street in London, two dogs, two servants and a knight.

'He's going to bite me – can't you move him?' Wat cried, close to tears.

'Alymer – *move*!' William shouted without looking.

Instantly the dog circled warily around Wat and walked to a patch of scrubby grass where he lay down. It was at the same time that Toker felt the burst of excitement in his breast as he remembered that interesting little chest. Slowly he made an oath, pulled out his dagger and kissed the blade.

Jeanne could see that her husband was astonished at the Coroner's words.

Baldwin blinked and stammered, 'How . . .? But who?' Harlewin was evidently delighted to see how his words had stunned the knight. The Coroner chuckled fruitily, drained his jug of ale and tossed it towards Edgar, who just managed to catch it.

'Fill that, man. Well, Sir Baldwin, the beheaded man, Philip Dyne, was an abjurer.'

Jeanne raised an eyebrow meaningfully at Edgar, who stuck his nose in the air and sniffed scornfully before walking out.

Harlewin continued without noticing: 'Philip Dyne had raped and murdered a girl here in Tiverton – Carter's daughter. Caused quite a stir. Managed to get to St Peter's and hide in the sanctuary. Of course I went and demanded that he should give himself up, but he wouldn't: demanded his forty days of sanctuary. So that was that. I posted guards, hoping that one of them would sleep and give him a chance to escape so we could hunt the bastard down, but he knew he was safe in there. So, we held a formal ceremony of abjuration and off he went.'

'Carter's daughter?' Simon cried.

'Yesterday. Didn't get very far, did he?' He looked up as Edgar passed him a jug. It was filled, but the Coroner winced at the taste. 'God's bollocks, man! This is practically undrinkable!'

'It is the normal ale, sir.'

Jeanne looked away, trying not to giggle. Edgar's distant manner, his offhandedness, was as near to an open insult as a servant could go.

Baldwin frowned. 'But so what? If the man made his confession and left, he was protected. He should not have been killed.'

'No, Sir Baldwin, he shouldn't. Unless, of course, he tried to commit another felony. Or left the road ordained.'

'And that is what you think happened?'

Jeanne watched Harlewin as he drank. An unmannered man, he belched and wiped his mouth with his hand before picking his ear with an enquiring finger, studying the wax

adhering to his nail with interest. Jeanne had the impression
that he wouldn't be capable of any flights of intellect. He was
a simple man at heart.

Harlewin rolled the wax into a ball and flicked it away.
'Yes, Sir Baldwin, I think that's what happened. The fool
saw the knight in among the trees and nipped in after him.
While he was there, he stabbed Sir Gilbert and took his purse
but then he was ridden down by two law-abiding men who
took off his head for his crime.'

'And who were these two upright men?' Baldwin asked,
and Jeanne could hear the sarcasm cloying his voice.

'Andrew Carter and Nicholas Lovecok. They should be
here by now. Would you like to hear their evidence?'

Andrew Carter reluctantly gazed down at the bodies deposited on the cobbles; the knight with his clothing all awry, his
long *cyclas* or surcoat ridden up about his waist to show his
gambeson beneath, the linen stuffed with rags or wool to
make a protective quilted jacket.

Alongside him, the headless corpse of Dyne looked
scruffy, the cloth of his tunic filthy with the blood which had
been spilled over it, the material loose where it had merely
been draped over the body. His head sat alongside, resting on
the ground with his eyes left open so that he looked alive, as
if he had been buried up to his chin in the cobbled yard and
the headless body was that of another man.

A ring of men stood around them, four and twenty or
more, with several male children among them – the jury. The
priest was already there, unpacking his roll of vellum or
whatever he used, setting his reeds and inks just so on the
trestle-table put up for him. He glanced up and met Andrew's

eye. There was a slight flicker there, but then he looked away again, and Andrew suddenly felt queasy. He should never have paid the priest to ensure the man's escape. The priest knew what he'd done.

At the far side of the men was his brother-in-law, and he walked slowly to Nicholas's side, reaching him just as Piers Bakere and William Small were led out.

'Nick?'

'Quiet! You know what to say.'

'Yes,' Andrew agreed and anxiously looked back at the two bodies.

Cecily stood with her husband at the back of the crowd. John Sherman didn't usually like seeing inquests, but this time he had insisted that they should go and watch. She had thought it was because of something to do with the Coroner, but now she wasn't sure. Sherman stood with a bitter scowl twisting his features. She put out a hand to his arm, and he looked at her as though he didn't recognise her.

'Husband?'

'I . . . I'm sorry. I don't feel well,' he said.

But she had seen that his gaze had been fixed with horror on the body of Sir Gilbert. She looked again. It was odd, she thought, the similarity. It could have been her husband lying there.

Two men were playing dice in the stable and one let out a shrill cry of delight at a winning throw just as Harlewin appeared, Simon and Baldwin following. In the sudden silence the shout was almost an abomination, like a heretic in church screaming his rejection of God.

140

Harlewin walked over to the bodies and glowered at the men all about him. 'Come on, lads, give me space, will you? You may be the jury, but I have to have room. Are you ready, Father?' Seeing the priest nod, he walked to Sir Gilbert's body and began to strip it. 'See here, all the clothing on this man. He was said to be a knight, and his clothing proves it. Now,' he said as he struggled with the quilted gambeson, then the shirt beneath. Soon both bodies were naked, and the assembled men were sombrely quiet. One or two of the younger ones, especially a boy of some nine or ten years, looked close to tears as the last shreds of cloth were pulled away; others craned their necks with fascination.

About the knight's neck was a small cord, on which was a crucifix and a small iron key. Harlewin took these and studied them a moment before tossing them on top of the pile of clothes. Baldwin reached down and picked them up.

Standing over Philip Dyne, Harlewin held up the head for all to see.

'I find that this man was beaten about the face. He was bound, laid down and had his head struck off by a blow from a sword or axe or similar weapon.' Setting the head down, he returned to the naked body and hauled it over and over. 'There are no stabs on his back, chest, or limbs. His hands have cuts at the fingers, which shows he struggled to defend himself, catching the sword aimed at him.'

He rose, blowing a little from his exertion, and walked to the knight's body. 'This was different. A tall, well-built knight. He died from a single stab-wound in his back, here.' He rolled over the body and pointed. 'I think it probably penetrated the heart,' he said, frowning thoughtfully as he stuffed his forefinger deep in the hole. Pulling it free, he studied the blood on it, then wiped it clean on the knight's shirt. 'Yes, he must have died almost immediately.'

He stood before the jury and set his hands on his hips. 'Does anyone have any comments to make?'

One grizzled old man nodded at the headless body. 'That man was Philip Dyne, the abjurer. If he left the road, he was outlaw, lawful prey of any man finding him. As outlaw he deserved beheading.'

'Yes, yes, yes, and someone *did* behead him,' Harlewin noted testily. 'What of this knight? Anyone know anything about him?'

William spoke up. 'He was Sir Gilbert, my master and a Knight Bachelor. He was on his way here and went into the woods to seek the felon. Those men told us Dyne had gone,' he added, pointing at Andrew and Nicholas.

'Sir Gilbert was found stabbed in the back without his purse,' Harlewin noted. 'That was with Dyne, together with the knight's knife – which suggests to me that Dyne killed him. Now, can you two gentlemen add anything?'

Nicholas stepped forward, his head bowed. His voice was low and humble – practically obsequious. 'My lord, I never thought this fellow would comply with your commands. Andrew and I rode after him to watch and make sure he adhered to his oath of abjuration as you had instructed him. He didn't. We saw him in the woods and realised he must have chosen the life of the outlaw. As law-abiding men we rode after him. It took us some little while to find him, in among the undergrowth, but we managed to . . .'

'Did you beat him?' Harlewin growled. 'Look at the state of the poor bugger's balls!'

'Not more than we needed to catch him. And when we had caught him, we beheaded him. As was our duty.'

'What of the other man?'

Andrew shoved his way forward. 'We had no idea about him being there, Coroner. We saw this man and his servant in their camp and asked them whether they had seen Dyne pass by. This servant said he'd seen a face in among the trees. Who else could it have been? We went into the woods. The good knight, I suppose, came after us, but we didn't see him.'

'I think it's clear that this man Dyne took the knight's knife and stabbed him to steal his purse, then met with you two. You executed him, rightly, but you failed in your legal duties,' Harlewin said, and slowly an unpleasant smile spread over his face. 'You wanted no one to know what you had done, did you? You failed to confess. More to the point, you failed to bring back his head!'

He stomped over to the bodies and picked up the head once more. 'This man was a confessed felon who had sworn to abjure the realm, and as such you should have brought his head back here to be lodged in gaol. I fine you five shillings each.'

Nicholas put out a hand to Andrew. Andrew had taken a quick step forward on hearing this large sum announced, but feeling his brother-in-law's touch, he pursed his lips silently, breathing stertorously through nostrils flared like a horse's.

'May I put a question or two, Coroner?' Baldwin enquired mildly, and when Harlewin nodded, he turned to the two men. 'I find it odd that you came back from the south. You must have already passed Dyne.'

Nicholas nodded. 'That's correct. We rode past him earlier in the day and carried on to a tavern near Silverton to eat. Then we came back.'

'And your first thought was naturally where this felon had got to?' Baldwin mused. Dyne was a felon – he had confessed to rape and murder. Baldwin had every reason to wish to see justice, and that included justice for the dead girl; he was not minded to throw the first stone at a man who avenged his daughter. But he was intrigued by the death of Sir Gilbert. 'I cannot see how this feeble-looking young man could have grabbed the dagger from a knight's belt and stabbed him.'

Nicholas shrugged and gave Baldwin a thin smile. 'Sir, you of the fighting class can understand this kind of thing more easily than us. We are merely merchants.'

'True enough,' Baldwin agreed, but with a puzzled expression. 'But there are aspects which seem curious. For example, did Dyne still have the knife when you came across him?'

'He dropped it,' Andrew said. 'It was in his hand when I saw him. I knocked it away with my sword.'

'So you, a merchant, could defend yourself against Dyne when he was armed although an armed knight could not,' Baldwin noted. 'Was anyone else about?'

It was William who answered. 'There was a woman.'

'Did you recognise her?'

'No. She was well-dressed,' William said musingly. He allowed his gaze to drift over the crowd watching. 'She wore a hooded cloak, green, but her face was covered.'

Standing at the back of the crowd, Cecily felt her husband's grip on her shoulder. He pulled her roughly around. 'You don't have a green cloak.'

'No, husband. Why?' she asked and then allowed the acid to enter her tone. 'Did you think *I* had killed him? Me? Murder a knight I had never met?'

He stared at her with his brow furrowed like a man who was going mad and could feel his sanity teetering on the brink. 'You were there with your man.'

'Husband, how many times do I have to tell you? I don't have a lover,' she said with slow, pained deliberation.

He curled his lip in disbelief but could not tell her he knew she was lying. That would mean confessing to following her.

Turning on his heel, he walked from the court.

CHAPTER THIRTEEN

Sir Peregrine of Barnstaple walked through the streets of Tiverton plunged deep in thought.

Other men tended to move aside when he approached. He always found his path clear, no matter how crowded the road or alley. It was the natural order exerting itself on his behalf. Sir Peregrine was a lord, one of the *Bellatores*, the fighting class, and if another man stood in his path or offered an insult, Sir Peregrine was wealthy, powerful and strong enough to force him to regret his rashness.

Sir Peregrine was relatively content with the way things were progressing. He had much to do still to persuade Lord de Courtenay to his own way of thinking, that it would be sensible to set up an alliance with the Marcher Lords, but the matter would be easier to deal with now that the Despensers' emissary was dead.

It had been alarming to hear that Sir Gilbert had met Lord Hugh. Sir Peregrine had heard by a chance remark from one of his gatehouse men: while Sir Peregrine was out comforting Emily, Sir Gilbert had arrived and asked to see Lord Hugh. Lord Hugh met him in his private solar and they spoke for some little while. Sir Peregrine himself returned before Sir Gilbert had left and instantly set a man to follow him. It was that man who had seen Sir Gilbert's horse. 'He's from the Despensers, Sir Peregrine.'

That was a complication Sir Peregrine wished to do without. He had no desire to see the cautious progression of his own persuasion wrecked by Sir Gilbert. It was *crucial* that Lord Hugh should join the ranks of the Welsh Marchers. Sir Peregrine himself was an enthusiastic supporter of theirs and had no wish to find himself fighting at the side of Lord de Courtenay against those he thought should be their friends. Better by far that he should persuade Lord de Courtenay to join his *natural* allies. After all, although the Despensers were exiled, that was no guarantee that they wouldn't return. King Edward II had recalled Gaveston; he could as easily ask his lover Despenser to return.

Sir Peregrine found his steps slowing as a pensive mood came over him. Surely a messenger would have brought something to prove his master's integrity: some form of reward for friendship? Sir Gilbert of Carlisle would not have come empty-handed to the castle.

He lost his train of thought as he arrived at Emily's house. It stank, and the refuse all about made him curl his lip, but he had to know how she was. 'Emily? Are you there?' Ducking under the low lintel, he gazed about him with consternation. The hovel had been cleaned and swept, the table moved, the bed tidied.

While he stood there dumbfounded, a woman entered behind him. 'She's dead.'

'Emily?'

'Childbirth. Baby killed her. They bury her tomorrow.'

Sir Peregrine swallowed but kept his face set. He nodded coldly, pushed past the neighbour and made his way back towards the castle, taking deep breaths as he walked.

Dead! His child gone, taking his woman with it. Sir Peregrine had never married and Emily had been the closest he had ever known to a wife: gentle, kind, grateful for the small presents he had given her.

Sir Peregrine had never been able to win the affection of a courtly lady. There had been one once, a woman in Barnstaple over fifteen years ago, but she was dead now. Emily had attracted him with her ready smile, her soft voice and calmness. It seemed impossible that she had gone for ever. The thought made him stumble, and when he recovered himself, he found his eyes had filled with moisture and he had to blink it away.

He felt as though someone had cut out his heart.

Father Abraham scratched as quickly as his reed allowed, stopping regularly to resharpen the tip, occasionally discarding old ones and picking up fresh, hating the work.

It wasn't that the task was difficult, but the ability to write was a God-given gift, and as such it deserved the concentration and dedication necessary to produce the most beautiful work possible. This hurried scribbling was an insult to Him; it was no better than a usurer's records.

Looking up, he saw the knight from Cadbury, Sir Baldwin, stare at the ground for a moment before returning to his questions. He appeared to take the matter seriously, but as far as Abraham was concerned, the whole issue was immaterial. The felon was dead after committing a second horrible murder. He had received his just deserts.

Baldwin looked at Andrew with an air of thoughtful enquiry. 'How long were you at the tavern?'

'I don't know. Not long. We only had a quart of ale each and a pie.'

Father Abraham scribbled and scratched in his shorthand, and tried to control his growing impatience. He had services to conduct. The implication of Sir Baldwin's questioning was clear enough: he thought the two men had been trying to ambush Dyne. Likely they had, Father Abraham considered, scratching at his bald pate with his reed and incidentally smearing ink over it – but so what?

At the back of his mind was the fear that his own part in that previous evening's events might become common knowledge. It made him anxious and fretful. If only Father Benedict hadn't demanded the last rites; Father Abraham wouldn't have been out on that road so late, so near the woods.

As Baldwin finished his interrogation and returned to Simon's side, Father Abraham threw Cecily Sherman a scowling glance. She was standing serenely and saw his look, giving him a slight smile that made the priest sneer. And what were you doing there, whore? he thought to himself.

Simon saw that Baldwin was frowning thoughtfully at Aylmer. The dog was sitting tied to a post, head tilted to one side as he observed the deliberations of the jury and Coroner. 'What is it, Baldwin?'

Baldwin murmured, 'The dead dog: if a dog launches himself at a man, he aims for the throat or arms, and the only way a man can defend himself is by cutting the animal's neck or stabbing him in the side of the chest once the jaws have closed on him. Only a brave man or a trained fighter would stand his ground and wait until the dog leaped, holding out his blade to pin the hound in the air. And if it were a long blade, the animal would be held at the full extent of the weapon, unable to reach an arm or leg.'

'So?'

Baldwin scowled at the jury. 'Although Dyne had no sword, he escaped being bitten.'

'What of the knight's knife?'

'Ah well, Simon. There we have another little mystery, don't we? First we wondered how the felon got a knife, then we saw he must have taken the knight's. But someone stabbed the knight, so we have to swallow the frankly ridiculous: that the knight and his dog allowed a man to ambush them, disarm and kill the knight. Only then did the dog attack, being himself slaughtered for his temerity.'

Simon chuckled. 'I see your point. And then the thief is discovered by a fat merchant who has no difficulty in knocking the felon's knife away.'

'Precisely. A fat merchant can succeed in a fight where a knight has failed? I find it incredible.'

'But if *he* didn't, who did?'

'Well, now. There I think ...' His pensive mood was destroyed as the court rang with a shriek of horror.

'Philip! Oh, God, no! Philip!'

Spinning, Sir Baldwin saw a young woman run to the ring

of the jury, then stop, hands flying up to her face as she stared petrified with horror at the head and torso of Philip Dyne.

Her figure was slender but strong and sturdy, that of a peasant girl who often had to put herself to labour in fields. Auburn hair dangled where her wimple had come adrift, hanging down the back of her cheap green tunic.

Without speaking again she collapsed. Baldwin sighed. Glancing at Edgar, he motioned to his servant to carry her indoors.

Jeanne took upon herself the duty of nursing the girl with Petronilla's help while the men stood huddled in the hall. Harlewin had decided that there was little more to be decided, and while the girl was carried indoors by Edgar to be installed on a cot in the solar, he declared that in his capacity as Coroner he was satisfied that Philip Dyne had murdered Sir Gilbert of Carlisle and had then been discovered by Andrew Carter and Nicholas Lovecok who had obeyed the law and beheaded him. For their misbehaviour in not bringing the head back to town for the Coroner to set in the gaol, they were fined. Apart from that, Baldwin himself swore to Sir Gilbert's Englishry and although he was not a member of the man's family, Harlewin agreed that his word was sufficient. In the case of Dyne, since he was a confirmed felon legally executed, there was no need for anyone to swear to his Englishry.

Father Abraham blew heavily on his paper and studied it pensively. Even with the hideous scar running though it where the girl's scream had made him jump, it was legible, which was all that mattered. Rolling it up carefully, he tied a short length of scarlet ribbon around it and began packing up his reeds, inks, knives and scrapers, storing them painstakingly in his wallet.

It was growing late. He had to hurry to return to the church and say Mass. There were bound to be many of his congregation waiting, especially on this, the vigil of St Giles. Market traders would be there asking the saint for his help to ensure a profit. Later he would have to write up Harlewin's inquest on poor Emily too.

He sighed and stood. She could wait. Divine services came first. Nodding to Harlewin and Simon – Sir Baldwin had gone inside with his wife – Father Abraham walked past the thinning jury, scarcely glancing at the two bodies.

'Father?'

Father Abraham turned to Harlewin with a feeling of resigned annoyance.

'Could you arrange to bury the knight as soon as possible? In this heat . . .'

There was no need to say more. Father Abraham gave a nod. 'Bring him to the church tonight. I will read the *Placebo*, the Evensong of the Dead, and arrange for the hearse and some deserving poor to sit up with him.'

'Thank you, Father.'

The priest walked out into the street. A hundred noxious scents assailed his nostrils, and he unconsciously hurried his steps as he made his way to his church.

Poor Emily, he thought. Her death reminded him that the minions of the Devil were waiting here, ever-present in the world, to ensnare any man who was foolish enough to submit to the temptations they offered.

That was the reason for anointing those soon to die, to keep devils away. After anointing, the soul lived in a shadow world until death came, and anointing protected the body. It meant devils couldn't use the corpse, flying on it through the air to upset townspeople.

Those who died suddenly and without preparation were often saved by God's Own grace. Although this knight would not be. *He* was an excommunicate. An evil heretic. Father Benedict had told him so. Sir Gilbert was a Templar.

Back at her house, Cecily Sherman waved her servants away and sat quietly with a jug of wine drawn from the best barrel in the buttery. Her husband was safely installed in his shop dealing with clients, and she was safe for a few moments of peace.

It was a good house, this. She glanced about her at the tapestries, the lamps, the thickly carved screen, the silverware, then, with a smile of self-satisfaction, at the pewter jug and small tankard on the table at her side. Yes, it was a very good house.

Oh, her husband wasn't as bad as some. He was a bit dim on occasion – luckily! – but for the most part, if she was careful she could prevent the worst excesses of his temper. He'd only given her a beating the once, and well, she had been a bit obvious when she looked at that man in church. It was natural John should think she had insulted him: she had! It had been painful, though. He'd taken a willow wand to her, thrashing her until her back was bloody. She had been careful ever since to make sure that he wouldn't ever feel the need to punish her again.

He wouldn't. She would never give him reason again. He'd hurt her because she'd hurt his feelings, and beating his wife was a man's right in his own house, just as he could beat the living daylights out of his maidservants – and menservants too, if it took his fancy.

No, she would never let that happen again. Since then she had always been careful to ensure that he couldn't suspect her of infidelity. And yet he appeared to know something about her and Harlewin.

Harlewin the Coroner. Vain – yes; occasionally foolish – yes; large – without a doubt. But fun and essentially a risk-taker like her. Like her, too, he thrived on sex that was dangerous. He enjoyed her body, but both thrilled to the pleasure that came from their secret trysts. Every so often, not too regularly, they would ride to his place down near the river, miles outside town where he owned a mill, and spend the night in each other's arms. As they had that night.

Somehow her husband knew something. He had been away, he'd said he had business in South Molton. A thought made a fist of ice clutch at her heart. He could have followed her; could have seen her there with Harlewin!

That was the fear that had so petrified her in the woods. But he hadn't been there when she looked. It wasn't him. Rationally she knew her panic was misplaced. If he'd seen them at the mill, he would have run in and killed them both. That was how his temper went. Fast and insane. He lost his veneer of calmness at the slightest provocation.

No, he couldn't know. It was only a suspicion. Nothing more.

But the niggling concern kept pulling at her consciousness. Perhaps she should get an independent witness to give her an alibi – ask Father Abraham to confirm that she had been with him. Judging by his shame when she had seen him with the knight's horse, he would be amenable to her plea.

He wouldn't *like* it, she thought – but then, he didn't need to. This was the price of her silence.

It was more than an hour before the girl was capable of seeing anyone, long after the Coroner and his clerk had left, the one to eat, the other to perform a Mass, before both attended the inquest of Emily and her baby in childbirth.

When Jeanne at last came down to the hall from the solar with a slow, thoughtful tread, she found Simon and her husband sitting in the hall, both holding large pots of wine.

'How is she?' Baldwin asked.

'Not well, but what would you expect after seeing her brother's decapitated body?'

Baldwin gave a low whistle. 'She was Dyne's sister? My God, the poor girl.'

'Her name is Avicia Dyne. She was horribly shocked and I've told her she needs to rest, but she wants to speak to you.'

Baldwin glanced at Simon, who shrugged. Simon knew what Baldwin was thinking: they had both seen people in every stage of distress and knew what to expect. There would be spirited denials of Philip Dyne's guilt, closely followed by accusations against those in authority for having accepted bribes to divert the blame to him. Both men had seen the same situations repeated over and over again. 'Come on, Baldwin, we may as well get it over with.'

'Very well,' Baldwin sighed, and followed his wife, Simon bringing up the rear.

Jeanne led them to a small, warm room that overlooked the court. It held little in the way of furnishing: a chest at one wall, a three-legged stool, and a small table with a jug of ale on it was all, apart from the modest little bed, which had no drapery, just a low wooden base with a palliasse on top. Thick, soft woollen blankets covered the girl.

In the yard Simon had been struck only by her misery on seeing her brother. He had hardly seen her features, but now he studied her with interest. Against the darkness of the room two candles had been lit, and their yellow flames illuminated the golden tints of Avicia Dyne's hair, making it gleam in surprising contrast to the grey tone of her skin. Her eyes were sunken and dulled, her lips, pale and thin; her whole demeanour was one of despair.

She looked at them wanly as they entered, and Simon saw a single tear spring from the corner of her eye and leave a trail glistening in its wake as it slipped down her cheek. It was that, the lack of hysteria or any other emotion which struck him most forcibly. It was as if her whole life was ended and she had no more energy.

Simon stood at the back of the room in the darkness while Jeanne glided quietly to the girl's side, pouring her a beaker of ale. Baldwin stood behind his wife.

'Sir, I am grateful to you,' Avicia told him, her voice stronger than he had expected. 'I know you think I am only a mean-spirited thing, weak and emotional because of my brother's death.'

Baldwin waved a hand as if in rejection, but she carried on swiftly before he could speak.

'Please let me finish. Sir, my brother hasn't received justice. This good lady has told me what the Coroner decided, but there are things you should know. Sir . . .' She tried to sit up and her face worked with passion as she sought the best words to convince him. 'Sir, my brother couldn't have killed Joan. He loved her.'

Baldwin smiled sadly. 'I have no authority here, child. Your brother confessed his guilt and was found away from the road. That is an end to—'

'No, I can't believe it!' she said, shaking her head and making her hair swirl about her shoulders. 'Sir, he couldn't have hurt her, he *couldn't*. He loved her, he was going to marry her. He wouldn't have hurt her for anything.'

'We often find that it is those who love who are the cause of the loved one's death,' Simon said quietly.

'But he and she were handfast,' she protested. 'And Philip was never a lecher.'

'What of it?' Baldwin asked.

'The Coroner killed Joan and put the blame onto Philip to clear himself. Perhaps he told Philip that if he accepted blame the Coroner would allow him to escape and to find a new life abroad. It was the Coroner who urged Andrew Carter and Nicholas Lovecok to chase after him and murder him.'

Baldwin ignored the word 'murder'. Their execution of Dyne had been perfectly legal. 'Andrew heard your brother admit to killing his daughter,' he pointed out reasonably, 'and Nicholas Lovecok heard him confess to killing his niece. What would be more natural than that they should follow the man who had confessed and execute him?'

'But Philip couldn't have done it! He wasn't a murderer!'

'Was he trained in fighting?'

'No – why?'

It was not much, but it added to Baldwin's feeling of wrongness. Commonly a close family member of a murderer would disbelieve his guilt, but the knowledge did not make Avicia's distress any easier to bear. 'Child, you know he confessed?' He held up his hand to stop her before she could protest. 'It is the truth, Avicia! He admitted killing Joan Carter after raping her – otherwise he wouldn't have been allowed from the sanctuary to abjure the realm. The first rule is that a man must confess.'

'But a man might be allowed to claim a pardon from the King if he was innocent!'

'Well, of course. But in this case he—'

'Philip was going to leave the country, yes, and he swore to abjure the realm, but he was innocent.'

Simon broke in, 'Why would he do that? If he knew he was without guilt, he should have stood before the court and made his case.'

'How can you say that, Bailiff? The jury here would have presented him to the court as a criminal and he would have been convicted. How could he defend himself?'

'How could he expect to prove his innocence as an exile abroad?' Simon pressed her.

'Easier than if he remained here and hanged!'

'This can get us nowhere,' Baldwin muttered.

'Then seek the murderer! When you know who caused Joan to die, you'll have the murderer of her, of that knight and of Philip. And I can tell you who it was: it was Harlewin, the Coroner!'

CHAPTER FOURTEEN

When he had completed the Mass Father Abraham left hurriedly to attend Emily's inquest. It was a depressing affair, sad and demeaning somehow for all who took part. The woman with the blood still drenching her legs, the child looking so innocent at her side, mute proof of the reason for her death.

The priest was surprised to see Sir Peregrine in the crowd, his long face sad, and when the Father had packed his few items, he found the knight falling into step beside him as if wishing to talk – or perhaps confess? It gave Father Abraham a wild sense of hope that the worldly knight might be tempted to ask him to shrive him.

His hopes were dashed. Sir Peregrine certainly wanted companionship in his loneliness, but the very last thing he needed was idle conversation. The death of his woman had left a pain that could not be assuaged. Since he had heard of her death he had wandered about the town, but that brought no mitigation of his suffering. Walking about and seeing how happy others were was no comfort to him. It merely added the poison of jealousy to his anguish. Toker's words had been nothing more than an irritant, given his mood, and he had sent the man away. Stories of a London man defending himself against Toker's boys were not important. Not now.

Father Abraham for once recognised that chatter would be unwelcome and the two walked to the church in silence.

Which was why they found the two of them.

As Father Abraham opened the door, he was welcomed by the sight of Hick the rat-catcher's hairy backside, ramming up and down as Felicity, beneath him, complained about the cold floor and entreated him to get a move on. As a scene, it was one guaranteed to send Father Abraham into a paroxysm of rage.

At least Felicity hung her head in a show of contrition and held her tongue when Father Abraham berated her.

'How dare you even *think* of coming here with your revolting clients!' he thundered. 'The . . . the shame of it! Don't you realise that you were fouling the church itself with your disgraceful, lewd . . .'

'I tried to tell her, Father,' Hick interrupted helpfully.

'Shut up, you pervert!' Father Abraham roared.

'I couldn't take him to my rooms, not at Fair time. The landlord could have evicted me!' Felicity protested.

'That was no excuse for fornicating in my church!'

'I told her you wouldn't like it.'

Felicity turned on Hick, hands on hips. 'You were happy enough to come here when I suggested it.'

'Only 'cos you wouldn't go to my dwelling.'

'Dwelling? *Dwelling*? Don't make me laugh! The place is practically falling about your ears, and you expect me to rut on the dirt floor with you?'

'It's no worse that the floor here.'

'It's covered in filth and mud, Hick!'

'Silence, the pair of you! *God* give me patience!'

Sir Peregrine left them to it. The mundane little squabble was irrelevant. He had no wish to witness it, and he walked slowly over the church's yard while he thought about his Emily. Her body, displayed like that for all the lewd-minded to see had left a bitterness in his mouth.

He was at the picket fence when he heard the church door creak on its hinges, and, in the dim light from the candles within, he saw the girl slip out. She had rearranged her clothing and now little of her form could be discerned beneath the heavy tunic, skirts and apron. Walking swiftly, she crossed the churchyard to him.

Under her layer of grime, he thought Felicity attractive. She had a long, slender frame with a heart-shaped face; her chin was small and the nose slightly snubbed, but her features were pleasantly regular. She approached him hesitantly.

'Sir Peregrine, I was sorry about Emily.'

'Thanks. I miss her.'

'And the child.'

'Yes,' he agreed sadly, looking away. 'That is why I am so lonely now.'

'If you want comfort . . .' she offered quietly.

He looked at her and she continued in a rush, 'The King has a marshall of the royal prostitutes; I see no reason why *you* shouldn't make use of one.'

'Perhaps,' he said with a dry chuckle. And yet when he thought about it, maybe another woman would help ease the burden of pain. At least she could help him forget for a while.

Felicity smiled at him sympathetically. She was a sharp woman: not yet twenty years old, she needed to be. Both her parents were dead, and since she had lost her job in the merchant's house she'd endured every insult the world could fling at her, but the diminution of her social position had not decreased her intelligence.

The knight did look miserable. Not that his troubles worried Felicity overmuch. She had her own problems to think of, and his money would come in useful.

She could weep to think how low she had sunk, degraded and reviled by all the women who should have been her friends. Instead she was shunned – all because a certain man had raped her systematically and regularly, and then thrown her over. If there was any way to make the shame rebound upon him, she would happily sell her soul to achieve it.

Felicity eyed Sir Peregrine warily. She'd no wish to be caught working during the Fair; in fact, she'd intended leaving for the duration but she'd been held up when the Coroner oiled round, the revolting old cockscomb. He'd said he wanted information about poor Emily, but it was obvious to Felicity that he wasn't thinking of the inquest when he stared at her breasts. It wouldn't have been the first time she'd done business with him, but not immediately after asking about Emily: that was disgusting! As if a mere whore was of no importance, had no feelings or common decency.

It was his hypocrisy – and unintentional insult to her – which so enraged her. She told him to piss off, she wouldn't sleep with him: he might report her. That was why, when Hick came round a little later, she had only agreed to take his money provided they went somewhere else. She didn't want

Harlewin to see her with Hick. He'd certainly have taken her in then – for accepting a shabby little man instead of him.

But it was terrible that the priest had found her in the church with Hick. She could have screamed at the unfairness. The inquest into Emily's death should have run on for longer and the priest shouldn't have returned so early.

Poor Emily. One of the few women who had been her friend, and now, almost before her body had cooled, here was Felicity chancing her luck with Emily's lover. Sighing, she hooked her arm through Sir Peregrine's. His face relaxed slightly in gratitude, but all she felt was loathing and self-disgust.

Father Abraham watched Hick sweep, rage making the priest's eyes gleam vindictively as the hapless rat-catcher plied the sexton's broom over the floor. Before he allowed Hick to leave, the priest made him donate two pennies to the church for his attempted blasphemy.

'And think yourself lucky, you heretic!' he hissed as Hick disconsolately passed him the coins. 'Do you have anything to confess?'

Hick scratched at the flea-bites on his neck. It was one of the inevitable results of his trade, this constant itching. Rats held fleas, and some would always end up on their killer. 'I don't know, really,' he began lamely, and then caught sight of the expression on the priest's face. Quickly Hick knelt and began telling the history of every falsehood he had told, each covetous dream he had enjoyed and the times he had lain with Felicity when he should have been about his business or at church.

'Is that all?' Father Abraham demanded curtly.

'Yes, sir.'

'Good. Do you realise the danger you're in? No, I don't suppose you do, do you?'

Hick looked up slowly, anxiously. The priest's voice held a depth of loathing that the rat-catcher had never encountered before. Revulsion he had experienced, aimed at him by the wealthier women in the town who enjoyed having someone to look down upon, but never before had he seen the contempt, the near-hatred that now distorted Father Abraham's features. Unknowingly he withdrew, leaning back on his heels as the priest's visage loomed nearer.

'Your fornicating with that drab whore makes you no better than a dog with his bitch. You're foul; beastly. If you sink any lower, you'll be *worse* than a beast, and then you will have sacrificed your immortal soul. You understand me?'

Hick nodded swiftly, his head bobbing up and down. Hick knew that when the priest warned him, he'd better take note. If he didn't, he'd be burned for eternity. Father Abraham had told him so.

'You'll become no better than the lowest of all men, a sodomite and paederast, slobbering and foul, like one of those damned *Templars*! You've heard of them? That Sir Gilbert was one of them. Evil! Evil and depraved! They were so disgusting in the sight of God that they all had to be burned at the stake – do you want that?'

'No, Father,' Hick squeaked.

'You know how they began? They were the holiest warriors in Christendom, until they went out to the Kingdom of Jerusalem, and that is why we lost the Kingdom. The Knights Templar took on the ways of the Moors; they lusted after gold and women and forgot themselves so much they learned the arts of witchcraft and devil worship. They would spit on the cross or urinate on it, and they murdered babies on their intolerable altars deep in their foul temples, then ate the child's flesh!' His voice broke with religious horror. 'Can you imagine that? *They used to eat children.*'

Hick's mouth was agape. Slowly he shook his head.

'God was so offended by their insufferable pride and disgraceful behaviour, their hideous facsimile of the Mass, their worship of images of horrible creatures, that He sought to punish not only them, but all Christian men. He didn't only throw the Templars from Jerusalem, he showed his rage by taking away Jerusalem and giving it to the Moors. He allowed them to kill the unrighteous and prideful Christians, to punish them for tolerating the dreadful evil of the Templars. They cost us Christ's own land!'

The priest's voice was tortured, his face suddenly sunken like a man about to die, and he cast his eyes up to the altar, making the sign of the cross as his eyes filled with tears. It made Hick feel guilty and scared, to think that he had brought this depression to the priest – but he recoiled when he caught sight of the other man's features again.

Father Abraham leaned forward and pointed a finger which shook with conviction.

'The Templars were and are cursed. They lost us the Holy Land because of their execrable activities, even though they started as a religious Order. They sank to the depths, just as you have started to. If you befoul the church with your degen-erate activities, you will deserve the same terrible punishment. Your soul will be dragged down to Hell to eternal damnation, where it will roast for ever! Do you want that?'

Gulping, Hick shook his head.

'Then get out of my sight, you contemptible little man!'

Hick rose to his feet, gabbling his thanks, promising never to bring Felicity to the church again, tripping and stumbling as he made his way backwards to the door, and thence into the clean, bright sunlight.

'Phew!' he gasped and wiped his brow with a dirty forearm. Pulling his cheap felt hat on, he glanced up and down the street. With relief he saw that Mistress Tan's alehouse had a small gorse bush tied over her doorway. She must have ale for sale. After the shock he had just endured, Hick needed a drink – badly.

He wasn't quite certain what had angered the priest. Surely it couldn't have been a natural transaction with a whore. That was normal. But something had upset him. He'd practically spat when he was talking about the Templars. Still, it wasn't anything to worry Hick. He scratched at his groin and remembered Felicity and a certain unfinished business. Maybe Mistress Tan would be amenable to selling him something other than ale. She often would when she was hard up for cash.

Baldwin and Simon left Avicia a short time later, Jeanne joining them as they stood outside in the narrow hallway. Petronilla appeared carrying a tray and took it in for the stricken woman.

Baldwin closed the door behind her. 'What do you think, Simon?'

'If I had to bet, I'd say she believed what she said.'

'So would I, but her personal opinion cannot be considered final. It could be that the shock of seeing her brother dead was enough to unbalance her humours.'

Simon agreed. It was well-known that women suffered from diseases from which men were immune. The vapours attacked women because of the noxious fumes produced in their organs. The uterus was the worst. It could prowl danger-ously about the body, especially after shock. Then it could move to the chest, where it caused diseases in the heart and lungs, and only by burning foul-smelling things beneath the poor woman's nose could a physician or midwife force it to move away.

Both men knew this, and they glanced covertly at Jeanne, who stood eyeing them with folded arms. 'Well?' she demanded imperiously. When neither answered, she snorted, spun on her heel and rejoined Petronilla and Avicia.

Simon took a deep breath. 'I suppose she could think she's telling the truth. Does that get us anywhere?'

'The Coroner has declared the result of his inquest.'

'So what's the point of chewing on the same old bone?'

'There is something wrong with all this. Dyne could not have killed the knight and the dog. He was too feeble. The dog alone would have tested him.'

'He had the knight's purse,' Simon reminded Baldwin.

'Yes, but if he found the knight dead, he would have taken it. An outlaw, not knowing where his pennies could come from would be bound to snatch a dead man's purse.'

'That was his fault. He should never have been off the road.'

'Oh, Simon, really! Think about it: he'd been passed once by Carter and Lovecok – what were they doing out there? Obviously they were looking for revenge, and Dyne knew it. He realised he must get off the road if he wanted to live. If he was so determined to run away, why was it William and the dogs saw or smelled him for much of the day?'

Simon mused. 'Perhaps the dogs saw someone else?'

'That *is* a thought. My God! Simon, you're right. Of course there was someone else there!'

'Eh?'

'Raches! They hunt by scent, not sight: the dog ran after whoever was there, following along his trail and, as soon as the dog caught the man, he ran it through with his sword.'

'Baldwin,' Simon said patiently, 'Dyne didn't have a sword.'

'Precisely.' Baldwin stared into the distance, his face hardening as his conviction grew. 'Simon, there has been a great injustice here. That fellow Dyne was too scared to carry on along the road, so he hurried to the woods for safety, where he was slaughtered. And he is to be blamed for killing Sir Gilbert.'

'I don't care about that,' Simon said pragmatically. 'Dyne was a felon. He deserved his end. It's no injustice if a felon is killed.'

'Rubbish! Consider the reverse: Dyne could not have killed Sir Gilbert and the dog. That means someone else did, and that someone will get away with murder unless we can stop him. A felon is escaping justice.'

Simon considered. 'You're convinced?'

'Sir Gilbert was a knight and a Templar. Believe me, a weakly felon like Dyne could not have stolen his knife, could not have made a stand against man and dog, could not have stolen the purse and run. Another man did all that. A murderer.'

'Then we must seek his killer,' Simon said, but uneasily.

'Something is troubling you?'

'The Coroner has declared the matter is closed. If we start stirring things now . . . Well, neither of us has jurisdiction here, but the Coroner has.'

'You're right,' Baldwin said musingly. 'Perhaps it would be easier if we didn't mention it to him yet.'

'I think so,' Simon agreed, frowning pensively. The Coroner removed from the issue, his mind turned to the crime itself. 'So you think it was Carter and his brother-in-law?'

'It is possible. One could have engaged the knight while the other stabbed him. But the two rode up *after* William saw the man in the trees. That implies someone else was also there.'

'Well, surely that was Dyne?'

'Maybe. But I'd have thought he'd have been making an effort to get away from the road.'

'Why should someone else have been there?'

'To keep an eye on Sir Gilbert?' Baldwin mused.

Simon stared. 'Why should someone do that?'

'Nobody trusts a stranger, Simon. Perhaps Sir Gilbert was a spy? He could have come from Despenser. There are many who would want to kill one of Despenser's men. Or maybe he was recognised as a Templar?'

'Who would care about a Templar now?'

'Not all Templars were entirely beyond rebuke, Simon. The Order's goods were confiscated after the Order was crushed. Many preceptories hid their wealth against the day when they could return and claim their property, but that day never came, so some Templars took what they could and ran away with it rather than leaving it hidden, and that has given rise to some folk thinking that Templars are thieves and outlaws as well as heretics.'

'Did that happen often?'

'Not very often. It was mainly in the territories in the north of the realm, places where the knights could simply pocket as much as possible and ride north to Scotland. Some were more organised: the treasurer of South Witham, for example, took everything. He disappeared with a small fortune in money and gold.'

'You still haven't said who you think could have wanted to kill the knight if it wasn't Dyne.'

'I have no idea. But I think we should try to find out.'

'So long as you don't upset the Coroner. What's your opinion of him?'

'A fat fool,' Baldwin said uncompromisingly. 'He has little intelligence, and the little he does possess seems to be devoted to womanising and politics, from what I have heard.'

'Politics seems to be a common failing of the folks here.'

'No need to sound so gloomy, Simon. Think what your position would be if you were a knight like me.'

'How do you mean?' Simon enquired as they walked into the hall.

'A knight is no more nor less than a useful pawn. Look at me: I'm not impoverished because I have a good couple of hundred acres, but that only brings in forty-two pounds a year, and out of that I have to comply with rules governing which equipment I should bear in time of war, pay taxes, protect the people of my demesne, and uphold the law.'

'Many would think that more than forty pounds a year would be a good living,' Simon observed with a smile

'Would they? When a destrier alone can reach over a hundred pounds? And every few years the King demands that all his knights get new armour or weaponry, and the weapons ranged against us improve so we need stronger armour than before, and all to be paid from our own pocket!'

'You find the costs of knighthood burdensome?' a strange voice intervened.

Baldwin peered ahead. This end of the hallway was darker – the sconces had not been lit yet. The voice had come from the shadows near the door, and he was sure he recognised it.

There was a chuckle, and Lord Hugh de Courtenay walked from the shadows. 'Don't look so upset, Sir Baldwin. I was sitting there, mulling over the sad news when I heard your voice. You know how it is, when you are sitting in the shade and looking at people who are well-lit – one assumes that if one can see, one must inevitably *be* seen. And my mind was far away.'

'I suppose you were thinking of our dead friend,' Baldwin said quickly. Behind Lord Hugh were two hard-looking men with swords at their waists and suspicion in their eyes.

'Sir Gilbert, you mean? Yes. It seems so long since I last met with him. He was with the Templars then, you know.'

Baldwin smiled thinly. 'We heard he was trying to see you, my Lord.'

'Me? I wonder why.'

'Perhaps he had a message?'

Lord Hugh said nothing, sitting on a bench.

Simon found him an interesting man. The bailiff had seen Lord de Courtenay many times over the years, for Simon's father had been a steward to Lord Hugh's father, working on the de Courtenay estates. The present lord was older than Simon's thirty-four years; casting his mind back, Simon couldn't remember the age of the man, but from the look of him he couldn't be younger than forty, a strong-looking fellow with broad shoulders and thickening belly. The de Courtenays were not the wealthiest family in Devon, but Simon knew that this man had influence beyond that of wealthier men.

Baldwin surveyed the lord for a few moments. 'Did you see Sir Gilbert?'

'How could I if he died on his way here?'

'We heard that he left his servant before he died. Perhaps he came here?'

'Perhaps,' Lord Hugh shrugged agreeably.

Baldwin sat at another bench. 'You have long been a thorn in the King's side, my Lord. You were with Bishop Stapledon when the Ordainers curbed the King's power back – oh, more than ten years ago. And then you helped Thomas of Lancaster to seek out Piers Gaveston, the King's friend.'

'That was difficult,' Lord Hugh said. 'But Gaveston had been lawfully exiled and insisted on returning. Lord Thomas saw to his execution.'

'Are you for Lord Thomas?'

'Me, Sir Baldwin? I am not entirely *for* anyone, as you would put it. I am not like others, bound by their oaths to one grouping or another. Everybody is tied to one master or another,' he smiled. 'I acknowledge only the King.'

'Yet now the King fears losing another favourite . . .'

Lord Hugh made a small gesture of indifference. 'I think you'll find that the King has already lost his latest favourite. The Despenser family is exiled, if my information is correct.'

There was a snigger from one of the squires and Baldwin saw Lord Hugh's expression harden. He did not like his servants to listen to his conversations, let alone show amusement. However he said nothing, merely waved a hand and both guards reluctantly moved out of earshot.

He continued more quietly. 'Sir Baldwin, in a town like Tiverton some people will have allied themselves with men for whom I feel little affinity. Some will owe duties to other men. Even Coroner Harlewin owes his position to Thomas of Lancaster. How many others owe service to the Lords of the Marches or to the Despensers?'

Baldwin held his gaze. 'Were you expecting Sir Gilbert or another messenger?'

'I am expecting, as you put it, messengers from all sides.'

'From which do you think Sir Gilbert would have come?'

'He could have come from the King to demand my loyalty, or the Marcher Lords asking for my help, or the Despensers to beg for my assistance. Maybe even Thomas of Lancaster threatening me, should I help any of the others. Which do *you* think he would have come from?'

Baldwin was quiet a moment. 'Most likely Despenser. The Lords of the Marches have taken their armies to London and have all the help they need; Earl Thomas is not with them and has little need of your assistance, nor would he fear your enmity. But Despenser, he would want any help, any support he could win. He knows he is to be thrown from the kingdom.'

'He has been,' Lord Hugh said smilingly. 'But, tell me. Which of all these great men would you advise me to support?'

Before Baldwin could answer this difficult question, he was interrupted.

'My Lord, I am glad you have managed to speak to Sir Baldwin. It was a shame that he was not present during the meal, but I am sure he will be able to eat with you soon,' Sir Peregrine said, striding in.

Baldwin saw a fleeting annoyance pass over Lord Hugh's face, but for his own part he felt only relief.

CHAPTER FIFTEEN

Sir Peregrine watched Sir Baldwin narrowly. He could kick himself for spending so long with Felicity, but at least he felt some kind of release. She had soothed him, cradling him in her arms for a while, stroking his back and murmuring gently as he wept. Afterwards the guilt of not having been with Emily when she died returned, but he had enjoyed a moment of peace with the whore.

As soon as he had got back to the castle Toker told him that Lord de Courtenay was in the hall. It was the last thing he needed, his lord talking to an ally of Bishop Stapledon and being swayed into believing that the banishment of the Despensers was illegal, which was why he had marched straight in, giving Baldwin a suspicious look, wondering what the knight had discussed with Lord Hugh; he only prayed that Baldwin hadn't persuaded Lord Hugh to side with the King as Bishop Stapledon no doubt wanted.

'How are you, my Lord?' he asked. With relief he saw that one of the guards with Lord Hugh was Owen, one of his own men. He would be able to find out what had been said.

Sitting, he glanced at Baldwin again. He was convinced the knight was an emissary from the Bishop of Exeter, Walter Stapledon, and Stapledon wanted the King to be allowed to invite the Despensers back; however he saw no shiftiness in Baldwin's eye.

'We were talking about the dead knight,' Lord Hugh said.

Sir Peregrine forced a smile to his face. 'Really?'

'It does seem odd to me, you know, Peregrine,' Lord Hugh continued. He leaned back contemplatively and stared up at the window with a slight frown. 'This man was a Templar knight, someone trained with all forms of weaponry. He was out with a massive dog, I understand, and yet one single cut-throat managed to steal his knife and kill both him and his dog. Doesn't that strike you as curious? I would have thought it was more the work of another trained fighter.'

'I doubt another knight would have attacked him,' Sir Peregrine said, but Baldwin saw how his face looked quite grey.

'Very curious,' Lord Hugh murmured. 'A warrior like him allowing his knife to be stolen.'

'It must have been the felon,' Sir Peregrine asserted.

'Stabbed in the dark,' Baldwin mused, frowning.

'What of it?' Sir Peregrine demanded. 'It's how an outlaw would strike, isn't it?'

'Perhaps. But if another man struck him down, perhaps the felon merely arranged the corpse neatly and took his purse. Since the knight wouldn't need the money again, an honourable man could do that.'

'Oh, really!' Sir Peregrine sneered.

'It could be one explanation. It is easier to believe that another trained man-at-arms of whatever rank killed him rather than a weakly abjurer.'

'I hope you don't mean to suggest . . .'

Baldwin smiled. 'What could I mean, Sir Peregrine?'

The bannaret stood coldly, plainly angry. His eyes held Baldwin's with a glittering intensity.

Simon wanted to interrupt them but daren't. If he was not careful, he could insult one or the other and precipitate a duel.

It was Lord Hugh who relaxed the tension. 'Come, Sir Peregrine, there's no need for weapons to be drawn. Sir Baldwin meant you no insult.'

'Certainly not, Sir Peregrine,' Baldwin said guilelessly. 'I was thinking aloud, no more.'

'I apologise, then. I am becoming peppery. It must be this sad death. Sir Baldwin, Master Bailiff, would you walk with me in the yard while we await our evening meal?'

'Naturally,' Baldwin said, allowing the tension to leave him. The three took their leave of the lord and walked down the stairs to the yard. Baldwin had to flex his fingers to ease the clenching where he had bunched his fists, but more than Sir Peregrine's sudden temper, Baldwin was fascinated by the reason behind his apparent loss of control.

William Small the sailor sat drinking ale. His guard had been removed when the Coroner decided he had no case to answer and now he sat alone, back against the ladder which led up to the walkway along the walls. Behind him was the doorway to the storeroom from which he had fetched his drink.

The sky was light, the clouds tinged with a vivid salmon pink as the sun followed its course down to the horizon, far out of sight from here, hidden as it was by the curtain wall of the castle. With its passing the yard was thrown into shade and the night chill was overtaking the place although the cobbles and stonework still gave off a little warmth.

It was ending a good day after all. He had feared that he might be attached to appear at the next court, having to pay more money in fines, but somehow he had escaped. It looked as though he was free. Everyone assumed that poor Sir Gilbert had been killed by the felon, and that suited William; it meant he need not be held for long here.

His belongings were all in the tack-room at the side of the stables, and as he sat near the hall, he noticed a man loitering nearby, in the doorway. For some reason William found himself studying him. He was a man-at-arms, a smartly turned-out fellow, who leaned as if casually against the door-jamb, but William was convinced that there was a watchful set to his shoulders. William had been a soldier, he could recognise the attitude of another who was on the scrounge.

William settled back with a smirk, certain that someone was inside the room rummaging through his things and those of the good, dead, Sir Gilbert. They were welcome, he thought. They'd find nothing in all his stuff. William had already been through the lot, looking for the money. It wasn't there.

It must have been that day when the knight left him and went on alone, returning late reeking of wine. He had taken the bags with him, because William had searched through the camp after he'd gone and there was nothing there. But Sir Gilbert didn't bring it back with him: it was all gone when the knight was found dead.

What the hell! Some you win, some you lose. William rested his head against the ladder. The beer felt good in his belly, he was fed and he was as contented as a man could be. Although he loved the sea in all her moods, he was happy to be living safely on land for a while.

There were footsteps nearby, but he ignored them, closing his eyes. He didn't want to chat; he wanted a good sleep and an early start. Hardly had he begun to doze, however, when he heard a low, rumbling growl. The man outside the tack-room had also heard the noise and was standing fearfully, staring at Aylmer. Seeing such a large man worried by the dog made William grin to himself.

Then the humour was wiped from his face as he recognised the man: the scene from the street outside the tavern in London came back to him and he was suddenly struck with a quick fear. That man had been pinned to the wall by Aylmer before.

He was about to call out when a blade rested on his throat, a blade that felt as sharp as a razor, as cold as only polished steel could be, and a voice hissed in his ear. 'If you call that sodding hound, you'll die.'

'Perhaps it was fortunate,' Sir Peregrine continued when the three were once more outside, 'that Sir Gilbert died, if he was a messenger.'

'Fortunate?' Baldwin enquired casually. The callousness of the bannaret's attitude shocked him, but he wanted to discover all he could from the man. 'Ho, Aylmer! Leave that man alone.'

He watched smiling as the great dog padded gently away from Perkin, trotting to Baldwin's side. Baldwin tickled his ears while they spoke.

Sir Peregrine eyed the dog warily. 'At least as an excommunicate he wasn't anyone to be mourned. And the felon dying with him was more or less a proof of God's justice. Others deserve more grief, don't you think?'

'If he was a messenger, couldn't he have carried a message from the King?'

'I would doubt it, Sir Baldwin. The King has his own men – why should he use a renegade Templar?'

Baldwin gave a brittle smile. 'I suppose not.'

'But of course Despenser would have wanted to bring Lord de Courtenay to his camp if possible.'

'You think so?'

Sir Peregrine shot him a look. 'There's no need to try to sound disinterested, Sir Baldwin. You and Bailiff Puttock here are friends of Walter Stapledon. He's mentioned you both in my presence and a friend of the good bishop's will know his views, won't he?'

'He rarely conceals them,' admitted Baldwin.

' "Trenchant", I have heard them described. I think he became disgusted with court politics earlier this year, and I can't blame him, but that doesn't mean he's right now.'

'You mean he is wrong to declare the banishment of the Despensers to be illegal?' Baldwin wanted to know.

Sir Peregrine made a gesture of irritation. 'Of course he is! The bastards had to go. Look at them! Greedy, vain, never satisfied, the pair of them. Always looking out for more advantage.'

'Yet if they were wrongly exiled . . .?'

'The pair are a danger to the realm. If they stayed in power, putting whoever they wanted into every official position, stealing any lands they fancied, throwing honest men into prison on their whim – aye, and poisoning the King's ear with stories about other men – the country would soon have gone to war.'

'They had to go, then?'

'It was inevitable.'

'And what now?' Baldwin asked quietly.

'We must ensure that the Despensers never return. That would be a disaster.'

'I see.'

'No, Sir Baldwin, I don't think you do.' Sir Peregrine halted. They were at the well and Sir Peregrine sat on the low wall that surrounded it, gazing up at Baldwin with the air of a teacher instructing a wayward pupil. 'If Hugh Despenser, the young one, comes back to England, there will be war. It may be Lancaster who precipitates it, it may be the Marcher Lords, it may even be the King himself – I don't know – but if the Despensers come back, there will inevitably be civil war.

'If the Despensers win that war, the whole realm will become subject to Hugh and then no man will be safe. Can you imagine the country under his boot? He steals what he wants. Power is the only authority he understands. That is why we have to support the Marcher Lords and Earl Thomas of Lancaster.'

'If the King himself supports the Despensers, my choice is made,' Baldwin said steadily.

'Sir Baldwin, I beg you to consider whether it is better that the King should be supported by a council of wise advisers, with decisions agreed by all for the fair government of the land, or that the King should be led by the nose by an avaricious devil like Despenser!'

Baldwin smiled. 'Is it better that a man should forget his oaths of loyalty to his King or abide by them?'

'In this case we should be upholding the King's power and authority, protecting him from advisers who would destroy the peace of his realm. By defending him against the evil advice of the Despensers, we should—'

'Yes, I understand the drift of your argument. I shall have to consider your words.'

'And you, Bailiff – what would *you* do?'

'Me?' Simon asked with surprise. 'I have no idea. After all, I am no knight.'

'Ah, but you could be! There are fines for those who can afford to take up their knighthood and who do not. Perhaps you ought to be a knight.'

'If I were a knight, I would obey the man to whom I owed allegiance,' Simon said. 'To do otherwise would be to earn the title "Traitor".'

Sir Peregrine smiled thinly. 'Is that what the Despensers have led us to already? A man who wishes to save the realm is now to be termed a traitor to his King?'

Baldwin met his gaze. 'Someone who has given his oath to his King would certainly be a traitor if he went over to another man.'

Sir Peregrine appeared irritated by his coolness. 'I hope you aren't implying that I have broken my vow?'

'Certainly not.'

Sir Peregrine's face did not reflect satisfaction with Baldwin's response. 'Do you think I killed Sir Gilbert then? That was what you implied in the hall.'

'I implied nothing, Sir Peregrine,' Baldwin said soothingly. 'I was speculating on what could have happened, nothing more.'

'You can stop speculating about *me* at once!' Sir Peregrine said, colouring. He realised straightaway that he had over-reacted but couldn't stop himself. He had lost the sense of ease and calmness which lying with Felicity had given him and the knowledge that Emily was dead was a rasp across his sore nerves. He tapped his foot, avoiding Baldwin's eye. 'What's that blasted dog doing?'

Aylmer had crossed to the door to the tack-room and now stood growling. Baldwin shrugged. 'Maybe he's hungry.'

'Well, if it keeps up this row, it'll get his fill – of steel,' Sir Peregrine said impatiently, fingering his sword hilt. Then he turned on his heel and stormed off to the stairs that led to the gatehouse.

Baldwin slowly walked over to the hound. The animal seemed nervous, not angry. He put out his hand to pat Aylmer's head. 'What is troubling you, old friend?' He opened the door and Aylmer walked in stiffly, full of menace, crossing the room to a door at the far end, which he sniffed at carefully. Then he went to Sir Gilbert's pile of clothes.

'Is that it? You wanted to be close to your master's things?' Baldwin laughed.

Aylmer sat and watched the two men.

Simon glanced at Baldwin. 'I fear you've succeeded in antagonising Sir Peregrine.'

'I think we have learned quite a deal. Especially from Lord Hugh.'

'What did we learn from *him*?'

Baldwin smiled at his disbelieving tone. 'Simon, a man like Lord Hugh is trained to conceal much, but he did confirm that he had been expecting a messenger. And he did not reject my reasoning that pointed to Sir Gilbert being a messenger from Despenser.'

'You think that takes us further?'

'I am convinced that there has been a crime, that a murderer is free, and that Sir Gilbert died for a reason which has something to do with politics. Yes, I think that takes us further.'

He laughed, walking from the room. Simon shook his head, but followed him, closing the door behind him.

Aylmer sat a while longer, frowning suspiciously at the door. When he was sure that all was quiet, he stood, circled round his dead master's belongings two or three times, then lay down with his head on his paws as if to sleep, but at every noise from the yard his eyes snapped open.

Later, Jeanne and Baldwin were leaving the hall with Simon after their meal when Jeanne saw Edgar at the far side of the court. She thought little of it at the time; she was too full of good humour to consider why her husband's man should wave at her. In any case, it was late, she was weary and her bed was calling to her. Baldwin and she had to share their room with another couple but the thought of resting on her mattress was enormously appealing. She thrust her arm through her husband's and smiled up at him.

'Tired, my love?' he asked.

She yawned in answer. 'The journey was not so tiring as I had expected, but it is exhausting to have to meet so many people whom I have never seen before.'

'Yes,' he agreed. 'Especially when some of them are dead.'

'It would be nice to be able to accept what the Coroner said,' Simon said.

'Very nice,' Baldwin said scathingly. 'But how can one trust that fool's judgement? A man who thinks a Templar could have his knife stolen and be stabbed with it!'

'Couldn't he, though?' Jeanne wondered. Her attention was wandering. Edgar had caught her eye again and now he gestured urgently, his lips pursed with concern. 'Husband, excuse me a moment. I must see what Edgar wants.'

She left them speculating on the reasons for Sir Gilbert's death and crossed the yard.

'My Lady, I am very sorry to have interrupted you, but I thought it better that you should help than that I should call for another.'

'Why, what is it, Edgar?'

'Petronilla.'

She followed him out to a little storeroom. Inside she could hear drunken sobbing. Glancing at Edgar, she saw him nod slowly.

'Something happened to her today,' he said.

Jeanne muttered a curse and entered. Edgar followed more slowly. He felt unqualified to assist with the girl. He had seen how the Coroner had molested her, and was sure that the last thing the girl needed was another man offering her sympathy.

The two women soon appeared, Petronilla weeping and leaning on her mistress's arm. Jeanne had to ask. 'Edgar – are you responsible for this?'

Edgar blinked in shock, but it was Petronilla who threw out a hand in extravagant denial. 'Of course it wasn't Edgar, my Lady. He saved me from him. Edgar's my hero.'

Jeanne sighed at the slurred voice. 'Well, your hero can help me take you to your room. I can't get you there alone in this state.'

She was right. Edgar took one arm while Jeanne kept hold of the other, but even then it was hard to half-carry Petronilla back to the women's rooms where she was supposed to be sleeping. In the end Jeanne stopped, breathless. 'Edgar, if we get her to the room she'll wake everyone else. Help me put her in the hayloft. She can sleep there the night. Then you go and tell Baldwin that I'll stay with her most of the night, and see the child's nurse. Stephen must stay with *her* tonight, not Petronilla.'

Soon they were hauling her up the small staircase to the low loft.

'It's love that matters,' Petronilla declared as Edgar shoved her rump upwards.

Jeanne pulled her arms, snarling, 'There'll be little love around here if you aren't silent, my girl.'

'My little son loves me,' Petronilla continued, throwing her hand out emphatically and nearly sending the three of them back down the ladder.

Snatching at her wrist Jeanne spoke through gritted teeth. 'That's fine because right now your mistress certainly doesn't!'

'He loves his mama. Not that Coroner, though, the filthy bastard!'

Edgar pushed but the girl was resisting. Glancing up he saw that Lady Jeanne was near the end of her tether; he made a quick decision. Stepping back, he allowed Petronilla to topple a little. As she gave a short squeak of alarm, he set his shoulder to her waist and caught her about the knees, climbing quickly up the ladder and depositing her giggling in a thick pile of hay. She rolled over and tried to stand. 'Again! That was fun.'

Jeanne groaned as the girl made as if to throw herself down the ladder. Edgar grabbed her at the last moment and lowered her back onto the hay.

'Lady, you should go to bed.'

'She can't be left a moment, can she?'

Edgar shook his head.

'This was all the fault of that Coroner?'

Edgar explained how he had found them and Jeanne scowled angrily. 'Molest my maid, would he?'

'I think it would be best to leave the matter,' Edgar said. 'If you accused him, he could make life difficult. Better to let things lie. I shall see that Petronilla is safe from him.'

'He's my hero. Edgar must love me too!' Petronilla gurgled happily from the straw.

On the morning of St Giles's feast, it was a sad little group which attended the church for Sir Gilbert's burial service. Father Abraham stood before them and began speaking in a quiet, low monotone.

'Dirige Dominus meus in conspectu tuo viam . . .'

Baldwin found it was difficult to concentrate. He had decided to attend with Jeanne to represent the Order which he and Sir Gilbert had both served, and yet now he was here he hardly knew why.

He had known Sir Gilbert from the time when the other knight had been at the Temple in Paris. Baldwin had been there as well, and the two men had been on nodding acquaintance. Nothing more than that, but it meant that there was a certain confusion of emotions as he stood watching the priest before the large hearse, the metal frame sitting over the dead bodies with the dark, threadbare cloth of the parish pall hanging over and concealing the corpses beneath.

Standing there at the final ceremony of a man who had once been a comrade in arms, a companion warrior-monk in his Order, Baldwin felt a rush of grief that threatened to overwhelm him for a moment. It was as if the death of this man was symbolic of the end of the Order which they both had served; as if Baldwin himself was the sole survivor of their warrior caste. It made him feel exceptionally lonely.

The service ended before he was ready, his mind still whirling with despair. He wished he could have told Jeanne about his membership of the Templars and about his present desolate mood but it was difficult: although he trusted to her solid commonsense he had never discussed the Templars with her. Many people believed the Church's malicious propaganda against the Order and Baldwin could not tell how she would respond to hearing that he himself had been one. In any case, one look at her this morning told him that after sitting up much of the night with an inebriated maidservant, his wife was in no mood to listen.

Jeanne and he walked out with the bearers and stood staring down at the hole in the ground. The plot was not far from the church but was not in the yard itself.

Baldwin and his wife waited as the coffinless body wrapped in its cheap winding-sheet was rested in the bottom of the grave. Hick, who today was the gravedigger, wandered over and gazed down speculatively, leaning on his shovel. The priest was still in the churchyard seeing to the similarly shrouded figure of a woman. Baldwin gathered from listening to others witnessing her interment that she had died in childbirth. A woman and many children stood by her hole, staring down into it as the priest tossed soil onto her face. A young girl holding the hand of an older sister burst into shattering sobs.

Meanwhile Father Abraham strode towards Baldwin and Jeanne, the family trailing after him as he walked to a patch of clear ground outside the yard but near the wall. There Baldwin saw a woman standing with a tiny corpse, and he guessed it was this child's birth which had caused the woman's death. The priest spoke for a short while, begging God's forgiveness for the baby's sins, pleading for the life which had scarcely existed, that God would take his soul up to Heaven.

Baldwin sourly thought to himself that the child could hardly be guilty of many sins.

'Sad business, that,' said Hick. He eyed the family weeping at the small graveside. 'Shame children can't be buried in the yard with their mothers.'

'In most parishes the priests allow them to be,' Jeanne said, and hearing the tightness in her tone, Baldwin smiled and put his hand through her arm.

'That a fact?' Hick said, and spat on the ground. 'Not here. Our Father Abraham, he sticks to the rules, he does.'

Baldwin was hardly listening. He was staring down again at the figure of Sir Gilbert.

Seeing the direction of his attention, the rat-catcher motioned towards the body. 'You knew him?'

'Not really,' Baldwin said. 'But I helped to find his body and investigate his death. He was a stranger to the town, and I knew he wouldn't be allowed a grave in the yard.'

'No, course not. Can't have strangers buried in a Christian yard. Poor old sod! And he seemed so cheerful.'

'Yes, poor devil,' Baldwin agreed absently and then started. 'What do you mean, "he seemed cheerful"?'

But Hick had no time to answer; Father Abraham was with them. Baldwin swallowed his urgency and concentrated while the priest ran through what sounded like a very terse version of the funeral rite. Finishing, Father Abraham stood looking down a moment, before suddenly hissing: 'Lie there in great opprobrium, excommunicate! *Your* heresy at least is finished.'

And before the astonished Baldwin could angrily demand what he meant, the priest had swept around and was marching back to his church.

CHAPTER SIXTEEN

After attending a short Mass in the castle's chapel, Simon went to the buttery and broke his fast with a hunk of bread washed down by a quart of thin ale. Feeling replete, he walked from the hall and stood in the doorway to the yard, idly scratching at an insect bite on his groin while he studied the servants and guests milling about in the yard.

It was a busy place, this castle. Much more so than Lydford, which was little more than a simple gaol now, with its courtroom above. Women hurried past carrying pails of milk; men rolled barrels ready to be stacked in the buttery; a girl walked slowly and carefully from the kitchen, not yet ten years old from the look of her, frowning with concentration, her tongue protruding pinkly as she took an over-full pitcher of cream to the hall; a pair of grooms recently returned from exercising a pair of Lord de Courtenay's mounts rubbed them down with handfuls of straw; dogs snapped and barked, a pig wandered slowly rummaging through the detritus, and a cock crowed time after time while one of his hens called enthusiastically the loud cry that Simon's father had once told him meant, 'An *egg*, an *egg*, an *egg*!'

Simon rubbed at his back. He was one of a few men who had come alone, without a wife to keep him company, and, since bedrooms were at a premium even in a castle the size of this he had been forced to find a bench to sleep on in the hall near the fire. Men with wives were allocated rooms with other couples so that the women should be spared the draughty hall and the indignity of enduring the lascivious gazes of other men at night. Simon had spent an uncomfortable night while drunken guests snored, servants giggled, men and maidservants coupled in the dark and dogs scratched flea bites. Gradually, to add injury to insult, Simon came to realise that he too had caught fleas.

But the sun, already high in the sky, was welcome and after his ale he felt a little more comfortable and less snappish. He fetched a new pint of strong ale, and took it outside to a low wall near the stables where he could sit and nod in the clear sunshine.

'So, Bailiff. Did you sleep well?'

'Sir Peregrine, a good morning to you. Yes, I slept well, I thank you,' Simon lied cheerfully. 'I trust you did too?'

'I did not,' said Sir Peregrine bitterly. 'There were two couples in my room: one man snored so loudly I thought the foundations of the castle were endangered, while the other two held a whispered argument until almost dawn. I understood from it that the husband had been paying too much attention to one of the serving girls and too little to his wife. From listening to her,' he added grimly, 'I would have done the same.' Then he sighed. 'I feel I should apologise for my mood last night,' he said stiffly.

Simon smiled and proffered his pot of ale. Sir Peregrine lifted it in grateful salute and sipped. His depression had not left him. He would have liked to have witnessed Emily's burial, but he was his Lord's man and he must do his work.

'A good brew. Lord Hugh does himself well here,' Simon said.

'It's a well-run castle. With sensible advice the Lord Hugh should be able to keep it.'

Simon knew that Sir Peregrine was leading towards the previous night's discussion and swore to himself. He was about to deflect the bannaret's attention to another subject when they heard shouting.

'God's blood! What is it this time?' Sir Peregrine roared.

A man appeared in the gateway and, seeing Sir Peregrine, ran to him. Stopping before the bannaret, he had to pause to get his breath back.

'Sir Peregrine, can you come? A body has been found – a body in the river.'

'Here to see the man buried, Keeper?' Cecily Sherman asked, and she was rewarded by seeing Sir Baldwin start with surprise.

Exchanging greetings with him and his wife, Cecily thought that Sir Baldwin looked rather handsome in the morning's thin light, with the sun filtering through the thick columns of smoke which rose upwards in the still air from the cooking fires of the town. The sun treated him kindly, smoothing out some of the interesting, deep lines at his forehead and reducing the impact of the scar that reached from one temple almost to his jaw.

'You are here early, Lady,' he answered.

'I wanted to see the woman and her child buried. One always feels sympathy for a woman who dies in childbirth.'

'You have no children of your own?' Jeanne asked.

'No, my Lady, but I pray and hope.'

Baldwin indicated the hole nearby into which Hick was studiously shovelling soil. 'That knight Sir Gilbert – did you see him alive?'

'Me, Sir Baldwin? Heavens, no! How would I?'

'He was camped down at the river, I understand, but he was riding about the country the previous day. His man even said that he had come here to Tiverton,' said Baldwin, casting a glance at Hick.

'Oh, I fear I rarely leave the town. My husband might have seen him, though. He was visiting South Molton the night that this good fellow was killed.'

'You didn't see him in Tiverton?'

'Do I look the sort of lady who would wander the streets whenever her husband is abroad?'

'Oh, no. No, of course not. I didn't intend to imply . . .'

She waved aside his protestations. 'No matter, sir. No insult was taken, I assure you.'

Something in her tone made Baldwin shoot a look at her. Cecily looked demure, but when he caught her eye she gave him a fleeting, saucy wink. Instantly he reddened, and saw that she was amused by his reaction. It made him angry: a woman hardly half his age, and a momentary flicker of the eye could make him colour like Wat with Petronilla! His temper made his voice harsh. 'Is there anyone who can confirm you were at home?'

'My servants, of course.' She indicated a woman standing a few yards behind.

'Anyone else?'

'Sir Baldwin, do you suspect me of riding out to an assignation with this knight?' she asked archly. She determined that she would not confess to her affair in front of this fellow. 'In any case, I understand the man's dog died too. Do you think I would be capable of wrestling a hound to the floor?'

'The dog . . .' Baldwin frowned.

'And I thought the Coroner had closed the matter – saying that the felon killed the knight, then was himself executed.'

'Well, I believe that someone murdered Sir Gilbert of Carlisle – and, if he was distracted, a woman could have stabbed him as easily as a man.'

His words made her protest with apparent honesty. 'Sir Baldwin, what possible reason could I have for killing someone I had never met?'

That, Baldwin knew, was the nub: how could she have known Sir Gilbert? He would have left the Order in 1307 or 1308, and had not been here for years, if what William Small had said was correct. In those far-off days Cecily would not have been seven years old.

The spicer's wife glanced over Baldwin's shoulder to where the family stood near the other grave. She continued, 'It's so sad to look at poor Emily. And to think that her man has lost her.'

'Her husband?' Baldwin asked.

'Oh, he left her ages ago. Even when he was with her, the useless devil didn't bring in enough money to support the family. What little he earned he preferred to spend on ale and women in the taverns.'

'But all those children . . . weren't they his?'

'*Emily* had many,' she corrected. 'I understand the baby that killed her was Sir Peregrine of Barnstaple's.'

'Oh, the poor man,' Jeanne breathed.

Baldwin considered how Sir Peregrine had been the previous night: distracted, fractious, unhappy. 'I would like to speak to your husband,' he told Cecily, and she beamed at him flirtatiously. 'He is in the shop. Would you like directions?'

The Coroner slammed his front door behind him and strode away up the road, roaring at anyone who blocked his path.

It was so unreasonable of his damned wife! He had only gone to visit Felicity before the inquest on that blasted woman Emily and her child, the pair that died in the child's birth, last afternoon to enquire about the dead woman – it was his *job*, for God's sake! But no, his blasted wife Jenny had to assume the worst, didn't she? Always thought he was out for a quickie, trying to poke his dagger in another woman's sheath. The fact that she was right didn't ease his mood.

And Felicity hadn't been accommodating either, which didn't make things any better. She was usually so gentle and understanding, but yesterday she'd seemed in a hurry to get away; hadn't wanted to service him or answer his questions. 'I've got to go before the market opens tomorrow, you know the rules,' she'd told him. 'I'm not allowed in town while the market's on.'

It was a fair point, but her reasons were perfectly clear. She was upset at the death of her friend, the one dead from childbirth. No one liked tó lose a pal and drinking partner. Harlewin could understand that.

He walked along the main thoroughfare, past the church and up the road towards the castle. Here the wind was in his face, and the stench of excrement from the pots emptied into the street's single sewer was strong enough to make him wrinkle his nose. A hog rooted in the filth, chewing at a piece of flesh, and Harlewin watched it queasily. It was enough to put a man off his bacon. A bitch with engorged teats began barking at it, snapping at the hog's hindquarters until it moved off, still munching, and only then did Harlewin see it was chewing on a puppy.

Glancing up he realised where he was. This was the spicers' area; his feet must have guided him here unconsciously to see his woman. Looking up at the window he couldn't help but smile a little. He knew the room where she slept with her husband was at the back of the shop, in their solar, but he gazed through the opened shopfront hopefully. Seeing John Sherman with his new apprentice at the rear of the shop, Harlewin hurried off.

It was a relief to be away from Cecily's knowing gaze. That young woman was a little too sharp for her own, and other people's, good. Before Baldwin went to seek her husband, he stood fingering two bright penny coins at the gravedigger's side. 'Friend, I know the good Father Abraham takes coins for looking after the Masses for the dead, but I feel it is only right that a man who performs the physical duties for the dead body should also be rewarded.'

Hick studied the two coins, then his gaze rose and met Baldwin's, giving a short grunt of wary agreement. Taking the pennies, he dropped them carefully into his small purse.

Baldwin smiled. 'This knight. You had seen him alive?'

'Aye. He was here. I saw him.'

'This would be when?'

'Four nights ago. I was down at the alehouse near the castle and saw him with Master Nicholas Lovecok. They were coming out of the tavern further up the hill.'

That would be the night before his murder, Baldwin noted. 'What time?'

Hick scowled with concentration. 'It was just before Father Abraham was called to Father Benedict, so it was a little after Compline.'

'Father Benedict?'

'He was the priest at the chapel in Templeton. He was dying. Father Abraham spent most of the day with him, then came home for Vespers, but not long after a boy came to say that the Father was sinking fast and Father Abraham went back to ease his passing.'

Baldwin said, 'And you saw Sir Gilbert leaving the tavern with Lovecok?'

'Yes. And a moment later one of Sir Peregrine's men came out and followed them.'

'Why should that be, I wonder. Do you know who that man was?'

'No, sir.'

'Would you recognise him again?'

Hick screwed up his face. 'It was dark, sir. I saw the badges on his tunic, but not his face.'

Jeanne smiled engagingly at Hick. 'I suppose Nicholas Lovecok and the knight were very friendly?'

'Yes, my Lady.'

'Were they very drunk, do you think?'

'They could walk,' Hick said surprised. 'They just looked like old friends.'

'More,' Baldwin murmured looking down into the grave, 'than you could say for the priest. He seems to hate the man.'

'Yes,' Hick agreed. 'You should have seen him yesterday, when he was talking about him and the Templars like him. Said the Templars cost us the Kingdom of Jerusalem, that they had taken up devil-worship or somesuch . . .'

While Baldwin listened appalled, the rat-catcher rattled on happily about the priest's fearsome denunciation of the Templars.

'So that's why he hated Sir Gilbert,' Baldwin said when Hick was done.

'I expect so, Sir Baldwin,' Hick said, hopefully fingering his purse in case more coins might be forthcoming.

'But how,' Baldwin wondered, staring back at the castle, 'would a knight like Sir Gilbert have known a merchant like Lovecok? And how did Father Abraham know Sir Gilbert was a Templar?'

'Ah, you'll need to ask *him* that.'

'Yes, I shall, shan't I?' Baldwin said. He smiled at his wife. 'Shall we go and call on the good Father, my dear?'

They found the priest in his chamber, a small room with a pleasant fire crackling in the middle of the floor. Father Abraham was putting his book and vestments into a chest at the side of his table. Seeing who his guests were, he looked surprised, but was polite if not effusive in his welcome. 'Please come in. Can I serve you with anything, Lady Jeanne?'

'A little wine?'

'Of course.' He walked to a small barrel stamped with the mark of Lord Hugh and turned a small wooden tap, filling a bowl. 'Sir Baldwin?'

Baldwin was staring thoughtfully at the chest, which remained open. Propping the lid up was a long-bladed knife in a sheath.

Seeing the direction of his eyes, the priest smiled. 'A man must protect himself when the country becomes so dangerous. Even I, a priest, must carry a weapon to defend myself.'

'You should be careful, Father. Many a man unused to a dagger has come to grief against a man well trained.'

Father Abraham gave a short laugh. 'I pity the felon who attacks *me*! I was brought up in a knight's household and was trained to arms. I would be able to shock any outlaw, I assure you. Now, would you care for some wine?'

'No, thank you. I would prefer some mental nourishment.'

Father Abraham glanced at Jeanne, wondering whether she should be present, and asked, 'Would you like to come to the church, then?'

'No, Father. I wanted to ask how you discovered that Sir Gilbert was a Templar.'

Father Abraham froze. 'You heard my words?'

'It would have been difficult to miss them,' Jeanne said.

He looked at her coldly. 'Then I can hardly deny it, can I? I learned he was a Templar when I was visiting an ill colleague: Father Benedict of Templeton. He was dying, and I went to give him what comfort I could.'

'He has died?'

'I fear so. He died on the same night as the heretic and the felon. I was with him and could listen to his confession.'

'I see. And he told you that Sir Gilbert was a Templar?'

'While I was with Benedict the Templar went to the chapel. I believe he used to be one of the devil-worshippers who once lived there until our Holy Father the Pope showed us how evil they were. Then he scurried away like all the other cowards.'

Baldwin restrained himself with an effort. The priest was scathing about his comrades, about his Order. It was hard to swallow his pride and continue, but continue Baldwin must – and without letting the priest realise that he himself had once been a Templar. 'Did you speak to Sir Gilbert?'

'My God, *no*! Speak to a foul heretic?' His face showed his disbelief and disgust at the suggestion. 'I should rather cut out my tongue! I was there with the good Father Benedict as a kindness. Although he was once a priest in that foul Order, he recanted and remained to help the poor of his little manor; this proud Templar Knight never recanted. His presence there proved it! Do you know what he did? Eh? He walked into the chapel. He must have gone there to pray! He cannot have adopted the true faith if he still believed in the holiness of his foul Order. I was with Father Benedict for a long while, and Sir Gilbert remained in the chapel all that time.'

'When did you leave?'

'I don't know. It was late afternoon, I suppose. The sun was low in the sky.'

'Did you leave when the good Father died?' Jeanne asked.

'No, Lady. He was still alive. He died much later, at night. I was called to him by a boy from his parish.'

'You went back after dark?' Baldwin demanded.

'Why . . . yes. Why?'

'And which road did you take to go there?'

'There is a track that leads almost straight there.'

'And which also leads along behind the road to Crediton, does it not?' Baldwin said. He smiled, but his face had no humour. 'Along the woods in which Sir Gilbert, the man you hated so much, was murdered. By someone skilled with weapons.'

He was almost at the castle gate when Harlewin saw her, and his ruddy face beamed at the sight.

True enough, Cecily Sherman was not the most beautiful woman in Tiverton, but to Harlewin she was a breath of invigorating air. Cecily was short and dark, with the flashing eyes of a Celt. Her belly was full and round, her breasts large and appealing, her face a pleasing spherical shape: perfect and warm to cuddle up to on a chill evening, he reflected – unlike Felicity who was little better than a sack of bones. Cecily Sherman's complexion was fine and smooth, unmarked by the pox, and of a beautiful creamy-pink colour. She looked as ripe and wholesome as a peach just plucked from the tree, and tasted as delicious.

There was no shame in her, either. When she saw him, her eyes widened invitingly, her smile broadened. Her maid was with her, but neither Cecily nor Harlewin feared that rumours of their meetings would be spread abroad. Harlewin, when all was said and done, was the Coroner. He could invent almost any offence and have a maid installed in her own private gaol if she were foolish enough to give him reason.

'My Lord Coroner,' Cecily curtsied. 'It seems such a long time since I last saw you.'

'You think so? I swear to me it seems only yesterday, my Lady.'

'And yet for me the passing of even a minute without you seems like an hour,' she sighed.

'Rubbish, woman,' he growled as they passed into a shadow, and he grabbed her to him and placed a smacking kiss on her lips.

Chuckling throatily she pulled away and ducked beneath his second attempt to grapple her. 'Sir! Not in the street like a whore and her client, thank you.'

'Then let's go off to the mill.'

'Do you think me a fool?' she asked, and this time there was a trace of asperity in her tone. 'With all the people come to the town for the Fair?'

'Er, no. Perhaps you're right,' he agreed. He hadn't considered how many eyes could witness him riding off with her, but now she mentioned it, it would be foolish to risk so much. John Sherman already suspected their affair – he'd shown his suspicions in the hall when he'd almost accused Harlewin of corruption or whatever the damn-fool spicer was on about. Not that Sherman was a man to fear a great deal. If he wished to force Harlewin into a duel, so be it. Harlewin was reasonably sure he could win any bout with the fellow.

Cecily continued, 'Has that knight from Furnshill spoken to you yet? He's just been asking me all about that night.'

'Sir Baldwin has?' he asked. That put a new complexion on things. 'Why?'

'He doesn't seem to think that Sir Gilbert was killed by the felon. You should be careful. I don't want John to find out about us because of a meddling Keeper. Can't you silence him?'

He grinned and shrugged. 'We have nothing to fear. Perhaps if we were to go to the mill later we could talk about it?'

Cecily Sherman waved her maid away with a small frown. 'Later?'

They had reached the entrance to an alley. He shot a look up and down the street, then darted in, pulling her giggling after him. Kissing her, he lifted her skirts while she responded with enthusiasm, thrusting her hips forward to him, returning the ardour of his embrace with a quick wantonness that excited him beyond caution, and as suddenly she pulled away and patted his face with one hand while she let the other rest on his groin. 'Not here.'

'The mill this evening,' he panted. 'You must come.'

'How can I? My husband is no fool: he will suspect. Anyway, I have to be early to bed . . . no, Harlewin, not with you! John is entertaining merchants at our hall tomorrow morning.'

'He'll be at the castle with the other guests. You remain at home pleading a bad head, then ride for the cottage when he's gone.'

'A bad head? Good God, Coroner, you aren't very inventive, are you? It'd need to be better than that.'

'Well, you think up something. I'll leave the hall early and see you there.'

'You? But you'll have to be at the feast, too, won't you?'

He gave a low, animal snarl. 'You think I can sit and eat when I can picture you lying on my bed? Ach, woman, stop your teasing!' he said and pulled her hand from his groin. 'You can do that later – when we're alone.'

CHAPTER SEVENTEEN

Nicholas Lovecok ensured that the wines and ales he had
delivered to the castle were stored correctly for the feast. In
the storerooms and buttery he checked barrels to see that the
drink would flow, tasting wine and smacking his lips as he
sought to assure himself that he had not failed Lord Hugh.
De Courtenay could be a painful client if the level of service
he received fell short of his expectations.

Finished and generally satisfied, Nicholas sat on a barrel
and filled a jug with wine. So much had happened in the last
few days that he had a lot to muse over, and little of it was of
a pleasant nature.

Meeting Sir Gilbert had been traumatic. It had been so
long, fifteen years almost since they had last met, that Nicholas
had practically forgotten the man. Seeing him again so unex-
pectedly had been like getting a sword-thrust in the guts.

He had been walking back from the castle, on his way to
his brother-in-law's place, and had decided to take a detour,

to work up an appetite. Andrew's hospitality was good, provided you didn't mind a thick mess of food at each meal, enough to adequately feed a whole family. For Nicholas, whose bachelor existence had made him appreciate smaller but more varied dishes, the massive quantities Andrew saw as essential were almost sufficient to make him feel sick.

Perhaps that was unfair. Now he looked back on it, maybe it was more the impact of his sister which made mealtimes at Andrew Carter's house so much of a trial. Poor Matilda sat in her chair like a saint undergoing torture. Wan, unspeaking, anxious and fretful, she picked at her food, speaking seldom, rarely listening, sunk in her own gloom-filled nightmare. When she was spoken to, she snapped or merely stared uncomprehendingly. Luckily she had recovered a little since Dyne's death.

But then it had been a joy to get away from the mourning woman and her nervous husband. Andrew Carter had sat gnawing at his nails while he observed his wife gradually sinking deeper into her hysterical depression as they approached the hour when Philip Dyne would be released on his oath of abjuration. Nicholas had thought that his black mood would be replaced by elation when they had taken Dyne's head off, but it had only seemed as if the full horror of their action had somehow killed off a part of his emotions.

The beheading was a memory Nicholas wanted to erase but he couldn't. Like a picture painted upon glass, it was always in his mind: the flash of the sword swooping down and the first fine spray of blood from the man's neck; a moment later the huge gouts spurting as the head rolled away, the eyelids snapping wide, then fluttering, the mouth opening and shutting as if Dyne was cursing the two men. But without a voice.

Nicholas shuddered at the memory. It was wrong for him to have got involved. Joan was his niece, true, but she would have been as effectively avenged by hiring men to commit the deed, and then there would be none of this lingering horror.

He forced his mind to the other night, the one before Dyne's death. It was in the tavern. Boisterous noise: roaring and bellowing as ebullient traders drank to each other's health, knocking pots or jugs together as they toasted their success at the coming Fair; musicians with harp and bagpipe in one corner competing with a crowder scraping his bow frantically in another; two dogs fighting, egged on by a small group of bystanders.

The room was small, the atmosphere smoky from the fire. It had been like wandering inside a small oven, but welcome for all that, being gloriously free of Andrew and his consumptive wife.

Walking in with a sense of relief, Nicholas ordered himself a large pot of wine and, as he waited, noticed a face that looked oddly familiar. Sir Gilbert had been sitting near the corner, out of the way, and Nicholas, with that sixth sense which he had honed so well since he had first moved to Devonshire, had realised someone was fixing their attention upon him. Instantly he felt the old terror welling up, filling his soul, reaching out and clinging to his every organ and limb, making any movement feel clumsy and conspicuous, like a guilty man waiting to be arrested.

He had thought himself safe here in Tiverton. It was almost ten years since he had fled here, him, his sister and her young daughter. And now someone who knew him, someone from his past, had found him. He had to force himself to drink his wine casually, and then turned, determined to put a bold face upon whatever might come to pass.

And found himself looking into the face of Sir Gilbert of Carlisle. A brother Templar.

Sherman's shop was not far from the church and Baldwin happily snuffed the air outside. 'I always adored that odour.'

'Then you may buy me spices for the house,' Jeanne said.

'Oh, I did not bring money with me. All I have is a few pennies,' Baldwin protested.

'I am sure the good spicer will take your word and offer you credit, Husband.'

Baldwin submitted with a wry grin and held the door open for her. They walked into a small hall, with pots racked upon the shelves that lined the walls. Beneath were sacks filled with aromatic spices and herbs. The air smelled sweet and musty, and Jeanne sneezed twice as she entered.

A youth was serving, a thin and pale lad of not more than twelve or thirteen years. While Jeanne spoke to him, Baldwin walked to the door at the back; as he peered up at some of the pots above it, the door opened and John Sherman came out.

For a merchant, his visage held little of the gracious welcome that Baldwin would have expected. Instead the man looked nervous, smiling weakly. 'Keeper. What can I do for you?'

'Not me, Sherman. It is my wife.'

Sherman appeared relieved. 'Your lady? Ah, I see.'

Baldwin wondered at his change in demeanour. A devil made him ask, 'I hear you were away in South Molton the day Sir Gilbert died. What were you doing there?'

'Meeting a business partner,' Sherman said pompously.

'And who would that have been?'

'Why do you need to know?'

'A man was murdered.'

'That was nothing to do with me. It wasn't even the same road. And the matter is closed: the inquest found Dyne killed the knight.'

'Not everyone believes that,' Jeanne said distinctly.

'Which is why,' Baldwin continued, 'I might have to make sure you were where you say.'

Sherman threw a harassed look at his apprentice. 'You'd better come out here, Sir Baldwin,' he said and stood aside. Jeanne went off to investigate more spices, while her husband followed their host through the door at the back.

Behind was a small chamber, largely filled with sacks and barrels, and Sherman sat on an upturned butt, waving the knight to another. 'Look, I wasn't really in South Molton,' he said without preamble, 'but I don't want people hearing where I was. My wife . . . Cecily has been making a fool of me for some time. I can't trust her. I told her I was going to South Molton, but really I was going to follow her. Except she went out earlier than I expected and I missed her.'

'Did you ask her where she had gone?'

'How could I? That would mean admitting that I'd been spying on her!'

'You could have told her that someone had called here, and found her from home.'

'I didn't think,' he admitted gloomily. 'I just went after the man instead. Harlewin le bloody Poter! Fat sod! Only he'd already gone too, so all I could do was ride out in the direction I thought they'd have taken.'

Harlewin! Just as Avicia Dyne had alleged, Baldwin thought.

Sherman continued, 'He's in the pocket of Earl Thomas, you know. A year ago he let one of the Earl's servants escape justice, saying there wasn't enough evidence against the fellow. There were three witnesses, for God's sake!'

'You think Earl Thomas had reason to want Sir Gilbert dead?'

'Sir Gilbert was Despenser's man – it's common knowledge. The last thing Earl Thomas wants is messengers from Despenser persuading barons to follow *him*. That could make the Earl's position very difficult.'

'Surely others support Earl Thomas in town?'

'Carter and Lovecok, if I've heard right,' Sherman agreed grudgingly.

Baldwin considered a moment. The spicer was too keen to accuse – his judgement was fouled with hatred because of Harlewin's alleged affair with his wife. 'That night, you followed Harlewin where?' he said.

'South then west. He's got a share in a mill over that way.'

'And did you see either him or the knight?'

'No.' His response was too quick, too sharp, and Baldwin merely stared at him.

Sherman couldn't hold his look. He dropped his gaze. 'I swear I didn't. I heard horses coming through the trees. It was late, dark, and I thought my wife must have gone in to hide from me.'

'It wasn't her?'

'No, I rode in because I thought my wife must be there, hiding from me. I'd heard the noise and thought it was her. But while there I heard men shouting. I realised it wasn't

Cecily or the Coroner, so I left. I didn't want to have a blade in the back.'

Baldwin watched him as he looked up.

'That's all I know, Sir Baldwin.'

'Did you see anyone else beforehand – on the road on the way there? Was there anyone you knew?'

Reluctantly he nodded. 'Sir Peregrine. I saw him before I went up that road. He was riding back to Tiverton in a hell of a hurry.'

'Anyone else?'

'The priest. He was up ahead of me on the way to Templeton. No one else.'

'You never saw the Coroner or your wife?'

'No.'

Baldwin had been watching him carefully and noticed the slight hesitation. He was lying again. Baldwin was about to press him further when the door opened.

'Baldwin?' Jeanne peered at him anxiously. 'There's been a murder – that servant of the knight. Simon wants you back at the castle.'

'We must go,' Baldwin said.

'*You* must, Husband,' she retorted. 'Simon sent Petronilla to keep me company, so you can go back with the messenger.'

Avicia Dyne was in the castle's gateway, peering through from the darkened corridor beneath the gatehouse itself, staring into the yard, but she could see the group of men. They were playing, one man laughing and throwing his ball into the air, then hurling it to his friends. Each of them caught it and sent it on until the Coroner saw her. Roaring with

laughter, he beckoned her over, and she saw him take the ball and hold it behind his back. He smiled and waggled his eyebrows as she fearfully came closer, and when she was almost before him, he brought his hands around and threw it at her: Philip's head.

She awoke with a start, a feverish sweat breaking out all over her body once more. This was the fifth time she had woken, but now she could see daylight at the window and the rough doorway. Exhausted with her grief, dull from sleeplessness and despair, she slowly rolled over and pushed herself up from her low palliasse. Her day must begin.

Sniffing, she rolled her mattress into a cylinder and bound it before setting it against the wall. Fetching a bowl she tried to force down some oatcakes, but her appetite had utterly failed her. Without her brother, her very last relation, she had little desire to live.

She could remember leaving the castle as if it was a dream. When she had come down from her room, most of the men had left, and her brother's body was already gone, taken out to a room where it could be held until a place was allocated for its burial. She didn't care where he would be installed. It was irrelevant: God would save him; He would recognise Phil's innocence.

Shuddering, she then thought how she and her brother had always believed the words of the priests: that a corpse must be anointed to save it from being taken by the Devil. Lucifer was always on the lookout for a new soul, they were told. But God was stronger, she reassured herself;

He would surely not leave Philip in Hell for a crime of which he was innocent.

She was aware of the tears coursing down her cheeks once more and dripping from her chin. It was as if she had no further energy for depression. She was drained of all emotion. There was nothing left.

Nothing but hatred.

Avicia had not heard the conclusions of the inquest, all she had seen was her brother's beheaded body lying amid the dirt. She knew that Carter and Lovecok had executed her brother but she couldn't blame them. They had acted as they had because the Coroner had persuaded Philip to confess. Yet he was innocent. *She knew it.*

Sweeping her bowl aside, she knocked it to the floor and put her face in her hands. She felt so weak: useless and feeble. She couldn't see what to do. Then she had an idea. She couldn't go to the Coroner, and the previous day she'd seen that the Keeper and Bailiff didn't believe her, but there were two others who had an interest now. Harlewin le Poter's lies had made two men murder an innocent.

Slowly she lifted her head. Andrew Carter and Nicholas Lovecok had killed Philip believing in his guilt. If she told them the truth they would have to have Harlewin arrested simply to rectify their fault.

Filled with a new resolve, she stood and wiped her hands on her apron. She would speak to Andrew Carter. He would help find justice for Philip *and* his daughter.

Simon supervised the rescue of the body. It wasn't easy to haul the waterlogged figure free. William Small the sailor lay at the bottom of the castle's steep hill in deep water, and if there hadn't been a tree trunk stuck across some ancient boulders further down, he could have been halfway to the

sea by now. Not only was the bank very steep, making it tricky to lift him out, his clothing kept snagging on the bushes and brambles which predominated here, and none of the men appeared eager to join William in the water to get him out.

In the end Simon himself, swearing and contemptuous of the feeble efforts of the castle's staff, slid down the bank and, with Edgar's help, lashed a rope around the corpse's chest. Throwing this to the men still on the bank, he had them pull while he and Edgar manhandled the stiffening body from the water. Aylmer sat mournfully on the bank and watched. He sniffed once at William's body, then walked away to lie down.

'Not a handsome sight,' Edgar commented, looking at the body.

'No,' Simon agreed.

Sir Peregrine had watched their efforts with sardonic amusement from a little further up the bank. Now he slid down the incline to join them. To Simon's private resentment he didn't lose his balance and tumble into the water, but instead joined them both at the body.

'Christ Jesus! What's happened to him? He looks like he's been beaten to death!'

Simon couldn't help but agree. Although much of the blood had been washed from the face, the swollen jaw and temple where William had been kicked or punched stood out distinctly compared with the pale almost translucent flesh.

'Where is he?' Harlewin bawled from the top of the hill. Baldwin appeared at his side. It took some little time for the two of them to join the others. Baldwin himself almost skidded into the water, which would have lightened Simon's mood and given him some comfort after his display of horse-manship the day before, but before he could grin, Edgar caught his master's arm and rescued him.

'What's all this, then?' Harlewin said, squatting at William's side. 'Good God above, but he's been in a war, hasn't he? It's amazing what a fall can do.'

'He has been badly beaten,' Baldwin said, examining William's head. 'The jaw is broken and the head has been clubbed.'

Harlewin peered sceptically, then gazed behind them to the castle's wall high above them. 'You think so? I reckon he could have taken a pot of wine too many up on the wall and stumbled.'

'Quite. Only . . .'

'What?'

'How do you explain this stab-wound?' Baldwin asked politely.

The Coroner let his attention drop to the one-inch-long wound that Baldwin pointed to. He scowled. This was guaranteed to annoy Lord Hugh, and Harlewin didn't like to have his Lordship irritable.

It was definitely murder. The wound was in the top of the left side of the torso, a little below the collar-bone. Harlewin poked his finger into the hole, but it was plain enough that the wound went straight down to the heart.

'An assassin's stroke,' he muttered.

Baldwin studied the man's wrists. 'He was bound, too.'

'It could hardly be worse,' Sir Peregrine grated.

Harlewin agreed that they should remove the body up to the castle where it could be more easily inspected. It would be difficult to get a jury to this site.

Baldwin and Simon waited as the body was carried up the slope, Harlewin and Sir Peregrine scrambling up as best they could. Edgar remained with them – he had been Sir Baldwin's sergeant in the Templars and took the knight's security seriously. When Simon pointed towards a serviceable path which led towards the bridge, Edgar made off along it, his hand near his sword's hilt, to make sure there was no ambush.

'Not easy terrain this,' Simon noted.

'No,' Baldwin murmured. Looking back, the castle sat squatly at the top of the steep hill. He whistled to Aylmer. 'It is almost sheer. The castle's builders made best use of this perilous slope. I can't envisage men-at-arms rushing up it to take the place. Especially while men lived within and could tumble rocks or trunks from the safety of their walls. Look, there's nothing but grassed slope. Perhaps he was thrown from the wall.'

Simon pulled a grass stem and sucked at the stalk. 'But who'd want to do that?'

'Someone who thought he might have killed Sir Gilbert and wanted revenge? Someone who thought William had seen *them* kill Sir Gilbert and needed to remove an embarrassing witness? Or someone who simply wanted to rob him? Ah, God! Who knows?'

Simon threw away the stem. 'If he was thrown from the walls, someone should have seen. There are so many men-at-arms about this place, surely someone will have noticed?'

'I don't know. At night there are few men about. Only one man is needed up on the walls to keep an eye open. Most guards would be down in the yard or at the gate. If someone wanted to push a man's body over, I doubt it would be very difficult to arrange. What if it was one of the guards?'

'We need to ask Sir Peregrine how many men he posts each night.'

'Before we ask him, I have to tell you what I've discovered,' Baldwin said and told of his talks with Cecily Sherman, her husband and Hick.

The news made Simon eager to speak to Sir Peregrine. They sought him as soon as they entered the castle. 'Guards on the wall?' he echoed. 'I fear that I only have two men out at night: one at the gatehouse, one at the tower. It hardly seems necessary to have a full guard in peacetime.'

'Even with the threats of war?' Simon said.

'Oh, come, Bailiff! If war was declared tomorrow, how long would it take for the King's army to get here? Marching at ten to fifteen miles a day? Long before they arrived, we'd know of their approach. There's no need for guards to protect against that. No, the guards are to prevent enterprising villains from throwing a grapnel over the wall and attempting to steal my Lord's pewter or silver.'

'Not to prevent an assassin making an attempt on Lord Hugh's life?' Baldwin pressed.

'No,' Sir Peregrine answered simply. 'A killer would have to enter the gatehouse itself, through the only door, and then would have to pass by my own picked men-at-arms before breaking down my own door, which I always bar, and then breaking down Lord Hugh's. There's no need to leave a guard outside.'

'From interest, where were you last night, Sir Peregrine?' Baldwin asked.

The man's face hardened. 'I was in the hall for the meal with Lord Hugh, and then did my rounds of the grounds. No one saw me, so if you wish to assume I killed the man and threw him from the wall I would have had plenty of time, but Sir Baldwin, do not dare to accuse me of such a thing!'

'We have also been told that you were out towards the south on the night Sir Gilbert died.'

'By Christ! Do you dare accuse me of murder?'

'I accuse no one. I only ask where you were and what you did.'

'I had my reasons for going for a ride. That's all you need know. I am no murderer.'

'Not when you think that the kingdom's future could depend upon one man's death?'

After Baldwin's softly spoken words the tension was dangerous. Sir Peregrine stood as though frozen, so furious he daren't move lest his hand grab his sword. Simon stepped back while the other two stared at each other. Before either could speak and hasten their descent into open battle, Simon cleared his throat and asked if he could go up to the wall to take a look.

Sir Peregrine angrily slammed a fist against his thigh, but nodded. Simon walked between the knights, facing his friend, forcing the two men to break eye-contact. Baldwin nodded curtly and walked to the staircase with him.

They were silent until they reached the walkway. Here Baldwin let his breath gush out in a long sigh. 'I am glad you were there. That was close.'

Simon looked down towards the river far below. 'A nasty drop. You should be careful in case you find Sir Peregrine behind you one dark night.'

Baldwin grunted, standing with his hands on the battlement and peering down with a puzzled frown.

'What is it, Baldwin?' Simon asked.

'What in God's name could William have done or known that made his death necessary?'

Behind them, hidden in the shadows of the staircase, Toker watched and listened with Perkin. Speaking in an undertone, Toker said, 'That bastard knight from Furnshill is too interested in the sailorboy's death.'

'You want me to slip a knife in his back?' Perkin asked seriously, measuring the distance over the yard.

'While the bailiff's there? Don't be bloody stupid! No, we'll leave them alone for now. But I don't want the whoreson to keep asking questions about the place.' He considered. 'I'll follow him tomorrow and see what he gets up to. And then, if he carries on asking about the sailorboy, we'll kill him.'

CHAPTER EIGHTEEN

Jeanne chose not to join them to witness the inquest. She had come all the way to Tiverton with a view to visiting St Giles's Fair, and if her husband now intended questioning a number of people about a possible murder, Jeanne was content to leave him to it. She returned to store the spices in their room, kissed him, and begged that he should not spend too long at the inquest, but when he asked that she should take Edgar with her if she did walk about the Fair, she agreed happily. She knew Edgar was a useful judge of cloths and trinkets.

When about to leave they saw Wat in the yard watching sulkily as Petronilla fed her child watched by another young mother. Wat jumped up at the sight of his mistress and Edgar, and his expression of desperate eagerness made Jeanne relent. She agreed that he and Petronilla should join her, and Petronilla smiled, passing her boy to the other maid and refastening her tunic while Stephen gurgled happily.

The Fair was only a short distance from the castle and they were soon past the toll-booth and in among the shouting, excited populace. Flags fluttered from strings, children walked about with sugar sweets, mothers gripping their hands as they peered from one stall to another; men chewed pies or drank ale; hucksters of all kinds bawled their wares; scruffy dealers offered dubious goods half-visible within baskets or concealed under their coats while shiftily looking about for the watchmen of the Fair's court; and all about them were women and children munching on roasted fowl: thrushes, starlings, fieldfares and larks.

At one meat stall Jeanne allowed her empty stomach to direct her. She selected five honeyed larks for herself and Petronilla at one and a half pennies. A board demanded another one and a half pennies for the 'Fire, paste and trouble' to put them into coffins, and she asked him to put them all into a pie. Wat and Edgar shared three plump pigeons for another twopence-halfpenny.

Jeanne threw occasional glances at her maid. Petronilla appeared to have forgotten her trial of the day before. Fresh-faced, happy, calm, she looked as if she had never imbibed to excess. In comparison Jeanne felt like a doddery old woman; her head was light, her back ached, and someone appeared to have sanded the interior of her eyelids – all because she had sat up half the night with Edgar to make sure Petronilla didn't vomit and suffocate.

Although the Fair was not of the same dimensions as the one at Tavistock, where Jeanne had first met Baldwin, Tiverton had a respectable mix of goods for sale and she was soon immersed in the relative merits of the silks and velvets on offer.

Edgar too eyed the various materials. His wife-to-be was becoming demanding, now that he had put off their wedding day for so long, and a good fur trimming or piece of fine linen might soothe her impatient breast. He wasn't sure, but he was wondering whether she was the right woman for him after all.

He was so used to being a bachelor that the thought of having a woman in his home was daunting – all the more so since he had been granted the opportunity of seeing how a woman could affect a household. Watching Jeanne move through Baldwin's hall and alter tapestries, throwing out all the older and tattier ones, discarding chairs, replacing all Baldwin's comfortable white tunics with brightly coloured cloths made Edgar look askance at the idea of a woman in his life. He wasn't sure he could cope with it.

And there was always the temptation of other women. Edgar had always been attracted, and proved attractive to, women of all kinds. Cristine was a lovely woman – tall, slender, fair, with a caustic wit and an intellect that often made men quail before the lash of her tongue. She made Edgar laugh, and when he was with her, he was happy, but when they were apart, like now, he found himself thinking of other women.

And not only when he was away from Furnshill. He was just as sorely tormented there as well, especially now that Petronilla had come from Throwleigh. She too was tall, slim and fair, and when he looked at her, with her gentle manner and soft speech, he was struck by the difference between her and Cristine. The comparison was not favourable to Cristine.

It was a difficult business and Edgar was swiftly coming to the conclusion that he would be happier if he were to stick to the oath of chastity he had made as a Templar.

Unfortunately, he had sworn his hand to Cristine. He eyed a small selection of furs. Petronilla was roughly the same complexion as Cristine, he reminded himself, and he gauged the colour of the furs against her colouring: red-gold hair and blue eyes – although Cristine's skin was paler than Petronilla's since the tavern-girl spent so many hours indoors.

Catching a glimpse of his expression, Petronilla felt an anxious thrill. Since first meeting Edgar she had felt a warmth in his presence, but after his rescue from the overly-ardent Coroner she had become aware of something stronger – a feeling of security. But she knew it was wrong. Edgar was already betrothed to another woman. Although she was personally quite sure that she would be better for him than some common alehouse wench, she could not escape the fact that she had an illegitimate child.

That fact could make her weep. It made her look as common and foolish as a tavern-girl. Certainly she had always thought it would prevent Edgar from looking at her, but now she was struck with the thought that he might recip-rocate her feelings, and she was aware of a nervousness. Edgar was so worldly-wise and dashing, she was sure that she'd be an embarrassment to him.

She moved nearer to Jeanne as if feeling the need for support. Edgar was an enormously good-looking man, but she daren't encourage him. Unhappily aware that he was watching her, she was also aware of a guilty sympathy for Cristine. Petronilla had lost the father of her baby and felt for any woman who had her man stolen from her; she didn't want to inflict the same suffering on Cristine.

It was while Petronilla was miserably trying to convince herself that she could live contentedly without Edgar that

Jeanne drew their attention to a large bolt of blue velvet. Petronilla and Jeanne fingered it, adding to the grubbiness of the material's edge, but Petronilla was aware only of Edgar standing so close beside her that she could practically feel the heat of his body. His proximity made her shudder with longing.

Avicia Dyne walked through the Fair with a sense of unreality as she took in the noise, the bustle and the cheerful shouting all about her. It seemed incomprehensible to her that people could be capable of enjoying themselves when such an appalling injustice had occurred. To her the death of her brother was so hideous as to blot out any comprehension of pleasure. She saw people laughing and grinning, but all she recognised was the inane gambolling of apes.

Shivering, she wrapped her arms about herself and let her head fall so as to avoid the gaze of anyone else. In her misery she had no wish to meet the expressions of happiness in other people's faces. It would be too painful to see how others remained sublimely unaware of her depression.

When she had almost left the Fair, when she was out at the opposite end of the ground, she heard a voice she recognised. Turning quickly, she caught sight of Andrew Carter standing near an ale stall with a large pot in his hand.

Avicia stared at him. He appeared to be trying to put on a brave face, smiling and giving occasional short laughs as jokes were told about him, but all the time she could see that he wasn't himself. Usually he would be more expansive in his gestures, more emphatic. Today he was jerky, twitching his arms rather than sweeping them about him. His face held a grin, but all the time his eyes darted hither and thither, as if wary that at any moment someone might approach him with unwelcome news, or perhaps an accusation? she wondered.

Acting on impulse, she approached and stood nearby, waiting for him to catch her eye, but he seemed so taken up with the other men about him that he didn't notice her. At last, nerves wound taut as a ship's cable, she shuffled forward the last few steps and tugged at his sleeve.

'What?' He spun around and gave her a gentle smile. 'My dear young thing, what is it?'

'Sir, I would like to speak . . . about your daughter.'

His face went blank, and she saw for an instant the naked emotion behind his eyes. Fear, sadness, guilt all flashed through them, and then he wiped at his brow with a sleeve. 'She's dead,' he said brokenly.

'I know, and the wrong man was killed for it. He was innocent.'

Carter pulled back, his lip curling in revulsion. 'Child, that is all done. I want to hear nothing more about it.'

'But sir, I am sure that the Coroner was responsible!'

Carter suddenly turned and marched off, moving surprisingly swiftly for a man so heavily built. Avicia made as if to follow him, but a friendly voice at her side said, 'No!' and held her elbow. It was a woman.

'Let me go, I have to talk to him! He has to know my brother didn't kill his daughter.'

'Are you Philip's sister?'

'Yes.'

'You poor thing.'

'Who are you? Did you know Phil?'

Felicity nodded and smiled comfortingly. 'Look, take a pot of wine with me and tell me what's so important that you should tell Andrew. I'll let you know whether he'll be interested.'

'You know him?'

Felicity's smile widened, but somehow there was less humour in it as she glanced after the disappearing merchant. 'Oh, yes, I know Master Carter.'

When Baldwin and Simon returned to the yard there was no sign of the castle's gatekeeper, and for safety Simon wanted to walk out to the town. He was unpleasantly convinced that Baldwin was in danger of so enraging Sir Peregrine with his questions that Sir Peregrine could offer him a challenge.

Baldwin was deep in thought but shook his head, instead wandering to a bench and sitting. 'There is something very peculiar about all this.' He counted off the points on his finger. 'The knight, Sir Gilbert, died with his hound – I think the dog died because he chased someone who had watched the camp all day; the same evening or night Philip Dyne was executed by Carter and his brother-in-law Lovecok; the night before, Gilbert was here in town, apparently drinking with Lovecok. We don't know where he was before that.'

'And now there's this third murder with Sir Gilbert's man thrown from the walls.'

'Beaten severely first. And his was the fourth murder, not the third. You forget the girl Dyne was accused of killing.'

'The girl whom Dyne's sister insisted was murdered by someone else.'

'Yes, she said that Joan Carter was murdered by the Coroner,' Baldwin corrected. He glanced across the yard before walking to the room where Sir Gilbert's belongings were stored. Aylmer was still inside, lying with his head resting on his paws, his eyes flying open as they walked in.

'It's all right, Aylmer,' Baldwin said. At Aylmer's side was a dish of biscuits and dried meat. The dog hadn't touched it. Remembering how he had first met the animal, Baldwin commanded, 'Aylmer, feed.'

The dog stood, stretched, and sank his nose into the pan.

While he ate Simon and Baldwin rummaged through the accumulated belongings of Sir Gilbert and William. There was nothing much of value, for obviously men who went on a long journey wouldn't carry spare baggage, and with the country in its present state of turmoil there was no point in bringing expensive goods. They found little: three shirts of decent linen, tunics, some mail of fine blued steel, lightly rusted, Sir Gilbert's sword and dagger-sheath, with the belt and spurs of his knighthood, and shoes and boots, all well worn. There were a few coins in a purse, but nothing significant. Then at the bottom of his pack they found the crucifix and key that had been about Sir Gilbert's neck.

'Bugger-all money,' Simon said suddenly.

His tone of voice made Baldwin shoot him a look. 'So?'

'Did the Templar have no idea of travel?'

'Sir Gilbert would have had experience of much longer journeys.'

'Was he expecting to remain here?' Simon asked.

'Not if he was a messenger as everyone appears to believe.'

'Then how was he going to get back to his master?' Simon demanded, holding out the handful of coins. 'With this he'd not have had enough to get to Exeter.'

'No,' Baldwin breathed. He picked up the little key again and studied it.

'What is it?'

'This looks rather like some of the keys I used to see . . .' Even though his friend knew about his past, Baldwin found it hard to talk of his life with the Order. Yet this key was very like those he had seen in some preceptories for opening chests. English-made metalwork tended to be functional, but this looked well-made, with intricate patterns carved upon the shaft and finger plate. Turning it in his hands, he felt sure it was Templar.

There was an old Templar preceptory nearby – one which Sir Gilbert had known, Baldwin recalled, and meditatively tapped his teeth with the key.

'William was the only man who could confirm the details about what happened to Sir Gilbert,' Simon said quietly. He had moved to the door and stood leaning against the jamb with his arms crossed. 'If Carter and Lovecok had lied in any way, William might have tried to get a bribe to keep quiet. Perhaps they didn't like his demands.'

'There's no proof of any of that,' Baldwin said. 'But I certainly find it easier to believe in the two men ambushing Sir Gilbert, one holding him while the other stabbed him in the back. And since the gravedigger says that Lovecok knew Sir Gilbert, it may be useful to find out *how* they knew each other.'

He threw the key back onto the pile of William's belongings. 'Let us question Lovecok then. I want to find out what he was doing speaking to Sir Gilbert the day before his murder. I want to know if he had a motive to kill the knight. Although . . .' he frowned with confusion '. . . although it sounded more as though the two were old friends and comrades. And why should a man kill his friend?'

*   *   *

Andrew Carter hurried through the crowds until he reached the far edge of the fairground; for a moment he stood breathing heavily, staring back the way he had come.

Thank God the whining bitch was out of sight! He was safe from her. With an effort he controlled his breathing and tried to stop his heart from racing. Her appearance had given him a massive shock when she said who she was, and as for what she was saying . . . about Philip being innocent, the last thing Andrew Carter wanted was for the townspeople to hear that Philip Dyne had been wrongly killed!

He strode off to the toll-booth and went past it, marching steadily and firmly until he got to the door of his own house, and there he slammed the door closed with a firmness that rattled the plates on his sideboard.

'Sir?' His maid Rose, a thin, short girl of some fourteen years, stood nervously in the screens passage wiping her hands on her apron.

'Fetch me a quart of wine,' he demanded and tramped through to his hall. There he dropped into his chair near the fire and drummed his fingers on the arm until the maidservant returned, her face flushed with anxiety at the appearance of her master.

'Here, sir.'

'Put it down, then!' he snarled, pointing at the table at his side.

She did as commanded, then stood back downcast, not daring to meet his gaze.

Eyeing her, he sipped his wine. It was good, a fine flavoured drink. Gradually he felt his foul temper fade under its influence. By the time he had drunk the first pint, life appeared in a more pleasant light. True, that woman, Dyne's sister, could make life troublesome, but that was no reason why he should be concerned. He had good friends. If the worst came to the worst, he could humour her for a while and warn Harlewin that she had accused him of Joan's murder.

There was no need to worry, really, Andrew thought to himself. Rose was still standing before him, her head hanging. She really was a pretty little thing, he thought with satisfaction; in every way suited to his tastes. He smiled and set his cup down on the table again. 'Come here,' he said, and Rose looked up once, wildly, as though thinking of running away, but then she dropped her head submissively and obeyed.

Entering the tavern, Avicia blinked against the smoke. The place was ancient and had no chimney, just a baked patch of earth in the middle of the floor where a few logs glowed, surrounded by small rocks to stop the rushes being kicked in and starting a fire.

This wasn't a place she'd been to before, and as soon as she walked in from the road she winced: it stank of sweat, piss and puke. At the fire a slatternly woman crouched, rat's tails of hair dangling before her and concealing her face, stirring a pot that seemed to contain a thin broth. All about her men lounged on benches, some women draped near them, and another figure lay comatose near a wall. It was dark, foul, and noisome.

'This a new girl?' a man asked Felicity, and reached out to touch Avicia's arm as if to test the smoothness of her skin.

'Keep your hands off!' Felicity snarled and slapped his hand away. 'Does she look like a slut? She's a lady, so leave off.' She led the shrinking woman over to a table and sat her down. 'Now tell me all about it.'

Slowly Avicia ran through her tale. The Coroner had been having an affair for some months with Mistress Sherman, and . . .

'How do you know that?'

Avicia blinked. 'What, about him and Cecily Sherman? It's been going on for ages.'

'And you work for the Coroner?'

'No, I work for John Sherman. It was the only way that Phil and I could keep together when our parents died. Phil got me the job. At least Sherman doesn't fondle me when his wife's not looking.'

'The Coroner would?'

'You bet! He's a right lecherous goat.'

'But you've heard he's tupping Sherman's wife?'

'Yes. I saw them together once when I went into the hall, and heard them talking about meeting.'

'Where do they meet? In Sherman's house?'

'No,' Avicia laughed, 'they wouldn't dare – not with John Sherman's temper. No, they go to a place he part-owns out beyond Withleigh, a mill. The miller wouldn't dare complain, not if he wants to keep his post there.'

'I see,' Felicity breathed.

'*He* murdered Joan Carter. That's why he told my Philip to claim sanctuary and abjure, so that he could see to it that Philip was seen to confess, and then had him chased down and killed. That's what I have to tell Andrew Carter.'

'How could he admit to believing you? That would make your brother's death a mortal sin.'

'It wasn't his fault – he was lied to. Anyway, Andrew would want to see the man who killed his daughter receive justice!'

'She wasn't *his* daughter.'

'But . . .'

'Oh, I know he described her as his, but she was the daughter of Matilda and her first husband. The husband died, and that's when Matilda married Andrew, when they came down here from somewhere up north. When she first came back here with Andrew, you could hardly understand a word she said! My, her accent was strong.'

'So, you think he wouldn't want to avenge her?'

Avicia's voice was almost a wail of despair. Felicity put a hand over hers and smiled. 'I bet we can think of something.' Her eyes widened. 'What about speaking to his wife, to Joan Carter's mother? Maybe she can help persuade him?'

'Do you think she would listen when he wouldn't?' Avicia asked doubtfully.

Felicity ignored her. There was no point going today, not with the feast at the castle. Everyone, including Andrew and Matilda, would be going there. But tomorrow, that was a different matter.

'Of course she'll listen. She was Joan's mother, wasn't she?'

CHAPTER NINETEEN

Baldwin and Simon spoke to an elderly steward at the castle who told them that Nicholas Lovecok was staying with his brother-in-law Andrew Carter and gave them directions on how to get there.

Carter's house was in a part of the town Simon had never visited before, to the north eastern side. Like many towns, there were large areas of Tiverton which were very poor and shabby, and the two men had to pass through miserable quarters, past hovels which lacked doors and windows, with piles of human excrement lying in the shallow gutter that was the only drain, while in the shadows they saw rats scuttle. Women stood and murmured quietly as the two approached, only to fall silent, watching Simon and Baldwin with glittering eyes as if the men were dangerous killers or representatives from a hated lord.

'They don't seem to like us,' Simon grunted.

'An obvious comment – but I can't argue with its accuracy.'

'The thing that impresses me is how they always appear so clean,' Simon said, ignoring his friend's sarcasm.

'It astonishes me, too. When you look at the state of the road here, or the quality of the houses, I can never understand how they manage to get their shirts white or remove the stains from their skirts.'

Simon dodged a small pile of faeces and winced as a toddler walked through it giggling fruitily. The bailiff turned away and saw gladly that they were almost at the edge of the poor area. Ahead of them the sunlight glinted off clean cobbles and fresh-looking limewashed walls. The maidservants here looked more wholesome than the women in the poor alleys and byways.

To Simon it felt as if they were leaving an area of degradation and sickness. There was a miasma, a foul air, about it which was absent in the more expensive parts. It was a relief to walk along the clean cobbled road, with a goodsized gutter fed by a spring which washed away all muck before it could accumulate.

The odours were better too. Here an occasional dog rose or honeysuckle clung to the wall of a house, while the scent of drying herbs was all about them, as was the smell of cooking meats as people prepared meals. Only a few places held the stench of dried urine where a man had pissed against a house's wall, or the foul odour of a dog's defecation in the shadow of a building, and Simon only saw two corpses, one of a dog, quite fresh, and one of a cat, very far gone and disgusting in putrefaction.

They were soon at the merchant's house and Baldwin rapped smartly on the wooden door. There came a bellow from inside, a pattering of feet, and soon a girl was in the doorway. A pretty maiden, Simon thought; fourteen or fifteen years old, with a hanging head and cap awry, she gave him the impression of shame. Her embarrassment made him assume they had interrupted her in some carnal pursuit, and he peered over her shoulder expecting to see a bottler or steward tying his hose in the background, but there was no one.

Baldwin appeared to notice nothing amiss. 'Is Master Nicholas Lovecok here? We were told he was staying here with your master.'

'No, sir,' she said, and her voice was small and faraway. 'He's not here yet; usually he visits a tavern on his way back from the castle.'

'What of your master? We should speak to him as well.'

There was a call from the hall, and Simon was sure he saw a hunted terror in the girl's eye as she listened. Then, standing back a little, she let the two men enter.

Sir Peregrine was in the castle's yard when Jeanne and her small entourage returned. He smiled and bowed, but unenthusiastically. Wherever he looked, he seemed to see women. His eyes followed Petronilla, who cooed with evident delight as she gathered up Stephen. Sir Peregrine felt a stab of jealousy. 'Was the Fair to your liking, my Lady?'

Jeanne waved a hand at the overladen Edgar and Wat. 'I think you can tell that for yourself, Sir Peregrine!'

Seeing Petronilla hurry back to save a bolt of cloth tipping from Wat's arms into the dirt, Sir Peregrine gave a dry chuckle. 'It looks as though your child is carrying as much as he can.'

'*Child?*' Wat demanded, glowering.

Quickly Jeanne moved in front of him to conceal his furious scowl. 'Yes, I like to make the servants work for their keep, rather than letting them get slack so they have to be beaten.' This last was spoken directly to Wat, but in a moment she was facing Sir Peregrine once more. 'Have you seen my husband? Is the inquest over yet?'

'We have not held the inquest as yet. Too many of the jury are involved in the Fair, and Harlewin thought it would be best to wait until the Fair is over. Your husband went out, I believe. Perhaps he went to seek you?'

'If he did, he failed,' Jeanne observed with a faintly caustic tone to her voice. She would have liked Baldwin to have joined her. It was many months since they had attended a fair together. Ah well, she thought, he never liked wandering around stalls. And maybe he'd gone to try to find her and had missed her in the crowds. It would have been all too easy to miss each other in the hectic crush.

'No doubt he will soon return,' she said, motioning to her servants to take the stuffs up to her room and watching them closely until they had disappeared through the door to the hall. She would persuade Baldwin to join her at the Fair tomorrow.

'I have no doubt,' Sir Peregrine said.

'Then good day for now. I shall see you at the meal,' Jeanne said and walked off to follow after the others. At the top of the stairs she happened to glance back. Sir Peregrine was still standing in the yard, looking sad and pensive, and Jeanne felt a burst of sympathy for him. She had lost a husband, but her man had been a bully and it was a source of delight to her that God had seen fit to permit her to marry Baldwin. But Sir Peregrine had found his ideal mate and lost her in childbirth. That was an ironic twist of fate.

As she watched she saw Toker enter the gateway, nod to the porter, and go up to Sir Peregrine, looking about him all the while. He noticed Jeanne and gave her a sneering nod. She walked indoors with a feeling of disquiet. There was something cruel and unpleasant in Toker's face.

Later she would remember that moment.

Andrew did not rise – he saw no need to. These two weren't officials in this town and had no authority to investigate any matters. Waving to a couple of chairs, he took a gulp of wine and belched.

'We were hoping to find your brother-in-law,' Baldwin said, sitting.

'He's not here. What did you want to see him about?'

'Perhaps we should save that until we have a chance to speak to him.'

'But while we're here,' Simon said, 'we have a few questions for you about the death of the felon.'

'Dyne? The bastard was lucky!' Andrew said, eyeing Simon with distaste and gesturing again to an empty seat. Simon ignored his invitation and remained standing, arms folded.

Baldwin sniffed. 'He was severely beaten and executed – and so was another man last night.'

'Another?' Andrew looked at him with surprise. 'Who?'

'William, Sir Gilbert's servant. It seems most strange that the knight's own servant, a man who could have seen something on the night that Sir Gilbert died, should now himself be dead.'

'A coincidence, surely. Where did he die?'

'We found his body in the river. But the question has to be, *did* he see something incriminating on the night of Sir Gilbert's murder, or was he killed for another reason? And there are rumours . . .'

'In a town like this there are always rumours.'

'Really? Because, you see, there are stories that Dyne was innocent.'

Andrew dropped his cup. It shattered on the floor, shards of pottery bouncing in all directions, but he didn't notice. 'What? Do you mean – but they must be inventing it. It's peasants talking . . . blasted fools and cretins the lot of them! What do they know?'

'Often rather more than we do,' Baldwin murmured.

'Well, if he was innocent, who killed my daughter? And why did he confess, eh? Answer me that!'

'There have been accusations,' Simon said shortly.

Andrew shot a look at the bailiff. 'What sort of accusations?'

'You need not concern yourself with them,' Baldwin said. 'But we would like to check some points with you about last night. Where were you?'

'Most of the time in here, why?' His face hardened. 'Do you mean to accuse me of murdering this servant? By God, if that's what you mean, I'll . . .'

Baldwin had been leaning back contemplating the merchant, but now he sat forward and his eyes glittered with near-anger. 'Stop ranting, man! If you want to cause people to suspect you, you're going the right way about it.'

'You dare to come in here and accuse me of . . .'

'We are attempting to see who was *not* involved. However, you have to admit that from your point of view it would be best to clear yourself as quickly as possible.'

'Me? What do you mean?' Carter blustered.

'Simply this,' Baldwin rasped coldly. 'Sir Gilbert was murdered, and the only man who could have seen who did it is also now silenced. At the same time, we have discovered that the servant and his master had not enough money to rent a room here in Tiverton, much less make their journey back to London. There are some who might consider that they were robbed.'

Andrew's face was a picture of astonishment. 'Robbed, you say? What the hell would *I* want to rob them for? I've got plenty of cash of my own, for God's sake.'

'Where were you last night?'

'I went out to a tavern for a while, but most of the time I was here.'

'Alone?' Simon snapped.

'Why . . . no.'

'Who was with you?'

'My maid.' He broke off and bellowed, '*Rose!*'

It took only a moment for the girl who had opened the door to hurry in. Baldwin eyed her with interest, convinced that she must have been listening at the screens.

'Rose, tell these men where I was last night.'

She stared at the ground. 'My master was with me. In his bed.'

Simon shot the merchant a quick look. The bailiff was certain he saw a small smile of self-satisfaction in the man's eyes. Simon looked down at his feet with a small frown. Some men would happily take advantage of any of the women in their households, but to deflower a child as young as Rose seemed almost barbaric.

'For how long?' Baldwin asked.

'For most of the night,' she said slowly. 'From before dark to early morning. Then I had to rise to get on with my work.'

'Thank you, child,' Baldwin said, and she turned hurriedly and walked out.

'You see?' Andrew said smugly. 'Was with her all night.' His expression changed swiftly, and he licked his lips as he gazed from one to the other. 'But there's no need to talk about this, is there? I don't want my wife to find out, or—'

'Or your brother-in-law?' Simon asked sharply. 'You mean to tell me you spent your time with your maid when your wife's brother was here?'

'He wasn't about last night.' He stopped, a hand flying to his mouth as he realised the implication of his words.

'Really?' said Baldwin smoothly. 'And I wonder where he would have been, then?'

'I don't know. Up at the castle, probably. He delivers much of the wine to my Lord Hugh.'

'When did he get back?'

'Not until late.'

'Where did your wife think you were?' Simon asked.

'My wife and I were married because it was convenient. It was useful for me and useful for Nicholas. That doesn't mean I have to enjoy sleeping with her.'

'She knows you sleep with her maids?'

'I have not slept in the same room as her for years. She likes her bed in the front of the house, where she can look out over the road. Her chamber is above the hall here. I like mine at the back, where it's a bit quieter. Nicholas sleeps here in the hall like any guest.'

'And the servants?'

'Most are at the back. There's a small hall for them all out there.'

'And each night you call Rose to your room?'

'She is paid well for her services,' Andrew stated, and there was a small smile on his round face again as he realised what Simon and Baldwin were thinking: they were jealous of him! Well, and so might they be. With girls like Rose in his household Andrew was jealous of no man. 'She is very experienced, you know,' he began confidentially. 'She . . .'

'I have no wish to listen to your vulgar bragging about how you have raped your servants,' Baldwin interrupted sharply. 'Suffice it to say that I think it a disgrace that a man should so forget his common humanity as to take a girl of that age to his bed.'

Andrew sank back in his chair with a sneer.

'But,' Baldwin continued, 'I do want to hear about your brother-in-law. You say he returned late. How do you know, if your room is at the back of the house? If he slept here in the hall, he'd have come in through the front door, wouldn't he?'

'No, he came in through a door at the back, in the alley that runs behind the house. I heard the man who guards the gate asking who was there and opening it.'

'Would that have been towards the middle of the night or later?'

'About the middle of the night. It was black as pitch outside.'

'When you executed Dyne, were you together with Nicholas all the time?'

'No. We separated to find the man.'

'Who found him?'

'Me.'

'Why did you beat him so harshly?'

'He had a knife. I had to beat him to make him surrender. Nick arrived later. Why?'

'Yet you told the Coroner that you knocked his dagger away with ease,' Baldwin reminded him. 'The night before you found the felon and killed him, were you with your brother then?'

Andrew frowned with the effort of recollection. 'No, I don't think so . . . *No*, I was here. That's right. I'd been with him for much of the day, and we had food prepared, but he sent a ragamuffin brat to us to say that he had been detained at the castle and would feed himself there or at a tavern.'

'What time was he back?'

'Again, it was after I had gone to my chamber,' Andrew said dismissively. 'And Rose was competent to remove any interest I might have had in affairs outside.'

'But it was late?'

'Oh, I suppose. Yes, he would have been quite late home.'

'There is one more thing. We heard at the inquest that there was a woman dressed in green at the scene. Do you know who that was?'

'No. I've no idea,' he said coldly.

'Husband, there is no need to lie for me.'

In the doorway stood Matilda. Baldwin thought her suffering was almost tangible. She was as pale as a corpse, with bright eyes that spoke of plentiful weeping.

Andrew stood. 'My dear, you shouldn't be up. Why not return to your bed and rest?'

To Simon he sounded unnecessarily solicitous, but then the bailiff remembered the tenor of their conversation and realised that Andrew was terrified that his wife might have overheard his confession of adultery with his maids.

Matilda waved aside his concerns. 'You wanted to know who it was in the woods, Keeper? Well, it was me. I was there to try to kill that hideous man Dyne. I wanted revenge.' She crossed the floor and took her husband's arm, a cool, elegant woman with the pallor of mourning lying heavily upon her.

Baldwin studied her with interest. 'You must have been furious when you heard that Dyne was to be exiled.'

'Why should he live when he killed my daughter? The evil wretch deserved his end.'

'My wife had nothing to do with his death,' Andrew said heavily. 'She didn't see what happened. We sent her home first.'

'You went?' Baldwin asked her, ignoring Andrew.

She met his gaze. 'No, of course not! I waited in the woods out of sight. I saw it all.'

Simon noticed Andrew's face at this point. The man had gone quite pale.

Matilda continued, 'He received a fitting death; I was satisfied. It was the least I could do for Joan and for her father.'

Baldwin glanced at her, then her husband. 'She wasn't *your* daughter, Carter?'

'No.'

Matilda smiled faintly. 'Joan was the daughter of my first husband. I was widowed. That was why Nicholas and I came here. And here I met Andrew.'

'I am surprised your brother could bring his whole business down here. Why did you not remain with him at your old home?'

'At Witham?' The name seemed to make her realise she had said too much. She appeared suddenly flustered, making a short angry gesture with a hand. 'Nicholas was living with my husband and I. When my husband died we both chose to leave. That is all.'

'Please, go on.' Baldwin nodded encouragingly. Simon, having noticed the woman's apparent slip and swift recovery, glanced at his friend but could see only eager interest in Baldwin's eyes. It was the name she had mentioned, he was sure.

Matilda looked up at her husband's face with pride. 'I went off after Dyne with every intention of killing him, but then I saw my man here. Dyne was in the road at the time. When Andrew rode off without killing the wretch I realised that he and my brother were going to lay in ambush farther along the road. I decided to follow Dyne myself, both to make sure that he didn't escape back to Tiverton, but also in order that I could see his death.'

She paused but Baldwin motioned to her to continue.

'It was a while before it became dark and then I saw the evil creature stop dead in the road. Ahead of him there was smoke rising from a bowl in the ground near the river.'

'That would be where Sir Gilbert had camped,' Simon noted.

'Perhaps. I thought – and I reckon Dyne thought – that it was an ambush. He darted into the trees. Fearing he might escape, I turned my horse in as well, meaning to track him, but with the noise my horse made, I couldn't hear a thing. Not until I heard an awful row: a man riding full tilt through the undergrowth. I'm afraid I screamed with fear. One hears such horrible stories about outlaws.'

'Who was it?'

'I know it sounds silly, but it was Sir Peregrine. He was making off back towards the northern road, back towards Tiverton.'

'Ah yes. That would be the road to Withleigh,' Baldwin confirmed. The same road which Harlewin and Cecily Sherman would have taken, he reminded himself.

'Then Nicholas my brother heard me. He suddenly appeared on my right, horrified to find me there. He told me to return home.'

'But you didn't?' Baldwin pressed.

She shook her head. 'I knew my husband and brother were going to make Dyne pay for his crime but I had to witness it.'

'What exactly did you see?' Baldwin asked. Andrew opened his mouth as if to speak but Baldwin silenced him with a cutting gesture of his hand.

She glanced down. 'I saw my husband ride off one way, my brother the other. I followed Nicholas at a distance. I don't know how long we went back and forth in the woods. It was cold and I felt miserable, but determined to see whatever I could. And then Nicholas came to an open space and went through it to the other side. I heard a dog bark, then a scream. It wasn't Andrew, and I was convinced it was Dyne. I set off towards it and when I came to a clearing I saw Andrew kicking the boy on the ground.'

Baldwin glanced at Andrew. He had gone white as if recalling the horror of the evening. Baldwin couldn't condemn the man for killing the lad in revenge. Anyone would have done the same.

Andrew met his gaze. 'He was going to run. I had to beat him to keep him there. Then I tied him up and waited for Nick.'

'It's true,' Matilda confirmed. 'I stayed there and watched. Dyne begged to be released, but Andrew hit him over the head and Dyne fell over. Then Nick arrived. He grabbed the boy, held his head back and made sure it was Dyne, then made him kneel, holding his arms behind him, and he screamed as Andrew swung his sword . . . It was over in a moment.'

She was silent, grasping her husband's arm for support. Baldwin could see that she was exhausted, worn down by the grim events of her daughter's death and the aftermath.

His voice was more gentle. 'Did you see anyone else in the woods or along the road?'

'Yes. After I turned back, I saw Father Abraham on his way to comfort Father Benedict at Templeton. When I had passed him I heard another horse and hid in the trees. It was far from the nearest house and I didn't want to be caught by a footpad.'

'Who was it?'

'John Sherman, and what a filthy mood he was in! Swearing about his wife, calling her all kinds of names.'

'Thank you,' Baldwin said and bowed. 'I am sorry to have asked you to recall these sad events, my Lady.'

'It was necessary.'

'Yes.' Baldwin walked to the door, but before he left the room, he turned to face her once more. 'When did your brother leave the Templars?'

A hand went to her throat and she staggered back as if struck. 'My brother? He . . . He was no Templar. What makes you say that?'

'Nothing, my Lady. Just a guess,' Baldwin said suavely, and left.

CHAPTER TWENTY

Baldwin and Simon were up at the battlements once more, peering over at the dreadful sheer fall down to the river.

'Nicholas was a Templar, you think?' Simon asked at last. His friend's comment had surprised him as much as Matilda Carter.

'Perhaps,' Baldwin said. 'But for now, I want to concentrate on William the Small. I am convinced that he died because of his master, for some reason.'

'You think the same man killed him as murdered Sir Gilbert?'

'I don't know. What if Sir Gilbert was carrying something? A secret that could help him take Lord Hugh to the Despensers' side, for example. His servant might have heard of it. There are several men who might wish to silence someone like that.'

'I think it's most likely that Carter and Lovecok killed Sir Gilbert. There were two of them there. Maybe they killed him in the dark and only later realised they'd got the wrong man; then William came along. They left him alone, but killed him later to silence him.'

'Why didn't they kill William at the same time as his master, then?' Baldwin asked, turning to walk back to the yard itself where Jeanne waited. 'Why leave him for so long, giving him ample time to blab to all who wished to listen? No, I can't think that's right.'

'By the same token,' Simon pointed, 'why should you think that someone else was involved? I see no reason to think anyone else was there. It was probably a mistake in the dark, maybe followed by an attempt at blackmail by William.'

Baldwin shook his head. The more he thought about it the more certain he grew. 'There is nothing for certain,' he said, 'but I tend to the view that Sir Gilbert knew something or carried something that could be useful to someone else, or might possibly be harmful to the alliance against the Despensers. An ambassador will always bring something – a letter, information, money . . . I reckon he was killed for it – and I think William found out about it.'

'And was killed after being tortured for his secret?'

'It would make sense,' Baldwin said. 'Murdered to keep his mouth shut and tossed over the wall like a sack of manure.'

'We should question all the servants and men-at-arms in the place,' Simon said, looking about him gloomily, considering how many men lived within the castle's walls.

'Yes, but not yet. It is more important to find out who killed Sir Gilbert, and why. When we know what it was he had, we can see whether it would justify two murders. Then we may discover whether the two deaths were connected or not.'

* * *

Toker watched them stride to the hall's entrance, a wave of cold anger breaking over him. Why were these two men still thinking about the shitty sailorman? Small was dead. It was none of their business who did it or why. Why did they insist on investigating things that were none of their business?

He was still there when Owen came out of the dark carrying a large pot of ale. Toker took it and drank deeply. 'That knight from Furnshill wants to find out who killed the man here.'

'So?' Owen shrugged.

Toker grabbed him by the shirt and pulled him forward. The smaller man stumbled as he met Toker's furious stare. 'Don't speak like that to me, you little bastard, not unless you want me to cut out your tongue! The knight's getting too interested in our business, right? I think we'll have to stop him before he learns too much.'

Sir Peregrine sat in his small room above the gatehouse and stared at the fire. He had attended Evensong with Lord Hugh in the small chapel in the solar block, a privilege granted only to those men Lord Hugh trusted. Now he waited while his master prepared for the feast.

But all the time his mind wandered over the deaths. First Sir Gilbert and now William were dead, and Sir Baldwin and his friend appeared to have an unhealthy interest in both cases. It was curious that a man should have so much interest in their deaths but Sir Peregrine had a shrewd idea that Baldwin and Simon were trying to find out more about Sir Gilbert's visit to Tiverton. Sir Peregrine slammed one fist into the other. The god-damned knight from Crediton was too persistent with this constant enquiring after people;

especially when he had the temerity to ask Sir Peregrine where he had been when the servant died. It was an insult.

If only Emily hadn't died. His thoughts should be more clear and logical, but each time he tried to consider what course to take, her face returned to haunt him.

Sir Baldwin's determination was not normal. It wasn't the behaviour of a man who was visiting his lord. Such a one should be spending his time demonstrating his courtesy with the women and his peers among the guests, not traipsing over the town looking for clues in a murder hunt when the Coroner had already declared that there was *no murder!* And in the case of the servant last night, that was probably just a cut-purse trying his luck with a drunk who retaliated and paid the price. A dead servant was hardly a fit subject for Sir Baldwin's enquiry. It was the duty of the jury to provide clues to the Coroner in a matter of suspicious death, their duty to accuse the man they thought guilty, not that of an impoverished Keeper of the King's Peace from a benighted town like Crediton.

Impoverished – the word hung in his mind like a flag fluttering and he recalled his thoughts of the previous day.

If a man thought there could be gold in an investigation, he would be tempted. There was nothing to indicate that Sir Gilbert had money on him – yet Sir Gilbert was the emissary of the Despensers. He should have brought a present, a sweetener, for Lord Hugh if he wanted the lord's influence, so where was it? Sir Peregrine bit at his lip. If it wasn't money, could there be something worth money – a note from the Despenser family which made dangerous offers? Such a letter could be useful, especially if it promised attractive inducements to Lord Hugh.

The last thing Sir Peregrine wanted was for a letter to be found which promised something worthwhile after Sir

Peregrine had spent all his efforts persuading Lord Hugh that the Despensers were best left alone, and that Lord Hugh should bend his support towards the Marcher Lords; if his work so far should be ruined, his credibility as an adviser would be wrecked. Not only that, his whole position in the castle could be demeaned. If Lord Hugh were to go over to them, he'd hardly be likely to entrust the guardianship of his gate to the very person who had told him never to go near the Despensers. He would send Sir Peregrine away, to a place like his holdings down towards the Cornish border.

With a shudder, Sir Peregrine called the place to mind. Bleak was a word which scarcely did the area justice.

Hearing steps above him, he rolled his eyes. It must be time for the meal. Cursing softly under his breath, Sir Peregrine strode to his washstand and rubbed soap into his face and neck, rinsing and then drying himself on a towel, trying to calm the desperate beating of his heart.

In the staircase he met his lord coming down, two men with him, his wife a few paces behind.

'Ah, Sir Peregrine. Are you ready to eat your fill and beyond? Come. Let's feast for Saint Giles.'

Leading his wife into the great hall, Baldwin was struck by its magnificence. It soared above, a massive room hung with flags and tapestries to show the importance of the lord who lived here. Even he, a man who had visited some of the greatest halls in Christendom, was struck by its splendour, a splendour enhanced by the rich clothing of the people within.

Entering from the screens passage, he was momentarily deafened: music played above him in the gallery and people were trying to chatter over it, creating a racket that made him wince. Then his wife gave his hand a little pressure and he became acclimatised.

A short time later Lord Hugh entered with Sir Peregrine and a sense of expectation filled the room as the lord walked slowly to his table and sat. Servants appeared, young squires and heralds with towels over their left arms and about their necks, carrying large cloths. As Lord Hugh sat, these men swiftly spread cloths over the table in front of him, first one over the edge facing the hall, then a second over the tabletop, smoothing them out carefully until not a wrinkle could be seen.

The guests took their seats, those who were unsure being directed by young squires, and then more cloths were brought in, these not so fine as that of the lord, and when all were seated Baldwin was pleased to find that he was given a good trencher of bread. He wasn't keen on the modern fad for wooden platters. They didn't soak up so much juice, and couldn't be used to feed the poor. A napkin was placed at his side, and he pulled his spoon from his wallet ready to eat.

Now the salt was brought to the top table and placed directly before Lord Hugh, a massive cellar in the shape of a crouching dog made from cunningly fashioned silver. The carver opened the salt and delicately used his knife to spread a little on his lord's trencher. Baldwin watched while Lord Hugh's knife and bread were both kissed and wiped clean by his cupbearer to *assay* them, to prove that no poison had been spread on them, and then the cupbearer tasted the water before Lord Hugh washed his hands.

As soon as he was done the food was brought in.

This first course was not too fearsome. Five dishes of meat, five with birds, one of fish and several pastries. There was little here that was designed to cause anxiety, but still Baldwin, whose stomach was queasy in the presence of heavily spiced foods, peered at the offerings with anxiety, only to be overcome with relief. All the dishes appeared to have only roasted or boiled meats.

He ate with gusto. It felt like an age since his last meal, and he consumed thrushes smothered in cinnamon, some snipe and a slice or two of swan.

While he ate he gazed about him. He was seated against one wall, while on his right-hand side was the dais with Lord Hugh. Near Lord Hugh was Sir Peregrine, and Baldwin noticed that Simon was almost opposite. When he caught Baldwin's eye, he raised his pot in a toast, his mouth filled, and slurped happily.

'I think Simon will regret his drinking tomorrow,' Jeanne said thinly.

'He has never learned that the way to avoid a foul head is to avoid drinking too much,' Baldwin agreed, sipping at his own drink again. After walking about the town he was desperately thirsty. 'I have always been moderate.'

'I would have expected him to associate the two by now: quarts of wine followed by a morning head that, if it were to fall off, would only be a blessed relief.'

'Simon resolutely denies that the two are connected in any way. He believes always that it is the quality of the food that causes his hangovers. I have seen him consume ale, then wine, then mead, and when his head seemed to labour under the impact of sixteen hammers all together the next morning, he put the blame squarely onto a single bad egg that he ate.'

Jeanne chuckled. As they spoke the servants had darted about the room again, and now the first course was removed and the subtlety was brought in, a splendid ornament of whole marchpane, which the cook had managed to fashion into the image of a hind.

'What is that?' Jeanne asked.

'If I remember my history correctly, St Giles was hit by an arrow from a king when the king was hunting a hind. He fired at her, but she took refuge with the saint and the arrow struck the saint instead. I think the cook has done his best to remember that event.'

Jeanne watched greedily as the hind was cut into pieces, and took hers with delight. She always had a very sweet tooth, and loved the almond flavour of the marchpane.

To her the sight of the next course was a pleasure. The same was not true for Baldwin. Servants brought in dishes filled with a rich mixture of pounded and minced, battered and coloured, beherbed and spiced foods. One concoction of blue and green pastes quartered in a large bowl gave him particular cause for concern and he found it difficult to draw his eyes away from it, emptying his wine with a gulp. A bottler refilled it.

Jeanne nudged him. 'What is it?' he demanded, taking another nervous gulp of wine.

'Sir Peregrine seems hardly able to keep his eyes from you.'

'Hmm? Maybe he has a sense of humour and expects me to explode,' he grumbled.

'I don't think so,' she said. Even as she spoke a servant entered and ran to Sir Peregrine. He listened, his eyes on his trencher, and then nodded. The servant hurried across the room to Harlewin le Poter and whispered in his ear. While Jeanne watched, Harlewin rose, bowed to Sir Peregrine, walked to Lord Hugh, bowed again and shrugged expansively in apology.

'My lord, I fear duty . . .'

Lord Hugh waved a courteous hand. 'Of course, we must all be obedient to our responsibilities, mustn't we?'

With another low bow, Harlewin turned and marched from the room, head high and proud.

Jeanne would have thought nothing of it, but then she glanced back at Sir Peregrine, and this time she saw he wasn't looking at her husband. Following the line of his eyes, she saw he was staring at another man.

'Yes?' Baldwin asked, feeling in his mouth for a fishbone. He had hoped the fish pie would be safe from spices, but it had been filled with so much mace he couldn't detect the fish except by the large quantities of bones.

'Look.'

He saw John Sherman half rise, lick his lips, shoot a look at the high table, and make as if to get up. Sir Peregrine muttered to a servant and sent him to Sherman. Sherman wanted to leave, but he sat back with a bad grace, his attention fixed upon the door through which Harlewin had just left.

At the far side of the hall, Father Abraham had seen the Coroner go and the sight made his lip curl disdainfully. He hadn't missed the absence of Cecily Sherman and he guessed shrewdly that the Coroner was off to his harlot.

It was repellent the way the woman flaunted herself like a bitch on heat. She flirted with every man she came across – unless her husband was in the room, in which case she was a little more circumspect – but generally she was a shameless whoring wench who deserved to be exposed for her adultery.

Sherman had gone quite pale. Father Abraham sneered at him, shaking his head. If the priest had been married to a bitch like Cecily Sherman, he would have left her and taken the tonsure for escape, and even if he hadn't the strength for that, he would have thrashed the devils from her.

Yet her husband made no move to stop her affair. The priest wondered at that for a moment. Was it because Sherman was worried that she knew something, that she could harm him if he beat her? There were rumours about his business – that he was less than generous in his measures, but would that be reason enough for him to leave her alone?

Father Abraham doubted it, but he eyed the merchant with interest for the rest of the meal, wondering why a man should allow himself to be so publicly cuckolded.

It was much later that Toker saw the mass of guests leave the hall.

He knew the routine of events like this perfectly well. It was the same as any other castle or hall. The first to leave were the women, who chose to go to their beds before they could be molested by drunks other than their husbands; after them came the wives who hoped to tempt their alcoholically-lecherous husbands to bed before they could drink too much. Soon the less inebriated men would come out, some to walk about the yard, some to talk in undertones about the political situation away from listening servants, others to vomit or urinate. Then, in varying degrees of drunkenness, the rest would pour from the hall, some upright, one or two crawling, many stumbling, and a few being carried by servants.

Usually the servants would eat with their lord and his household in the hall, but tonight, with so many guests visiting the place, men-at-arms and others had to eat in parallel, taking their own food where they may. Toker had avoided the service held over a small portable altar set up in the small hall near the gatehouse, preferring to sit in the open air with an ale rather than indoors while some fool of a chaplain preached about St Giles's saintliness.

Compared with many, Sir Peregrine was as sober as normal, but Toker was sure he had drunk plenty of wine from the way he walked so precisely and cautiously. Lord Hugh was just behind him, belching happily while he gripped his belt with both hands as if fearing that its weight might lead it to fall to the ground. As he went to the gatehouse he giggled in that high tone of his as he recalled the jokes told at his table, his wife still exclaiming at the feats performed by jugglers and acrobats.

Sir Peregrine gave Toker a good night, but as Sir Baldwin and his lady passed Sir Peregrine, Toker heard his voice change. 'Damn you, Sir Baldwin,' he hissed. 'If only someone would rid me of you, my Lord would be safer.'

Toker smiled to himself. 'Always a pleasure to oblige you, Master,' he muttered under his breath.

Returning to her room after the feast, Matilda sniffled as she drank another pot of wine. Andrew had gone to his own room again, leaving her to cope with her desolation alone. He rarely came to her bed now.

It was chilly tonight, or was it her? It was hard to tell nowadays what she felt about anything. Since her girl had died.

In a way she was relieved that he didn't want to be with her. It would have been too much to bear if he had demonstrated more affection when he had banished Joan to the servants' hall. His decision to leave his wife alone had given Matilda a sense of unity with her daughter, although it was tempered by her guilt. Andrew's rejection of Joan had made Matilda feel as if she had betrayed her daughter, her last remaining tie with her first husband, Paul.

Pulling off her clothes, she let them fall to the floor and sat on the edge of the bed.

She drew away from memories of Paul like a child regretfully pulling away from a plate of sweetmeats; she would have liked to wallow in vivid recollections of him. Her time with him had been so good, so full of pleasure and fulfilment, that to recall those years to mind was almost to commit mental treachery against Andrew. And if she were capable of committing treason in her head, where would she stop?

No, she would put all thoughts of her first husband from her. She had a duty, one which she had sworn to, towards Andrew. And Duty and Honour were important concepts to her. They had to be.

Nicholas had been a Templar at the small Preceptory in South Witham when Matilda married Paul, a local knight. Her marriage had been a delight to her, fulfilling and pleasurable. And then one morning her brother appeared, shocked and horror-struck, and blurted that his Order, the greatest, most devoted army in Christendom, had been disbanded. Templars who refused to surrender were declared outlaw and excommunicate. Paul had preferred to trust to his own King's judgement rather than listen to the French King's accusations. He took Nicholas in, protected, fed and clothed him.

They would all be there still, and Joan would be alive, if the second disaster hadn't struck shortly afterwards. One day while out hunting, Paul had been thrown from his horse, and although Matilda had been worried about his head, in which there was a gash from striking a rock, a small scratch on his arm went septic. Two days later, he died.

His lord was apologetic, but with the political situation he couldn't afford to leave a feeble widow and her daughter in the manor, and neither was he prepared to trust an excommunicate Templar: he needed another knight. He evicted Matilda, giving her a small purse of gold in memory of her husband's service, but nothing more. She had often thought that if Joan had been a boy-child, he would have let her remain.

Nicholas had taken over; she was his responsibility. Luckily he had saved money while he was a Templar. He took her purse, not trusting a woman with money, and the three of them made the journey to the south. At first Nicholas had intended going to Bordeaux to see what opportunities existed in the English King's lands, but when they arrived in Oxford, a wrong turning took them to the west, and Nicholas decided to see what the farthest-flung parts of the realm were like. Thus they ended up in Exeter.

It was good fortune that led to Nicholas meeting a merchant who needed a little money, or so Nicholas always said. The merchant had been glad of the purse of gold, agreed to Nicholas's terms, and swiftly the purse had doubled in value. Then Nicholas began dealing with a ship-owner and helped fill the ships with wine, until within a few years he had a share in a ship of his own.

A frequent visitor to their house in those days was Andrew Carter. Then he had been lean and hungry-looking, still waiting for the opportunity that would make him wealthy, but before long Matilda realised that Andrew was observing her with an eye of admiration, not one of mere courtesy to a partner's sister.

She had not at first thought much of him, but gradually his generous compliments, his overblown admiration and fervent statements of desire had persuaded her that life with a husband could be preferable to life without. Or was it that Nicholas had seemed so keen to see her handfast? Maybe that was it, she thought; maybe there had never been love on her side, but she wanted to obey and please her brother, just as before she would have done anything to satisfy her Paul.

Not that there was much possibility of satisfying her husband now. He never came to her. Hadn't for months. He was like Nicholas; he'd looked on Matilda as an asset to be traded. Nicholas had wanted to be free of Matilda and Joan, and Andrew had wanted to be tied to the successful trader. The marriage fulfilled both their dreams. There was no reason to expect any other feelings than duty in a marriage after all.

It hadn't mattered until Joan died, of course.

She felt the tears begin again and blinked them away. Waves of remorse washed over her. For years she had left Joan in the servants' hall at her husband's behest, only rarely seeing her own daughter, and when she did it was always with Andrew in the room at the same time. She had been no kind of mother. No mother at all.

Riven by sobs, she turned and threw herself down on the soft mattress and hid her face in the counterpane as the keen poignancy of her sadness caught her up once again.

CHAPTER TWENTY-ONE

While Matilda wept for the daughter she had now lost for ever, a fire burned brightly in a small cottage four miles away.

Harlewin smiled at the naked treasure before him. He had ridden here as quickly as he could in order to sample the delights of Cecily's body, and seeing her here was enough to justify his urgency.

'It was a work of brilliance to say that a man had fallen in a well,' he laughed as he picked her up and carried her to the bed.

She twined her hair around a finger. 'It seemed the best means of rescuing you from the interminable feasting. Was John there?'

'Yes, and he looked daggers at my back when I left,' Harlewin said and dropped her onto the bed.

She squealed with delight. 'The fool! So long as he never knows for sure that we've met.'

Harlewin let his sword belt fall to the ground, his fingers pulling at the laced neck of his shirt. 'Are you sure you'll be all right? I hate the thought of him taking a switch to your arse or belting you.'

'Oh, you really would mind that, wouldn't you?' she said, reaching up and touching his face with her soft fingers.

'Course I would,' he returned gruffly, untying his hose from his tunic and letting them drop beside his shirt. 'If he hurt you, I'd challenge him.'

'To a duel?'

'Of course.'

'That's nice.'

'I must confess to a certain surprise that you don't seem to be scared he might find out about you.'

'That's easily answered.' Her face lost a little of its gaiety and in its place she wore a colder, more calculating expression. He had never seen such a look on her face before and it made him pause a moment. 'I *am* scared that he could find out. That is why I am very, very careful. He isn't that bright, and provided I carry on being careful I should be safe enough.'

'You'd have thought the dumb bugger would have got the message, wouldn't you, eh?' Harlewin said. He tugged his tunic over his head and threw it to the ground.

'Not really, no. I can be devious when I want,' Cecily said, pulling a long tress of her black hair to her mouth and sweeping it in teasing flicks over her lips and chin while she watched him. 'I usually make sure he's busy before I come out.'

'What about tonight? He'll be back after the feast and wonder where you've got to – especially since he knows I left the place early,' he said, kicking away the last of his clothes and climbing into the bed beside her.

'You have your alibi arranged?'

'Yes. The fool wouldn't dare cross me,' he said, and nuzzled at her breast.

She giggled and cupped his head to her but after a moment he pulled away and looked up at her.

'But what will you say tomorrow when he asks you where you have been?'

'My husband doesn't trouble me in my bed of a night. I lock my door and my maid will tell him I am asleep if he knocks.'

'He could knock the door down and see you aren't there.'

She touched his lip with a finger, smiling. 'No. He will return home drunk and bang on my door angrily demanding to see me. His rage will make his frustration and impotence all the more painful for him. Rather than cause more of a stir in the household, he will swallow any story. He can't face confrontations, you see. My maid will tell him I am asleep and he will go to his own chamber and collapse in a furious stupor. Tomorrow I shall be back before he wakes. I'll leave here before dawn.'

'So long as you don't doze off.'

'Am I likely to get bored?' she asked innocently.

Baldwin awoke with a head that thumped madly and a belly that rebelled at the very thought of food. His bladder demanded release, but he couldn't stand. The mere thought was an exquisite torture.

It was not only that he had eaten too much rich food last night, it was the fact that it was so late at night. They had finished their meal long after he would usually have been in bed. Looking back on it, Baldwin was quite certain that the priest would not have had time to retire to bed before going to his church to hold the nightly services. They were supposed to be conducted at the middle of the night, after all, and by the time the meal was done it was close enough to the middle watches.

Perhaps he had drunk a little too much as well, he amended as a dagger of pain stabbed at his temple.

'How are you?' Jeanne asked at his side.

He grunted. There was sympathy in her voice, but a certain tartness indicated that where he had passed an uncomfortable night, his movements and snoring had ensured that she suffered a sleepless one.

'Do you want some wine?' she asked, motioning to the jug on the chest.

'Yes. A small pot, with water.' He felt hot and shivery. The muscles of his hand wanted to clench for some reason and his stomach rumbled and hissed. It was some time before he could rise, not so much because of his head, but more because of his stomach. The thought of breaking his fast made him nauseous. Miraculously the wine helped.

'You look dreadful,' Jeanne observed. She had risen from the bed and covered her nakedness with a thin robe, standing near the window.

They were alone now. The other couple using the room must have already risen. He wondered whether they too had slept badly. With him as a neighbour he assumed they had.

'Thank you, my Lady,' he said and sipped. The wine slipped down more pleasantly than he would have expected.

Jeanne stood with the sun behind her, filtering through the thin gauzy material of her night-gown and showing her body beneath. Baldwin swallowed, feeling better after the wine. His smile grew broader and he patted the mattress beside him. 'Lady, there is a comfortable bed here. We didn't make good use of it last night, but now . . .'

'Oh, no, Baldwin. We can't. The household is up. They'd know.'

'My wife, that doesn't concern me,' he said, stalking after her as she backed away.

'Baldwin, we have to get dressed!' she protested, but her voice was quiet and sounded on the brink of a giggle.

'We shall get dressed,' he murmured, adding, 'later.'

'What if someone should hear us?'

He caught an arm and tugged her towards him. She was trembling with laughter as he wrapped his arms about her, but then she kissed him slowly and he could feel the pace of her breathing alter. He picked her up and took her to the bed, settling her on the mattress before he slowly opened her robe.

'Hurry, husband,' she said and held out her arms to him. He went to her and as their lips touched he felt the blood pounding in his head.

It was matched by the pounding on the door. With a muttered curse Baldwin recognised Simon's voice: 'Baldwin, are you there? Are you awake?'

Jeanne froze, then was convulsed at the sight of the expressions that flew over her husband's face: disbelief, shock, anger and finally, despair. 'I think you should open the door, husband,' she chuckled and pulled away from his embrace to hide behind a screen.

'Baldwin? Wake up, man!'

Taking a deep breath, Baldwin went and unlocked the door.

'That knight Furnshill and his friend Puttock the bailiff were here looking for you yesterday,' Andrew said as he broke his bread and dipped a crust into his pottage.

Nicholas had been pouring himself a pot of thin ale, but on hearing his brother-in-law's words he started and spilt it over the table. 'Me? Why?'

'Something to do with the death of another man. Sir Gilbert of Carlisle's servant: the one who pointed us to where Dyne was in the woods.'

Nicholas set the jug down and shrugged. 'We've told the Coroner all we know.'

'They were asking about the night before that, too. Wanted to know where you were, what time you'd got in and so on.'

'Did they say why?' Nicholas enquired casually.

'No.'

Their breakfast completed, Andrew said he would be going to the Fair to see how his stalls were doing. Nicholas said he would go along later, but in the meantime, he waited until Andrew had disappeared, then hurried to his roll of clothing in his chest near the hall's doorway. Searching through it, he pulled out his old sword belt.

The blade was as clean and unmarked as when he had first been given it, almost twenty years ago now, in Lincolnshire, by a grizzled old warrior who had taken it from a Moor outside Acre. Nashki script ran along the fuller, saying, according to the older man, 'Praise to God' – although Nicholas had never learned Arabic or the strange letters that flowed over the metal like some kind of liquid fire. Now, as he studied the metalwork, he felt a little of his courage return. Any man who tried to make him out to be a heretic would have to fight him.

Putting the belt about his waist, he was tying the cords when his sister entered.

'What are you doing with that? Has Andrew told you about Sir Baldwin?

He stood upright once more. With the comforting weight at his side, he felt more like a soldier-monk again, as if the mere carrying of his weapon reminded him of his duty and of honour. 'I am preparing to meet with Furnshill. He's learned about me from someone.'

Matilda went to a chair and, fell into it as she stared up at her brother. 'He knows you were a Templar. He asked me yesterday – before the feast.'

Nicholas gazed at her. He had never confessed to her that he had stolen his money from the Order. She still believed that he had saved money while he was a Templar, as he had told her. Much of his wealth now was based upon the shrewd investment of his money and hers, but it was all founded upon his theft.

'What will you do?' she asked, worried by his anxious but determined mien.

He gave a slow, sad smile. The money he had taken was legally the King's. If he was discovered, Nicholas knew he would die. 'I have no idea what I should do, Matilda. No idea at all.'

In the roadway, Felicity saw Andrew and then Nicholas leave the house. 'Right,' she said. 'You have to come with me now and tell your story, if you want to hear what really happened to your brother.'

Avicia nodded, but she was still unsure why they had come. 'I just don't understand why we're here. If, like you say, Andrew Carter is not particularly bothered about his daughter's murder, what good can it do, me saying that Philip was innocent?'

For answer Felicity led the way over the road to Andrew Carter's door and knocked.

'But he's gone! We just saw him,' Avicia protested, more confused than ever.

As the door opened and Rose peered out, Felicity pushed the door wide. 'Tell Mistress Matilda that Felicity would like to speak with her.' She paused, and an unpleasant smile transformed her features. 'And if she asks who I am, tell her I'm Felicity the Whore and I know who *really* killed her daughter.'

It was the tapping at the door that woke him from his dreams.

Harlewin was drifting delightfully. With Cecily warm, soft and plump at his side, he saw no need to waken. His eyes opened once, took in the little room, the fire now dead in the hearth, the packed earth floor without even rushes, the chest owned by the miller. The only item of value was this, the miller's bed, which Harlewin himself had bought for the man and his family. Harlewin wanted a good bed when he came here to sleep with his woman. It was a small price to pay, the fact that the miller and his family slept in it all the time Harlewin wasn't here. When the Coroner wanted the place, the miller and his brood went and slept in the mill itself.

Closing his eyes, he was annoyed to hear the tapping again. 'Bugger off!' he roared.

His bellow made Cecily jump, and before she could properly open her eyes and take in the sight of him, he closed them again with kisses while his hand rested first on her hip and then stroked its way down to her thigh. She moaned and rolled onto her back, and he felt her legs part slightly, just enough, and then snap together as her whole body went tense.

'Come on, my love,' he whispered, 'let's just—'

'Christ *bollocking* Jesus!' she blurted.

He blinked, startled, and gazed down at her. 'What on earth . . .?'

'I fell asleep, you fat twerp! My husband!' she snapped and leaped from the bed grabbing at clothing, pulling her tunic over her head and letting it settle anyhow, before drawing a shift over it. In the chest she kept a change of clothing, and now she went to this and pulled out various dresses and skirts, muttering to herself all the while. 'God! That I should be so *stupid*! How could I have fallen asleep? I must be a complete fool! He'll want an explanation this time.'

Harlewin leaned on his arm and watched as she pulled on a skirt and patted it smooth, then a clean shirt, cotte and surcoat. 'How do I look?'

'Fine, once your hair is done.'

The miller's daughter shyly obeyed Cecily's bellowed command and Harlewin watched while the two worked swiftly to repair the damage of the previous night, and then the red-faced maiden was sent out. Cecily quickly went to his side and patted his cheek.

'You should have covered yourself. She hardly knew where to look.'

He grinned widely. 'I thought she knew exactly where to look!'

'Don't make the poor girl jealous for things she can't touch.' He kissed her.

'You should be gone.'

'Yes. You will be careful?'

'Don't think of me,' he said, and his brow creased. 'You make sure *you're* safe from that husband of yours.'

Edgar could see that his master was not of a mood to tolerate jesting. He quickly sent Wat away to fetch wine and Petronilla for bread and cold slices of meat: a simple diet to help his master's head.

Baldwin sat at a bench and sourly eyed the folk about the room. Two men who had drunk more than was usual for them were still snoring near the fire, but most guests had risen earlier when the servants appeared to begin preparing the place for the new day. Lord Hugh had eaten in his chamber, Edgar told Baldwin, and the knight grunted his jealousy. Edgar smiled and left his master to his meal.

Simon chewed happily on an old mutton bone he had found in the kitchen and took a pint of ale, smacking his lips and giving a loud grunt of appreciation as he finished.

'Have you no feeling of queasiness when you think of what you ate last night?' Baldwin asked.

'It was good food, wasn't it?' Simon said happily.

At Baldwin's side Jeanne snorted. 'I'm surprised you can remember it, the way you sank so many pots of wine.'

'It was good wine!' Simon protested defensively. 'Baldwin liked it too. Why shouldn't a fellow take a little wine with his food? A man has to drink!'

'Man has to breathe; fishes need to drink,' Jeanne noted caustically.

'I find both help,' Simon said cheerfully. 'Do you want that fat?'

Baldwin winced as Simon stabbed the thick, yellow pork fat that he had left at the edge of his trencher. Simon studied it closely: it was crisp and burned at the outside, and he beamed as he put it in his mouth. 'Ah, good, that!'

'Shall we go?' Baldwin said, standing.

'Nothing more to eat?' Simon asked hopefully.

Baldwin looked at him.

Matilda remained in her chair when the two girls were shown in, and waved an imperious hand to halt them some few feet from her.

Avicia felt overawed by this woman, who wore on the fingers of one hand more wealth than Avicia could ever hope to earn. The house itself was magnificent, as she would have expected. Large, imposing, with a multitude of small decorative works carved into the beams and lintels, she could only gawp around her in awe. It was far finer than the Shermans' place.

The lady herself was different. She was the picture of depression. Looking into her eyes Avicia could see her own misery reflected. One woman mourning the loss of her daughter, the other the loss of her brother; both had lost their own flesh.

'Is this some sort of a joke, Felicity?' Matilda said at last. 'You bring me the sister of the man who murdered my daughter on the pretence that I might learn something?'

'The wrong man was killed,' Felicity said flatly.

'I am supposed to take your word for it?' Matilda sneered.

'Your husband had me thrown from the house. Do you know why?'

'You were a nuisance. He told me you were sleeping with the men in the yard. A common whore!'

'I am now. I had no choice when your fine husband threw me from here. But when I lived here, I had only one lover: your fine husband.'

'Rubbish! *Rose!*' Matilda shouted. 'These women wish to leave.'

Felicity turned to the pale girl. 'Oh, it's Rose now, is it? He's been after you, hasn't he?'

Rose coloured, and her head dropped in shame.

Matilda opened her mouth to offer a snide comment, when something in the maid's demeanour caught her attention. 'What do you mean? Rose? Are you all right?'

Felicity turned back to face her. 'Can't you see it yet? Your husband always picks the best of the maids, the youngest, the most impressionable, the most appealing, and takes them. Haven't you realised? Are you *blind*?' She stepped towards the seated woman and held out her hands in appeal. 'Andrew Carter, your husband, forces any maid in the house who takes his fancy to share his bed. That's what he did with me, and by the time he was finished with me, what else could I do? He ruined me.'

'Well? And what of it?' Matilda said proudly. 'He is a man, and we women all know what men are like. But he is also my husband and the head of my family, and as such I owe him my loyalty. Perhaps he does sleep with my maids – well, he wouldn't be the first man to do that – and if he does, there's little harm in it.'

271

' "Little harm!" ' Felicity repeated with disbelief. 'Look at *me*! He made me what I now have become, a used woman, a whore, a common stale – you call this *nothing*? He has taken my life. I could have been happy, could have married a good man and raised my own daughters . . .'

'You still might – if you can find a man who can forgive you your sinfulness.'

'It is not my sins but *his* that need forgiveness. Do you remember how long ago your husband made me leave?'

Matilda shrugged. 'Years.'

'Yes. Six years ago. That was when he threw me over for his new lover.'

'What has this to do with me? Are you merely boasting to upset me?' Rising, Matilda made as if to walk from the room.

'It was six years ago he took your daughter for the first time.'

'*NO!*' Matilda gasped. She fell back into her chair, a hand flying to her mouth. There was a seething motion to the room. She was sure that the walls were moving as if about to tumble down, but she couldn't look at them; her attention was fixed upon the woman before her. 'No,' she said again, and this time she shook her head in denial.

'He raped me, then went on to Joan. That was why he had her installed in the servants' quarters, so she wouldn't be missed from your chamber when he called her.'

'No. He couldn't . . . He wouldn't . . .'

'He took her every night, and when she found her own lover, a man who adored her, your husband grew scared. He didn't want her to tell her man what he had been doing to her all those years. She may only have been his step-daughter, but the Church frowns upon a man who takes advantage in that way. He is still guilty of incest.'

Matilda swallowed. There was a feeling of weakness in her legs and she couldn't trust them to support her if she were to try to stand. Her heart was pounding painfully as if it would soon break free from her breast. There was a thick sensation in her throat as though a ball had lodged there, and her head spun. It felt as if she were whirling around, weightless and formless.

'And not only the Church would want to see him punished. Can you imagine how Joan's husband would feel if he heard later that his bride was already deflowered, and by her own father? He would want his revenge.'

'Air ... It is so hot ... Open the shutters,' Matilda wheezed. It felt as though there was an iron band about her breast, slowly squeezing the air from her lungs.

Felicity sent the maid for wine, walked to the window and opened the shutter wide. By the time she was done, Rose was back, bringing Clarice with her.

As soon as she saw her mistress, panting and gasping, she threw a bitter look in Felicity's direction. 'Couldn't you have saved her from this? What good will it do to ruin her life now?'

Felicity watched as Clarice took a little wine in a bowl and used it to dab Matilda's temples, murmuring all the while, 'Come now, mistress. Don't worry what the whore says. She will soon leave us and you can go and rest, and then we'll—'

Thrusting her arm aside, Matilda stared into her face. 'Is it true?'

'What, mistress?' Clarice asked, but Matilda read the answer in her frightened eyes.

273

Felicity walked to Rose's side. 'Don't ask me, don't ask Clarice: ask Rose. Ask her when your husband first started taking an interest in her. When did he first demand she should join him in his bed?'

'Rose, come here!' Matilda said.

The girl stepped forward slowly, reluctantly, her head hanging so low her chin almost touched on her breast.

'Tell me, Rose. Has he told you to join him in his room?'

'Mistress, I never wanted to!' Rose burst out. 'He just can't keep his hands off me, not since your Joan died. Since then he's wanted me almost every night, and when I tried to refuse, he told me to look at what happened to girls who turned him down.'

'What did he mean by that?' Matilda asked quietly.

'He meant I'd become a whore like Felicity or . . .'

'Or die like Joan,' Felicity finished for her.

CHAPTER TWENTY-TWO

Harlewin leaned against the doorpost while he settled his tunic and tugged his surcoat over his shoulders more snugly. Ramming his hat upon his head he idly kicked a pebble, then sauntered slowly to the mill. He tossed a coin to the grinning miller, said, 'Keep your mouth shut about it,' and wandered round to the back of the place where his horse was already saddled and bridled by the miller's boy. Reaching into his purse Harlewin found another coin and flipped it to the lad before checking that the harness was as he liked it, the saddle tight enough, the bridle properly placed.

All done, he stood on a chair and hoisted himself into the saddle, taking up the reins and setting off homewards.

The mill was close to the road here, and it took him little time to climb up the incline to the thoroughfare, where he turned off towards Tiverton, whistling happily. He felt replete. Cecily Sherman was a perfect lover: she wanted a lot in a short time, but then she would be content to leave

Harlewin alone for several days while her husband's doubts died down. Harlewin grinned. Sherman was plainly a fool. He trusted her when he shouldn't, and then accepted her excuses at face value. A complete cuckold!

Taking the shorter lane to Tiverton rather than following the trail round to the north, he felt the oppressive nature of the woods about him. The trees here were tall and threatening on either side, their lower trunks hidden by the tangle of weeds, brambles and bracken that clogged the ground here. Here the boughs were so close together that the sun could scarcely break through and the air was perpetually chill. Although an occasional breath of wind soughed through the branches, it could only be discerned by the rustle as of dried paper as leaves moved against one another.

With a shiver Harlewin recalled that night. It hadn't been his fault: he had been scared, riding alone here in the dark, and Sir Gilbert had been a stern, fearsome figure in the gloom beneath the trees. When Harlewin first caught sight of him, he had thought the man was a ghost, dressed as he was in his white tunic, his pale features almost gleaming in the dark. At least Sir Gilbert hadn't seen Cecily. That was a relief. She had ridden on beforehand; she was out of the way.

And then there had come that scream filled with terror. Harlewin knew immediately that there was no need for him to remain. He had a way to go to return home and kicked his horse onwards.

Luckily Harlewin was out of the woods now. Above him the warm summer sun shone so brightly that for a while his eyes hurt, the contrast with the shadowy space beneath the trees was so extreme. He was on the busy road to Exeter. Here the Keeper of the King's Peace in Tiverton had exerted all his efforts and forced the local peasants to clear the verge for many yards in order that outlaws would find ambush more difficult and Harlewin could go at a faster pace.

Moving at a comfortable canter that was not quick enough to overtire his mount but which would eat the miles easily, Harlewin le Poter made his way homewards.

Nicholas drank a quart of ale before he felt ready to face whatever questions the Keeper might pose. He felt his stomach complain. It wasn't that his belly rebelled against the morning whet, for after all that was a normal drink first thing in the morning; it was more a reflection of his nervousness about meeting Sir Baldwin de Furnshill.

Baldwin had acquired a reputation in Devon for being fair but rigorous, and when necessary, ruthless. It was said that he had caused the number of hangings in Crediton to increase in the last four years because men were convicted on his word when in the past they wouldn't have been; men knew they could trust his judgement. They had never trusted his predecessor's.

Nicholas had heard much about the Keeper of Crediton. The town wasn't far from Exeter, and any official who was apparently innocent of corruption was a figure of some interest, if only for novelty's sake.

The noise in the tavern was growing. Nicholas could hardly think in here, and even if Baldwin was waiting outside, he needed air. He went out and stood blinking in the roadway. Momentarily dazzled by the brightness after the gloomy fug indoors, he stood squinting and confused. When he heard hooves approach, he hardly connected them with any danger, but then the Coroner was almost on him, and with a, 'Move aside, you clumsy bugger!' he passed.

Nicholas's hand went to his sword as the words of challenge rose to his mouth. It would be so easy to throw down the gauntlet to this arrogant popinjay, the first time in years. He was no weakly coward, he was a trained soldier and knight, a man of honour. Hadn't he taken the threefold vows of chastity, poverty and obedience? He had remained faithful, had he not? Never had he taken a woman since giving his oath; never had he forgotten his obedience to the Order, even when he stole the Order's money. At the time the Order was destroyed and he had taken the money not from his companions, but from the King, who was trying to take anything moveable from the Templars before handing their properties over to the Hospitallers. As for poverty, he had been forced to make money to help his sister and poor young Joan. When he died he would be laid in a sombre coffin without adornment, laid in a plain winding sheet, and buried without pomp or show of any sort. It would be stated in his will when he was ready to die. He had adhered to his vows. Many hadn't.

The internal justification stiffened his resolve, but the near-accident had renewed his pride as well, and when he heard the calm voice of Sir Baldwin, he was able to turn graciously and face him with a refreshing sense of resolve.

'I was looking for you, Keeper. You have some questions for me, I understand.'

Matilda stared at them all before curling her lip and practically screaming her rejection. 'You mean to tell me that my own husband deliberately murdered my daughter? You're mad! Insane! How could you think that – it's obscene!'

Felicity held out her hands as if pleading. 'Yes. Your husband killed your daughter.'

'So *you* say, whore! Why should I believe you? Did you see my daughter with him? Did any of you? *No!*' Matilda leaned back in her chair, a hand raised in a gesture of denial. The prostitute had taken it upon herself to accuse her husband and had simultaneously set herself up as judge and jury, but her motives were clear: she had been dropped by Andrew in favour of Rose, a younger, more attractive girl. All the other stuff was lies, pure invention. Of course her Andrew wouldn't have slept with Joan, much less killed her. He probably hadn't even been out that night.

He had, though, she recalled; he had come back late that evening, and when she asked where he had been, he laughed oddly and said he had been drinking. She thrust the thought aside. Felicity was after revenge, that was all. She was warped, vicious, *stupid*. 'Rose, go back to your duties. Clarice, I shall want to speak to you later. As for you two, leave my house! You have done all you can to wreck my faith in my husband, but you have not succeeded.'

Avicia could only gape. Matilda covered her face again, making Avicia feel sorry for her once more; Felicity stood back with Rose, with what Avicia thought was an unpleasant smile twisting her features. Clarice rubbed her mistress's neck and back, murmuring soothingly but Matilda pushed her away; her ministrations were intolerable. 'Don't touch me! Tell that whore and her friend to go. I will not listen to them!'

'Will you do nothing? Will my brother never be proved innocent? Won't your daughter be avenged?' Avicia burst out with a wail. She couldn't believe that this last possibility was being shut off to her.

Matilda leaned back in her seat and cast an eye over her. 'What are you doing here? Are you here to enjoy my grief?

Do you want to wallow in my despair? Is it pleasing for you to witness my misery?'

'Oh, mistress, how could I wish someone else the same misery I myself feel?' Avicia gasped.

'You can know nothing of my feelings,' Matilda said shortly. 'I have lost the life I created, the last remaining link with the husband I loved. You can know nothing of my loss.'

Felicity sneered, 'And you cared so much for your first husband, so much for your only daughter that you will ignore the facts. He killed your daughter to keep her silent. You know it is true.'

'You're a liar! You were thrown from this house . . .'

'Yes. He ruined my life. Luckily he didn't need to kill me – but with your daughter he felt he had no choice. If she told her lover about his drunken fumblings beneath her skirts, then Philip Dyne could have attacked him. Ask Rose again; ask Clarice – ask *any* of the other girls you employ. *You know it's true.*'

'No,' Matilda said, but her voice was losing its force. Andrew had been most peculiar that night. And Rose had admitted his attentions to her had begun just after Joan's death . . . A spark of loyalty – or maybe it was pure defiance? – made her square her shoulders. 'No, that's rubbish.'

The whore stepped forward. 'This girl is like me, like Joan. She's a victim of your husband's passions. She deserves the same consideration as I do, that Rose does, that your Joan would have.'

'You think to claim that you deserve my sympathy?' Matilda asked, her tone rising to a shriek. 'After *this*? Go! In God's name, leave me! And don't return!'

* * *

Baldwin and Simon took seats at a bench while Nicholas toyed with a tankard of wine opposite them. Rather than enter the tavern, they had chosen to sit outside in a shaded part of the alehouse's yard. Here Simon gratefully stretched his legs while Baldwin radiated discomfort.

His hangover had returned: his body was heavy, slow and hot; he felt sweaty in the sunlight and his hands wanted to shake. He had to keep flexing them to stop them from clenching into claws – and all the time his belly bubbled and spat bile up into his throat.

To forget his ill-ease, he turned his attention to Nicholas. The merchant had long fingers, he noticed, with carefully cleaned nails and almost perfect smooth skin which showed no calluses or warts. He was the image of the wealthy, well-to-do merchant.

'Well, Sir Baldwin. What do you want from me?'

'First, where were you on the night before last?'

'Me?' Nicholas was unsettled by the knight's pale, angry-looking glower and short manner. 'I was here in the tavern. Ask the landlord.'

'I will. You know that Sir Gilbert's man was killed that night?'

'I had heard.'

'Did you know him?' Simon pressed.

'I don't believe so, no.'

'We have heard that you met with Sir Gilbert the night before he died,' Baldwin said. 'I want to know how you knew him and what you found to talk about.'

'I have met many people in my life. Some I have met about Exeter, others further afield while I travelled.'

'And Sir Gilbert?'

Nicholas stared into his pot. 'I knew him many years ago when he and I lived far from here. When we saw each other in the tavern, was it surprising that he and I should speak?'

'I don't know. That depends upon how you last separated.'

Nicholas's eyes rose to meet Baldwin's steady gaze. 'We separated as honourable friends, men who had done many things together, and who had experienced hardship and privations.'

'You're wearing a sword today,' Simon commented.

'Should a merchant go undefended? Why should I not wear a sword?'

'I've not seen you with one before.'

'There's not been much need for one.'

'And you feel there is now?' Baldwin pressed.

Nicholas snapped, 'What do *you* think after the news from London?'

Baldwin could not disagree with that. He continued more mildly, 'What did Sir Gilbert speak to you about?'

'He was happy. He'd come to speak to Lord Hugh and had seen an old friend, Father Benedict, the cleric at Templeton.' Nicholas drained his pot. 'He wanted to know all about the politics of the town. Who supported whom, who could be bribed, how expensive such men would be. Especially Sir Peregrine, whether he could be bought.'

'I see. And you were able to help him?'

'I have some experience, Sir Baldwin.'

'I expect you have. What did you tell him about Lord Hugh?'

'He wasn't interested in our lord. He wanted to know about other folks, especially those who supported Earl Thomas of Lancaster.'

Baldwin frowned slightly. 'Why?'

'To be honest I think he was himself wondering whether to look for a new master. Despenser is exiled and Sir Gilbert didn't want to follow him.'

'I see. How long was he with you?'

'A good hour – perhaps more.'

'And then he left to go in which direction?'

'Down the hill. I thought he was heading towards the stables near the castle.'

'That would make sense,' Baldwin agreed. 'Did he give you any clue as to his reasons for being here?'

'He made no bones about it. The Younger Despenser had sent him to try to sound out Lord Hugh and the townspeople. And if possible bribe them to support the Despensers' return.'

Simon interrupted. 'With what?'

'Eh?' Nicholas hesitated.

'I said: "with what?" The man had nothing on him.'

'His purse was stolen by that little shit Dyne, yes, but he must have had more.'

'Where is it, then? There was nothing on him or at his camp.'

Nicholas turned his hands palm-up in a gesture of indifference. 'How should I know where it is?'

Simon said slowly, 'You are the first person to have hinted that Sir Gilbert had any money with him. Yet there isn't any.'

'Do you mean to suggest that I stole his money?'

'No,' Simon said after a moment's consideration. 'Not then, because his man, William, said that Sir Gilbert returned from town cheerful. I suppose that was because he had seen you, and he was more confident of succeeding in his mission to help the Despensers. So you didn't take his money then. And although you met up with him later, when Sir Gilbert followed you into the woods and died, William must have had the gold with him in the camp.'

Baldwin scowled thoughtfully at the table. 'Unless the gold had gone the day before.'

'Eh?' Simon drained his pot and held it up to a serving-girl.

'You want more?' Baldwin cried disbelievingly. 'Ah, your belly must be made of leather!' He watched with near disbelief as the jug was brought and Simon served. It was with an effort that he brought his mind back to the present. 'What I wondered was, whether Sir Gilbert could have disposed of the money before he came here.'

'Why would he do that?' Nicholas asked doubtfully.

Simon took Baldwin's point. 'He wouldn't want to leave temptation in the way of his servant, a man he scarcely knew if William's evidence was honest, and yet who would want to wander around a town like this, alone, with a fortune on his back? It would have meant selecting the lesser of two evil courses. Of course he might have brought the money into town and delivered it to someone for safe-keeping . . .'

Nicholas paled with anger. 'So you do mean to insult me? I could have you indicted for this kind of villainous talk.'

'No, no, Nicholas,' Baldwin murmured dismissively. 'The fact that from all we have heard Sir Gilbert didn't know anyone to speak to in Tiverton means he would hardly have brought the money with him. He had not *expected* to meet you.'

'Well, if it's not here and it's not at his camp, where is it?'

Neither answered. After a moment Simon asked, 'It was the day after you saw him here that the felon abjured, wasn't it?'

'Yes,' said Nicholas, shooting him a curious look, wondering what new avenue of questioning he was being led down.

'Was the Coroner keen to let him escape? Not all felons are permitted to abjure.'

'Andrew and I offered money.'

'Why?'

'Bailiff, if it was your niece, your daughter, wouldn't you want a chance to win justice? I went to the priest and gave him a large purse for the Coroner . . .'

'Why go through the priest?' pressed Baldwin.

'Father Abraham is fond of winning rewards here as well as in Heaven.'

Baldwin nodded and motioned for him to continue.

'The Father agreed to ensure that Dyne was released to go and seek exile. It was all Andrew and I wanted. We were there when he was freed, with a few men from alehouses, but the Coroner stopped us killing him there and then. He said we'd have to leave him alone, the hypocrite! All he meant was, we'd have to wait until he was outside the town.'

'And as soon as he'd gone, you rode off after him,' Simon continued.

'Yes. We gave him a while, then cantered down the road to Exeter. And there he was. We almost killed him on the spot. It would've been so easy, just a knife and that was that, but a group of fools were on the road and could see us. I pulled Andrew off him, and forced him to keep on going. We went down some way, keeping an eye on the travellers wending their way to the Fair. As soon as there was a good gap, we cantered on a way. It was late, and I think most people had decided to halt at the last inn, so we had a clear field.

'We rode back but Dyne had left the road. We came up to Sir Gilbert and his man, but we'd agreed the night before that we shouldn't admit to knowing each other. So I simply said we were hunting a felon, and while I spoke William pointed to where he'd just seen a face. It was all we needed.'

'It could have been anyone,' pointed out Simon. Baldwin was silent.

'Yes, it could,' agreed Nicholas. 'But we were sure it was him, and we were right. We rode straight for the point William had indicated, and then on. After a while we came to a glade, and there we separated. Andrew blundered off right, I kept on straight ahead.

'It was hard to gauge how long it was since Dyne saw us, so I couldn't tell how far he might have run. And with the gathering dusk it became hard to see. I knew we'd missed him when we came to a road. We turned back into the woods and that was where we met my sister.

'She screamed at the sight of us. Probably thought we were outlaws! I calmed her and she agreed to go home. Meanwhile we turned back into the woods. The horses didn't like it, I can tell you. Neither did I, for riding like that, when you have little idea what might be underfoot, is damned dangerous, and a knight should always look to his mount. Branches threatened to knock us from our saddles.'

'I know,' said Simon ruefully. Baldwin didn't laugh but peered all the more intently at Nicholas.

'Some short way in, there was a loud crashing, and I saw Sir Gilbert riding towards me. He told me that if this was a genuine felon it was his duty to aid us. Well, I thanked him and he rode off to my left, widening our area still further.'

Baldwin was still peering intently at him. 'How long did it take you to find the fellow?'

'I couldn't say. Andrew found him. He told me he rode back some way without luck but when the moon came out, he lurched into a clearing and there before him was Dyne. Andrew spurred round to cut him off, and shouted for me, but I didn't hear at first, what with the sound of twigs breaking and so on. So Andrew blocked his escape and bellowed for me.'

'What did you find when you got there?'

'The boy was on the ground and Andrew was kicking him.'

'Poor devil,' Baldwin muttered.

'It wasn't your niece he raped and strangled,' Nicholas said hotly. 'I picked him up by the shoulders and held him kneeling. Andrew took up his sword. I think the boy realised what was happening, because he gave an awful, shrill scream as Andrew swung, and . . . well, that was that.'

'There is one thing that I am convinced of, then,' Baldwin said.

'That he was far from the road when we saw him? I tell you this, he was breaking the law and his oath long before we saw him.'

'Not that,' Baldwin said irritably, resting a hand on his belly. 'I meant Sir Gilbert must already have hidden his money somewhere if he was prepared to leave his camp in William's hands.'

CHAPTER TWENTY-THREE

At her house Cecily Sherman walked sedately into her hall. Inside were several men with their wives, all gripping pots of wine and talking. Cecily smiled at faces she recognised and inclined her head to others when they made her welcome. It was easy for her to be friendly with several of the men here, for two of them had been her lovers and one in particular she had earmarked for when Harlewin lost his lustre.

Only one man appeared to be unimpressed with her entrance. John, her husband, stood with his back to the fire and glowered as she walked in. She approached him with her head a little downcast and halted before him, curtseying. 'My Lord.'

'I was expecting you earlier,' he grated. 'After you couldn't join us last night, I thought you would sleep so well that you would be able to be punctual this morning.'

She met his gaze innocently. 'But my Lord, didn't you receive my message? I sent to let you know that I would be delayed because I had stopped at the church.'

'You "went to church?"' he mimicked cruelly. 'What time was this, my dear?'

'Before dawn, Husband,' she said, permitting a faint tone of hurt to creep into her voice.

'Truly! What a religious wife I have, to be sure. I had no idea.'

'I was so unwell last night that I prayed to be cured, and it worked: I slept. When I woke this morning I went straight to church to celebrate Mass and give confession in gratitude, Husband,' she said, her voice registering still more pain.

He smiled, but without humour. 'Oh, well perhaps I shall go and thank the priest myself later. And I can get myself shriven at the same time, can't I?'

'You can thank him now, good my Lord,' she said.

'How? Do you expect me to leave all our guests to gallivant about the town? He might well not be there.'

'He isn't, Husband. He walked back with me,' she smiled and stood back to introduce Father Abraham.

It was a shame, Jeanne felt, that her husband was once more investigating crimes when she wanted him with her to help select goods for the house.

Jeanne was no shrew but she would have liked to have had her husband's company a little while in this new town, especially since he knew that they needed new linen and cushions. Not that he would have been able to help much, she considered as she led Edgar and Petronilla through the narrow alleys between stalls. Edgar was more interested in clothing and fashion and he had an infinitely better eye for detail than Baldwin.

She adored her husband but she would never have described him as fashion conscious. That was a modern fad: men with particoloured hose, or velvet jackets with expensive linings, cut carefully to show a man's figure. They spent more time primping and preening than womenfolk, Jeanne sometimes thought. It must be a reflection of the time and the King's own habits.

Every so often she glanced around, and twice she thought she caught a slightly odd expression in Edgar's eyes. It was when he had been looking to his right, as though watching Petronilla – but he wouldn't, surely . . . Jeanne scolded herself for trying to see love, admiration, lust, whatever, wherever she looked. It was all too easy to imagine that others were feeling the same urges as she, her love for Baldwin was so strong. It almost made her want to cry out for sheer pleasure.

She took a right turn down an alley she had missed the day before. Here she saw a gorgeous scarlet, a bolt of bright red cloth that shimmered in the sunlight from fine metallic threads woven into the material. 'Oh, look!' she gasped, and glanced at Petronilla.

The girl's face was a picture. Petronilla was not so adept an actor as Edgar, and her features, turned towards him, radiated affection of the most obvious and intense kind.

'Oh-oh,' Jeanne breathed. 'That will delight Baldwin; just what he needed to round off the perfect trip to Tiverton. A servant who's about to break his engagement vow, and a woman about to take his manservant to her bed.'

Toker waited at the street corner. There was only the one entrance to the tavern and he had three men with him – Owen he had left in the castle; the Welshman didn't fill him with confidence when it came to fighting, he was too much Sir Peregrine's man. All the escapes were blocked: that was the good thing about having a small company of men to command. They could ambush even the most determined of victims.

Picking his nose, he wiped the solid residue on the house's wall behind him and snorted, then hawked and spat. Before long, if Sir Peregrine was right, they would be at war again. Then towns like this had better be wary! If he could, he'd love to break in and have a look around a place like Sherman's or Carter's. Both had nooks and crannies filled with rich stuff, silver and pewter plates, gold-chased cups, no doubt, and lots of spoons. When he had been in the service of Lady Maud, he had seen her spoons. She had more than twenty; he had often dreamed about owning such wonderful pieces of craftsmanship himself.

It was war that gave opportunities for a man to get rich. Only in war could a man prove his valour. And once he'd done so, he might be allowed his own *chevauchée* – a licence to ride out over nearby territory to see what could be won: gold, silver, wine, women – whatever. That was the life! Better by far than standing idle in a shit-stricken dump like this and hoping to remove some knight who'd become a threat.

France, that would be a good place to go. Tough, of course, because the French had the biggest and best army in Christendom, the most numerous knights, the heaviest cavalry, but in a land so wide a man with a small company could get lost and, with a little ingenuity, could become very rich very quickly. There was so much money out there, it would be a miracle if a fellow with his head screwed on right couldn't take a bit for himself.

To get rich in war, a man needed a good war-leader, and Toker was satisfied that Sir Peregrine was potentially just that: shrewd, cunning, and well-connected. Under him, Toker was sure he could take a fortune.

It was still a cause for regret that he had failed to get his hands on Sir Gilbert's little chest in London. No doubt it had contained enough for him to have been able to afford a tavern of his own and retire. William had told them Sir Gilbert had had it when they camped, but when the knight was bumped off, the money had gone. Toker knew that William would have told them where it was if he had known. He'd have been *glad* to tell them by the time they'd finished with him, especially when Perkin kicked him in the bollocks. The memory made Toker smile: how William's eyes had popped! Yes, if he'd known where the money was, he'd have told them, all right. Once he'd stopped puking.

And now this other knight was causing trouble and needed to be disposed of. Toker was happy to oblige. As far as he was concerned if Sir Baldwin de Furnshill was annoying folks, he had to be removed. If he was arrested for his part in this, Toker knew he could rely on his friends for aid. In Tiverton's courts two men held all the power: Lord Hugh and the Coroner. The Coroner answered to Lord Hugh and the man who told everyone what Lord Hugh thought was his reliable, trustworthy gatekeeper, Sir Peregrine.

No, if Toker or any of his lads were caught and accused of murder, they'd be set free at the Court of Gaol Delivery before they could even get put into prison.

Toker leaned back against the wall and contemplated the road once more. This was dull. He daren't go into the tavern to seek Sir Baldwin, for that would be too obvious, but it was boring out here, especially knowing that Sir Baldwin and his mate were sitting at a table and enjoying a quart of ale or something. Just what he could do with, Toker thought.

His eyes narrowed as someone appeared in the doorway. It was Nicholas Lovecok, and Toker relaxed slightly, but then he saw the two men behind and he stiffened with anticipation.

Wat had been glad to avoid walking about the Fair. It was beneath him, staring at all those stupid lengths of cloth, having to listen to all the 'Oohs' and 'Aahs' that Lady Jeanne and Petronilla, whom he generally credited with far better brains than most other girls, would gasp when confronted with arrays of coloured and gaudy strips of materials. Women's business! Far better to be here in the castle learning how a man-at-arms could serve his lord.

Not that Wat had managed to learn much so far. His first essay into the skills of service had led to him trying to bring a cup of wine to a guest: he had gone to the buttery before the steward, who had cuffed him about the head when he tried to pour wine, telling Wat to leave off the Lord Hugh's stocks, and took the filled pot from him to carry to the hall. Wat had tried to explain he was helping, but his expostulations had led to his almost tripping the steward, and he earned a second clip around the ear for his efforts.

Then he had gone to watch two men-at-arms practising with swords and daggers, and in his attempts to follow what they were doing, had convinced them that he was apeing their efforts. Both stopped their bout to hurl stones at him. One caught him on the rump, the other on his forehead, and now a trickle of blood ran down his face.

He scuffed the dirt, wondering moodily how a boy was supposed to learn the skills of arms or courtesy if no one was prepared to help teach them. He was out near the gateway, watching while guests of Lord Hugh wandered in and out. Some had their own boys with them, several already wearing long daggers or swords, and most of them younger than he. That was his trouble, he knew. He had been born to a cattleman, so he was expected to follow in his father's footsteps and become a cattleman in his turn.

When Sir Baldwin had asked him to help in the house, his father had been enthusiastic. 'Look, boy, it'll keep you indoors more, not out in the freezing cold in winter, or smothered with flies in summer. You can learn lording properly, always having a filled belly and a pot of wine never far from your hand.'

It was attractive the way he had put it, but Wat could see from the boys here how he had been wrong. Wat could never learn fighting. He was a country peasant, no more. To be a gentleman in a great house you had to have been born to it, so that your parents could send you away to learn your business at an early age, ideally about eight or younger. He would have been sent away to a friend of his father's, or maybe to his master, and trained in fighting.

Across the yard two boys were dragging a friend, who was seated upon a wheeled wooden horse and gripped a lance, across the cobbles towards a quintain. When he hit his mark, they all crowed with delight, but their pleasure only served to increase Wat's gloom. He would never know such simple happiness. His was to be a peasant's life.

Head down, he kicked a pebble and scuffed away towards the hall's door, wondering who might be inside. At the door was Sir Peregrine of Barnstaple. He didn't seem to notice Wat, but Wat was used to being invisible in this castle. Men tended not to notice him; he was merely one of several brats about the place. The only time, Wat had discovered, he was likely to be seen was when he didn't want to be, such as when he had just dropped a bowl of wine and splashed the stuff all up a wall, or when he was caught in the kitchen filching biscuits.

Idly he watched as Sir Peregrine walked across the yard to the gatehouse and entered. Wat wondered whether he could slip into the buttery and serve himself a pot or two of wine.

Harlewin le Poter felt good as he left his house. With an expansive gesture he stretched, reaching his arms up to the sky, and groaned with pleasure as he felt bones crack and muscles slip over each other. It felt good to be alive.

The Fair was still on, and so far he'd seen hardly any of it, so he set off, sauntering cheerily towards the noise, considering what he could buy his wife as a present. Probably a pleasant little necklace or ring, he thought. Nothing too expensive, but a trinket such as she would like. Luckily he and Cecily had agreed a while ago that they would never purchase anything for each other. There was no point when nothing they received could be put on show. It wasn't as if she was going to be able to fasten on a new necklace in front of her husband and say, 'Nice, isn't it? Harlewin gave it me.'

With that thought the Coroner gave a broad smile. It was the attractive aspect of a lover: this simplicity. A wife would complain, 'You never buy me presents, you can't love me,' whereas a lover was grateful for a more basic, no less sincere, proof of adoration.

He had to cross several poorer areas, and he moved down the alleys and along streets with no urgency, but a constant caution, a man always on his guard and aware of his surroundings. At fairtime even a small town like Tiverton could attract petty thieves prepared to knock a man on the head for what he carried in his purse – and a friend of Earl Thomas should always be on guard in these troubled times.

At the end of the last alley he came into bright sunlight and stood a moment sniffing the air. Over the way he saw the tavern, Simon and Baldwin in the doorway.

Toker pushed himself away from the wall as Sir Baldwin stepped out into the street. Resting a hand on his dagger, Toker tested it in its sheath – it moved easily enough, as it should after the amount of grease he had rubbed over it from the kitchen's pots. There was no need for a sword for a quick assassination like this, he knew. One swift stab upwards into the knight's heart and lungs and he would be gone. No more trouble.

Sir Baldwin and Simon were walking away, their backs to him. He made to walk over the cobbles but a horse passed, slowing him. Once it had gone he moved forward and gave a significant look at his men in front. They walked into the street lazily, and paused as if to chatter. When Toker glanced left he saw Perkin coming level with him. Soon the men in front would pull out their knives and the sight would make the knight and his friend pause in surprise, then in anger, and before they could pull their blades free, they would be dead, stabbed in the back. Toker and his men had done it all before.

But as he placed his hand on his dagger's hilt, there was a shout from behind him.

Harlewin was dubious about joining the knight. Sir Baldwin could be an unsettling companion, and the Coroner was of a mind to leave him. He was about to turn away and walk up a sidestreet when he noticed the two men just in front pushing their way through the crowds and gaining on Sir Baldwin. Every nerve in his body screamed caution at the sight.

'Sir Baldwin and Bailiff Puttock! How good to see you again!' he bellowed, and stepped forward, nudging Perkin heavily and shoving him from his path as he went, then faced Toker, his hand already on his sword, shaking his head.

Toker took his hand away from his dagger slowly registering his confusion, but then he smiled and marched back the way he had come.

Simon had turned at the first call, and was just in time to see a man go flying. Nearby was the Coroner, a massive figure, and before him was a scruffy, nondescript figure with his back to Simon. 'What the . . .'

Baldwin reacted faster. He took in the scene, but then whirled around to face forwards again, and now his sword was free of its sheath, and the bright blue blade glistened and shone wickedly in the sun. Its colour was a dismal threat to any man who wished to threaten him.

A woman screamed, another took up the cry, and in a moment the street was almost empty.

Now he knew there was danger, Baldwin could see that two men were acting oddly. Both were tattily clothed, both large men, with faces that betrayed their dismay at the loss of surprise. One had his hand on a dagger, but under Baldwin's intent stare, his hand fell from it. The two ambushers exchanged a glance before backing away carefully. Both had knives, but a knife was no defence against a man trained from his youth in sword-play. They retreated, then darted up an alley, and Baldwin heard their footsteps hurrying away.

When those two had disappeared, Baldwin turned just in time to see the last of the other men scampering away while a roaring, furious Simon aimed a weighty kick at his arse, making him scream with pain. Simon walked with a faint limp as he returned to his friend, although his beaming face showed that he did not regret the mild pain.

'We owe you a great debt of thanks,' Baldwin said to Harlewin.

'They shouldn't be allowed to escape,' Harlewin muttered grimly. 'The bastards could attack someone else.'

'I think they have likely lost their taste for waylaying men in town,' Baldwin noted. 'And they didn't actually do anything.'

'They were going to rob you,' Harlewin growled.

'And thanks to your vigilance they failed.'

'It was my pleasure. Well, and my duty, I suppose. I am the Coroner, so my job is to see to it that felons fail and are arrested.'

'Did you recognise them?' Simon enquired.

'I have seen them before,' Harlewin admitted. 'Didn't you know them? They are from Sir Peregrine's entourage.'

'Good Lord!' Baldwin breathed.

'God's Bollocks!' Simon declared. 'The shit set his men on us? Why, for Christ's sake?'

Baldwin scowled thoughtfully. 'We should ask *him* that. Perhaps he didn't? They could be freebooters.'

'Well, there's little point in hurrying to him,' Simon considered. 'Those buggers of his will get there before us and explain their failure, so he'll be briefed with an alibi before we get to the castle.'

'They are staying in the castle, Simon,' Baldwin said urgently. 'They could have grabbed William and executed him.'

'Why should they do that?'

'Maybe it was a brawl – or perhaps there was another reason. I find it hard to believe that William's death was not somehow related to his master's.'

Harlewin smiled thinly. 'I have declared the good Sir Gilbert's death to have been caused by the felon.'

'Ah, yes,' Baldwin said. 'I am sure you are correct.'

'But you're treating it as a suspicious death?'

Baldwin smiled innocently. 'Would you care to join us in a celebratory drink, Coroner? You may have saved our lives, after all.'

CHAPTER TWENTY-FOUR

John Sherman broke off a profitable conversation as the priest came closer, chewing on a pie with an expression that would have soured milk.

'It was good of you to bring my wife back, Father. The streets can be dangerous during the Fair.'

'It was a pleasure.'

His voice hardly expressed enthusiasm, Sherman noted. 'She was with you early, she said.'

'Yes. A little after dawn,' the priest said with conviction.

'And you listened to her confession?'

Father Abraham looked at Sherman unblinkingly. 'I can't discuss that, of course.'

'Of course, Father. I wouldn't dream . . . No, I was just worried about her. When she wasn't in her room this morning.'

'Then you shouldn't be. A woman needs to attend church as often as possible.' The priest's gaze flitted over to where

Cecily Sherman stood talking and laughing with a group of three men about her. In a lull, she looked over the room and her eyes met Father Abraham's. She smiled and lifted her cup in a toast, and he turned away guiltily.

'Do you mean my wife in particular?' Sherman asked.

'No.'

Sherman shook his head.

Taking pity on him, Father Abraham gave him a smile. 'Sherman, God has given you health and wealth. You must concentrate on how to improve the lot of those poorer than yourself rather than worrying about things which do not matter. Give alms to the poor, help the Church to look after peasants who have a vocation for the religious life, and share your money with schools to help men to spread God's goodness with the rest of mankind.' Sherman smiled, but as he walked away to talk to another man, Father Abraham saw his expression, and it was grim and forbidding.

'No more than the whoring bitch deserves,' the priest muttered to himself.

'We have been talking to Nicholas,' Baldwin said, leaning back as the serving maid set jugs and pots before them.

'He told you about Sir Gilbert meeting him in town?' Harlewin asked shrewdly.

'Yes. It seems to have been innocent from Nicholas's point of view.'

'That was what I thought when he mentioned it. And of course the knight got back to his camp. If Nicholas wanted him dead, he'd have stabbed him here in the town. Why let him escape and have to go through the charade of executing Dyne nearby?'

'He was able to tell us a bit more about how Dyne was caught as well,' Simon said pointedly.

'Aha?' Harlewin's expression implied that he was fighting manfully to show interest.

'He told us he paid for Dyne's release.'

'Bollocks.'

Baldwin blinked. 'But he told us he and Andrew Carter paid to ensure that Dyne was allowed to escape so that they could go after him and execute him.'

'He lied. No one bribed me: no one ever has. I only let go those who I think deserve to be freed or those who the law says I must.'

'So Nicholas never paid you?'

'No.'

Simon chewed his lip. 'Baldwin, didn't he say that they paid Father Abraham, and he agreed so as to ensure the release of Dyne?'

'Yes . . . But the priest told them the money would go to the Coroner.'

'More fool them. If they wanted to know how to influence me, they should have asked me, not sought to buy me through a con man. So, you are still enquiring about Sir Gilbert's death?'

Baldwin was evasive. 'We did want to follow up a couple of points.'

'When you know I've already closed the matter?' Harlewin demanded testily. 'I am the Coroner here, you know. On what grounds do you claim the right to investigate the affair?'

Baldwin and Simon exchanged a look. The Coroner was quite right. They had no jurisdiction – Harlewin had full authority in this matter unless they could appeal him for incompetence or corruption.

Simon smiled soothingly. 'We don't want to step on your toes, but—'

'*Balls*, Bailiff, if you'll pardon the expression. You want to look into it because you think I took someone's money.' Harlewin scowled, but then gave a short sigh. 'Oh, very well. I daresay an order to you both to leave the matter would have as much impact as telling Father Abraham to leave wine alone.'

Baldwin smiled and ran a finger round the rim of his pot. 'Did you mean the good Father Abraham was taking bribes?'

'Can you call it a bribe when he never intended to do anything for the money? I suppose if I hadn't agreed to release Dyne, he would have told them that I had behaved dishonourably, but what could he do? I had taken the money and then failed to comply with their wishes. Disgraceful!' He laughed. 'I can hear the old hypocrite saying it!'

Simon still looked doubtful. 'You mean you never take bribes?'

'Bailiff, I know all Coroners are tarred with the brush that says they are corrupt as hell, but I seem to recall hearing that all bailiffs are thieves as well. Does that make you a felon?'

'A good point,' Baldwin grinned. 'So the worthy priest is taking money. That puts an interesting slant on things. Tell me, how do you find him?'

'He's a fool. Full of himself, and likes the chink of coins in his purse, but he's a good clerk. Keeps the Coroner's Rolls neatly. What more can I say? He charges too much from people for writing up his notes, but many clerks do. Beyond that, he doesn't like little boys, which is good in a priest, and doesn't go whoring after any wench in a skirt, which makes him rare. But he will go on at people who fail in his eyes, which can be tedious.'

'He often rails at you? Baldwin guessed.

Harlewin raised a pot and smiled.

'What for? Women?'

'How did you guess?'

'How many obvious failings are there?' Baldwin wondered aloud. He had not altered his original opinion of the Coroner as fat and foolish, but he had to admit to himself that Harlewin had a certain charm about him. Baldwin could see how some women could be attracted to the man.

Harlewin finished his pot and topped it up.

'How was your corpse last night?' Simon enquired.

'Bailiff, the man effected a wonderful recovery. He had been bruised badly on his forehead and everyone thought he'd been hit by a club, but it happens he came to and declared he'd walked into a door while drunk. Clumsy, but no need for a Coroner.'

'So you returned immediately?' Baldwin pressed him.

'No, Sir Knight. It was out on my lands towards Withleigh, and I thought I'd rest there the night. There seemed little point making the journey back here in the dark.'

Baldwin had to smile at the man's confidence. It was plain as the nose on his face that he was lying, for only the death of an important man would justify the Coroner's leaving his lord's feast. The corpse would still be there in the morning, and yet Harlewin had jumped up from the table as soon as the message had arrived. Only an obvious corpse would justify sending a messenger in the middle of the night, and yet this man had apparently leaped to his feet as soon as

Harlewin arrived. There was no point in sending to verify the tale – Harlewin had said as much by letting them know the fellow was from his own estate. 'I am glad he recovered. Naturally if someone was to go and check his wound they would find him badly bruised?'

Harlewin grinned but said nothing.

It was with a feeling of intense relief that Father Abraham heard the bells ring; he could now decently leave the house. Rising, he made his apologies to John Sherman, who scarcely paid him any heed, he was so deeply involved in a talk about Mediterranean wines and how to acquire them safely when Venetian galleys kept raiding shipping.

Walking to the door, the priest was about to leave when he felt a tug at his sleeve, and found Cecily Sherman at his side.

'Are you leaving so soon, Father?'

'I have much to do for the next service.'

'Oh, don't be so formal, Father.'

'How do you expect me to behave with a woman who has blackmailed me?'

She chuckled. 'Come, now. It's nothing too dangerous, is it? And if your conscience gives you trouble, why, remind it that I would have been forced to suffer indignities and pain if you hadn't backed up my story.'

'You forced me to *lie*! You threatened to tell everyone otherwise.'

'About your taking the knight's horse? Yes, well, I hardly think that's blackmail. I only pointed out that I should have reported your theft, after all.'

He glared at her. She was plump and attractive, but at this moment all he could see was how slender her throat looked.

If he had the courage he would put out his hands and grasp it.

She continued, 'And if everyone would then think, "Aha! so it was Father Abraham who killed the knight," that would hardly be my fault.'

'I didn't kill him!'

'No? Well, you have to admit it looks rather suspicious.' She patted his cheek, smiled, and whirled around to return to the hall.

'God forgive me, but I hate that bitch!' Father Abraham hissed under his breath as he walked from the door and into the street. From here he could see his church, and he hurried to it, his steps given more urgency by his loathing of the woman behind. Only when he was almost at the gate to his yard did he slow, forcing himself to breathe more evenly and calmly.

At the church's door he heard voices, and he paused, listening. After a moment he frowned and entered.

'Felicity? And Avicia Dyne – what are you doing in here?' he thundered.

'So you weren't seeing Cecily Sherman last night?' Simon enquired mildly.

Harlewin choked on his drink. 'Christ's Bones! Who on earth . . .?'

'We've been told you were with her the night Sir Gilbert died,' Simon continued imperturbably. 'That is why, it was put to us, you decided to murder Dyne – because you were womanising with Joan Carter, and something went wrong. You killed her to hide your rape, and arrested Dyne to conceal your crime.'

'Me? *Me* rape her? Good God, man, do you realise what you're saying? She was pleasant enough, but I wouldn't have touched her – she was little better than a servant.'

'John Sherman said you were in Earl Thomas's pay,' Baldwin mentioned as if idly.

'I have helped him on occasion.'

'For money?' Simon pressed.

'No! Anyway, what of Sherman? He's not the most reliable man, you know. He keeps false measures. If officers go to check on him, he hides his bad ones in a compartment under his floor and shows only the good ones.'

Baldwin was not interested. 'That is hardly our concern. Tell the Fair's court. More important is that people have said you had Dyne confess so that your own crime would remain concealed and, when you could, you released him so that he could be killed by the girl's father.'

Harlewin stared, then made a weak gesture. 'You've certainly listened to a lot of gossip. All I can say is, it's rubbish. I didn't touch the girl. To be frank, Cecily Sherman has taken up my spare time lately, and when she wasn't available, there was always Felicity or another prostitute in the town. I never had reason to hurt a woman who didn't want me.

'As for this stuff about Dyne – I *didn't* arrest the sod, he escaped! He ran to sanctuary as soon as he realised he was being sought. I spoke to him there, but that was all. It's my duty to speak to a felon claiming sanctuary, to ask them to surrender to arrest, but he refused. Said he knew he'd never get a fair trial.'

'How did he seem?' Baldwin asked.

'Scared. How does any felon look when he's been surrounded by the posse? He was there at the altar clinging onto that filthy scrap of linen they use for an altar cloth staring at me like he couldn't believe he'd been found out.'

'Or perhaps he couldn't believe that he had been accused of killing his woman?' Simon suggested.

Harlewin gave a dismissive snort.

'Maybe he was simply horrified to learn that the woman he had intended marrying was dead,' Baldwin mused.

'It's fine to speculate – all I know is that he was accused and confessed.'

'Did he give any reason why he'd never get a fair trial?'

'Made up some cock-and-bull story about the girl's father seeing to it he'd never be freed. Said Andrew Carter would pay off the jury.'

Baldwin scratched his ear. In his experience, when a jury presented the facts of a case before the justices, all too often the matter had already been decided in the jury's collective mind. Usually that merely reflected the jury's acceptance that the felon was a man with 'common fame', a notorious criminal; they would have him installed in gaol as quickly as possible. But often a rich man would seek to ensure the result he wanted by bribing officials or jurors to release his friends and adherents – or to punish his enemies. Philip Dyne would naturally have feared Carter's reaction. Carter was rich: he could afford to bribe any number of jurors against him.

'What then?' asked Baldwin.

'When he'd completed his time in there and made plain his willingness to abjure the realm, I made sure he confessed before witnesses and set him loose. No bribe, no arrest, just performing my duties. And when Andrew Carter and his brother looked dangerous, I held them back. I even drew my sword against them, if you would believe it!'

'Where were you on the night Sir Gilbert and Philip Dyne were killed?'

Harlewin opened his mouth – Baldwin was convinced he was about to lie – but then the Coroner shrugged and grinned. 'Why should I lie? I was with Cecily. As I was last night, really. Why hide it, if you already know her name? I was with her on the night those two died, at a mill I own to the west.'

'Near Templeton?' Baldwin asked.

'Not far from it, yes. I rode back from there with Cecily during the night. We heard a lot of noise in the woods, and I sent her on to protect her, drawing my sword. Only a few moments later a man came out. Now I know it was Sir Gilbert, but then all I knew was that he looked dangerous to me: he had his sword out, and when he caught sight of me he demanded to know who I was. Well, I told him I was the Coroner, and he looked relieved. He said he was helping apprehend a felon and I promised to stay in the road in case the felon darted back that way to escape. Then Sir Gilbert turned and rode back into the woods.'

'What did you do?'

'I waited there quite some while, but saw nothing of Dyne. Actually I have to confess that I was surprised to hear that the fool had decided to turn outlaw. I wouldn't have expected it of him. However, it had to be true if a knight like this fellow Sir Gilbert was helping seek him.'

'Did you hear anything of Sir Gilbert's death?'

'I remained there for a while. There was one Godawful scream – I assumed it was Dyne. I saw no sign of anyone and it didn't seem a good idea to go wandering about in the woods with three armed men on the loose so I just headed for home.'

'Did you see anyone else on your way?'

'There was no one on the road. Well, only one person, but he couldn't have had anything to do with all this.'

'Who was it?'

'Father Abraham. I saw him come out of the woods and ride back for Tiverton as if all the hounds of Hell were on his arse.'

Much later, when Harlewin had left them, Wat waited until the last of the servants had left the buttery, and then wandered inside and filled a pot of wine. It tasted good and he finished it swiftly, refilling it.

The castle wasn't so bad really, he told himself as he took a comfortable seat between the barrels behind the bar. It was just a bit quiet, and if he was lonely, surely that would change as people came back from the Fair. For now this was a pleasant, quiet room, and he might as well sit here with a drink while he waited.

Hearing voices from the yard, he jerked awake. Too often in the past his master had found him in the Furnshill buttery and tanned his hide. Hurriedly Wat emptied his pot and rose to his feet, dashing from the place. At the doorway, he was about to slip out when he saw the Coroner outside.

'Hey! You, Toker, come here!'

Wat waited until they should have gone before slipping out. Harlewin was talking in a low voice to Toker, but soon the two parted as another man entered the castle's gate. Toker beckoned him, calling, 'Perkin!'

Before Wat could fix an innocent expression to his face and go out to the courtyard, he saw the two approach. Swiftly he dived back into the buttery, ducking down between two of the farther barrels.

'Kicked me right up the arse, did Puttock, the bastard!' the man called Perkin was complaining. 'If I can get near him he'll never do that again, the shit!'

'I've already said you can kill him, all right? But the knight too, the black-bearded sodomite from Furnshill – we take him as well,' Toker said. 'There's no point killing the bailiff alone. We have to kill his friend too.'

CHAPTER TWENTY-FIVE

Nicholas strode indoors and called for wine. Marching through to his brother-in-law's hearth, he stood staring at the glowing embers, rubbing his hands with a slow, pensive action.

It was a fascinating thought and Nicholas couldn't think why it hadn't occurred to him before. Of course Sir Gilbert had arrived in town with money! What would he bribe people with, if not gold? But he didn't have anything on him when he turned up the night before he died – Nicholas could swear to that. There was nowhere for him to have hidden it: his horse was at a stable, he'd said, and he wouldn't have left a hoard of gold and jewels in a saddlebag to be rifled through by some unknown ostler. No, he would have deposited it in a safe place, easy enough to find, but secure from prying eyes.

He realised the maid hadn't arrived, glanced up, cried, 'Hey there! I want wine!' and returned to his musing.

Sir Gilbert surely didn't know enough about Tiverton to be able to conceal his gold safely. It was possible he had left

312

it in his camp with his man, but that fellow William Small had hardly got a penny to his name when he died. If he *had* stolen from the knight, he'd surely have bolted with it that same evening. He wouldn't have hung around like he had.

No, Nicholas thought. The servant hadn't taken it. It had been hidden somewhere by Sir Gilbert: in a place he knew, where he was comfortable that it would be safe. There must have been a special location nearby.

His brow slowly cleared, and Nicholas almost held his breath with joy as he realised.

Sir Gilbert – the Templar Knight *from Templeton.*

Father Abraham listened with the disbelief twisting his features into a cynical sneer as Felicity told of their meeting with Matilda.

'What do you want of me?' he demanded. 'You say that this girl was killed by someone else, and that your brother the felon was—'

'Philip was not a felon, he was murdered!' Avicia declared hotly.

'He never killed Joan – he wouldn't have,' Felicity stated.

'And how can you be sure of that, woman? Did you know him well?' Father Abraham demanded pointedly.

Felicity smiled. 'No, Father, I didn't. But I *do* know Andrew Carter.'

'So? What of it?'

'He murdered Joan so that she couldn't tell of his incest.'

Father Abraham rose and walked to the altar. Kneeling before it, his mind worked furiously as he considered. If it was true that the merchant had carried on an incestuous affair with his step-daughter, he was guilty of a crime and deserved to be punished. Yet if he truly was guilty, then Avicia was quite correct and her brother had been killed wrongly – which meant that Andrew Carter was guilty of murder, and Nicholas his brother must surely be guilty of conspiracy.

It was a difficult matter and the priest had to remain on his knees for some considerable time while he thought through it all. If only it was as straightforward as the Knight Templar; that man's guilt was known, was confirmed by the Pope himself, the leader of all the world's Christians, more powerful and important than any king. Templars were condemned, excommunicate. They were anathema: accursed; consigned to perdition for all time. Sir Gilbert was an example of the most loathsome of mankind, a man who resorted to devil-worship for his own benefit.

At last he stood, grimacing as his arthritic joints complained. 'You have made serious allegations. Before we go anywhere, I want you to swear to me that you are telling the truth. Come!' He led them to the great book where it sat on its own pedestal. 'Here, put your hand on the Gospels and swear it is the truth.'

He watched carefully while the two women made their oaths. 'Very well,' he sighed. 'Let us seek the Coroner.'

Simon and Baldwin sat a while longer when Harlewin had left them. Baldwin's head was gradually returning to normal under the influence of the strong Bordeaux wine, and his belly felt pleasantly numb, if a little acidic. Simon had ordered a pie and consumed it quickly, but Baldwin didn't feel well enough yet to try the roasted coffins of gristle and offal that a place like this would offer strangers to the town.

'Are we any closer to some answers?' Simon asked as he settled back and began to pick his teeth.

'It would appear not, but I think we are learning much.'

'Such as?'

'We had thought that there were only the two men, Andrew Carter and Nicholas Lovecok, out there when Sir Gilbert and Dyne died. Now we know that not only were Harlewin and his woman there, but Matilda, Sherman and the priest, as well as Sir Peregrine.'

'And the knight's man.'

'I hardly think we need consider him. He's dead.'

'Now we know there was possibly money involved, I think we have to look at him again. Where is the money?'

'You mean William could have stolen it?'

'Of course. And if he did, perhaps he hid it out there near the scene of the murder.'

'You are wrong.'

Simon blinked at his friend. Baldwin sat thoughtfully, but there was no uncertainty on his face. He was quite convinced that he knew the truth. 'How do you know?' Simon asked.

'Because Sir Gilbert wouldn't have taken the money with him to town, neither would he have left it in William's hands. I believe he went off that evening before he died and hid it himself.'

'Where?'

'I am a fool. The priest told me when I spoke to him. I will take you there, if you wish,' Baldwin said and finished his wine.

Father Abraham knocked on the Coroner's door and waited. Soon a manservant appeared and took the three of them to the Coroner's hall.

'Father – what can I do for you?' Harlewin asked curtly. He had not long returned, and wished only for peace. He recognised Avicia by sight and studied her with a frank interest that made her redden with embarrassment, and she let her head fall so that she wouldn't have to meet his eyes. Felicity, however, smiled broadly when he winked at her. He had been, and would probably be again, a good client. She couldn't hold a grudge about Emily's inquest, even if she preferred the gentle Sir Peregrine.

'Carter,' Father Abraham snapped sharply, having noticed Harlewin's greeting to Felicity.

'What of him?' Harlewin asked, calling for wine and sitting. His grin faded as he listened, his eyes hardening, and when the priest finished, saying, 'And these two women have sworn on the Gospels that all this is true,' the Coroner glanced at Felicity.

She nodded. 'I swear it on my soul.'

'You mean that this bastard raped the girl he was supposed to protect, then murdered her to keep her silence? The *sodomite*!'

'Worse than that,' Father Abraham continued. He was feeling ill with horror at the terrible allegations made by Felicity and supported by Avicia. 'He enlisted the aid of his brother-in-law to kill Philip Dyne.'

Harlewin hesitated. Even in the midst of his anger he could think clearly. 'I think that Nicholas is innocent. He was as convinced as you and I over Dyne's guilt. Damn Carter! Yet the lad confessed before us all, didn't he? Why should we think he was lying?'

'It is Felicity's evidence that raises the suspicion,' Father Abraham said.

The wine arrived and Harlewin threw his head back, emptying his pot at a gulp. 'Then let's go and confront the bastard!'

He picked up his sword belt and tied it on before leading the trio up the road towards the merchant's house. Father Abraham halted.

'Are you well, Father?' Harlewin asked. The older man was waxen and faltering in his steps.

'I am shocked by all this. I . . . I find it hard to believe, yet I *must* believe it.' Such a hideous sequence of actions was difficult to absorb. The priest had never liked Carter, but to think that he could have killed his own daughter! And after committing incest with her, too. 'I shall meet you at Carter's house. I have to return to the church for a moment.' He needed the solace that only the Gospels could give him. Perhaps he could clear his mind while praying. Prepare himself to meet Carter.

'Very well, Father. We shall see you there,' Harlewin said and continued on.

They missed Nicholas, who was at that moment climbing aboard a sturdy rounsey, and as the door was opened for them, Nicholas trotted off towards the castle, westwards, before taking the road to Withleigh, thence to Templeton.

'I want your master,' Harlewin rasped when the door finally opened.

'He's not here, sir.'

'Then we'll wait.'

It was after noon when Simon and Baldwin returned to the castle. They went straight to the stables and ordered their horses prepared. While they waited, Simon irritably tapping his foot, Baldwin sent a servant to see if his wife had yet returned. The man was soon back, shaking his head, and Baldwin nodded and turned to watch the grooms saddling his mount.

'Sir Baldwin? Sir Baldwin, I must speak to you,' Wat whispered.

'What are you doing here? Have you been drinking?' Baldwin asked, his eyes narrowing as he took in the sight of his cattleman's son's pinched, anxious features. He was about to crouch and sniff at Wat's breath when the lad's next words made him stop.

'Sir, I heard men saying they'd attack you. They said they would go for you first,' Wat said.

'And they did. Where was this?'

Wat glanced about him. 'Here in the yard, sir. They said you'd hit them and they wanted their revenge; said they'd .kill both of you, Sir Baldwin.'

Simon glanced at Baldwin. 'They said we'd hit them? That must mean they were talking *after* the ambush. They intend to kill us.'

'So it would seem. Did you see them, Wat?'

'Yes. They are men from the castle here. I don't know whose.'

Baldwin and Simon exchanged a look. The knight was the first to speak. 'Can you see them now?'

'No, sir. I think they went back to the buttery.'

'We'd better wait until Edgar returns so at least we've got his protection at our backs,' Simon recommended.

'That is all very well, but if we wait here, this is where the danger lies; if we go to the Fair to find Edgar, we could be ambushed again – this time successfully. We may just as well go out to . . .' Baldwin noticed a groom listening with interest and lowered his voice. 'To where we were going.'

Simon saw his look and motioned to the groom. 'Piss off! Don't listen to the conversations of your betters.'

'Betters?' the man enquired as if with genuine doubt. As Simon's face reddened angrily he laughed and strolled away.

'Arrogant swine!' Simon muttered.

'Forget him. As I say, we may as well go.'

'Very well, but leave a message with Wat here.'

'Good idea. Wat, you will wait here to see Lady Jeanne and when she returns with Edgar, you will tell them what you just told us and let them know that we are going to Templeton.'

'Yes, sir.'

'And you will watch the gate after we've gone. If anyone seems to try to follow us, you will tell Edgar who they were and how many.'

'Yes, sir.'

'Good. Come then, Simon,' Baldwin said and walked out into the sunlight with his horse. He hesitated, passed his reins to Simon, then darted back into the stable. When he returned, he was slipping a necklace over his neck – Sir Gilbert's crucifix and key.

They mounted and clattered under the gateway. Aylmer rose and followed them. Baldwin noticed the dog when they reached Tiverton's timber bridge, where they asked a man for the best way to reach Templeton. He pointed them to a road heading almost due west. It was too late to take the dog back to the castle and he loped along beside them as they rode.

* * *

Matilda sat composedly while Clarice combed and brushed her long hair. In the mirror she could see that her long tresses had become quite grey and straggly. Rose, she noticed, avoided her eye. 'Are you well, Clarice?'

The sharpness in her tone made her maid start. 'Yes, Lady.'

'Then why do you look so miserable?'

'It is nothing.'

'It was all true, wasn't it?'

'What?'

'What those two sluts said. Has he been bedding you too? How often?'

'I'm too old now.'

With an inward shiver Matilda saw the pained sadness in Clarice's face. 'He used to take you before?'

'When I was younger. What could I do to refuse him? He was my master.'

'When did he start with Joan?'

'I don't know.'

'Liar! It's all over your face that you know.'

'I think Felicity told the truth.'

'You mean . . .' It was hard for her to breathe for a moment. Her heart was pounding deafeningly in her ears as Matilda swallowed. 'Tell me the truth. You think he began raping my daughter as soon as he threw Felicity out?'

'Yes.'

'Leave me.'

Once Clarice had gone, Matilda rose unsteadily. She put her hand to her face and walked to the wall opposite her window where she had a small cross hanging. 'Please, God, don't let this be true,' she begged, but she knew there was nothing He could do to alter the hideous facts.

She went to the small chest in which her daughter's few belongings had been stored and pulled out a tunic, then a robe and cloak. The things Joan had worn on her last day. They were the best clothes she possessed, selected carefully to impress the man she loved. Matilda laid them out on her bed and smoothed them, weeping. Then she threw herself on the bed and gave herself up to her overwhelming grief.

Toker was leaning against a house outside the castle near the gate when Lady Jeanne, Petronilla and Edgar returned to the castle's court. He had a small knife in his hand and was carving at a piece of leather as he waited. As people approached the castle he looked up, but each time his men shook their heads. One was at one end of the street, a second at the other so that when the knight and his friend came back, Toker and his companions could take them right here. No one would expect to be ambushed so near to the castle's walls.

He didn't raise his eyes from his leatherwork when Edgar shouted for Wat in the yard and cuffed the boy over the ear for his slowness, nor see Wat going up to the hall clutching the armfuls of cloth and parcels that his mistress had laden him with. The hall was inside the castle and Toker knew that the knight and his companion were out. He had sent Perkin and Owen to follow them. Toker had no idea where they could have gone, but he was content to wait until their return and then see how best to spring his attack.

If he had kept the door to the hall under more careful observation, he would have seen the door open a fraction and Edgar and Wat peer round it at him.

CHAPTER TWENTY-SIX

The roadway was almost empty and Simon and Baldwin made good time as they cantered to Withleigh. The whole of the town was behind them now, and Baldwin felt a lightening of his spirits as he trotted on. Towns were all very well for those who could abide living squashed together like rats in a hole, but Baldwin was a man bred to space and freedom; he hated being bound up in the strict confines of a town. Out here, with trees covering the gentle hills at either side, he felt as if a cloak of intrigue and danger had sloughed away and at last he could relax his guard a little.

Not, he reflected, that he had been very careful. It was ludicrous that he should have found himself the target of an ambush and that a man like that buffoon Harlewin had been able to save them just in time.

'Simon, do you think those men could have been ordered to kill us by Lord Hugh?'

'Nothing's impossible,' Simon grunted doubtfully. 'But why should Lord Hugh want to assassinate you? Wouldn't Sir Peregrine be a more likely enemy?'

'Yes. And he would be a likely candidate to try to remove Sir Gilbert, too.'

'He was in the woods on the night Sir Gilbert died, riding away at speed,' Simon recalled, '*and* he was in the castle when William was murdered.'

'True, but Sir Peregrine is no murderer. He would always send one of his henchmen to do the nasty work,' Baldwin considered. 'I think you're right – it was Sir Peregrine's men who attacked us, although I have no idea why he would want to kill us.'

'Who else is continuing to investigate Sir Gilbert's death?'

'You think that is it? He wants to silence us, just so that the matter is left alone?' Baldwin asked. 'I find that hard to believe.'

'We know Sir Peregrine wants the Lords of the Marches to be supported by Lord Hugh, while Sir Gilbert was an agent of Despenser. Perhaps that's all there is to it. A simple political murder.'

'Possibly,' Baldwin agreed. 'But I don't find it convincing. Sir Peregrine knows that the Marcher Lords are in the ascendant and the Despensers are gone. Why should he bother to kill Sir Gilbert? Those who had supported the Despensers have all gone to the side of other magnates. Sir Gilbert would hardly have been likely to persuade Lord Hugh to join him in serving the Despensers just when everyone else was deserting the man.'

'Who else could it have been? Father Abraham looking to remove an excommunicate from his parish?' Simon chuckled.

Baldwin set his head on one side. 'It is possible, Simon. He is a curious man, that priest. Prepared to curse a man being installed in his grave, for example. Anyway, let's hope he didn't have more of an idea about Sir Gilbert's visit to Templeton than he let on.'

'Is that where you are taking me, then?'

Baldwin smiled. 'If Sir Gilbert had money, he wouldn't have left it with a sailor whose trustworthiness was questionable.

'Why do you suppose William Small's loyalty was questionable?'

'Look at it from Sir Gilbert's perspective: he was a trained Templar. Forget how he has lived recently, for he wouldn't count it as important. He was taught as a Templar and that is how he would think.'

Simon nodded. He knew that Baldwin had himself been a Templar and trusted his judgement.

'Very well,' continued Baldwin, 'could a man like Sir Gilbert trust a man like William? No! Sir Gilbert would trust a man who was bound by oaths as strong as his own; he wouldn't trust someone who could choose to leave his craft on a whim. That is what William did, from his own testimony.'

'All right, we'll take that as a reasonable hypothesis.'

'If he could not leave the money in William's hands, it is perfectly clear that he couldn't take it with him to Tiverton either. Where could he leave it? He would not wish to carry it with him wherever he went; that would invite trouble. Fairs attract thieves, cut-purses and more vigorous felons. It would be madness to walk about with it.'

'Couldn't he have placed it somewhere safe?'

'With whom? If Sir Gilbert had visited Tiverton, how long ago was that? Could he be sure that any friends he used to know would still be alive? No! He would want to ensure that the treasure was concealed far from a robber's eyes.'

Simon gave an elaborate yawn. 'Does this mean you're getting close to the point?'

'Patience, friend! We know that Sir Gilbert was a Templar and we also know that he came from Templeton.'

Simon slapped his forehead. 'So he would be aware of any number of places to hide the stuff!'

'Precisely.'

Originally their path had taken them along the side of a small stream which meandered down towards Tiverton where it joined the Exe, but now they left it behind and entered a thicker section of woodland. The sun was still high overhead, and the men and their mounts began to feel the heat. With no breeze to cool them, it was immensely warm and the dust beneath their horses' hooves stirred and rose to choke them. Aylmer sneezed regularly, shaking his head comically. It was a relief to all of them when they found themselves at the bank of another river with a mill.

They dropped from their beasts, Simon dipping his hands into the water and dashing his face before drinking deeply. Aylmer lapped fastidiously at the edge, while Baldwin rinsed a cloth and spread it over his face a moment before tasting the water.

As they rode on past the mill, Baldwin stopped and nodded to the miller in his doorway. 'Is this the mill of Harlewin le Poter?' he asked.

The miller – a short, scruffy individual with a bald head and guilty smile, nodded shortly.

'Was he here the night before last?'

The miller chewed his lip before venturing, 'Yes.'

'Alone?'

In reply the miller went red from his shirt upwards. His obvious discomfort made Simon laugh aloud. 'Don't worry, miller. He has already told us about Lady Cecily Sherman.'

The man's face relaxed instantly and he seemed to sag with relief.

'Did they leave together?'

'No, sir. They always left separate. She went first, he a while later.'

'Thank you. Now . . .' Soon they had directions to the village and were on their way once more. Their path took them northwards, up narrow tracks, between thick hedges, and on one side Baldwin could hear the munching of cattle although he could see nothing. Every now and again there came a loud roaring from a bull and he hoped that the beast would not be able to escape from its field. In a narrow lane like this a bull could easily create mayhem and kill or injure both Simon and him.

As they arrived on a broad plain they could see the little ramshackle manor to their left and they turned off on the small untended road which led down a slight hill to the small chapel. From the look of the lack of graves, the ground was not consecrated.

'My God! What a sad place,' Simon said in a hushed tone.

'There was once a large staff here,' Baldwin said sadly. 'It was a thriving little manor bringing in enough money to cover the cost of a Templar Knight. And it has been left to rot.'

He knew that many other Templar sites had suffered the same fate. The lands had been taken by the King together with all their moveable property. But the Templars had not owned the lands – they were owned by the Church. The Pope decreed that they should all pass to the Knights of St John of Jerusalem, the Hospitallers, to ensure that the wealth that they represented should continue to be put to the use intended. Unfortunately, the Hospitallers did not have the manpower to administrate so many properties, and King Edward II had an expensive court to maintain. He still, from what Baldwin had heard, had not passed over the deeds to any of the Templar manors; this meant that local men had plundered the little that the King's own Keepers had left. Everything of any use whatsoever had long since been carted off.

The lands had fallen into disuse. Some farmers had taken over fields and houses, encroaching ever closer to the main precincts, for although some had heard of the sins of the Templars and feared contamination by excommunicates, many had never been told of the hideous crimes the Templars were supposed to have committed.

Only fifteen years before, Baldwin thought bitterly, this place would have been bustling, filled with hurrying servants. There would have been a brewery, storehouses, a small mill down to the west, orchards filled with pears and apples, cattle being driven to and from the dairies, men and women, the lay-workers, busy at work, ensuring the profit from the manor's lands that would help pay for a knight to protect pilgrims.

And now it was all waste, as devastated as a farmstead after a marauding army has passed. It struck a blow at Baldwin's heart. He had seen this kind of place at its prime; to see it like this was hideous.

'It's not what I expected,' Simon said softly. His wife only rarely accused him of empathy, but seeing his friend's face Simon could share a little of Baldwin's despair.

327

'I had not realised how they had simply left the preceptories to ruin.'

Simon glanced about him. There was little remaining. Roofs had collapsed and the walls wouldn't stand much longer. Doors hung from torn and broken leather hinges; shutters had fallen away. Peering inside the shell of a house Simon was surprised to see that a bowl still stood on a table as if the owner had rushed out to chase a dog from his sheep.

'Come!' Baldwin said gruffly and resolutely swung himself from his horse. 'There is no point in a mawkish display. I knew my Order was destroyed. There! Let us seek this wealth.'

'Yes, Baldwin,' Simon said. He tied his horse to a ring in a wall, testing it doubtfully to see whether it would take the strain. Waiting while his friend tied his own to a post, he didn't glance behind him until Baldwin was done, and then he saw another horse tethered. 'Whose is that?'

'Perhaps when we know that we shall know more about the whole affair,' said Baldwin, patting Aylmer's head. But as they set off to the door Baldwin's hand slipped to his sword.

Andrew Carter was about to cross the road and enter his house when he paused. The noise in the street was loud enough, but he was sure he heard the barking, harsh laugh of the Coroner, and even as the merchant stared up and down the street, his ears told him where that voice had come from: his own hall.

It wasn't unusual for the Coroner to come and see him, but such visits were usually foreshadowed by some form of warning. Still, Andrew Carter prided himself on being a good host and he was prepared to make le Poter most welcome. Especially since he had hopes of discovering more from the fellow about the Lord Hugh's plans.

Before he could go inside, however, he spotted the hurrying figure of the priest. 'Father, were you coming to see me?' he smiled.

'Do you have anything to confess to me, Carter?' His voice was as cold as a moorland stream.

'What is it, Father? Have I upset you?'

'Is it true? Did you sin against your own daughter?' Abraham hissed.

Carter felt as though his blood was congealing in his veins. 'M-me? Sin against poor Joan?'

'If you have, confess your sins to me now! The Coroner is in there with Felicity and another to arrest you. Is it true? Are you an incest?'

His face frozen into a blank, Carter merely inclined his head. 'May I make my confession now?'

'Is it true you killed your daughter?'

'Yes.' Carter glanced at his door. It was hard to believe, but he now knew that his life was about to change utterly. He wondered how he could escape.

'You are evil! *Evil*! You knew that you were yourself guilty, yet you murdered Philip Dyne!'

'How else could I escape? May I make my confession to you, Father?'

'No, you pervert! You can go inside and admit your crime to Harlewin le Poter. Then, when you are in your cell I shall come to you to hear your last confession.'

'But Father . . .' Carter reached for him, pleading, but the priest recoiled.

'Don't touch me, murderer! I will give you no absolution. You raped your own daughter, then killed her, and blamed another man, murdering him as well. Don't look to me for sympathy! If you won't admit your guilt, I shall tell them all myself!'

'You can't, Father. I have confessed to you because you are a priest. You must not tell any others about my crimes,' Andrew smiled thinly.

Father Abraham spat at the ground between them, then darted past Carter and in through his door.

Carter daren't enter. He was no fool: if Felicity was there with Harlewin, she must have convinced the Coroner that Carter was guilty – he must have believed her. Slowly, cautiously, Carter backed away from his door. He couldn't walk through the screens to the back of the house to grab a horse, for he would be seen. There were private stables in town, and when he weighed his purse in his hands, he thought there might be enough there to rent one, but that would use up all his money, and there wouldn't be enough to take a room for an evening – not even enough to buy a meal. He couldn't rent a horse.

He was being stupid! His stables gave out onto the back streets. All he need do was walk around the house and command a groom to saddle his mare. Then he could be off.

With this resolve he hurried around the corner and out to the back of his yard.

Wat glanced upwards. Edgar was frowning as he stared at the man leaning at the gateway.

'Are you sure, youngster?'

Wat bridled at the note of doubt in Edgar's voice. 'What do you think? The master, he listened to me, he said to tell you – he never thought you'd not trust me.'

'It sounds very peculiar,' Edgar noted. 'However, as you say, I've been ordered to protect my Lady. How many did you say went out after Sir Baldwin?'

'Two, sir. They went out as soon as they could, taking some horses from men who had just come back from hunting and their mounts were tired.'

'That is all to the good, anyway.' Edgar stood a moment longer. As he watched he saw Toker stiffen, the knife still in his hand as he stared at the gateway. A moment later Edgar heard horses, saw Toker nod and settle back into his lounging attitude as a pair of horses rode in. 'I see. They are watching for Sir Baldwin's return – or that of their men,' he breathed.

He walked from the door. 'Stay here and let me know if he moves from that spot,' he said before striding off.

Jeanne was sitting in her guest room in the solar with a cup of wine, imperiously instructing Petronilla as the maid stacked cloths in a priority known only to Lady Jeanne. Edgar smiled and bowed. 'My Lady?'

'What is it? Can't you see we're busy?' Jeanne scolded him mockingly. 'Don't you know better than to interrupt a lady and her maid when they are ordering their purchases?'

'Your husband has ridden off, my Lady, but this morning he was attacked and the men he beat are here lying in wait for him. My orders are to remain here with you, but with your permission I shall wait in the yard where I may be able to help Sir Baldwin if he is attacked in the gateway.'

Jeanne had frozen when she heard the word 'attacked' and now she passed her wine to Petronilla before stepping up to him. 'You are sure of this?'

'Wat told me,' he said dismissively, 'but I have confirmed to my own satisfaction that the men in the gateway are planning an ambush.'

'Then go! Take Wat with you and send him to me if you need anything. I shall wait here,' she said.

Perkin jogged along uncomfortably. 'Are you sure about this?'

'Oh, shut it!'

Perkin reached over and grabbed Owen's jack, hauling him half off his saddle. He hissed, 'You try telling me to shut it again, and I'll tear out your liver and feed it to the dogs, understand?'

'Yes.'

Releasing him, Perkin glared irritably at the road ahead. They had already taken two wrong turnings; Owen maintained it was because the earth was too dry to leave tracks, but Perkin suspected it was because the little Welsh sod didn't fancy a fight. Perkin himself wanted to see Simon disembowelled. He hadn't been kicked before, and he wouldn't let the bastard who had done that to him live. Perkin would kill Simon before the day was over.

Unfortunately, to catch Simon he had to depend upon this gibbering fool from Wales.

It would have been much easier if they had set off after the knight and bailiff as soon as the two left the castle, but Toker, that clever, smarmy git Toker, hadn't thought they'd be buggering off so soon. It was only when they saw the missing horses that they realised.

Perkin sneered. Toker hadn't managed to get much right at all in the last few weeks, had he? He'd got them to London where that bastard sailor-boy had beaten them while they had their eyes on the chest. Toker hadn't been hurt, of course, and neither had Perkin, but Perkin wasn't fool enough to attack a man wielding a sword when he only had a dagger. Especially when it was a man like Sir Gilbert who had held his sword so aggressively, his face a mask of rage. Perkin had seen faces like that before, and he knew well enough that it brooked no argument. He'd backed off, especially when the hound streaked towards him.

Nah, Toker hadn't got them anywhere. He was the leader; it was his job to get them money and there had been little enough of that recently.

'Where are they?' he shot out. That was why they were here – to see whether the little chest had been hidden out here. And whether it was or not, Perkin was determined to kill Baldwin and Simon. He wanted revenge for the kick on his arse. Not that Owen was likely to be much use. The little bastard looked like he hadn't the guts to kill a rabbit, let alone a man. 'Well?'

Owen bit back the reply and merely jerked with his chin. 'We're following their trail. What more do you want? Hold on!'

Perkin grunted his displeasure as the Welshman kicked his feet from his stirrups and slipped to the ground. He immediately crouched, his face near the dusty soil. They were at a junction, a common on the right, a lane off to the left. 'I think they went down there,' he pointed.

'There?' Perkin hawked and spat out a gobbet of phlegm. 'What would a Keeper be doing in a place like that?'

CHAPTER TWENTY-SEVEN

The chapel was quiet, but at least it had a roof still. At the door Baldwin glanced at Simon. The bailiff nodded, and Baldwin quietly pulled the door open.

Inside all was bewebbed, but not dirty. There was a fusty smell, the odour of damp and decay, and fungus had crept up the woodwork and plaster of the walls. It was swept and clean, but neither noticed as they walked in, their boots ringing dully on the heavy flags. Their attention was on the dark figure ahead of them, who crouched at the altar.

'Have you found it yet, Nicholas?' Baldwin called.

Nicholas spun around, astonished. 'What are you doing here?'

'Probably the same as you. Looking for whatever Sir Gilbert left.'

'How did you . . . Did you follow me?'

Baldwin smiled. 'A Templar Knight, who must surely have possessed a large sum, would look to conceal it in a place he knew, wouldn't he? And he knew of this place for he used to be a Templar here. But what of you, Nicholas?'

'Me? What of me?'

'You too were a Templar, weren't you? That was where you knew Sir Gilbert from.'

'No, not me.'

'There is little point denying it. Your sister more or less told us by accident. And at the tavern you said a knight looked to his mount. You were a knight, weren't you?'

Nicholas felt a fist of ice clench in his belly. 'Of course not. What makes you think I'd . . .' His voice trailed off. He couldn't maintain the pretence any longer. His whole life for fourteen years had been devoted to hiding his past, and now that this Keeper had guessed at the truth, the whole edifice Nicholas had so carefully constructed seemed to collapse.

'You were a Templar. At Witham. Did you kill Sir Gilbert?'

'No! Why should I?'

'Because Sir Gilbert could betray your secret. You thought he might tell other people about your background.'

'Why should that worry me? If he did, he'd have to tell everyone about himself.'

'Ah, but would you have cared about him? You would be more worried about your friends and business partners finding out about your background. They might not care for a man who had once given his oaths to the Temple.'

Nicholas stared, then guffawed with laughter. 'You honestly think those ignorant, avaricious arseholes could give two damns about my history? Merchants are not devout religious, you know; not members of an Order. They only care for one thing, Sir Knight, and that is the ability to make money. If other merchants think I can increase their wealth, they will invest with me. If I begin to falter they may discover a new religious fervor and move to other men.'

Baldwin gave a small frown. Simon glanced at him and grinned. 'I think he's got a point there, Baldwin.'

'Which makes the matter rather more intriguing, doesn't it? If he knew that his brother merchants wouldn't worry about his background, why should he conceal it? Especially as Templars were known to be thoroughly competent with money. His life with the Order could have helped guarantee riches. Couldn't it, Nicholas?'

'Some might not have reacted so favourably,' the merchant said. 'What about that priest?'

'Abraham? Yes, I concede that he could have been troublesome. Perhaps more than that, for his beliefs seem to preclude the concept of forgiveness.'

'How could a priest forgive a renegade heretic? An excommunicate? It is not within his power. No, I simply wanted to avoid any accusations – any difficulties.'

'Where was your preceptory? South Witham?'

Nicholas tried to smile as if unconcerned. 'You have heard of it?'

'I have heard that a Templar there called de Gonville was the treasurer and that he took all the money from the preceptory and disappeared.'

'Interesting, but hardly . . .'

'What were you doing here?' Simon asked.

'I came to pray.'

'There is a church in Tiverton.'

'It is not so peaceful as this small chapel.'

'This is precisely the place to which a Templar would turn. How did you get started as a merchant?' Baldwin asked mildly.

'My sister's money. It was a good purse.'

'And that was enough to set you up?'

'Yes. I fear I didn't inherit, as the younger son.'

'Nicholas,' Baldwin said gently, 'let us stop beating about the bush. You were a Templar. Your name was de Gonville and when your Order was destroyed you took the money and fled, bringing your sister and her daughter with you.'

'What else could I do? There was only death and ruin if I stayed – the Pope had set the Inquisition upon us! You know what that means – no access to a lawyer, no defence considered, because if you refused to confess you could be imprisoned for life until you did, and all the time you would be tortured.'

He suddenly fell to his knees, the scabbard at his side crashing loudly on the flags, and covered his face in his hands.

'You can't imagine how it was – first the Order collapsing, then my brother-in-law dying and leaving me to look after Matilda and little Joan. When she was told she couldn't stay in her manor, we didn't know what to do. What was the point of leaving all that money to go to waste? It was better to use it, to look after all three of us. And that's what I did. I used it for the good of my sister and I. And when I had begun to make enough money, I paid more than I needed in alms for the poor to help those who hadn't been so lucky.'

Baldwin raised his eyes to Simon. The bailiff was watching the merchant with a sympathetic expression and Baldwin knew he was thinking how a man would behave when he found his profession declared illegal, his sister and her child and he himself suddenly homeless.

'I think there is no need for us to mention this to anyone,' Baldwin said. 'Your secret is safe with us, Nicholas.'

'Thank you, Sir Baldwin. You are kind to promise that.'

'But if I hear you have lied to me, I will not hesitate to denounce you.'

Nicholas sniffed and wiped his eyes.

'Is there anything else you can tell us?' Baldwin asked.

'Perhaps,' he agreed. 'When I met Sir Gilbert in the tavern, one reason why I feared being noticed was that one of Sir Peregrine's men was there and seemed to be watching us. It was an impression, no more, but when Sir Gilbert and I left the place, I saw him rise too. I think he followed Sir Gilbert.'

Simon suddenly recalled the bowl. 'Has someone been living here?'

'The old priest, Benedict. But he's dead now. Died the night Sir Gilbert was killed.'

'What was he doing here?'

'He was the priest when this was a Templar manor. He stayed on.'

'That's why this chapel is still quite clean.'

'And died here alone,' Baldwin mused sadly.

'No, Father Abraham was here.'

'Of course.' Baldwin nodded. That was why Harlewin had seen the Father on the road that night.

'Will you help us to look for the money?' Simon asked.

'Can we share it three ways?' Nicholas enquired hopefully.

'The bollocks we can!' Simon exploded.

'I think my friend is pointing out that the whole amount is owned by the King,' said Baldwin suavely.

Nicholas smiled thinly. 'I don't think you need me getting in your way, then.'

Simon's sympathy had evaporated. 'Do you mean to suggest we'd take it for ourselves?'

'Oh, I suppose you'll put it straight into the King's own hands, won't you!'

'Hold your tongue!' Baldwin thundered. A twinge of pain shot through his head and he glowered still more angrily. 'Remember this, cretin! I am a King's officer, and I will do my duty as I have sworn. That means that this wealth, if I find it, will be taken straight to the Coroner, Harlewin le Poter, for him to dispose of. If any man has a legal right to it, he can appeal the justices when they arrive on their tourn.'

'You mean to tell me you'll give it to *that* thieving bastard?' Nicholas burst out. 'You might as well throw it in the Exe for all the money the King will see from it.'

'You idiotic fool! Do you think the owner will readily forget all this? You know whose money it *is*, don't you?'

Nicholas faltered. Baldwin's angry conviction made the merchant quail. 'It's Despenser money, but what of it? They've been exiled.'

'Who is Hugh Despenser's best friend and ally? The King! Who will receive an account of the full sum here? The King! To whom will he pass it? His friend Despenser. And before you whine, "He'll keep it for himself", remember that the King's favourites have a habit of returning when Parliament has forced him to exile them. If you steal this money, the King will know about it, and so will the Despensers. And they will come to ask what has happened to it.'

'I've had enough of this!' Nicholas said, throwing his hands into the air. 'You mean to take the money – that's fine, but don't try to convince me you'll take it to that fat fool in Tiverton. That's trying my credulity too far.'

'Where are you going?' Simon demanded.

'Back to Tiverton. If you want to see whether you can get the gold, go ahead! You're welcome to it.'

He stamped out, slamming the door shut behind him, and instantly ran on light feet to his horse, untying the reins with a panicked urgency, his attention focused on the church. There was no doubt in his mind that the two men were going to take the hoard for themselves, and he feared that they might try to silence him. He expected them to come storming through the door at any moment.

But as he swung his leg over the saddle, hastily finding the stirrups, he saw no one rushing to catch or kill him. Breathing a sigh of relief he realised that they must have been so lured by the thought of the money that they had decided to remain and seek it out. Stupid, he considered. If he had been them, he would have ensured the silence of any witnesses before searching.

There was no point in hanging about. If he did, they might see him and kill him. He couldn't trust a man in authority; he knew how he himself had behaved when he had last been entrusted with someone else's gold. No, he would go back to town, and just to make sure that they couldn't get away with their theft, he'd broadcast news of their find ahead of them.

He felt sure that this would be the very last thing they would want. That idea appealed to him and he pulled his horse's head around and kicked her up the slope. Riding up, he passed two scruffy-looking men and eyed them with cautious curiosity as any man would who passed strangers on a quiet road, but the two appeared to be more interested in the lane ahead than him.

Andrew Carter sidled in by the rearmost gate to his stable. In there he found a stable lad and sent him to the house to fetch a loaf of bread and a wineskin. Meanwhile Carter ordered a groom to saddle and bridle a horse.

'Husband? Why didn't you come to the front door?'

'Matilda – my dear,' he said a little stiffly. She looked odd. There was something different. Her dress. It was familiar but looked out of place on her somehow; unsettling. He put it from his mind. 'A man is asking me to prove my credit, so I have to ride to Exeter to get papers signed. I should be back before long.'

She was watching him closely. Foolish woman. He wanted to be away, couldn't she see that? He shot a glance to the doorway behind her, thinking he heard someone approach.

'Is something the matter, Husband?'

'Nothing. No, not at all. I should be back in a couple of days.' The dress did not fit her perfectly. It was the wrong style for her . . . and yet it was familiar somehow.

'That is a shame, dear,' she said and smiled. 'But I am sure you will return as soon as possible.'

'Oh, yes,' he lied. I'd say anything to get rid of you, you stupid raddled old bitch, he said to himself. Then he looked at her smiling face again. A small fist of trepidation clenched in his bowels. Something was wrong. She was too calm, too composed. She hadn't been like this for days. Not since the death of her daughter. And that dress – *what was it about that dress*?

'You like my new tunic?' she asked, swivelling her hips to let the skirts open.

The fist in his guts became a sharp pain that almost made him gag: it was *her* dress; Joan's. It was the one she had worn when he killed her. He felt the sweat break out on his forehead. She was mad! His wife had lost her head. The vapours had got to her at last. He started to move away, but her calm voice stopped him.

'Your horse is almost ready. Would you kiss me before you go?'

'Of course,' he said, trying to smile. She lifted her face to his, eyes closed as always, and he thanked his stars that with luck he might never have to see her again. 'Goodbye, my love.'

'Good*bye*!'

There was a flash, and he stared in disbelief as her eyes opened vindictively, then narrowed as she thrust the blade into his chest.

He hardly recognised the scream as coming from his own mouth.

'Where could he have shoved it?' Simon demanded.

Baldwin pulled the key on its necklace from beneath his tunic. 'In a box or chest. You see,' he continued, tapping at the flags near the altar, 'when the Order was destroyed, most of the Temple's places near London, Winchester, York and Oxford, were quickly taken by the King's men, but preceptories in outlying areas like this, had a little more warning sometimes. They *occasionally* concealed some of their wealth.'

'In case the Knights wanted it for themselves?' Simon asked doubtfully. 'It sounds a bit . . . well, sacrilegious.'

'Not for themselves; for the Order. Most of us couldn't believe that the Pope or the French King could seriously believe the propaganda they were putting about. We honestly thought that after a few weeks we and our Order would be reinstated. Few of us realised that it was a coordinated attack to extract every last item of value, so we hid our wealth where we could retrieve it and use it for the honour of the Order when we were back in business.'

'And you think there might be a cache here? Why?'

Baldwin paused and threw him an exasperated look. 'Simon, *I* don't know anything about this place – but someone else *did*!'

'Sir Gilbert!'

'Of course. He served here. If he came here to hide his money, he knew there was somewhere to put it. And a man determined to save his money for the good of God would hide it somewhere near the altar, wouldn't he?'

Simon nodded amiably as Baldwin roved over the altar itself, then tapped at the wall behind. All the time Baldwin's face grew longer and longer, and Simon found himself offering up a prayer that they might succeed. It would be ridiculous for the secret of Sir Gilbert's hoard to remain hidden. He allowed his eyes to rise to the window. It still had glass, a thick, heavy-looking glass, set in the thick stone wall. There was a large window-ledge.

He blinked.

'Um – Baldwin?'

'Not now, I need to think.'

'Do you think he'd have stuck the lot in a box?'

Baldwin frowned at him. 'What the hell are you on about?'

'In a box like that one up there?' Simon pointed.

CHAPTER TWENTY-EIGHT

'Shut up,' Perkin snarled. 'You want them to hear you whingeing?'

'But this is a Templar place,' Owen declared nervously.

'You scared of them? They've all gone long ago.'

'You shouldn't be so sure about that. They were dreadful.'

'Not as dreadful as me, Owen, and I'm right here.'

Owen glanced at Perkin, then looked away. He didn't want to be here; he was happy enough to go about his work just as he was ordered, but sitting here, waiting to waylay a man on Templar land felt wrong. It was worse than robbing a cleric somehow, doing it here, on Templar property. The Templars were all evil. His French priest had told him so when he had been to church back at home in Harlech. Owen had never thought he'd be forced to visit a Templar site like this.

Perkin was a miserable, brutal sodomite. Owen was quite sure in his own mind that Perkin would kill him for the slightest reason. Perkin liked killing. He was mad.

'Hush!' Perkin whispered. 'I can hear something.' Owen nodded disconsolately, nocking an arrow to his string. 'Get ready,' Perkin instructed and strung his bow.

Harlewin heard the scream and was out of his chair, his sword already in his hand before he got to the screens. Almost as soon as he reached the threshold to the yard behind the house he stopped, gaping.

The screaming had ended, and staring out he saw Andrew Carter stumble forward, his shirt a red, sodden mass. Mouth working uselessly, he reached for Harlewin pleadingly, but his eyes closed in pain and he stumbled to his knees.

'Help! Bring help!' Harlewin roared over his shoulder. As he did so, he heard another shriek, this time from inside as one of the women saw Andrew. Harlewin lurched past the dying man and out to the yard itself. 'Come, Matilda. Drop the knife.'

'The knife? Oh. Yes.'

Seeing it fall, he kicked it away before sheathing his own blade. Matilda smiled at him sleepily, as though vague from drink. In every way she looked the same as normal, except she was wearing a different dress. With a shock of horror he recognised it as Joan's. It was the tunic which Joan had worn when she died.

Then it had been clean enough. Now the sleeves were smothered in blood. Andrew Carter's blood.

'How on earth did Sir Gilbert get up there?' Baldwin had muttered, adding uncharitably, 'There must be an easy way if *he* could get up there without a problem.'

Simon ignored him, staring up at the ledge. Then he walked to the tower. Inside was the ladder, which still rose up to give access to the bells and the roof above. He grabbed it and pulled it through to the chapel, set it against the wall and waved to Baldwin. 'After you, Keeper.'

Baldwin smiled thinly. Simon knew about his vertigo. 'Get up there, Bailiff.'

The box was solid and heavy. Simon had to call Baldwin partway up the ladder and pass it to him, for the weight was too great for him alone, and together they manhandled it to the ground. The box had a heavy hasp through which a thick padlock had been thrust.

'This box comes from here. It has the name Templeton engraved here,' Baldwin said as he lifted the necklace over his head. He put the key into the lock and turned it. 'So, what have we here, then?'

Simon hadn't been sure what to expect, but as the lid came up, he saw a pair of small sacks. Opening one, he whistled. 'Christ's bones!'

Inside was a collection of gemstones. Rubies and sapphires, emeralds and garnets trickled through his fingers. 'This is a fortune.'

'So is this,' Baldwin said. He had unwrapped the contents of the other sack and now held up a silver salt formed in the image of a ship. 'It must be immensely valuable.'

Simon was struck with a sense of awe and nervousness. 'This is much more than I'd expected to find. Is there anything else?'

Baldwin had already been looking into the bottom of the box. 'Only a few small items,' he said. 'The communion plate and some bits and pieces of wood.'

'What are they?' Simon wondered aloud, picking up a couple and turning them over and over in his hand.

'I fear you now hold the things that the servants of this preceptory held most dear,' sighed Baldwin. 'Their only decent plate and some relics. Maybe they thought these were part of the Cross.'

Simon hastily dropped them back into the box. 'You think so?'

'This chest was the chapel's reliquary. I think that when the Templars here realised that they were to be arrested, they put their valuables together into a chest and shoved it up out of the way. Father Benedict probably saw no reason to move it.'

'We should take the hoard to Lord Hugh. It was intended for him.'

'No, to the Coroner. We have no real knowledge to whom this belongs, nor for whom it might have been intended. But the plate and pieces of wood remain here.'

Simon was going to argue, but he saw the expression on his friend's face. Baldwin would brook no argument. These were Templar goods, and Baldwin thought they should remain in a Templar chapel. 'Very well.'

They locked the casket once more and replaced it, lighter now, on its ledge, then Baldwin took the ladder back to the tower. Outside, Simon threw the bundle over his horse's withers. Slapping it, he grinned. 'Never thought I'd carry this much money with me!'

'He hid it in the only place he could think of,' Baldwin mused as Simon mounted. 'Everywhere else was fraught with danger. He must have been constantly fearful of being robbed.'

347

'As we must be now,' Simon said.

'Yes,' Baldwin said. 'Hey – what's the matter with the dog?'

Aylmer was bristling, walking stiff-legged towards the hedge. As Baldwin spoke Simon saw a wood pigeon heading for a tree a short distance beyond. He snared pigeons when he could: tasty creatures. This one looked good and plump, he thought, and as he did so it veered away from the tree at the last minute.

'Baldwin, go hell for leather up that road!' Simon hissed.

'What? Why?' Baldwin climbed onto his horse and eyed Simon with surprise.

'Don't ask, just ride!'

Both clapped spurs to their horses and they sprang forward suddenly, rushing up the slope. Simon hauled his sword free, crouching low and spurring the animal with enthusiasm, and when the arrow flew, it missed him, flying low over his crouching back and uselessly striking a stone at the roadside. Baldwin was with him a moment later, and the two men galloped up to the common land, where Simon reined in and gazed back down the road.

'Who was that? Nicholas?'

'You think he could use a bow? No, it was someone else. Perhaps we were followed from Tiverton.'

'Should we see who it was?'

Baldwin was tempted, but: 'No, we're responsible for the hoard. We can't afford to take any risks. Come! Let us return and dispose of it as soon as possible.'

Nicholas reached town in the late afternoon and left his horse in the street before Andrew's front door. His temper had deteriorated as he rode back. He had hoped that the treasure hidden by Sir Gilbert would be a useful addition to his mercantile ventures; instead it would go to others, for Nicholas had no doubt that Sir Baldwin and his friend would be able to locate it.

'Wine!' he bawled as he entered the house. Without waiting for a response he strode into the hall and then stopped dead. 'What in God's name are *you* doing here?'

Father Abraham scowled. 'Don't blaspheme!'

'My apologies, Father, but—'

'Quiet!' Harlewin rasped. 'Lovecok, your brother-in-law's dead.'

'Andrew?' He glanced over to the far wall of the room. 'My God – what's happened? Matilda! Are you all right?'

'I'm fine, Nicholas.'

And she was. All the gloom which had assaulted her for the previous weeks had gone as soon as her husband had died. She was filled with a sense of happiness. Her daughter was avenged, and the depression which had filled her was replaced with a fierce delight. She felt calm, satisfied, as though she knew that she had performed the final, most important service for her child.

Harlewin continued, 'She killed him. That's not her blood, it's *his*. She stabbed him to death outside.'

'Why?' Nicholas demanded, and then his face lengthened as he heard the full story. 'This can't be true!' he said with a broken voice. 'You mean I am guilty of murder?'

Father Abraham nodded. 'You were persuaded to kill an innocent man by an evil soul. He dragged you down into the filth of sin at his side. You helped provide the backing to the rapist and murderer of your own niece and then helped him murder the only man who could point to his guilt.'

'Oh, my God!' Nicholas said and collapsed into a seat. His whole body trembled as a cold panic washed down his spine, the full horror of his position dawning on him. 'My God! What have I done?'

'We will need another inquest. And I am afraid your sister must be arrested,' said Harlewin.

Sir Peregrine crossed the yard to the hall. Looking out at the road, he wondered where Sir Baldwin and Simon could have gone. The two of them were potentially a threat, and at this difficult time he didn't need the extra worry. He had enough to occupy him already.

Two of the guests at Tiverton Castle had been set upon by townspeople after they had tried to push farmers from their path in the road, and now both were being treated in a room above the hall. One had a bad cut to his shoulder where a knife had slashed him, the other had a broken arm from a cudgel; the skin wasn't punctured, so he should survive.

Then there were the rumours of the King's anger at being forced to exile his favourite. Edward had made his feelings known, and there were stories circulating that he was already considering inviting the Despensers back to England. The Marcher Lords were content that they had saved the nation, but now Sir Peregrine was unpleasantly certain that the King would vacillate and complain until he had reversed any decisions made under duress. He had done so over the sodomite Gaveston, he had over the Ordinances, and he would over the Despensers, too.

Which meant war.

He was about to ascend the stairs to the great hall, when he saw a man watching him from a storeroom's doorway under the stairs. Sir Baldwin's manservant.

'Good afternoon, Sir Peregrine,' said Edgar and bowed courteously.

'Do you know where your master has gone? He should be here soon.'

'I am sure he will return soon, Sir Peregrine.'

'Good.' Sir Peregrine began to walk up the stairs, but as he reached the top he glanced back. Edgar was still watching him, and for some reason Sir Peregrine found his expression very unsettling. It was like an accusation.

Harlewin left Father Abraham with Nicholas and his sister. Both had need of a priest, although Harlewin was not convinced that the austere cleric would be the best man to comfort them.

It had been a long day and he felt the strain. Andrew Carter's last scream still stuck in his mind, and Harlewin was looking forward to a pot of strong wine when he got back to his own hall. Shutting his door behind him, he had the fleeting sense of calm which closing his door against the outside world always gave him, but then he saw a dog and heard men's voices in his hall and had to stifle a groan. More business.

'Sir Baldwin, Bailiff Puttock – how may I serve you?' he enquired wearily.

'It's more the other way around,' Simon said. 'Look!'

To the Coroner's astonishment the bailiff lifted a small sack and up-ended it on a table. A stream of gemstones fell and formed a pile. 'What is this?'

'It is what Sir Gilbert of Carlisle was bringing to reward all the friends of the Despensers,' Baldwin explained, scrabbling on the ground to pick up a fallen ruby. 'I suppose the larger share was to go to Lord Hugh if he agreed to offer support, but who can tell? There's also that,' he added, pointing to the salt.

'Christ alive! What a hoard! Where did you find it?'

'We'll want a receipt,' Simon pointed out. 'I think that would be sensible for all of us.'

'Er yes,' Harlewin said, his eyes still transfixed by the glittering pile. He called for a servant and sent a boy to fetch Father Abraham. 'He won't be in a good mood.'

While they waited for Father Abraham to arrive, the Coroner briefly told Baldwin and Simon about the terrible murder of Andrew Carter.

When the priest arrived, he hardly spoke a word to any of the men, but stamped to the table where he scribbled down the numbers and approximate sizes of all the stones there, as well as recording a detailed description of the silver salt.

The Father's demeanour intrigued Baldwin. 'Father, are you quite well?'

'I am.'

'You seem angry.'

Father Abraham turned on him. 'Angry? Yes, I am. This . . . this *stuff* is the lawful property of the Church if found at that accursed site.'

'Templeton?'

'Where else? It should all go to the Church, not to the King for him to fritter away on his frivolities!' The priest picked up a gemstone at random and sneered at it.

'Look at it! A pretty bauble, yet it is defiled. It has been touched by a Templar!' He spat at it and dropped it back on the pile. Finishing, he passed the wax to Harlewin and the three men made their marks to validate the roll. The priest took it with him, striding out of the house as quickly as he could.

'What do you think will happen to Matilda Carter?' Simon asked.

'Her? She's not much liked, but which jury would want to convict a woman for avenging her daughter? I expect she'll escape the rope.'

'I suppose she is fortunate to have a rich brother.'

'Yes,' Baldwin said. 'It seems harsh when you look at a case like this, the fact that all a felon's wealth escheats to the King. And there can be little doubt that Andrew Carter was a felon.'

Harlewin poured himself a third pot of wine. His mood was improving, his temper growing more calm as the soothing liquid flowed into his veins. 'It's only fair that a felon who upsets the King's laws should lose everything.'

'We have heard that another man was seen out on the road the night Sir Gilbert was killed,' Baldwin said.

Harlewin groaned and lifted a hand to his brow in an elegant display of boredom. 'Not that again! I have decided that he died, as I told you, because a felon murdered him for his purse.'

Baldwin grinned drily. 'Didn't you see Sir Peregrine? Someone else told us he was there.'

'No. No, I didn't. Only Father Abraham.'

Baldwin nodded, but almost instantly Simon saw a frown fleet across his features. 'So Sir Peregrine must have disappeared in the woods too. Who else might have done?' He wondered aloud.

Soon Simon and he were making their way back to the castle, but all the way Baldwin kept silent, his attention fixed upon the ground.

Toker saw his man up on the right alter his position. The man peered up the road then gave a low whistle to attract Toker's notice. Toker waved to his other lookout. With any luck it was Perkin and Owen and they might come back laden with gold and with a story to tell about two dead men.

There was no haul. He could see that at a glance.

Toker waited in the road while the two approached. 'Well?'

'They saw us or something,' Owen said, his voice a whine of self-justification.

'Saw us my arse! There was nothing *to* see. This sod missed. Only a couple of feet away, and he missed. Pathetic!'

'They came past at a gallop – the best archer in the land would have missed them,' Owen said, glowering.

'Call that a gallop?'

'What would you call it then? A trot? You know sod all about horseflesh, but even a—'

'Yeah? Even a what?' Perkin said, reaching over to grab Owen's jack again.

The Welshman leaned away on his pony and spurred it out of range, spitting in Perkin's direction. 'If you'd fired, I'd take my part of the blame, but you couldn't even get your arrow nocked.'

'Shut up!' Toker said quietly, but his voice carried authority and anger. 'Where are they now?'

Owen scowled at the ground. 'They rode past us so fast we lost them.'

'Did they find anything?'

It was Perkin's turn to evade Toker's eye. 'They had something; they threw it over a saddle before they rode past. It was in two sacks, I think.'

'Good. Perhaps they'll bring it back here,' Toker smiled. Taking Perkin's bridle, he smiled up at him. Suddenly he caught Perkin's foot and thrust upwards. Perkin gave a roar, but before he could stop himself he was flying over his horse's back, then falling headfirst. He hit the cobbles with a loud crack.

Owen's horse skittered nervously, moving backwards into the castle's wall and he cried out, 'No, Toker, no!'

Toker scarcely glanced at him. 'Get Perkin inside. Useless pile of dung that he is! Owen, take his horse and see that both are looked after. Then meet me in the yard.'

Owen nodded. He slowly dismounted, his eyes on Toker's back, while the nearest lookout caught hold of Perkin's legs and hauled him into the yard. Perkin's horse was standing quietly, blowing every now and again through his nostrils, and Owen caught up his trailing reins and led him under the arch of the gatehouse with his own mount, but before he could enter the yard, he felt a knife at his throat.

'But Owen, my little Welsh friend, if I ever hear that you've failed again, I'll slit your guts from groin to gizzard – understand? This'll remind you!' A dull dragging sensation caught at Owen's cheek and he automatically raised a hand to it as Toker shoved past him and swaggered inside.

When he felt the flap of skin dangling, the bile rose in Owen's throat even before he saw the blood on his hand.

CHAPTER TWENTY-NINE

Edgar saw the weeping man cross the yard to the stable and install the horses there, watching while a groom took them and began the long process of removing harnesses and brushing them. As far as he could see, the men had all come in now, so he sent Wat in to inform Jeanne of this and to ask her if he could see Petronilla for a moment.

She left her child and was soon at his side.

'I think that man over there in the stable is one of the outlaws who tried to ambush Sir Baldwin,' Edgar told her. 'Could you speak to him and see whether you can find out anything about him and his master? Offer him some help with his cut. And ask how he got it.'

Petronilla nodded slowly. She hadn't much hope of discovering anything, but the man certainly needed help.

It was demeaning being commanded like this. Edgar had no right. She had hoped that he had asked for her to join him because he wanted to speak to her in private, but instead it was merely to send her to entice a man into performing an indiscretion. It was tempting to give him short shrift and storm off, but then she saw the anxiety in his eyes and the concern that creased his brow, and felt her heart swell at the knowledge that he had asked her for help in this.

Not, she reminded herself, that there was anyone else he could ask in this place.

'I shall constantly be within a few yards of you. You need not fear that he could hurt you,' Edgar whispered as they walked slowly over the yard.

Petronilla avoided a pile of horse dung and skirted around a sow suckling her young. As Edgar paused at the wall to the stables, she walked on to the side of the silently weeping Welshman.

'Are you all right, master?' she asked, setting her tone at a quietly sympathetic level. 'Ooh, your cheek! It's deeply cut, you need some cloth. Come here into the light.'

Owen found himself being led into the late afternoon sunlight, where Petronilla examined his wound carefully.

'It isn't as deep as I'd thought,' she murmured as if to herself. 'Come, I shall fetch cloth and clean it for you.'

'No, it's not hurting or anything,' he lied, ashamed now of his tears, but she shook her head solemnly.

'Do you want to have it fester and give you a fever? Stay there. I'll get wine.'

She was as good as her word. In a few minutes she was back with a jug of wine and a pot. She filled the pot and gave it to him to hold while she dipped her clean cloth in the horse trough, wiping away the blood. 'This may hurt a little,' she said, soaking the cloth in his wine and gently washing the edges of the wound.

Owen winced and his shoulders clenched with the sharp sting, but although he closed his eyes firmly, he gave no cry.

'Are you part of the garrison?'

He nodded, hardly trusting his voice: the wine burned like fire.

'So you serve Lord Hugh?'

'Yes. I am one of Sir Peregrine's men – except he's put me with Toker's band.' He drew in his breath sharply as she dabbed too hard.

'Oh, sorry, sorry. What's your name?'

'Owen, Miss.'

'Well, Owen, you've travelled far from your home, from your accent.'

'This is nothing. We're only just back from London.'

'London? What's it like? I've never been so far.'

'It's a great huge city, but it was dangerous when we were there. All the great lords were rattling their swords outside the city while the King decided what to do.'

'That must have been exciting.'

'Toker, he's used to excitement. He's served many different lords,' Owen agreed dismally. 'All over the country, and in the King's lands in Gascony.'

'Why are you here now, then? It sounds too exciting for you to be content to stay in Tiverton,' she said, sitting on the edge of the trough, finished.

Owen indicated his wound. 'This is as much excitement as I care to take,' he said wryly.

'Did a cutpurse do it?'

'Ha! No, it was Toker. He wanted to show me . . . well, he wasn't happy with me.'

'That's terrible! It's one thing to thrash a servant, but to scar you for life like that!'

'Well, I failed, see. So I got punished.'

'What didn't you do?'

Owen shuffled his feet. 'Never mind that. It's nothing, really.'

'It must have been something pretty important for him to cut you like that. Maybe I should ask someone to complain to Sir Peregrine for you.'

But Owen was no longer listening. In the roadway he heard horses' hooves, and now they rang on the cobbles under the gatehouse.

Simon and Baldwin rode across the yard to the stables and chatted happily as they dropped lightly from their mounts, then strolled to the hall. Owen hardly noticed them. Bleakly he took in the sight of the two saddles. Both now empty of sacks.

'Oh, bollocks,' he said sadly.

Baldwin saw Sir Peregrine walking to greet them as soon as they entered the hall. 'Look out, the bannaret is coming.' It was with a feeling of considerable satisfaction that Baldwin saw an already partly drunk guest engage Sir Peregrine in conversation. The bannaret tried to break away politely, but the guest was persistent.

'You were delayed long, Husband,' Jeanne said. She had been waiting at the door for their approach, and now she joined them.

'It will soon be too hot in here for a person to keep from perspiring.'

Glancing about him Baldwin could see what she meant. The hall was filling quickly as guests arrived for the celebrations of the morrow of St Giles's Day. It was not so splendid an occasion as the previous night, but the women were all dressed in their finery, the men wearing their best velvets and furs. Men-at-arms in the de Courtenay colours stood at the walls, while servants wearing Lord Hugh's livery moved among the people with silver plates piled high with pies and drinks.

'I have a terrible feeling I've been here before,' Baldwin told himself, and grabbed a handful of pies and a large pot of wine. The knight felt horribly under-dressed in his dusty and faded riding tunic, but even as he considered leaving the room there was a change in the atmosphere.

Simon sniggered, but before he could reply he, too, noticed the subtle difference in the conversation as Lord Hugh himself walked in. He stood a short way into the room smiling at his guests, taking a large cup of wine and lifting it in a toast.

'I think we should make our presence known,' Baldwin said softly and walked up to the lord. Jeanne looked from him to Simon, then followed her husband.

'My Lord, I thank you for inviting me here,' Sir Baldwin began.

Sir Peregrine at last broke away from the unwelcome conversation of the drunken man and he marched to Lord Hugh's side.

Baldwin acknowledged his presence with a polite smile, then resumed: 'Lord Hugh, I thought you should know that a treasure has been discovered. I and the Bailiff here found it at Templeton. We think it was owned by Sir Gilbert of Carlisle and concealed in the chapel there by him.'

'I am glad to hear it is held safely,' Lord Hugh said, and his eyes held a happy twinkle. 'It would be terrible for such a find to be made by a wandering outlaw.'

'There was no risk of that, my Lord. Now it is safely installed with the Coroner.'

'Harlewin le Poter? Good. In that case there is little more to be said about it. Such a shame about the knight himself. I understand Sir Gilbert was an experienced man. He could have been invaluable as a member of my household, don't you think?'

'I scarcely knew the man, I fear.'

'Anyone who could come all the way here carrying a treasure trove would be an interesting man to meet, wouldn't you say, Sir Baldwin?' Lord Hugh said mildly.

'Interesting to meet and talk to, I suspect,' replied Baldwin.

A few moments later the lord excused himself and went to make conversation with someone else farther along the room. Sir Peregrine hesitated, then stepped after him.

'I think the bannaret wanted to speak to you,' Simon said pensively.

'Probably. But there's nothing much for us to say to each other, is there – not now he knows that the Despensers' cache is lost. He realises – I hope – that his ambitions to see the Marcher Lords win ascendency in Lord Hugh's court will probably succeed. He has no need to worry about Despenser money going to bribe anyone. I hope, too, that he realises there is no longer any point in ambushing us. We can't give *him* the money either!'

Jeanne frowned from one to the other. 'What are you talking about?'

'We had a little trouble in town today,' Simon began.

'Not trouble exactly,' Baldwin hurriedly interrupted. 'Just a near . . .'

'Husband, please leave our friend and me to talk unhindered,' Jeanne said with poisonous sweetness. 'So, Simon. I had heard a little of this, but I should appreciate a few facts. You were saying?'

'It was nothing. Some men tried to ambush us, but they failed. The Coroner saved us.'

'That in itself must make you both unique,' she observed caustically.

'The interesting thing is what we heard from the Coroner,' Baldwin said and told her of the arrest and murder of Andrew Carter.

'All very fascinating, but it hardly helps to show us who killed the knight,' she pointed out.

Baldwin pondered. 'No, it doesn't. But I think we are getting close to discovering who it might have been.'

Simon held up his pot and inspected the wine within. 'The trouble is there seem to have been so many people who could have wanted him never to get here.'

Baldwin nodded. 'From Sir Peregrine there, trying to keep his master from accepting Despenser's bribe, to Cecily Sherman and Harlewin le Poter, wishing to conceal their liaison. The priest, if he knew Sir Gilbert was a Templar, and Nicholas himself, to prevent anyone hearing about his past.'

'What past?' Jeanne asked.

'I forgot to mention it,' Simon said, missing Baldwin's swift look. 'Lovecok used to be a Knight Templar.'

Baldwin was sure he felt his heart stop. He dared not meet his wife's gaze for a minute in case he saw her face transfigured with disgust at the thought that a man she had met might have been a part of that hated Order. When he heard her response, he could have grabbed her and kissed her before all the assembly.

'So what?'

Owen held a cloth to his cheek. It had stopped stinging now, and instead the slash felt like a burn across his cheekbone. 'That's what I saw,' he stated stolidly. 'All the stuff was gone.'

'Damn!' Toker said. He and his men were in the undercroft below the great hall. It was one of the few places where they could talk in peace. Perkin was upright again, glowering sullenly in the corner and holding his bruised and battered head. The others were ranged about the floor or on barrels.

He knew that they were looking to him for a lead as usual, but for once he felt lost. All depended on where they had put the money: if it was hidden somewhere nearby so the Bailiff and Keeper could collect it later, Toker might be able to get it. He couldn't afford to lose face among his men. Chewing his lip, he turned away from the little Welshman and strolled to the doorway. A short distance away was a girl throwing pebbles at a stick in the ground, while a man sat nearby watching her. Toker didn't know Petronilla or Edgar except as vaguely familiar faces about the castle ground, so he only gave them a cursory look.

The question was, *had* they hidden it? If they had, they could be 'persuaded' to say where it was.

Toker's mind turned to Perkin. People told Perkin all they knew when he started punching them. He knew where to hit for maximum pain. Perkin could persuade the knight to tell them where the contents of the box were stored, all right. All they had to do was catch Sir Baldwin.

And if it proved difficult, Toker thought, drawing his knife and kissing the blade as he made his oath, the knight and his friend would die.

Baldwin took another pot of wine with a feeling of satisfaction. He had done all he could to ensure that he and Simon would be safe from any form of attack. Now Sir Peregrine knew the hoard was safe in the Coroner's hands, Baldwin felt secure.

Harlewin arrived a while after most other people, nodding to many and smiling at Simon and Baldwin like an accomplice. However, he moved off swiftly as Baldwin became aware of a man behind him. When he turned he saw it was Cecily's husband, John Sherman.

'Master Sherman?' Jeanne said. 'We were very impressed with your stock. I couldn't recognise some of it. It all looked very impressive.'

The spicer glanced at them as if he hadn't heard. 'Eh?' Then, recollecting himself, he gave a broken smile. 'Oh, thank you. Yes, I try to stock as much as possible. It's not always easy, but . . .' He ran on, speaking of his trade with France, with other countries, his fine collection of cardamoms, the quality of his peppercorns, his exotic nutmegs and how they could flavour a wine fit for a king.

Baldwin could see that his attention was equally split between Jeanne as a prospective customer, and his wife Cecily, who had gathered a circle of admiring men about her like a candle attracting moths. Some of them, Baldwin thought to himself, could soon end up scorched. If looks could burn, many of Cecily Sherman's entourage would be singed already.

While his wife listened attentively, Baldwin's mind wandered. If there was any fairness in the world, Philip Dyne would have been left alone to leave the country. Perhaps he would have been able to rebuild his life abroad, found a new woman, married and produced children. Except he was unlucky enough to have Andrew Carter on his trail, a man who sought to kill him to conceal his own crime.

If life were straightforward, Sir Gilbert would have been overcome by the lad, his knife stolen and used to stab him. Except Baldwin knew that a trained knight would not easily submit, far less permit an unarmed thief to steal his dagger. And as for his dog sitting by and waiting until his master was dead, before leaping forward to be spitted on a dagger – well that beggared belief.

Baldwin racked his brains, thinking again of the people who could have wished Sir Gilbert dead. Nicholas Lovecok, to keep his secret; the Templar-hating Father Abraham, who had also been there. Harlewin and his lover had passed by the road to the west of the scene of the murders, although Harlewin had remained on the road to stop Dyne's escape. John Sherman had been there too, and Matilda, and today she had proved that she could kill by slaughtering her husband.

Harlewin and Cecily Sherman had ridden past, she first, Harlewin following, until he met Sir Gilbert. Sir Gilbert had turned back and ridden into the woods, and presumably had never seen Cecily.

There was always Nicholas. It was possible that he or Andrew Carter could have come across the knight in the dark and slayed him by accident, thinking he was the felon. Matilda would have tried to back them up, if she had seen them kill the wrong man, perjuring herself to protect the men who she thought were trying to avenge her daughter.

Suddenly Baldwin felt a tingle creep up his spine to his neck: *the knight had surely died on his feet; not on horseback.*

When Harlewin had seen him, Sir Gilbert was still riding about in the woods. For some reason his dog was not with him. Baldwin was suddenly sure that the dog was already dead. When he had seen Uther dying it was natural to crouch at his side to comfort him. Surely Sir Gilbert would have done the same. Was it possible that someone could have killed the dog beforehand, as a trap, and that Sir Gilbert had seen the hound's body and gone to help it?

Sir Peregrine had been there. He had ridden off as if the hounds of Hell were after him. Perhaps that was right and a hound *was* after him, Baldwin reasoned – if Sir Peregrine was the mysterious man in the woods who had been watching William and Sir Gilbert that day. When the dog was released, it must have chased after the man it had noticed before: the man whose scent it had caught on the wind. Everyone who had seen Sir Peregrine said that he was riding at speed.

And behind him, Sir Gilbert saw his dog. Riding in Sir Peregrine's wake, he had come across his hound's dead body, perhaps. Like Sir Baldwin, Sir Gilbert would probably have dropped from his horse – not that it would have helped the dog. What then? Did Sir Gilbert remount and chase after the killer of his dog? Could Sir Peregrine have been attacked by Sir Gilbert and killed him in defence? No. Sir Gilbert was struck in the back. Could he have been stabbed that way while on horseback?

His horse! A great heavy creature – a destrier. It still hadn't appeared. Suddenly Baldwin was sure that he had found a crucial clue. The mount should have turned up by now, unless it had been stolen or . . .

He turned sharply to his friend. 'Simon – that horsedealer we went to. Didn't he have one mount which stood out?'

Simon gazed at him uncomprehendingly. Sherman was less subtle. 'What in God's name are you talking about?'

'Think!' Baldwin urged his friend, ignoring the spicer. 'When we went in to talk to that man about horses, there was one decent mount in there, wasn't there? A large animal, just like a destrier.'

'I suppose so,' Simon agreed. 'But it looked a mess, just like all the others.'

'Simon, we are fools. If stupidity was a felony we would deserve to be thrown into gaol. Come with me!'

Jeanne sipped her wine as Baldwin gripped Simon's elbow and half-dragged the bailiff from the hall, giving his wife a brief wave as they went.

'Is he mad?' Sherman asked, bewildered.

Jeanne smiled, but coldly. '*I* find him perfect,' she said, but as soon as she saw the hurt in his eyes, and the way he guiltily cast a look at his wife, chatting so easily and happily with her circle of male friends, Jeanne felt embarrassed for him and ashamed of talking so curtly. 'Would you like more wine?' she asked gently, and he nodded gratefully.

CHAPTER THIRTY

Toker was sitting in the undercroft listening to the babble of all the people in the room overhead when Perkin, who was at the door, hissed and beckoned. 'It's them!'

On his feet instantly, Toker joined him in time to see two men walking swiftly past under the gatehouse. 'You sure?' he demanded, but he so wanted Perkin to be right that he already had a hand reaching out for his sword to test the blade in the sheath.

In answer Perkin grabbed his favourite weapon, a staff some six and a half feet long, and set off at a jog. Toker waved at the others and they climbed to their feet grabbing their weapons and following Toker.

All but Owen. He hung back in the doorway.

He was content to attack an enemy in battle or raid, but ambushing the innocent felt wrong. The very thought gave him a queasiness in the bowels. Even two or three men fighting against one was all right, to his way of thinking, but trapping men like this was wrong. It was no better than the behaviour of a felon and Owen was no felon. He was Sir Peregrine's man, not Toker's. He had had enough.

The girl was still tossing stones at a target. Owen was sickened by the band – especially by Toker. All he wanted to do was to sit and talk with this pretty, fair woman. Toker was standing at the far end of the gateway watching, and Owen felt a twinge of anxiety curling in his belly. The other man had scarred him for life for missing with an arrow – what would he do if Owen neglected to take part in this? The knight had made the gang look like a bunch of amateurs and Toker wanted to punish him.

Catching the Welshman's eye, Toker meaningfully drew his dagger and kissed the blade. Owen shivered at the sight. He knew what that meant: Toker would come to find him. Toker would kill him. But Owen was no footpad. He watched their leader turn and stride from the yard, and as he looked about him, Owen saw a figure he recognised. He walked over to Edgar. 'Are you the knight's man?' he asked.

'Yes,' Edgar said, peering after Toker and his men distractedly.

'You must go after them. They intend catching your master and killing him. He's got their gold – and Perkin wants revenge for the kick the bailiff gave him.'

Edgar didn't say a word: he was already halfway to the gate. Owen saw him halt at the porter and point back. Two guards glanced at each other and came to arrest Owen, but before they got to him, Edgar had disappeared.

'Here it is!' Baldwin declared and pounded on the door. It was wide and tall enough to allow a wagon to enter or a man on horseback, and the timbers rattled as he banged.

'Hoy! Stop that row!'

Baldwin turned to see a woman glaring at him from a window on the opposite side of the street. 'I want to speak to the groom running this place,' he shouted.

'Well, you can't – he's not there.'

'Do you know where he is?'

'Maybe I do, maybe I don't, but you start that banging again and I'll get the Constable onto you.'

'You fool! I am a Keeper of the King's Peace, so tell me where this damned horse-trader has gone.'

'If you were a Keeper you'd be up at the castle in your finery instead of rattling people's doors at this time of night, so go on, bugger off!' She banged the window shut.

'That damned . . . What are you laughing at?'

Simon shook his head in innocent denial. 'Nothing, Baldwin. But since the man isn't here, why don't we go to the nearest alehouse and see if he's there having a drink?'

'All right, but when we get back I'll rattle that miserable old besom's doors too,' Baldwin muttered vindictively as they walked up the road to where a bush bound to a pole over a doorway showed that drinks could be bought.

It was a poor woman's hovel: there was hardly space inside for the seven men who sat at a table staring at the dice with bleared eyes and supping ale, while the alewife squatted on the floor. She looked up when Baldwin entered, ducking under the low lintel.

The hackneyman was at the table. He recognised their faces and instantly a smile transfigured his features. 'Sirs! You require more mounts? I have the very ones for you. Good, comfortable and biddable beasts. Perfect for a short run into the country or a longer ride if you need. Excellent turn of speed, too.'

He stood with little apparent regret. Simon was convinced he had lost heavily. The bailiff pulled a coin from his purse and passed it to the man, who glanced at it, smiled more widely, finished off his ale and led the way up the street to his stable.

The light was fading swiftly now. Twilight was darkening the streets, and in the shadow of the tall buildings Baldwin thought he caught a glimpse of movement. At first he thought that a rat had scuttled away – a common enough sight at the best of times – but then he heard a scrape and recognised the sound of metal being pulled from a scabbard.

All at once he realised that his message of giving up the hoard, mentioned so confidently in the hall, might *not* have filtered down to the felons who had tried to attack him and Simon earlier. He cleared his throat to warn Simon, but before he could say anything the attack was underway.

Perkin sprang into the street, a heavy staff held cross-wise over his chest. He grinned, saying, 'Remember me, you bastard? You kicked my arse . . .' His tone dropped to a malevolent rasp. *'Now I'll eat your liver!'*

Baldwin felt someone at his back and just had time to leap aside and whip out his sword as Toker's first slash scythed through the air. Baldwin caught the blade on his own as he lifted the flashing blue steel to guard his right flank. Toker's eyes narrowed, and he stamped forward, his blade whirling left in a feint, but Baldwin had seen his swift change of foot and was ready when Toker darted right, knocking the blade away with almost contemptuous ease. He would have continued with a lunge to Toker's throat had he not, from the corner of his eye, seen Simon crumple as Perkin's heavy staff caught him at the base of his skull. 'Simon!'

Then there were four at him, Toker and another with swords, a short villein with one eye but two long-bladed daggers, and Perkin with his long, iron-tipped staff. That was the weapon Baldwin feared most. A good staffman was a dangerous adversary with a greater reach than a swordsman, and this man knew how to hold his. He kept himself away from Baldwin, fighting like a man-at-arms, gripping it like a quarter-staff, one hand near the middle, the other at the farther end, thrusting at Baldwin, shoving him whenever he got his blade within a few inches of Toker or the others. The two swordsmen were biding their time, waiting until Baldwin was tired, and when he was they would come at him from either side. If they failed, the man with the daggers would finish him off.

Baldwin gave more ground, feeling the inevitability of his doom. Simon groaned, Baldwin saw him roll, trying to get on all fours, shaking his head, but although Baldwin hoped none of the men would hear, hoped that Simon might be able to come to his aid, he saw the man with the daggers glance over his shoulder.

'No!' Baldwin bellowed, but he saw the man flick a dagger up, catching it by the tip of the blade ready to throw. There was a flash as a blade caught the light, a scream, and Baldwin felt his heart lurch.

But Simon hadn't screamed. The bailiff was shaking his head like a groggy fist-fighter, falling back to rest on his haunches, while the felon with the daggers was staring at his handless stump, at the blood flying upwards in a fountain and at the hand holding a knife which had fallen to the ground before him.

Toker saw Baldwin's attention waver and moved to take advantage, but a fine spray of blood misted into his face and he

shouted a curse, wiping it away with disgust. Vaguely through it
he saw a figure loom, a figure who shrieked '*Beauséant!*' before
flying at him; dimly he recognised Baldwin's servant Edgar.

He fell back, almost tripping, his sword up to defend his
chest, but the flying sword aimed first at his breast, then his
legs, swiping quickly at an arm, then at his throat, almost so
fast that Toker couldn't see it move.

The battle cry brought a stinging lump to Baldwin's
throat. *Beauséant*, the battle cry of the Knights Templar, the
call of the men to rally, the name of their flag, the call that
meant 'be good, be noble.'

'*Beauséant!*' Baldwin roared in his turn. He could have
wept for joy.

He heard a fresh shout: 'Take that, you thieving bastard!'
There was a crack and Baldwin saw Perkin collapse like a
steer with a spike hammered in his skull, eyes wide with
astonishment. Behind him Baldwin caught a fleeting glimpse
of the stableman gripping a pair of cudgels and aiming a
vicious kick at the fallen outlaw's groin.

Now Baldwin had only the one man attacking him, and
this was a man he knew he could beat. His concern for
Simon, his shock at the sudden violence, and the sheer rage
at being waylaid, lent his arm more vigour than he would
have thought possible, and his regular practice showed in the
way that he plied his weapon.

'Yield!' he demanded, but the felon, though frightened by
the sudden turn of events, merely slashed and cut at him.
Baldwin roared again, this time a wordless bellow of pure
animal ferocity. He drove forward, his sword up and then
swept it low, taking his enemy's blade on the cross-guard
and knocking it out of the way, before reversing the

manoeuvre and thrusting forwards and up. Baldwin shoved his body forward, his whole weight behind his blade, saw the point sink in below his opponent's chest, rammed the metal into the man's body, feeling his hand become slick with blood, ripping upwards through his torso while the man gave a high, keening scream.

The man's sword was still in his hands, but Baldwin was close enough to grab at it and tug it from the now-feeble grip. He jerked his own blade higher, sawing through bone and slicing deeper, higher with his sharp, peacock-blue blade, wrenching it further into his enemy's body. The fellow shivered twice, then slumped, and Baldwin kicked him to release his blade. It came free, smeared as if with a thin oil and, panting, he looked about him for Toker and Edgar.

They were a short way farther up the lane, and Baldwin ran to them, shouting again, 'Yield! Yield!'

Toker daren't take his eyes from the whirling man before him. Edgar moved like a fluid dancer, constantly changing his position, but always with his feet coordinated, flat and stable on the ground before striking forwards or taking a defensive position. Toker couldn't shake him or get him off-balance, couldn't make him slip. He was too good. Toker was giving way almost steadily now. At first he'd managed to make Edgar retreat a little, but now he doubted whether it was genuine. It felt more like Edgar had been gauging Toker's ability, allowing himself to be pushed so that he could see how powerful Toker's blows really were, see how quickly Toker could respond to a counter-attack after launching a stabbing thrust. Now Toker was beaten – it was only a matter of time before he felt the blade slicing through his jack. He felt the presence of the knight nearby, and risked a short glance. Baldwin was too close, less than a yard away, and Toker couldn't defend himself from a man that near. He shifted his weight and made to leap away, but a sharp pain stopped him.

It was stupid. He knew that as it happened: his foot had turned on a loose cobble. He felt the tendons snap, a curious sensation like lightning shooting through his ankle, and felt himself begin to fall. And then something supported him. Something was holding him up. He coughed as the thick bile rose in his throat, choking him, and he couldn't breathe easily. It was odd, he thought, especially the dragging sensation at his breast.

When he looked up, he saw Edgar's face only a few inches from his own, then he felt himself fall as Edgar, with a moue of distaste, twisted his sword and let Toker's body fall from it.

Harlewin was soon with them, and when Owen had been called and explained the reason for the attack, the Coroner declared that there was no crime to be investigated: felons had tried to murder innocent men and those men had defended themselves. The amputee with the stained tourniquet about his wrist and the snoring Perkin were taken away to the gaol.

When the impromptu jury had dispersed and the priest was rolling up his wallet of pens and ink, Baldwin thanked the groom. 'Without your help I might well have died.'

'My pleasure. Seeing the bastard spring out like that got me angry.'

Baldwin gave a lopsided smile. 'I know how you felt.'

And in truth he did. A mist of hatred had enveloped him, a mist composed of anger and loathing, which had lent him the energy to keep the men away. He was helped by his training, but then, when he had seen the attack form on Simon and saw Edgar appear as if from nowhere, the mist had turned to red and he wanted only to kill, to slaughter those who would attack him, those who would murder his friend. It had hardly been the behaviour of a humanist who valued human life – it had been the reaction of a man of war when threatened. He felt no shame, for the men would have killed him if they could, and the reversal of their fortunes was a fact which he could not regret.

'The good bailiff has recovered himself,' Edgar said.

'I owe you a life now, Edgar.'

'Sir Baldwin, you saved my life once and I am happy if I can provide you with any service.'

Baldwin smiled at his servant. Edgar appeared embarrassed by his gratitude. Rather than cause him more, the knight gripped his forearm and held it a moment.

'Is there any wine in this benighted street?' Simon asked.

He was fit enough, so far as Baldwin could see, although his normally ruddy complexion was pale and he wore a vague frown.

'Come, gentlemen, I have a small barrel of wine in my stable. If you can tolerate the scent of horses, I'd be happy to celebrate our victory against these miserable, thieving bastards,' the hackneyman said.

Trying to smile, Baldwin accepted. It was not easy, for the man who had helped to save his life was still a fawning fellow, too sycophantic for him to respect, but they were comrades-in-arms now and it would have been rude to refuse. Helping Simon with an arm each, he and Edgar walked behind the hackneyman to his stable. At the door Baldwin realised that Harlewin was with them. 'Friend Coroner, could you leave us here? We shall see you back at the castle very soon.'

Harlewin looked upset at being dismissed this way, and Baldwin had to smile.

'Coroner, my wife is back there worrying about me, and I would consider it a generous act were you to return and let her know that the bailiff and I are perfectly fine, apart from Simon's headache.' His voice dropped. 'It would be churlish to refuse the hospitality of a man who may have saved my life, but I look upon it as a duty more than a pleasure, and I swear I shall soon be with you.'

The Coroner gave a faint smile at his explanation and swore to carry word to Jeanne before anyone else. Before long he was striding with the priest along the road towards the castle.

At the stable door the hackneyman began laughing at the recollection of the man he had hit. His loud guffaws caused the shutter opposite to swing open again. 'Will you be quiet you ignorant damned peasant!'

In answer, the hackneyman picked up a lump of horse dung and flung it in a deadly accurate arc. There was a brief squawk, a horrified splutter, then the shutter was hurriedly slammed shut. 'Always wanted to do that,' he said contentedly. 'What a day! What a day!'

Inside, seated upon empty barrels, Baldwin took a cup of wine from him. Simon and Edgar too had cups but these three appeared to represent the total of the hackneyman's drinking vessels for he himself was forced to sup from a wineskin.

'Your health,' Baldwin said in toast, and the others all echoed his sentiment. Taking a sip, Baldwin set the drink down at his side fervently hoping that someone would knock it over. It was sweet, heavily spiced and, to Baldwin's taste, almost undrinkable. 'And my thanks for knocking down that mad staff-man.'

'He was big, but he fell fast enough.'

'You are good with a pair of cudgels.'

'A man who spends his life dealing with some of the lowlifes who hang around a stable needs to know how to defend himself. I learned how to use cudgels when I was a lad, but they are just as effective for an old sod like me as a boy of ten,' their host declared with satisfaction.

'You must see many strangers here,' Baldwin considered.

'Oh, I get all sorts. Travellers from all over.'

'Did you know the felons that attacked us?'

'Toker and his mob? Oh, yes. They were often down here. Not that I wanted too much to do with 'em. No, they weren't the sort I wanted hanging about. Gives the place the wrong sort of reputation, having private armies in here.'

'Tell me, friend: have they ever brought in horses for sale?'

'Them?' Baldwin was watching as he answered, but there was not the faintest hint of deceit as he gazed at the knight and declared without hesitation, 'No.'

It was his openness that made Baldwin jerk his thumb at the stable. 'There was a large, scruffy horse here when we first came to see you. It had mud over it.'

'Ah, yes. You are a good judge of horseflesh, that is certain, Master,' the man said. 'That one should fetch a . . .'

'Friend, we have fought off felons together,' Baldwin said with a degree of sharpness. 'You don't have to give me your usual patter. Just the facts.'

The hackneyman looked innocent. 'But there is no patter to it, Master. Only the horse isn't for sale yet.'

'May I see it?'

'Of course.'

He led the way to a series of stalls out at the back of the stables. Muttering to himself, he counted down to one, at which he stopped, gazed over the rail which served as a gate, then nodded. 'This is the one.'

'Let's see it,' Baldwin said, and darted under the bar.

'No, sir, just let me . . .'

Baldwin ignored his sudden nervousness and patted the beast's flanks confidently to soothe it. The mud, although dried, still adhered to neck and rump, but Baldwin had a good idea why. He grabbed a handful of straw and rubbed at the muck. Soon the dusty mess was falling away and he was rewarded by seeing the marks he expected.

'Come, now,' he said sternly. 'This horse is not yours to sell, as you know well.'

'It is a good working horse, sir.'

'You know better than that. This is a heavy animal, certainly, but it was never used for draught. It's a knight's.'

'Oh . . . I *did* wonder.'

'Of course you did. You know a good mount when you see one. But we are comrades: I have no interest in betraying your secret.' Baldwin ducked under the rail again. 'Just tell me this: did you find it yourself or did you see it in another's hands?'

The hackneyman tilted his head as if assessing his risks. 'I didn't find it, sir, it was brought here to me.'

'And who did that?'

'John Sherman, sir.'

CHAPTER THIRTY-ONE

At the stairs to the hall Baldwin paused and stopped, staring up at the doorway.

He was still there when Edgar returned from helping Simon to a bed in the gatehouse. 'Sir Baldwin, are you well?'

'I am fine,' he replied testily, but it was not the truth. The elation which had filled him after the short and bloody battle in the street had left him and now the reaction was setting in: a dark mood had fallen over him like a blanket, dampening his spirits and filling him with gloom.

The hall was filled with the guests, and as he stood in the doorway, many heads turned to stare at him. Among them was Sir Peregrine's. The bannaret's expression was hard to gauge. Baldwin assumed it must reflect sadness that his plans had failed, rather than any shame or embarrassment.

'Edgar,' he said, 'see if the man with the broken head is awake yet. If he is, bring him here along with the last remaining man from Toker's band.'

Lord Hugh and Sir Peregrine were beside him now. 'My good Sir, what has occurred?' Lord Hugh asked. 'You left us in such a steaming hurry. Have you been hurt? And where is the good bailiff?'

Baldwin was quiet a moment. He surveyed the room. 'This is a pretty gathering, isn't it?' he said in a strong voice. 'All these fine people here, and treachery and murder stalk the streets.'

His anger was bubbling and rising to the surface, but he was beyond worrying as the room fell silent.

'A good man, a noble and honourable knight, was stabbed to death; near him a man thought to be a felon was also killed, his fiancée having been murdered; the knight's servant then was killed; and tonight my friend and I were set upon. Simon is injured and two more men have died while their two friends are in gaol.'

Lord Hugh said mildly, 'This is hardly the time or place for such reminiscences, Sir Baldwin.'

'My Lord, with respect I think this is the ideal time. Before witnesses.'

Lord Hugh met his gaze, then gave a slow nod. 'Very well, tell us what you have discovered.' He beckoned a servant who hurried forward with a seat and the lord sat while the guests shuffled and glanced at each other.

Baldwin ignored the audience.

'My Lord, our kingdom is riven with fear. All men are terrified of a fresh war and they seek to defend themselves as best they can. Some look for money, some for other rewards. They try to bend you to the will of their masters in return for promises of power.

'Sir Gilbert was here to bring you to the Despensers' fold; others wished to ensure he failed. Sir Peregrine wants your support for the Marcher Lords; Andrew Carter wished you to give your backing to Earl Thomas.

'And Bailiff Puttock and I make such men fearful because we only seek to *serve* our lords, not to influence them. That makes us appear threatening . . .

'My Lord, Philip Dyne was no criminal. He never committed rape or murder: he was simply an innocent who thought he would be killed if he went to court. Everyone assumed he was guilty, so he would never be able to escape the rope.'

'What proof do you have for this?'

'Andrew Carter is dead. He admitted his guilt to Father Abraham: he committed incest with his step-daughter and killed her to ensure her silence when he realised she was in love. I expect he was unhappy when Dyne escaped – he almost certainly wanted Dyne to be caught by the posse and summarily executed, but his wish was denied him. Instead Dyne reached sanctuary. No matter what else one may say about Father Abraham – and there is much I could say about him – he does at least consider the sanctity of his church to be sacrosanct.'

Baldwin became aware of a rumbling of anger in the crowd, and when he turned he saw the priest spluttering with indignation. 'What do you mean by this? What would you dare to say to me, Sir Knight? I have never heard such ridiculous words from someone who is supposed to be in a position of authority.'

'Then today shall be a novel experience for you, Father,' Baldwin snapped. 'I say you are dishonest and corrupt. You take bribes from people to write up your records although you already receive payment for them. Then you compound your avarice with bigotry and theft.'

'What! You dare accuse me of . . .' The priest had gone puce with rage and he quivered with emotion. 'How dare you! You'll apologise or I shall excommunicate—'

'Be silent!' Baldwin roared and took a step forward. His anger was unfeigned. This priest had cursed a knight purely because he had been a member of Baldwin's own Order, burying the man in unconsecrated ground to the harm of his soul just like a common felon, and compounding the insult by cursing him. Baldwin pointed, not caring that his hands were still covered with the drying blood of his foe. 'You saw the dead body on the night Sir Gilbert died, didn't you? I shall come to you in a moment.'

Father Abraham licked his lips but remained silent.

Baldwin looked at the other faces in the room. 'It has been difficult to piece together what happened in those woods that night. There were many people there, each of whom had their own reasons to wish to see Sir Gilbert silenced.

'What really *did* happen there? I think we have to look at the day *before* Sir Gilbert died. In the period between his arrival and his death, someone decided to kill him. So where did he go and what did he do?

'He went to Templeton before anything else, if Father Abraham can be believed. He wanted to see his old chapel and hide the goods he carried for safekeeping. It would be too dangerous to wander the streets of Tiverton with such a fortune on his person. That accomplished, he rode to Tiverton and went to the castle.

'The next we know of him, he was seeing Nicholas Lovecok in a tavern. What happened before that? I do not believe Sir Gilbert, a messenger from the Despensers, would sit drinking and wasting time had he not yet spoken to you,

Lord Hugh. Surely he came here to the castle before going to the tavern!'

'Yes, he did. He came to see me during the afternoon.'

'You knew that your bannaret wouldn't want you to see him, for Sir Peregrine supports the Lords of the Marches, not the King's favourite. So you met Sir Gilbert in private?'

'Yes. I saw him in my chamber.' Lord Hugh glanced at his guests, and spoke out strongly, so that all present could hear. 'He offered me a huge bribe to support the Despensers and let them land in Devonshire. I refused.'

'Did he leave immediately?' Baldwin asked.

'No, he remained talking for some time. In fact, he asked me for advice. He said he hadn't expected me to take a bribe; it was his conviction that the Despensers were a broken reed, that they could not be permitted to return to the kingdom, and asked me who I advised him to support.'

'At the inn, Lovecok noticed that Sir Gilbert was being followed. I think that although you tried to conceal your tryst with Sir Gilbert, you failed. Sir Peregrine knew he was there. Not only that, he had the man followed when he left here.'

'This is nonsense!' Sir Peregrine exclaimed. 'Why should I do that?'

'In order to know what he was doing. You had a man follow him back to his camp, and the next day you yourself went there to keep an eye on him. And it was then you caused the first death.'

'You dare to accuse me of murder?' Sir Peregrine grated. He marched towards Baldwin, his hand on his sword hilt, chin jutting aggressively. Two female guests gasped in alarm but their husbands leaned forward eagerly to watch with all the others.

'No, Sir Peregrine, I do not. You were there to keep this dangerous messenger under surveillance but no, you didn't kill him.' Baldwin turned back to Lord Hugh. 'One thing I could not understand, my Lord, was how the knight's dog died. It was plain to me that a weakly man like Dyne could never have killed the knight and the dog if they set upon him at the same time. This is what happened. The dogs had been restless all day and as soon as the knight let one off the leash, it raced into the woods and was never seen alive by Sir Gilbert again.'

'What are you accusing me of?' Sir Peregrine demanded.

'Sir Peregrine, I do not accuse you of killing the knight but you *did* commit a slaying that night.'

Bewildered, Lord Hugh looked at Baldwin. 'Dyne was killed by the other two.'

'Sir Peregrine killed Sir Gilbert's dog.'

Sir Peregrine took a deep breath. 'I am afraid that is true, my Lord. When the merchants appeared and pointed towards my hiding place thinking to catch Dyne, I set off back into the woods. I hadn't got far when the dog attacked me.'

'The hound saw or heard you that afternoon,' Baldwin told him. 'As soon as Sir Gilbert set off for the trees his dog caught your scent and ran after you.'

'He came straight at me. There was nothing I could do but run him through. I left him there and made off. But I swear I never killed Sir Gilbert.'

'You had the motive,' Baldwin said. 'You didn't want your lord to support the King's favourite.'

'Maybe not, but that is no reason to kill.'

Baldwin nodded thoughtfully. 'Sir Gilbert rode up, saw his beast lying hurt, dismounted and dropped to his side – and was stabbed. It was all over very quickly.

'Meanwhile, Dyne was being hunted. He was found by Andrew Carter and run down. His sole weapon – Sir Gilbert's dagger – was knocked away, and he was beaten severely by Carter before he was beheaded, probably so that he could not tell Nicholas about Carter's incest and subsequent murder of his daughter. All the while Sir Gilbert's body lay nearby, and the murderer, I expect, looked on.

'Many people were there near the woods that night. Harlewin was riding along the road when Sir Gilbert came out of the woods, and was asked to remain there to prevent the felon crossing over.' He turned to John Sherman. 'You were there.'

'Yes, I told you,' he admitted.

'Only you forgot to mention that you brought Sir Gilbert's horse back to town with you.'

At this, Lord Hugh exploded. 'What? *You* killed the poor devil, spicer?'

'No, my Lord, no!' Sherman felt people move away from him. 'It wasn't me! What would I have killed him for?'

'Tell us again what happened – and this time, make it the truth,' Baldwin said remorselessly. 'You were riding through the woods. Who did you see?'

'I had seen a woman on horseback riding along slowly and thought . . .' he stopped and glanced at his wife. 'I thought it was my wife. When she darted into the woods I believed that she had seen me and was hiding so that I wouldn't find her with her lover.'

'Did you see a man with her?'

'No, so I decided to follow after her and see what was happening. I had only gone a short way in when I heard a scream. That put me on my guard. A while afterwards I heard a heavy mount cantering towards me and I saw Sir Peregrine sweep back towards the road.'

'What did you do?'

'I continued, Sir Baldwin,' Sherman said and his back straightened a little. 'I may not be a very good husband, but if my wife was in there and was in trouble, I intended to find her and rescue her.'

'I see.'

'I edged forward slowly. There was a lot of commotion in among the trees. My God! It was horrible. And then I saw Father Abraham. He was walking, leading a horse. He stopped at the roadway and slapped it hard on the rump to make it flee.'

'What? This is nonsense!' exclaimed the priest angrily.

Sherman carried on. 'I turned into the woods and soon caught up with him; he seemed almost to jump out of his skin when I called to him.'

'What would you have done?' demanded Father Abraham. 'I thought it was an outlaw or someone.'

'The Father seemed furious to see me there. He wanted to know what I was doing, and when I said I had heard a scream and seen a woman hereabouts and thought it could be my wife, he told me that my Cecily *wasn't* there, and ordered me to leave and return home. However, just then there was another scream, a short cry of terror, and the priest crossed himself. I was scared but I felt I should go and see what was happening. I thought my wife could be in danger. I rode towards the sound, ignoring the priest's words, and came across Dyne's body.'

His voice trailed off. When Lord Hugh gave an impatient gesture, Sherman hung his head. 'I didn't want to be fined for being the first finder, so I came away as quickly as I could. What was the point of me being amerced and going to the inquest later? I just left the woods as quickly as I could, praying that Father Abraham was telling the truth and Cecily wasn't there. On the way home I saw the horse Father Abraham had been leading. I caught it and brought it back to town, leaving it at the hackneyman's stables.'

'Why didn't you bring it in to be impounded?' Lord Hugh asked. 'That's what should happen to a horse found loose.'

Baldwin answered. 'Because the horse he found had brands at neck and rump saying it was owned by the Despenser. John Sherman did not want that family to think he might have had a hand in any action against them or their friends so he took it to a dealer for safekeeping.'

'It looks suspicious, though,' Lord Hugh said. 'A murderer would steal a horse in the same way, concealing it to sell it later.'

Sherman felt his danger. He stammered, 'If . . . If anyone was guilty it was the priest. *He* was there, he caught the horse – who else could have killed the knight?'

Baldwin nodded his agreement. 'Quite correct – so he was. Father Abraham didn't pass Harlewin in the road, I think because he found a corpse and went to Templeton through the woods, avoiding the roads where he could. He knew of Sir Gilbert's Templar connections and Father Abraham hates the Templars, even to the extent of cursing the body of Sir Gilbert as he laid the body in its grave.'

'*I* didn't kill him!'

'But you did find the horse.'

'Yes,' the priest sighed. 'I found it. And I was thinking about keeping it for myself, but then I saw Sir Gilbert's body slumped over his dead dog and didn't want to be associated with a murder. Especially when I saw the Despenser brands. So I set it free.'

'Slumped over his dog?' Baldwin shot. 'So you left him in that position?'

'Yes. To my shame. I should have arranged him like a Christian, but I couldn't. I had to get away from there.'

'So there we have it,' Baldwin said. 'And who else saw you in there?'

'Cecily Sherman,' the priest replied. 'She saw me with the horse. She was there too and made it quite clear she thought I had killed Sir Gilbert. If it was anyone else I'd have laughed off her words, but I knew Sir Gilbert and knew he was a Templar. If one woman believed I had killed him, others would think I hated his kind enough to kill him.'

'And you don't?' Baldwin sneered.

'No! I am no murderer. Cecily promised not to tell anyone, but she obviously thought I was guilty. It scared me, as I say, for if a woman like her thought it possible that I could have killed a man to steal his mount, then any man or woman in my congregation might think the same. She blackmailed me. Forced me to lie to her husband for her, covering up for her fornication. Only this morning she arrived late in my church and demanded that I lie and say she had come to the church for early Mass. I didn't dare tell the truth in case she said she had seen me.'

'That night, she thought she was being chased, that her husband had lost his mind and was determined to catch her in her adultery and kill her,' Baldwin said slowly. 'She was going to meet her lover, but all the noise made her hide in the woods.'

'That was what I feared,' John Sherman said. He stared at his wife bleakly.

'And you thought *she* had killed Sir Gilbert, didn't you?' Baldwin said softly.

Sherman's face was pulled taut as though he was holding the tears at bay with difficulty. 'I didn't want to,' he protested. 'And when I heard the other woman was dressed in green I knew my wife was innocent. She doesn't have a green robe.'

'Nonetheless, you thought she was guilty of Sir Gilbert's murder, didn't you?'

'Oh, God help me!'

Baldwin watched his tears dispassionately. 'Cecily, perhaps you should tell us your side.'

Cecily stood up from her stool, her mouth working soundlessly, shaking her head.

Baldwin eyed her remotely. 'You were there: you saw the priest, you saw the horse. Did you stab the knight?'

'No! No, I swear it!'

John Sherman threw his hands out in appeal. 'My Lord, leave the matter to me. I will thrash the evil from her. In future she will be loyal to me, I am sure of it.'

Baldwin spoke quietly. 'John Sherman, I suppose you think she killed him almost in self-defence. "I thought my husband was hunting me: a horse came blundering up, and a man dropped from it. I heard him come closer, and then he fell to his knees. I thought he'd tripped and stabbed him to defend myself." It is a good hypothesis. What made you so convinced it was she who committed the murder?'

'No . . . No, I *won't* condemn her! She is my wife,' he said, throwing his hands down like a man pleading for his life.

'Sherman, your wife is innocent, I promise you. Why did you doubt her?'

He gazed at Baldwin blankly. There was an almost crazed hopefulness in his eyes at Baldwin's words, as if he scarcely dared dream that Baldwin was telling the truth. Slowly he said, 'It was the inquest. As soon as I saw Sir Gilbert's body I realised he looked just like me from behind. I thought she had seen Sir Gilbert and struck him down, thinking it was me.' His voice broke with the horror of what he was saying and he could speak no more.

Cecily licked her lips but had to clear her throat before she could speak. 'My Lord, why should I have tried to kill this man? I didn't know him.'

'But if you thought it was your husband, what better way to remove him?' Baldwin said coldly. 'You had hidden in the woods fearing that your husband might have followed you, hadn't you? And then you saw the man before you and struck. That is what your husband thought.'

'I couldn't have killed like that. I am no murderer.'

'No,' Baldwin agreed. 'You are not. The first thing my friend and I thought when we saw Sir Gilbert's body was that he had been murdered by an experienced man, a professional. This was no frenzied, fearful killing. It was a cold-blooded and deliberate assassination. Only someone with specialised knowledge could have done it.'

'But who?' Lord Hugh said.

'The murderer was a ruthless man, someone with a definite motive,' Baldwin continued remorselessly. 'Someone who wanted to remove a potential threat to his lord. Oh, and someone who knew that Nicholas Lovecok had already met him in a tavern. Someone who knew that Sir Gilbert was the emissary of Despenser. Someone who was alone, who was not seen in the woods when everyone else was there. *Harlewin le Poter.*'

The Coroner felt all the eyes in the room move to him and he gave a surprised smile, raising his eyebrows, protesting mildly, 'But I was at the road.'

'Sir Gilbert never came to see you at the roadside. You heard crashing about in the trees, and went in. Let us give you the benefit of the doubt: probably you wished to try to help. You are a King's officer. You rode into the woods and in a short time you came across a dog's body. When a horse came blundering towards you, you hid.'

'He just appeared and leaped down instantly,' said Harlewin, looking uneasy now. 'I thought he was after me: I wouldn't have attacked him otherwise.'

'You stalked the man while he was weeping for his lost dog. While he knelt at his dead hound's side, you stabbed him.'

'I thought he was going to attack me.'

'Liar!' Baldwin said coldly. 'You crept up behind him and stabbed him once, selecting the point which would kill. Then you mounted your house and rode back to the road. Those who saw you there didn't realise that you had already killed Sir Gilbert.'

'Why? Why should I have killed him?'

'It was something I have heard mentioned a couple of times: your corruption. Your reputation seemed unfair because from all I have heard, you have served the King loyally and without double-dealings, yet the stench of deviousness clings to you. It springs from the occasion when you released a man of Earl Thomas's from gaol. Some Coroners will take money to do such things, but your reputation seemed to be tied to Earl Thomas's. And Sir Gilbert wanted Lord Hugh to support Despenser.'

Harlewin allowed a fleeting frown to pass over his brow. 'But how could I have known that?'

'You told me yourself – you reported that Nicholas had met with Sir Gilbert. It was hardly surprising that Nicholas, a man who himself supports Thomas of Lancaster, should let you, another supporter of his lord, know that there was a dangerous ambassador in the town who had been to call on Lord Hugh.'

'If you are correct, why should I kill Sir Gilbert? If I knew about their meeting in the tavern, I would also have known that Lord Hugh was committed to the King and wouldn't change his allegiance.'

Nicholas cried, 'I didn't tell him that!'

'Are you sure?' said Baldwin.

'Of course I am! Sir Gilbert asked me about many things and told me he was here to negotiate with Lord Hugh on the Despensers' behalf, but he never told me the detail of his meeting. He wouldn't. It was confidential.'

Harlewin shook his head, but then turned and darted for the doorway. Before he could reach it John Sherman leaped forward, hurling himself at the Coroner. Grasping him about the knees, he brought Harlewin down, and when Harlewin looked up, he found himself staring along the naked blade of Sir Peregrine's sword.

'Coroner, you are arrested.'

'Not for long, Sir Peregrine,' he grinned. He stood and dusted his knees, smiling coolly. 'As soon as my Lord Thomas hears of my position he will have me released, be assured of that.'

Lord Hugh walked over to Harlewin, looking him up and down with contempt. 'He may well do that for so loyal a servant, Master Coroner. But before you celebrate, consider this: I have news which may not be so appealing to you. There are stories circulating in London that indicate Lord Despenser is back in the country at the invitation of the King and the bishops. The exile has been declared illegal.'

'Nonsense! The King wouldn't dare,' Harlewin blustered, but his face had gone pale.

'He did so before with Piers Gaveston; he has done so again. And when Hugh Despenser hears that you murdered his favoured ambassador, I think it won't matter who your lord may be. Guards: lock him up!'

CHAPTER THIRTY-TWO

Lord Hugh called for more wine for all his guests as Harlewin was led away to be locked in the gaol. 'I understand the reason for his crime, Sir Baldwin, but why was Sir Gilbert's servant killed?'

'I confess I wondered about that for a long time too, but if you will call for Toker's remaining men, they can tell us.'

Owen entered with dragging feet. As he surveyed the faces ranged there, he wished fervently that he had made his getaway from the castle as soon as Toker had left to follow Sir Baldwin. Even the fear of Toker's reprisals would have been preferable to this.

'You were one of that band which attacked me?' Baldwin said sternly.

'This afternoon, yes, sir – but I refused to take part tonight and warned your man.'

'You knew that they were going to ambush me?'

'Yes, sir.'

Edgar entered with Perkin as Owen spoke.

'Shut up, you bastard!' Perkin snarled. 'Don't tell 'em anything.'

'What of the servant William?' Baldwin continued.

Owen told of the encounter in London between the group and William. 'When we saw William in the courtyard here, Toker said we had to get rid of him. Otherwise he could expose Toker and Perkin for their felonies in London.'

'Did you take part in killing William?' Baldwin said.

'No, sir. Toker had Perkin with him . . .'

Perkin strained to leap forward but Edgar held him firmly. Instead he snarled, 'Shut up, or I'll feed your liver to the crows!'

'. . . It was them two who killed the servant. If they'd found the money, Toker and Perkin would have taken it and gone. They killed the sailor when he wouldn't say where the money was, and because Toker wanted to punish him for defeating us in London.'

'You did not help in killing William in any way?'

'No sir. Toker wanted the money for himself, I reckon.'

'Why were the Bailiff and I attacked?'

'You kept asking questions. Toker was worried you'd guess he'd killed the servant. Then he realised you'd found the money and he wanted to punish you for taking what he thought should be *his*. Bloody prat!'

'You can't keep us. Where's the Coroner? He can speak for us,' Perkin suddenly roared.

'Why should he speak for you?' Sir Peregrine demanded harshly. 'You deserve no protection.'

'We've done nothing wrong. Ask the Coroner. He'll tell you.'

Baldwin stood before him and considered him for a long moment before saying, 'I think your friend the Coroner would not be keen to help you now. You are arrested.'

'Toker might have done wrong, but I've done nothing, whatever that maggot says. Get the Coroner.'

'Do you work for him?' Baldwin asked.

'Sometimes.'

'The Coroner is in gaol, awaiting trial for the murder of Sir Gilbert.'

'What? Le Poter? The stupid, fat bastard!'

'He hired Toker to ambush you,' Owen explained.

'Shut up, you little shit!'

'I rather thought so,' Baldwin said. 'Sir Peregrine, I would ask that this Welshman be kept in decent lodgings away from the others. He warned my man and saved my life and that of the Bailiff.'

'Certainly. Take them both away! The sight of them hurts my eyes,' Sir Peregrine said.

After they had been manhandled away, Perkin shouting his defiance and cursing all in the room, there was silence for a short while which was gradually overtaken by an excited chattering as people started to discuss the dramatic developments. Sir Peregrine was grinning quizzically, head slightly tilted, but Lord Hugh still frowned with incomprehension.

'Tell me one thing, Sir Baldwin,' he said. 'This man Dyne . . . He must have been there. He must have seen Sir Gilbert's body, for how else could he have taken the purse and the knife?'

'I should think he did,' Baldwin agreed sadly. His mood was growing dark again. He was pleased to have solved the murders, but a black depression was clouding his mind and he longed for the forgetfulness of inebriation. 'Who can tell when he found the knight? I think that while he tried to escape from the posse on horseback he stumbled over the man and his dog. He saw that the knight was dead and arranged his body neatly, only taking the knife and money because they were of no further use to the dead man.'

Lord Hugh was quiet for a moment, sadly considering the story. 'He is the only man who comes out of this whole sorry tale with any credit, isn't he? Dyne was innocent of any crime, and when he found a dead man he treated the corpse with respect; whereas the priest tried to steal the knight's horse, Sherman hid from the facts because he was a cuckold, Carter was a murderer and incest, and God knows what the others were.'

'You have come out of the matter with honour, my Lord,' Baldwin reminded him gently. 'When Despenser made an attempt to bribe you with a vast sum you didn't accept it.'

'No. And I was glad to have done so.'

'Why, my Lord?'

Sir Hugh grinned crookedly. 'As I said before, Sir Gilbert was not so convinced of the Despensers himself. He thought that they had left the Kingdom for good, so he planned to travel north to Carlisle where he came from.'

'And join Earl Thomas's ranks?' Baldwin said.

'Yes – *with* the jewels.'

Baldwin whistled. 'So he proved a traitor to his master,' he said disappointedly.

'Don't judge him too harshly, Sir Baldwin,' Lord Hugh murmured. 'You may find yourself in a similarly difficult position before long. If the Despensers *have* returned we will all have many tough choices to make.'

'True,' Baldwin said. Then he frowned briefly. 'Why, then, did Sir Gilbert wait around? Why didn't he just head off north as soon as he had seen you?'

Lord Hugh cleared his throat and spoke in an undertone, with every appearance of embarrassment. 'He was waiting for me to prepare a message for Earl Thomas,' he said quietly. 'You see, even if you think I have come out of this well, I am not so clean as I appear. When the Kingdom is this close to war, a lord must seek the most advantageous alliances he may. And at present the Earl Thomas seems strongest. So you could say that I, too, am a traitor.'

He walked away shortly afterwards. Baldwin thought he was ashamed of his confession, but it didn't affect the knight. He was exhausted mentally and physically, and now that the murders were solved he felt himself sinking into a torpor.

John Sherman had stalked out while Baldwin talked to Lord Hugh, and Baldwin wondered where he might have gone. He could feel some sympathy for the man. Sherman now had proof of his wife's infidelity: the knowledge must be devastating. Of course it was mitigated by learning that Sir Gilbert's death was not a failed attempt by his wife to murder *him*, but Baldwin was not sure that was enough of a consolation. Sherman's wife had still betrayed him. Looking at his own wife, Baldwin wondered how he would react to learning that Jeanne had committed petty treason of that kind. Not well, he was sure.

Seeing his dejected look she smiled and joined him, linking her fingers in his. 'Are you truly all right?' she asked.

'I am fine.'

'I was terrified when I heard you had been attacked,' she whispered. 'I was convinced I was to be widowed again.'

There was a break in her tone, proof of her renewed fear that she might lose her man so soon after finding him. Baldwin squeezed her hand. 'Do not fear for me, Lady.'

No, he told himself. No one need fear for his personal safety while he could still wield a sword – but Baldwin recalled vividly that rending, tearing of flesh and bone as he hauled his sword up into his opponent's chest and the memory made him wonder for a moment what sort of man he was. He had always looked upon himself as a model of rational, humane behaviour, seeking to protect those who were weaker than he, and to prevent persecution and violence towards those who were unable to protect themselves – and yet he had *exulted* in the killing of that man. It had been a delight to end that life.

Jeanne's touch drew him back to the present. 'I hope we have a child soon,' he said.

Simon's head was not too seriously bruised. He was shaken and feeble for two days but then he began to recover swiftly. On the fourth day after the attack he went to see Lord Hugh in his great hall. The castle was almost deserted; the larger part of the guests had left and Simon found Lord Hugh sitting on his favourite carved chair on the dais with Sir Peregrine alone for company. 'You asked for me?'

'Bailiff, thank you for coming. The physician tells me you are recovering swiftly. How does your head feel?'

'I am fine now, I think. Good food and drink have helped me and your servants have all been most kind, I thank you.'

'I am pleased to hear it,' Lord Hugh said. Coming swiftly to his point, he jerked a thumb towards his companion.

'Good Sir Peregrine here has suggested that you should be knighted, Bailiff. What do you think of that?'

'I . . . I am most grateful, my Lord. It would be a great honour and privilege . . . um.'

'But one you would be happy to forgo?'

'My Lord, if I am to be honest, yes.'

'Why, in God's name?' Sir Peregrine demanded.

'Sir you are trained in warfare. I am not. If I were to be made a knight, I would be expected to fight as a lance in the army – and I have no idea how to. I could be called to tournaments with other knights and forced to fight, and if I lost, I would lose everything. I am not trained for such a service. And there is another thing . . .'

'Which is?' Lord Hugh asked.

'My Lord, I am conscious of the honour you do me, but surely I would be disloyal to my own master if I accepted a knighthood from any man other than he? My master is the Warden of the Stannaries, Abbot Champeaux of Tavistock. If I accepted a knighthood from you, you could call me away to wars in your host when my own legitimate lord wished me to remain with him or join his army. How could I do that to him?'

'A splendid argument, Bailiff!' Lord Hugh slapped his thigh, but Simon noticed that Sir Peregrine looked at him with a bleak distaste in his eyes.

Lord Hugh ceased laughing after a moment. 'There is another matter, Bailiff, on which I wished to canvass your opinion. The jewels that you and your friend Sir Baldwin deposited with the Coroner. They were clearly intended for me. What do you think I should do?'

Simon looked up into his shrewd eyes. 'That is something which is easily decided. The money is the King's. It was

401

found in a Templar chapel and before that was being carried by a Templar. All their possessions were confiscated by the King, so this too must go to him.'

'It is a small fortune!' Sir Peregrine growled.

'A King's ransom,' Simon agreed.

Lord Hugh appeared to have lost his amusement. 'You don't think I can claim it as my own?'

'You could try to appeal in court and prove that it was yours, my Lord.'

'Appeal against the King?'

Simon shrugged. 'As matters stand, I do not see you have any choice.'

Lord Hugh nodded, his face sour. 'Very well. I thank you for your advice anyway.'

It seemed that the meeting was over, and Simon walked out to the sunshine with relief at having escaped so easily. Things could have gone very differently and he could have been forced to become a knight. Not a pleasant propect.

Baldwin and Jeanne were outside in the yard, walking arm-in-arm, Sir Gilbert's surviving dog following them. Simon looked at the hound but forbore to ask. He knew that his friend inevitably attracted dogs of all types and assumed that this was the latest of Baldwin's acquisitions.

'Is the case all tied up?' Simon grunted after greeting his friends.

'I think so. We know why Sir Gilbert was killed, why we were attacked and why William was killed. Coroner Harlewin is awaiting the arrival of the justices as are the two men who survived from Toker's gang.'

'Apart from Owen, you mean?'

'He has already joined Lord Hugh's retinue. As an archer he leaves something to be desired, but he would be a good man-at-arms in a host.'

'How is John Sherman?' Jeanne asked.

'I believe he has left his wife to go and live in Exeter. His wife remains here. Whether she will be happy is a different matter. I believe she truly cared for Harlewin, her lover.'

'I wonder what will happen to Avicia?' Jeanne continued more thoughtfully. 'She has no protector at all in the town with her brother dead.'

'One can only hope she doesn't turn to the same trade as Felicity,' her husband said. 'The same thing could be said about Andrew Carter's servants. His wife has turned them all from the house.'

'Poor woman,' Simon mused. 'To learn that her husband had raped and murdered her daughter . . . it must have been appalling for her.'

'And for Nicholas too,' Baldwin reminded him. 'It was he who introduced Carter to his sister. He was responsible for his niece's death.'

Simon nodded. 'Where is Edgar?' he asked suddenly.

Baldwin looked at him coldly. 'He is with Petronilla.'

'Your maid?' Simon asked innocently, and then a grin slowly spread over his face. 'You don't mean . . .?'

Jeanne was unimpressed by his amusement. 'It's no laughing matter if he breaks his promise to Cristine.'

Baldwin nodded, but he had been struck with a sudden, delightful thought. 'It would be very bad if he were to do that. I would have to make sure that he was made aware of our feelings,' he said seriously, but as he spoke he could not help thinking that if his servant was to marry Petronilla instead, Edgar could remain in the manor.

Try as he might, he couldn't prevent the guffaw of laughter that exploded from him.

Edgar's release was much easier than Baldwin could have expected; to Jeanne's mind much easier than Edgar deserved. Cristine took his announcement and apology with stoical calm, a fact which caused Edgar no little hurt, having expected tears and protestations of eternal devotion. He had never before known a woman who had so willingly given him up, and it made him resentful.

Not, however, as resentful as he became a week later when he heard that she had married another man, one of the ostlers at the inn where she worked.

'I expect she took him on the rebound,' he remarked to Baldwin a short time after he heard.

Baldwin took in his piqued expression with amusement. 'You arrogant bugger!'

It was largely at Jeanne's prompting that Edgar and Petronilla were wed at the church door. Lady Jeanne was a sensible, cautious and worldly woman where Edgar was concerned. She knew that he was sleeping with her maid and she was satisfied in her own mind that the two had exchanged their vows and wanted to fix that thought hard in Edgar's philandering mind.

But the day was good, she had to admit to herself afterwards. The sun shone brilliantly, if coldly, for once in that miserable, damp December, and the two hurried inside the church with the guests to warm themselves with prayers and blessings once the formal oath-making was done. Baldwin had arranged for a feast afterwards, and when the wedded couple entered his hall for the meal set out for their celebrations, Baldwin had been quite touched to see Petronilla dissolve in tears of pure joy.

For once Wat managed to avoid ending up repellently drunk, which was a relief to Baldwin, the food was suited to the knight's plain taste, and he was pleased to see how all his servants appeared to enjoy themselves. The season of hardest work was done, the winter-time now called for rest until the first Monday after Epiphany, Plough Monday, when the ploughmen would begin the annual round of work with their teams of oxen.

Baldwin sat back and covered a belch. His wife threw him a reproachful look, but it faded when she saw his happiness. Her man was happy and content, and she felt a sudden warm affection for him which prevented the sharp comment about politeness at the table which had threatened. Instead she put her hand upon his and smiled. He saw her reflective, gentle smile, but simply thought she had drunk too much wine.

It was the very next morning that the news filtered down to them.

Baldwin and Edgar sat in the hall while women brushed and swept around them. Aylmer yelped as he was caught over the nose with a besom, and retreated to the kitchen where he hoped to be able to rest in a warm spot by the cooking fires.

'Good day, Owen. How are you?' Sir Baldwin said on catching sight of the Welshman as he entered.

'Well, thank you, my Lord.'

'And how is Sir Peregrine?'

'He is more calm and relaxed than before, sir,' Owen said, and a fleeting grin passed over his stolid features. 'He is happier now he has a new woman. Felicity has left her whoring and is keeping a chamber for Sir Peregrine a short way from the gate.'

His light-heartedness faded swiftly and Baldwin felt the sombre atmosphere sinking into his hall. 'It looks bad, then?' he asked, knowing that Owen hadn't ridden all this way to tell him about Felicity.

'Yes, Sir Baldwin. Sir Peregrine wanted to tell you that the clergy have declared the King's banishment of the Despensers as illegal since it was extracted from him by force of arms.'

'If they have, Despenser will soon be back breathing his poison in Edward's ear.'

'That's what my master fears. The Marcher Lords will not submit to his extortion without a fight.'

'So it means war.'

'We have heard that the Younger Despenser is already back.'

'Christ's Blood! Hasn't he done enough harm already?' Baldwin demanded rhetorically. 'I am sorry, I forget myself. You would care for some wine after your journey?'

'Spiced and hot would be best.'

Edgar left and Baldwin studied him. 'Well, Owen, your scar has healed well.'

'Yes, sir. I have your maid to thank for that,' he said, a hand going to his cheek.

'And I have *you* to thank for the fact that I am still alive. If you hadn't let Edgar know, I could be dead now.'

Owen looked away. 'I couldn't act like a common foot-pad. That was why my arrow intentionally missed you that day in the Templar village,' he added.

'Your survival was good enough reason – or so many others would have thought.'

'Perhaps. But all ended well.'

All ended well. Those were the words which Baldwin recalled later when Owen had gone to sleep in the stable and Baldwin, shivering, pulled the linen curtains around the bed.

Jeanne lay back beneath the sheets and blankets with a faraway look in her eyes. A short while before Owen appeared, Baldwin had told her of his position in the Templars and, rather to his surprise, she had been dismissive about it. Now he eyed her nervously, wondering if she had been silent from horror.

His wife was still silent, not meeting his gaze even when he slipped between the sheets himself and put out an arm towards her. She hesitated before wriggling towards him.

'Your feet are like ice!' she exclaimed.

He glanced down at her impatiently. 'What do you expect?'

'I could have wished for a husband who warmed his feet before entering his Lady's bed.'

'Be glad you have a husband who pulls your curtains for you,' he growled, and let his hand move along her soft flank.

'Not tonight, Husband. I am tired.'

As she spoke, young Stephen began to cry and Baldwin swore. He made as if to rise, but then studied her anxiously. 'Are you sickening for something?' he asked.

'No, no.'

He drew away and looked into her face, his own anguish apparent. 'Is it because of what I told you? You don't regret marrying me, now you know what I used to be?'

Jeanne stared a moment, then closed her eyes and shook silently with humour. When she opened them again, she reached up and kissed him. 'You clot! I love you.'

He kissed her back, radiating his confusion.

'Baldwin, dearest. I am tired because I am pregnant. You are to be a father.'

In the hall, Aylmer's head shot up at the cry from his new master's room and he stared fixedly at the ceiling as he heard Baldwin leap from the marital bed and perform a thunderous impromptu dance on the bare boards overhead. Then, when silence reigned once again, the animal stretched luxuriously in front of the fire, scratched at a flea on his neck and settled for the night.

Michael Jecks
Templar's Acre

The Holy Land, 1291.

A war has been raging across these lands for decades. The forces of the Crusaders have been pushed back again and again by the Muslims and now just one city remains in Crusader control. That one city stands between the past and the future. One city which must be defended at all costs. That city is Acre.

Into this battle where men will fight to the death to defend their city comes a young boy. Green and scared, he has never seen battle before. But he is on the run from a dark past and he has no choice but to stay. And to stay means to fight. That boy is Baldwin de Furnshill.

This is the story of the siege of Acre, and of the moment Baldwin first charged into battle.

This is just the beginning. The rest is history.

Hardback ISBN 978-0-85720-517-9
Ebook ISBN 978-0-85720-520-9